Praise for Candice Proctor and *Midnight Confessions*

"Proctor is in top form here. . . . A versatile author whose firsthand knowledge of the region and vivid descriptions infuse this story with a strong sense of place. . . . A gripping plot, arresting characters, and a thoroughly researched setting combine to make this a remarkable read."
—*Publishers Weekly* (starred review)

"This haunting story plunges the reader deep into the steamy New Orleans summer. . . . The author gradually peels away the veiled layers of reality and truth, showing the true complexity of life."
—*Rendezvous*

"Although this is a superbly suspenseful historical romance, the book's real appeal is its mood, for which Proctor has an obvious gift. The reader actually feels weighed down by the heat, humidity, despair, corruption, superstition, [and] sense of foreboding. . . . Even knowing that the two lovers will commit to each other doesn't lessen the drama leading up to the exciting ending."
—*Booklist*

By Candice Proctor:

NIGHT IN EDEN
THE BEQUEST
SEPTEMBER MOON
THE LAST KNIGHT
WHISPERS OF HEAVEN
MIDNIGHT CONFESSIONS

BEYOND SUNRISE

CANDICE PROCTOR

IVY BOOKS • NEW YORK

An Ivy Book
Published by The Random House Ballantine Publishing Group
Copyright © 2003 by Candice Proctor

www.ballantinebooks.com

ISBN 0-345-44718-2

Manufactured in the United States of America

First Edition: May 2003

OPM   10   9   8   7   6   5   4   3   2   1

~~Prologue

THE BLAME ALL lay with India McKnight's mother. Or at least that's what the Reverend Hamish McKnight used to say on those rare occasions when he'd look up from his collections of sermons and theological treatises long enough to give some thought to the existence of his only child. What had Mrs. McKnight expected, he used to say, giving the girl such an outlandish, heathen name? And the books the woman used to read to her—*The Arabian Nights* and *Marco Polo* and all manner of other ungodly tales that might have been precisely calculated to inflame a child's imagination and set her to dreaming of faraway, exotic places when she should have been practicing her stitches and learning her catechism.

But when he considered his daughter's future—which was admittedly seldom—Hamish McKnight found consolation in the thought that, eventually, India would be forced to give up her unfeminine thirst for adventure and travel, and settle into the predictable, conformable life of a wife, preferably to some sober, sensible vicar much like the Reverend McKnight himself. Because Hamish McKnight died before this comfortable illusion was shattered by reality, he never knew how wrong he was.

~~ Chapter One

THE TRADE WINDS blowing off the Coral Sea were warm and sweet, evocative reminders of faraway places that whistled through the rigging of the ketches and sloops riding at anchor in the sun-spangled Rabaul Harbor, and flapped the heavy skirt of Miss India McKnight's sensible serge traveling outfit.

"Very sorry, mum," said the middle-aged Hindu trader who stood before her, his short legs splayed wide against the weathered dock's unpredictable pitch, "but help you I cannot."

India McKnight, spinster, Scotswoman, and travel writer of some renown, was accustomed to meeting—and overcoming—resistance. When the trading captain made as if to go around her, India simply shifted her weight until she was once more in his path. Since the man was short and slight, and India stood five feet ten in her stockings, the maneuver brought him to a stand again. "I was told your ketch is for hire," she said, softening the overt belligerence of her blocking tactics with a smile.

The Hindu's head rocked back and forth on his shoulders in a motion that looked like *no*, but actually meant *yes*. "It is. But you don't want to go to Takaku. Not to the southern bay."

"On the contrary," said India, her voice calm and even, "I assure you that I most definitely do."

"It's dangerous. Very dangerous." The Hindu's eyes bulged out as he leaned forward and dropped his voice in the manner of one imparting a terrible secret. "Cannibals, you know. A man from the London Missionary Society went there last year. The Takakus listened to him read his Bible, and they let him pray over them, and then they had him for dinner. As the main course."

"I am not a missionary, and I am not asking you to accompany me on my expedition up the slopes of Mount Futapu. All you need do is anchor in the bay, convey me ashore in your dinghy, and wait some four or five hours until I return."

"The channel through the reefs at the southern tip of the island is dangerous." The Hindu squinted off across the brilliant azure water of the harbor. In the misty distance, far beyond Rabaul's golden shoreline and waving coconut palms, the jagged outline of the island of Takaku, with its towering volcanic cones and dark secrets, was just visible. "Very dangerous," he said again. "Rocky and narrow."

India tightened her grip on her large traveling reticule in a way that drew the trader's attention. "I'll pay you double your normal fee."

He licked his salt-cracked lips. "You want to go to Takaku? I take you to the northern end of the island, to the French port of La Rochelle. It's pretty. Very pretty. And no cannibals." An enthusiastic smile beamed, then dimmed. "Lots of French, though."

India shook her head. "It is the Faces of Futapu I wish to study, and they are far easier to approach from the southern bay than by an overland expedition from La Rochelle."

The Hindu stared at her, his full-cheeked, flat-nosed face becoming thoughtful. "Now I remember why I thought I had heard of you. You're that crazy Englishwoman writing a book about the Polynesians. There are no Polynesians on Takaku. Only black men. Headhunters." He paused. "Hungry headhunters."

"I am Scots, not English." India's tone was rapidly becoming less calm, less controlled. Near the end of the dock, a British naval captain standing with two other officers had turned his head and was studying her intently. "I know there are no Polynesians on Takaku now," she said, carefully lowering her voice. "But there are Polynesians on the island of Ontong Java, and on Tikopia, and if it's true that—"

"You want to go to Ontong Java? The steamer will take you there. It stops at many islands, Neu Brenen and

Ontong Java and Fiji, before going on to Samoa and the
Marquesas and the Sandwich Islands."

"I plan to visit many of those places eventually, but at
the moment it is Takaku I must see."

"Not from my ketch," said the trader, and before India realized what he was about, he darted sideways and
was around her, the intense tropical sunlight gleaming on
his sweat-sheened brown cheeks as he threw a panicked
look back at her and trotted toward the shore.

"Blast it," muttered India beneath her breath, for he
was the fourth trader she had approached, and she was
running out of options.

At the end of the dock, the British naval captain nodded to his associates and began to walk toward her.
He was a tall, big-boned man who looked to be in his
early thirties, with attractive, even features and pale gray
eyes that crinkled at the corners. "I beg your pardon,
madam," he said, touching one hand to the brim of his
hat as he came abreast of her. "But you are Miss India
McKnight, aren't you? The travel writer?"

India felt herself glow warmly with pleasure. The
Hindu copra trader had heard of her, too, of course, but
his opinion of her had obviously been less than flattering.
"Why, yes. I am."

An open smile spread across the captain's suntanned
face. "I'm Simon Granger. That's my ship out there, the
Barracuda." He nodded toward a sleek corvette riding at
anchor in the sun-drenched blue waters of the harbor.
"I'm afraid I couldn't help overhearing your conversa-

tion, and I must say, I don't think you're likely to find anyone here in Rabaul willing to put in to the southern bay of Takaku."

India met his engaging smile with one of her own. "You're going to tell me it's dangerous. The pass through the reef is narrow and rocky, and the natives there have reverted to their old habit of solving their problems by eating them."

He gave a startled laugh. "That's about what I was going to say, yes."

"Then I am all the more determined to go there. In my experience, the most fascinating and rewarding places to visit are always those I have been expressly warned to avoid."

He laughed again, then sobered as he stared thoughtfully into the distance. "There is someone who might be willing to take you to Takaku, if you truly are determined to go there. His name is Ryder. Jack Ryder. He knows the reef around Takaku better than most, and he's not afraid of cannibals."

India looked at Captain Granger with interest. "Why not?"

"Perhaps because he lived with them for two years."

India sucked in her breath. "He lived with *cannibals*? An Englishman?"

"He's not an Englishman, exactly. He comes from Queensland, in the Australian Colonies."

"I see," murmured India, for it explained much. They

had quite a reputation for lawlessness, the Australians. Not as bad as the island headhunters, of course, but bad.

"He has a small start-up copra plantation on Neu Brenen," the captain was saying. "There's a steamer leaving first thing in the morning that could drop you there."

"He lives on Neu Brenen? But that's a German island, isn't it?"

The captain's gently molded lips tightened. "The Germans think it is. And their gunboat in the harbor is the main reason Ryder settled there."

India knew a tremor of apprehension that mingled, contradictorily, with a quiver of interest. "He's a buccaneer, is he?"

"Not exactly. But he is a rough character. You need to understand that."

"Not too dangerous, surely, or you wouldn't have told me about him, now would you?" She held out her hand to him. "Our meeting was fortuitous, Captain. I appreciate your information."

Captain Granger clasped her hand in his, but shook his head. "There are many who would say I have done you a disservice, that I should have warned you to stay far away from the likes of Jack Ryder. And that I should have tried harder to talk you out of going to Takaku."

"That you could not have done."

Amusement deepened the crinkled edges of his eyes. "No. I don't think I could." He started to turn away, then paused to glance back at her, his brows drawn together as if by a worrisome thought. "If you do decide to look up Jack Ryder, it probably wouldn't be a good idea to mention my name."

"You are old enemies?"

He showed his teeth in a smile that struck India as cold and fierce and far from charming. "On the contrary. We were the best of friends. Once."

≈≈Chapter Two

THE SURF BROKE on Neu Brenen's offshore coral reef with a boom that was like a continuous, earth-shuddering volley of deadly cannon fire. Sometimes, Jack liked to climb the cliffs at the head of the bay and simply let the power of the crashing waves reverberate through him in a primitive, drumbeatlike evocation of eternity that made him feel both humble and oddly, exhilaratingly free.

But at the moment, Jack Ryder had a headache, and the endless bloody *boom-boom-boom* of the surf was about to drive him out of his bloody mind. Too much kava, he told himself as he staggered out onto the pandanus-roofed veranda of his bungalow. Finding the water bucket he'd left near the steps still half full, he upended its contents over his head, the breath wheezing out of him as the surprisingly cool liquid coursed down his naked chest and back, for he wore only a laplap wrapped low, native style, around his hips, leaving his legs and feet bare.

Shaking his head like a wet dog, Jack opened his eyes and squinted against the fierce tropical sun that turned the wind-whipped ripples on the lagoon below into a blinding panoply of diamond flashes. For a moment, he thought he saw a longboat striking toward his dock from the rusty old steamer riding at anchor in the bay. But then he thought, Nah, couldn't be, and shut his eyes again.

Above the din of the distant surf, the gentle patter of footfalls on the path around the side of his bungalow was barely audible. "I was wondering when you'd make it out of bed," said a young, cheerful voice.

Jack opened one eye, saw Patu's shining, smiling face, and groaned. Jack thought about leaning against the wall behind him, but the problem with woven bamboo walls was that you couldn't use them as a prop in a pinch. He went to sit at the top of the steps instead, and lowered his aching forehead to his updrawn knees.

"There's talk about an Englishman named Granger looking for you," said Patu. "Simon Granger, captain of the HMS *Barracuda*."

"I've heard."

"They say he wants to see you hanged. Him and his first lieutenant, who just happens to be a cousin of the bloody Prime Minister of England. They say he's *sworn* to see you hanged."

"I've heard that, too."

"You don't seem too worried about it."

"You think I should be worried?" Jack looked up to find that Patu was no longer smiling.

"I would be."

The boy had been with Jack for almost four years now. Patu said he was probably around fifteen or sixteen years old, although no one knew for certain and he was so small and slight that he looked even younger. His mother was a Polynesian from an island near Tahiti, his father one of a long line of Englishmen who had sailed through the islands and made love to a dusky-skinned, exotic beauty, and then sailed away again. Most people thought Jack had adopted the boy, perhaps as some sort of atonement for the child Jack himself had abandoned, but the truth was that Patu had adopted Jack.

"I think you've been around the *papalagi* too long," Jack said now. "You need to go back to the lotus-eating islands of Polynesia, where the days are spent laughing and swimming, and the nights are for making soft, sweet love on palm-fringed, moonlit beaches."

"Huh." Patu came to sit on the step below Jack. Unlike Jack, Patu wore canvas trousers, an open-necked shirt, and shoes on his feet. "I think you musta done too much lotus-eating in your day." It was the irony of their friendship that while Patu had attached himself to Jack in order to learn the ways of that long-vanished English officer, Jack was determined not to let the boy forget the other part of his heritage, the Polynesian part.

In the bay below, sunlight gleamed on an eddy of water turned by a flashing oar.

"What you lookin' at?" said Patu.

Jack raised one hand to shade his eyes. "That ship that's just dropped anchor in the harbor."

"It's the steamer from Rabaul."

"Yeah. And why's it sending a boat to my dock?"

"Did you order something?"

"Through that rat- and cockroach-infested rust bucket?" Jack made a rude noise and frowned against the glare of the sun and the bleary haze of too many nights spent indulging in the pleasures of sin and excess. "What do you think?"

Patu climbed to the top step and peered into the distance. "I think something's coming, whether you ordered it or not." He grinned. "Or should I say, *someone*. A mail-order wife, maybe? Although from the looks of her, I'd say it's more likely somebody has decided you need your very own missionary, to convert you to the ways of the godly and save you from the fires of hell and damnation."

A terrible pain flashed across Jack's temple, and he groaned and lowered his head again. "You talk too much, boy. Just go down there and tell her to go away."

"Not me," said Patu. "She looks bigger than me. And meaner than you."

It was a bloody missionary, all right, Jack decided, frowning at the woman who sat ramrod straight at the prow of the longboat, her gloved hands gripping the plain handle of an austere parasol, the collar of her ugly, drab-colored gown buttoned up so high around her neck he wondered it didn't choke her.

He was standing near the end of his dock, his bare legs straddled wide, his arms crossed at his naked chest, when her boat knocked against the rough wooden pier.

"*Kaoha nui*," said the woman, evidently mistaking him for a Polynesian.

"G'day," said Jack, giving her his nastiest smile.

She blinked up at him, her nostrils flaring on a quick, startled breath as she took in the brown, nearly naked, overtly hostile length of him. He had to give her credit: she didn't miss a beat. "You must be Jack Ryder." The accent surprised him: crisp, no-nonsense Scots.

"That's right." He shifted his hands to his hips and leaned forward. "I don't know who you are or what you're doing here, but you can just tell these men to turn around and take you right back where you came from."

He'd made no move to offer her a hand, so she simply closed her parasol with a snap and clambered unaided up onto the dock with an agility that both surprised him and gave him a quick glimpse of long, slim calves and un-expectedly neat ankles disappearing into sensible, lace-up boots. "I am India McKnight," she said, carefully shaking out her skirts before she lifted her head and fixed him with a steady stare. "How do you do?"

He'd actually heard of her, although he wasn't about to tell her that. He even had one of her books. *In the*

Footsteps of Montezuma, it was called. It had been written with a wonderfully dry wit and an acerbic way of looking at the world that had appealed to him. He remembered finishing it and thinking, Now, that's one Scotswoman I wouldn't mind meeting.

Just went to prove how wrong a body could be, he thought.

"I've come to offer you a business proposition," she said, when he continued simply to stare at her.

"Not interested."

"How can you know when you haven't heard what it is yet?"

Patu had been right, Jack realized. The woman was a bloody Amazon. She barely had to tip back her head to meet his gaze squarely.

She nodded toward the sleek, American-built yacht riding at anchor in the lagoon. "Is that your boat?"

The glint of sunlight off the water hurt his eyes. It wasn't fair, really, having to deal with this bloody shark of a woman and a hangover, both at the same time. He hadn't even had time to take a bloody leak. He thought about taking one now, right off the end of the dock. That would surely send Miss Priss-faced McKnight scurrying back to her rusty steamer, where she'd probably sit down and write all about it for her next book. He wouldn't have expected the thought to give him pause, but it did.

"She's called the *Sea Hawk,*" Jack said, contenting himself with giving her another of his nasty smiles. "I won her off a couple of Yankee blackbirders in a poker game a few years back."

"And are you a blackbirder, Mr. Ryder?"

They were the lowest of the low, blackbirders. They called it recruiting, what they did, stealing young Melanesians and Polynesians and taking them away to work in the fields of Queensland and Fiji and South America, but it was really just another word for slaving. If she'd been a man, he'd probably have punched her one for that. As it was, he took a hasty step forward, then drew up short. "What do you think?"

She kept her gaze steady on his face, her gray eyes dark and solemn in a way that almost made him regret baiting her. "I think I owe you an apology," she said after a moment. "I hear you are familiar with the passage through the southern reef off Takaku."

She so took him by surprise that he answered her without thought. "Familiar enough. Why?"

"I would like to hire you to convey me to the bay below Mount Futapu. If we leave first thing tomorrow morning, we should be there before eleven. That would give me some four or five hours to climb the slopes of the volcano and investigate the so-called Faces of Futapu, and still—"

"Whoa, whoa, whoa." Jack brought up both hands to clutch the sides of his aching head. "I'm not *conveying* you anywhere, lady."

She gave him a calm, appraising look that took him straight from annoyance all the way to full fury. "You're concerned about the recent reports of cannibal activity in the area, I suppose," she said in a self-confident, faintly condescending tone that would have been enough, by itself, to aggravate him. "I can assure you, you will be in no danger. I am not asking you to accompany me in my ascent to the summit. You may remain safely aboard your yacht in the harbor."

"I don't give a rat's ass about the bloody cannibals," Jack bellowed. The echo of the shout reverberated in his head, making him groan.

She gave him another of those critical assessments, and this time he'd swear he saw a gleam of amusement sparkling in her clear gray eyes. "From the looks of things, Mr. Ryder, I'd say you have what we call in Scotland a *deevil of a haid*. Is that why you're so cranky?"

He walked right up to her, deliberately intimidating her with his big, nearly naked, sweat-sheened, sunbrowned body. "I am not *cranky*," he said, enunciating each word softly and carefully as he leaned into her, close enough that his breath stirred an errant, chestnut-colored curl peeking out from her sensible bonnet. "Nor am I some bloody tour guide. I'm an antisocial renegade wanted by the British bloody navy for mayhem and murder, which means you've probably far more to fear from me than from any headhunting black men of Takaku."

He saw her chest jerk as she sucked in a deep breath, her eyes growing wide as she stared up at him. She was younger than he'd first supposed, he realized, twenty-four or -five at the most, with smooth cheeks and fine

eyes and the kind of clear-cut features that would probably be called handsome by those who admired that sort
of woman. Jack didn't.

He also saw that she wasn't nearly as self-possessed as
she liked to think she was. Her gaze skittered sideways to
the longboat that still bobbed, waiting, beside the dock.
She might not be afraid of cannibals, but a naked male
chest in close proximity was obviously something else
again. She probably would have gone away then and left
him alone if he hadn't spoiled it all by adding, "Besides,
the so-called Faces of Fatapu are a natural formation."

Too late, he saw the leap of interest in her eyes. "Natural? Are you certain? Because according to my sources—"

"Which sources?" Jack demanded, before he could
stop himself.

"Dunsberry," she said, with a little lifting of her head,
as if James Dunsberry were the definitive expert on the
South Pacific.

"Huh. Dunsberry never got within a hundred miles of
Takaku, let alone climbed to the summit of Mount Futapu. If he had, he'd have known that the Faces are just
weirdly folded upthrusts of old lava."

"You've seen them?" Her lips parted on a little gasp of
excitement that set him to thinking, for some reason he
couldn't begin to understand, that this was exactly the
kind of erotic, breathy noise she'd make when a man
took her.

Jack stared off into the distance, and willed a certain
wayward portion of his anatomy to behave itself. "Of

course I've seen them," he muttered, wishing he were wearing something more confining than a twist of cloth around his hips.

"If it's true, you understand what this means, don't you?" she said, for all the world as if she were having an esoteric scholarly conversation in some stuffy London drawing room, rather than standing at the end of a weathered dock on a flyspeck of an island in the middle of the South Pacific, with a half-naked Aussie no-account preoccupied with lascivious thoughts of what she might look like if someone could ever get her out of that ugly, high-collared dress of hers.

"If it's true," she was saying, "then it is more important than ever that I go to Takaku and verify what you're saying. Dunsberry used the Faces of Futapu as proof of an ancient link between the rock-carving traditions of Laos and Burma and the statues and marae of the Marshalls and Easter Island. But if he was wrong, if there never was a Polynesian rock-carving presence in Melanesia, then the break is significant."

"Just wait right there." Jack brought his bleary gaze and wandering attention back to focus on her animated face. "Where exactly do you think the Polynesians came from?"

"South America."

She said it with a tightening of her jaw and a steely gaze that defied him to laugh at her. He didn't laugh. But he did shake his head. "You're wrong."

"Am I?" Her tone told him she'd had this argument

before. "The Polynesians are concentrated in the eastern islands of the Pacific. The common consensus, of course, is that they were forced to keep moving through the western islands such as New Guinea and the Solomons because of the presence of the headhunting Melanesians. But what if they're found predominantly in the eastern islands because they came from the east? It's the prevailing direction of the trade winds, isn't it? Botanists have documented numerous native South American plants throughout the islands—the sweet potato and coconut palm and many others. And if the *vegetation* could move from east to west, then why not the human inhabitants? I have compared photographs of the statues of Fatu Hiva with those I have seen myself in the jungles of Central and South America, and the similarities are startling."

He stared at her through squinted eyes. "You're writing a bloody book about this, aren't you?"

A faint, unexpected hint of color touched her cheeks. "As a matter of fact, I am. I'm thinking of calling it *From Mandalay to the Cannibal Islands*."

"Huh. Given your argument, one would think you'd have started in the Americas, and called the book *From Peru to the Cannibal Islands*."

He was silently laughing at her, and her chest rose and fell with indignation when she realized it. "You made it up, didn't you? What you said about the Faces of Fatapu? They're not a natural formation. You just said that so I'd go away and leave you alone."

Jack let out a soft sigh. "That's why I said it, all right. But that doesn't mean it's not true."

"Prove it."

He should have told her he didn't need to prove a bloody thing to her. He should have told her to get the bloody hell away from him and stay away. Instead, he said, "You're forgetting about the cannibals."

She shook her head. "You told me you're not afraid of cannibals."

"I'm not. But you should be."

"Because I'm a woman?"

"Women make good eating."

He said it with a smile, meaning to scare her. Instead, a gleam of interest lit up her eyes. "Really? Have you ever eaten one?"

The question was so unexpected, Jack almost jumped. "Bloody hell. What do you think I am?"

"I heard you lived with cannibals once. For two years."

"Not here."

"Where?"

Jack half turned away, then swung back on her. "Look, you want me to take you to Takaku, or not?"

A flicker of surprise animated her expressive face. She'd make a lousy poker player, Jack thought. "Does this mean you'll do it?"

"For ten pounds."

"Ten pounds! But that's outrageous!"

He shrugged. "Take it or leave it."

She looked at him through the narrowed eyes of a woman who had haggled her way from Egypt to Mexico. "Five."

He grinned. "Eight."

"Seven and a half."

"Done." He jerked his head toward the German settlement of Neu Brenenberg, tucked into the side of the verdant mountain that rose dark and steep on the far side of the bay. "Have these men take you to a place called the Limerick. The old one-legged Irishman who runs it looks like a pirate, but he keeps a bungalow hotel you'll find considerably cleaner than that steamer you just got off. Unless you like rats, of course."

"Actually, I came to appreciate their presence on the steamer," she said with a slow smile. "They scared away the cockroaches."

He found he liked her smile, liked the way it banished that spinsterish pinch of earnestness and hinted at the existence of another side to this woman altogether. "I'll pick you up from the Limerick at first light," he said gruffly, and took a step back.

He stood and watched as, with the aid of one of the seamen, she clambered down into the waiting longboat. Then she paused, her head falling back and her brows drawing together as she stared up at him. "You will be there, won't you?"

It was his last chance to get out of it. For one, oddly

suspended moment, he was intensely aware of the golden heat of the tropical sun on his bare shoulders and the violent boom of the distant surf and the rocking of the dock beneath his feet. Then he said, "I'll be there. Now get the hell out of here, would you? I need to take a leak."

~~Chapter Three

On the deck of the HMS *Barracuda*, First Lieutenant Alex Preston paused to watch Captain Granger lean against the rail and lift a spyglass to one eye. Around them, the wind-whipped waves of the tropical blue sea surged, foam-flecked and empty. Captain Granger's jaw tightened in a careful checking of emotions that Alex could only guess at.

Already, the light had taken on a richly drenching golden quality that spoke of the imminent descent of darkness. Even after some six months of sailing these equatorial waters, it still amazed Alex how rapidly night replaced day here. One minute, the sun would be shining fierce and bright. Then, suddenly, the world would be bathed in a glorious tapestry of orange streaked with red and purple, a breathtaking panorama that disappeared all too quickly to plunge the earth into starry darkness.

"I thought you weren't expecting Ryder to show up until tomorrow, sir," said Alex.

Captain Granger lowered the glass, but kept his gaze on the wide, swelling sea. "I'm not."

Alex studied the other man's hard, closed profile. They'd been friends once, Captain Granger and Jack Ryder—or so it was rumored. That had been back in the days when they'd both been junior officers, before the Australian deliberately caused the sinking of their ship, the HMS *Lady Juliana*, and the death of more than half its company, including the *Lady Juliana*'s captain. As the only officer left alive, Simon Granger had spent six weeks with the surviving crew members in an open lifeboat before being rescued by Malay fishermen somewhere in the Dutch East Indies. The incident had made Granger a hero, and Ryder an outlaw.

But the Admiralty, like Disraeli's Conservative government, had been distracted at the time by events in South Africa and India, Afghanistan and Turkey. It had only been recently, with the victory of the Liberals and their leader, Gladstone—a near-cousin of the *Lady Juliana*'s ill-fated captain—that the Admiralty's determination to capture Ryder and bring him to justice had resurged.

It was the reason Alex was here now as first lieutenant, an appointment almost unheard of for an officer of his age and experience. For Captain Gladstone had been Alex's uncle, and the Prime Minister was cousin to Alex's mother. The appointment was a dream come true. Yet Alex felt the weight of his new responsibility and his family's expectations sitting heavily on his shoulders. They expected him to make certain Captain Granger didn't allow his past friendship with the renegade to interfere with the execution of his orders. Only, if the need were to arise, Alex wasn't exactly clear on how he, as a mere first lieutenant, could be expected to control his own captain. Even if Alex's mother's cousin was the Prime Minister of England.

"You must be looking forward to getting your hands on the man, sir," said Alex. "After so many years."

"Looking forward to it?" The captain's nostrils flared, his chest lifting as he sucked the salt-tinged air deep into his lungs. "I'm just following orders, Mr. Preston."

Alex kept his gaze fixed on the captain's face. There was no hint of impatient anticipation, no thirst for the chase. Yet Simon Granger had volunteered to be the one to bring Ryder in. "The man's a disgrace to the service and to England," Alex said, his voice rough with emotion, for Alex was a man with high ideals and little but contempt for those who fell afoul of them. "He never should have been allowed to roam free for so many years."

The captain turned his head then, his gray eyes narrowing as he studied Alex. "Tell me something, Mr. Preston; why did you join the navy?"

Alex lifted his chin with self-conscious pride. "To serve Queen and country, sir."

A slow smile curled the captain's lips. "Nothing else?"

Alex felt himself growing unexpectedly warm under the other man's scrutiny. "And to see something of the world." There was no need for Alex to mention the other reason—the one that had to do with being a gentleman's younger son, and the need to make his own way in the world. That was a driving force common to every officer in the navy.

"You're from Norfolk, aren't you?" said the captain.

"Yes, sir."

"And this is your first assignment overseas?"

"Yes, sir," said Alex, wondering where the captain was leading, for he surely knew Alex had spent his first years in the navy on a steam sloop based out of Southampton.

Granger swung away to stare once more at the surrounding sea, pale silver now in the vanishing light. The island of Takaku, with its steaming volcanic peaks rising up steep and wild, was only a dark silhouette against the fading orange of the horizon. "Ever make love to a Tahitian woman, Mr. Preston?"

Alex felt himself heat, once more, with embarrassed confusion. "No, sir. Why?"

Captain Granger pushed away from the rail and turned toward the stern, his voice carrying back to Alex on the warm trade winds. "Because until you do, I wouldn't be too quick to judge Jack Ryder."

India's encounter with Jack Ryder should have prepared her for the proprietor of Neu Brenenberg's bungalow hotel, but she still found the gnarled, one-eyed, one-legged Irishman who ran the Limerick a shock. The man said his name was Harry O'Keefe, although India had her doubts about the veracity of that.

He looks for all the world like a character out of Mr. Stevenson's Treasure Island, she wrote in her notebook later that evening. *One can't help but wonder what crimes this Australian and Irishman have committed, to make them so eager to live with the shadow of a German gunboat protecting them from the long arm of British law.*

Still, she thought, absently chewing on the end of her pencil, she had to admit that the appalling Australian had been right. The Limerick's rooms were unexpectedly, refreshingly clean, and she could find no fault with the hearty Irish stew Mr. O'Keefe had sent up for her supper. The lack of a lock on the door she had solved by shoving her trunk in front of it.

The sound of a child's laughter carrying through the open window on a fresh sea breeze brought India's head up. She heard a woman's laughing admonition, and a man's voice, deep with amusement. India hesitated a moment, then laid aside her pencil and crossed the room to where the light muslin curtains billowed in the warm night air.

Mingling moon- and star-shine bathed the scene outside her window in a clear, silvery-blue light. She could see the white line of the surf, breaking on the beach below, and the feathery, wind-ruffled darkness of the palms silhouetted against the night sky. It was early yet, the inhabitants of the tidy little German settlement of Neu

Brenenberg not yet having settled down for the night. Two men, their voices low murmurs, bent over a chessboard set up on the deep veranda of a nearby house. And, beyond them, India could see a young family, out for a stroll along the beach.

The child—a boy of about five, she decided—played at the surf's edge, shrieking with delight as he ran from each breaking, racing wave. From higher up the sand, his parents watched him. The woman had her arm linked through the man's. And as India stood at her window, watching, she saw the woman rest her head on her man's shoulder in a simple gesture of love and contentment that caught at something inside of India. Something that hurt, and left her feeling restless and sad.

Turning away from the window, she jerked the curtains closed against the night. Her gaze fell on her notebook, but she felt oddly disinclined to write more, and decided to retire instead.

By the time she parted the bed's mosquito netting and put out the oil lamp, the night had quieted. Yet she could still hear the child's laughter echoing through her memory, still see in her mind's eye the way the man's arm had slipped, warm and tender, about his wife's waist to hold her close.

Fluffing and refluffing her pillows, India shifted, wakeful, restless, in her lonely bed. She reminded herself that she remained unmarried by choice. That she was living the life of freedom and adventure about which she had always dreamed. It was true, all true. Yet as she lay alone in the darkness, her hand crept up to touch her breast, then slipped down to ride, thoughtfully, on her empty womb.

It was a long time before she slept.

She was up early the next morning, dressed in what she called her Expedition Outfit, which she had had especially made to her own design by a tailor in Cairo. She checked for what was probably the third time to make certain that her notebook and pencils were in her waterproof knapsack, also specifically made to her design. Then she slung the knapsack along with a canteen over her shoulder, and sallied forth to await Mr. Ryder's arrival on the bungalow's porch.

Dawn was just breaking in the east when she let herself out the hotel's front door. A rich panoply of pink and gold and orange light spilled in exotic splendor across the smooth silver water of the bay, and she paused, one hand curling around the edge of the half-closed door as the beauty of the moment stole her breath. Around her, the small, orderly German town still slept; the only sounds to come to her were the gentle sloshing of the incoming tide and the chorus of tropical birdsongs that filled the warm, steamy air. She felt both exhilarated and oddly humbled by the magic of the moment. And she thought, *This* is why I travel, why I have chosen the life I lead.

Smiling to herself, India went to stand expectantly at the top of the steps, her eyes straining to catch sight of

Mr. Ryder's *Sea Hawk* in the rapidly lightening bay below.

An hour later, the sun was well up in the sky and the village around her stirring. Mr. Ryder had yet to arrive. India was sitting in one of the porch's tattered wicker chairs, her gaze on the wind-rippled expanse of the bay, the toe of one boot tapping an annoyed tattoo on the plank flooring, when Mr. O'Keefe came whistling up the hibiscus- and fern-shaded path that ran around the side of the hotel.

"Blimey," said the Irishman, his head falling back as he stumbled to a halt at the base of the steps and stared up at the sight of India in her Expedition Outfit. The long-sleeved, belted blouse was nothing out of the ordinary, constructed as it was of a dark blue cloth woven loosely enough to allow good air circulation, yet sturdy enough to protect her from the fierceness of the tropical sun, as well as from snakes, insects, and savage vegetation.

But it was the rest of India's outfit that generally excited the most comment. The skirt was cut full enough to be modest, but not so full as to hamper the movements of a woman who made her living tramping through jungles and scrambling up cliffs. An unfortunate incident that had occurred while climbing to the High Place in Petra and had nearly cost India her life had convinced her of the wisdom of having the skirt discreetly split. And because nothing wears quite as well as a good Scottish plaid, India had had her Expedition Outfit cut from the McKnight tartan.

"Well, you'll be a hard one to lose in the jungle wearing that getup, that's fer sure," said Mr. O'Keefe, rubbing the tip of his nose with a splayed hand that did not quite manage to obscure his broad grin.

"That seems unlikely to become a problem," said India, who had long ago become inured to such reactions to her Expedition Outfit, "seeing as how Mr. Ryder has failed to put in an appearance as promised."

"Sure then, but it's liable to be noon or more before anyone'll be seeing Jack, given what I hear about last night's game, and him liking to have a good bottle of brandy at his elbow when he's got the cards in his hands."

India rose slowly to her feet. "Are you telling me that Mr. Ryder spent last night *gambling*? And drinking?"

Mr. O'Keefe's one remaining eye blinked. "Aye."

India stared off across the sun-sparkled, vivid blue waters of the bay. She'd always been frustratingly myopic, but if she squinted, she thought she could make out the shape of the *Sea Hawk*, still riding at anchor near Mr. Ryder's dilapidated dock. A rush of cold fury surged through her, surprising her with the shaking, blinding intensity of its passion.

"Tell me, Mr. O'Keefe," she said, stooping with swift decision to assemble knapsack, canteen, and pith helmet. "Where might I find someone willing to drive me to the far side of the bay?"

*   *   *

"You want I wait?" asked the woolly-headed Melanesian boy who had driven India around the bay in his rickety pony cart.

Standing in the sun-baked, grassy verge beside the cart, India looked down at the palm-shaded pandanus roofs of the scattering of small huts that had been built into the side of the hill between the road and the beach below. A start-up copra plantation, Captain Simon Granger had called this establishment. Well, India had seen several such places in her tour of the South Seas, but none as ramshackle as this one. Instead of the neat, iron-roofed, colonial-style bungalow one might expect, Mr. Ryder's home appeared indistinguishable from a common native hut. Nor could she see any significant signs of cultivation. There were a few racks of drying copra, their pungent sweetness filling the hot, steamy air. But as far as she could tell, Jack Ryder must simply lie around waiting for the coconuts to fall out the surrounding trees and into his lap.

"Miss?" said the boy in the cart.

India looked up into the boy's dark, flat-nosed face. "No, you needn't wait." She handed him the agreed fare, and a generous tip besides. "Thank you," she said, and adjusting the angle of her pith helmet, she set off down the narrow, muddy track to the primitive buildings below.

The leafy canopy of the jungle overhead came alive with a twittering, screeching, rustling protest as India pushed through a thicket of dripping ferns still wet from the previous evening's rain. The Australians had an expression for it: going troppo, they called it, when a white man abandoned the trappings of Western civilization and assumed the clothing and lifestyle of the natives. Well, thought India, it was difficult to imagine anyone going more troppo than Mr. Ryder.

Shaded by a stand of coconut and breadfruit trees, his house stood in a clearing on a spit of land overlooking both the bay and the thundering ocean beyond it. As she drew nearer, India realized the structure was slightly larger than most native huts, more like two huts put together. The walls were of woven bamboo, the roof of pandanus fastened with coconut fiber thongs to supporting purau-bough rafters. In place of window glass, bamboo blinds swung from the eaves, while on the porch, a young, dark-skinned, bare-breasted woman was squatting on a mat and grating a coconut. She looked up as India approached.

"Is Mr. Ryder at home?" India asked, hesitating at the base of the steps.

The woman was lighter-skinned than most of the Melanesians of the island, perhaps part Polynesian, or even part European. A bare-bottomed boy of two or three gazed up at India from his mother's side, his eyes big and blue in a pale, even-featured face. A terrible suspicion forming in her mind, India stared at the child, then back at the nubile, half-naked woman.

India was no innocent. She had heard of such things:

white men keeping dark women as their mistresses. But that didn't mean she found the thought of having to deal with such a man any less disquieting.

"Ryder inside," said the woman, her attention once more concentrated on the deft movement of her fingers. "You go in."

India mounted the steps, then paused again before the open, darkened doorway. The woman had told her to enter, but she couldn't quite bring herself to do so unannounced. Raising one fist, she rapped her knuckles sharply against the frame. "Mr. Ryder?" she called, then stood listening as her voice faded away into a silence broken by the gentle swish of palm fronds and the boom of the distant surf.

"Mr. Ryder," she called again, louder. Somewhere, a cockatoo screeched, but the stillness of the house's interior remained undisturbed. With a last glance at the bare-breasted woman on the porch, India stepped inside.

Although primitive, the house's interior was surprisingly pleasant, with tall, open rafters and a deliciously airy atmosphere a more proper plank-and-iron colonial structure could never have achieved. The pale, diffused light filtering in through the bamboo blinds showed her a scattering of island-made furniture: sturdy mahogany and teak tables and settees, and numerous tall bamboo bookcases filled, to India's amazement, with shelf after shelf of well-worn books. Overcome with curiosity, she was halfway across the floor toward them, intending to study their titles, when a faint stirring followed by a strangled snore froze her in her tracks.

Turning her head to search the shadowy recesses of the room, India found herself staring at a huge, elaborately carved Malaysian bedstead draped in filmy white falls of mosquito netting. From the crumpled depths of the bedding, a dark masculine arm emerged to flop over the mattress's edge and dangle there limply.

"Mr. Ryder," said India.

The arm didn't move.

Remembering the man's state of undress the previous day, India approached the bedstead with some caution. A tousled dark head came into view, then a naked back, well strapped with muscle and darkened by the sun. Letting her gaze travel slowly down that taut, curving spine, India found herself both relieved and oddly disappointed to discover a twisted sheet obscuring any further details of the man's anatomy.

"Mr. Ryder," she said again, louder, but received in response only another half snore that filled the air with incriminating fumes of brandy.

She thought about shaking the bedpost, but it seemed too intimate a thing, to actually touch his bed. Instead, she grasped the edge of a nearby chest for balance and, lifting one foot, used the toe of her sensible lace-up boot to jostle the mattress.

Nothing.

A soft, melodic laugh from the doorway behind her brought India around.

"You could dump him out of bed and it probably still wouldn't wake him," said the slim Polynesian boy who stood just inside the hut's entrance.

India threw a disdainful glance back at the man in the bed. "I hired him to take me to Takaku. He was to have picked me up at the Limerick in Neu Brenenberg at dawn."

"I know. I've had the *Sea Hawk* ready to go." He came forward as he spoke, and India saw that, like the Melanesian baby on the porch, this boy must be of mixed parentage, for his skin was surprisingly fair, his hair more auburn than black. His English was good, too, with only a vague trace of an accent. And unlike Mr. Ryder, the boy was decently clothed in a sturdy shirt and canvas trousers. "I am Patu."

"How do you do?" she said, extending him her hand, and wondering if this boy, like the one on the porch, counted the dissolute, naked Australian in the bed as his father. "It doesn't look as if we shall be making the trip to Takaku today."

"I'm afraid it's today or not at all," said Patu. "The *Sea Hawk*'s scheduled to start its run through the islands tomorrow, to pick up copra from the other stations, and we're late as it is. The weather's not likely to hold for much longer."

India knew a bitter combination of disappointment and rising indignation. To have come so close to reaching her objective, only to have the chance snatched away!

The man in the bed let out another brandy-tinged snore, then lay still.

"Stand back, Mr. Patu," said India, coming to an instant decision.

The smile on the boy's face faded. "Why?"

"Because I wouldn't want to get you wet." Spinning back around, she seized the water jug from Mr. Ryder's bedside chest and flung its contents in a well-aimed arc that landed with a sodden splash on the dark, disheveled head of the bed's occupant.

~~Chapter Four

H E WAS DROWNING.
   Choking and sputtering, Jack pushed himself up onto his forearms, his head bowed, his open mouth sucking in air, his brain confused and befuddled. Water ran into his ear and dripped off his nose. He must have gone outside and passed out. That was it. He'd gone outside to take a leak and passed out, and now it was raining.

Opening his eyes, Jack had a brief, confusing vision of mosquito netting and a carved bedpost. Then the room spun around in a familiar, sickening way. Groaning, he closed his eyes and sank down onto the sheets again. Wet sheets. Why were his sheets wet? He was in his bed, but he was wet. It didn't make any sense.

"We had an appointment today, Mr. Ryder," said a faintly familiar and smugly self-satisfied female voice. "Have you forgotten?"

Swiveling his head, Jack opened one eye and found himself staring at Miss India Bloody McKnight. She had a malevolent smile on her face and his water jug in her hands. His empty water jug.

"Sonofafuckingbitch." It came out hoarse and water-logged, but ferociously clear.

"An appointment to sail *at dawn*," she continued, as if she hadn't heard him, although he knew bloody well she had by the angry color in her cheeks and the unnecessary click with which she set the empty jug down on the chest. "The sun is now well up in the sky. You must bestir yourself."

She sounded like a bloody Sunday school teacher. She should have been a Sunday school teacher, he decided, rather than tromping determinedly around the world, writing her bloody books and trying to drown men in their beds.

Jack rolled onto his back, his hands coming up to rake the wet hair out of his face and rub his bleary eyes. Bestir himself. He brought his gaze into focus on her prim, self-righteous face. So she wanted him to bestir himself, did she? He'd teach her to come barging into a sleeping man's house and throw water on him.

His gaze still fixed on her face, Jack swung first one leg over the side of the bed, then the other, and pushed the dripping mosquito netting aside. She must have expected him to bring the sheet up with him, wrapped laplap style about his hips for modesty, because she didn't turn away. It wasn't until he thrust the covers aside and stood up in all his naked glory that she went skittering backward, her eyes opening wide, her tented hands flying up to press against her lips.

"All right," he said, spreading his arms wide. It being first thing in the morning, and Jack being the kind of man he was, he didn't even need to check to know that a certain portion of his anatomy was already wide awake and ready for action. "I'm up. Satisfied?"

He expected her to scream and run away. She didn't. Clasping her hands together, she let them fall to the front of her skirt—*her split tartan skirt,* Jack noticed, opening his eyes wider at the sight of it. He also noticed, for the first time, that Patu was standing behind her. Patu was not smiling.

"Mr. Patu informs me that the *Sea Hawk* is ready to sail." She drew in a deep breath that lifted her full breasts, but she managed to keep her voice steady, even business-like. And she didn't look away. "We will await your arrival at the dock." Then she turned slowly, her shoulders back, her head held high, her dignity and self-possession unshaken, and walked out the house.

"Well, I'll be damned," said Jack.

"Go ahead, say it." Jack turned his head to study the tight, serious profile of the boy beside him. They were some three miles out of Neu Brenen, running easily with a freshening wind, and Patu had yet to say a word to him that didn't deal with the rigging of the *Sea Hawk*'s sails or some other detail involved in setting out to sea.

Patu kept his gaze on the gentle swell of the foam-flecked, vivid blue waves that stretched back to the dark and jagged outline of Neu Brenen's high peaks, still visible in the hazy distance. "I have nothing to say."

"Like hell you don't. The way it's all churning around inside you, you're liable to spew if you don't spit it out soon."

Patu turned his head, his nostrils flaring. "All right, I'll say it. She's a lady. A European lady. And you . . . you did *that* to her."

"Bloody hell." Jack threw a quick glance toward the prow of the yacht, where Miss India McKnight sat cross-legged on a chest, her head bowed as she scribbled furiously in a little black cloth notebook. He lowered his voice. "She upended a jug of water on me."

"And you were supposed to pick her up from the Limerick. At dawn."

A hot urge to defend the indefensible swelled within him. Jack swallowed it. "Here, take the tiller," he said, and sauntered toward the prow, swaying easily with the pitch and swell of the deck.

He drew up some two feet from his pith-hat- and tartan-clad passenger. She continued writing, not even bothering to glance up, although his shadow fell across her page and she must have known he was there. Jack cleared his throat. "I was thinking maybe you might like a guide. On Takaku."

She kept her head bowed over her notebook. "Are you offering your services, Mr. Ryder?"

"Patu. I was offering Patu."

The pencil paused, then resumed its journey across the page. "Thank you, but I always travel alone, and I prefer to explore the various sites I visit alone, as well."

"Seems a lonely way of life," he said, surprising even himself with the words.

She did look up then, but only enough so that, with the pith helmet hiding the upper part of her face, he still couldn't see her eyes. "For a woman, you mean?"

He blinked down at her. "For anyone."

"I have never been troubled by loneliness," she said, and went back to her writing. "It is only in solitude that one finds the peace necessary for reflection and composition. I find that women companions have a regrettable tendency to chatter incessantly, while men . . ."

She paused, so that he had to prompt her. "Yes?"

"Men invariably fall into the habit of attempting to boss any female in their company—even if the female in question is paying their wages."

Jack stared down at the rounded top of that pith helmet, and knew an unexpected and totally inexplicable rush of rage so pure and sweet that it stole his breath. He started to turn away, but took only two steps before he spun back around to point his finger at her and say, "The way I figure it, we're even."

Her head fell back, slowly, as she stared up at him, her eyes narrowing against the glare off the water. "And precisely how do you *figure* that, Mr. Ryder?"

"I might have missed picking you up at dawn, but you threw a bloody pitcher of water on me."

Her entire body seemed to stiffen. "I see no correlation between the two events at all. If you recall, I was simply endeavoring to awaken you."

"Huh. I recognize revenge when I see it."

"Indeed. I didn't expect to hear you admit that I'd been wronged."

"I didn't say that."

She swung her head away to stare out over the surging waves, but not before he caught a glimpse of the intriguing smile that played about her lips. "Very well, Mr. Ryder. I accept your apology."

Jack almost jumped. "Bloody hell. I wasn't apologizing."

She brought her gaze back to his face. The smile was gone. "Then we're not even."

They could smell the island of Takaku before they saw it, a spicy sweet tropical aroma that came to them on the stiffening breeze. Then the island itself materialized from out of the haze, a wild, impossibly beautiful place of calm turquoise lagoons and sweeping, palm-fringed beaches backed by steep, wild crags clad in a luxurious riot of tangled greenery.

Far to the north, the island tapered off into leafy dales and marshy flats where the French had established a trading village they called La Rochelle. But here, at its southern tip, Takaku was a land of near-vertical gorges and high volcanic peaks that rose twisted and menacing toward the tropical blue sky. Steam still drifted from the various cracks and craters of the smaller and southern-most of these, Mount Futapu, thrusting up from the shores of a deep round bay that was itself the flooded caldron of an old volcano. Like most of the islands in this area, Takaku was surrounded by a lagoon formed by a largely submerged fringing coral reef against which the surf crashed in an endless, spray-dashing cannonade. Which meant that the only way into the bay at the base of Mount Futapu was through a narrow break in the reef made all the more dangerous by crosscurrents and an unpredictable wind.

Idling in the rolling breakers outside the reef, Jack hauled down the staysail. Then he took the tiller again, the yacht dipping and swaying with the swell as Patu scrambled up the mast.

"Is that necessary?" asked Miss McKnight, her head tipping back as she watched the boy's ascent.

"What'd you think?" said Jack, shouting to be heard over the roar of the surf. "That people told you the pass into the bay of Futapu was dangerous just so they could up the price of 'conveying' you here?"

"As a matter of fact, yes."

Jack grunted and brought the yacht's prow around until they were pointed at the passage. "And the cannibals?"

"Oh, those I believe in."

"And they still don't worry you?"

"They're a necessary risk."

Jack threw her a quick, assessing glance. The sun was

shining warm and golden on the smooth skin of her even-featured face. She looked young and excited and far more attractive than he would have liked. He gave a low grunt that came out sounding like a growl. "You're either very brave, or very foolish."

"And which are you, Mr. Ryder?"

Jack laughed. "Me? I'm just crazy."

After that, his attention was all for the dark blue ribbon of deep water that curled its way between the sharp, submerged shelves of rainbow-hued coral. Gulls wheeled, screeching, overhead, as Patu called down warnings and directions from his high perch. But although Jack was careful, he wasn't particularly worried, and it wasn't long before they reached the calm, flat safety of the inner lagoon.

"There's sails out there," said Patu, climbing down the rigging as Jack eased the *Sea Hawk* into the deep, round bay. "A frigate or corvette, by the looks of her."

Jack found his spyglass and raised it to his eye. A sleek three-masted ship hovered in the haze just off the southern tip of the island. After a long pause, he said, "If she's flying any colors, I can't see them."

Miss McKnight came to stand at the rail beside him, her narrowed gaze on the distant ship. "Surely you don't think it's pirates, do you?"

"Pirates?" Jack lowered his glass. "No, I don't think it's pirates." She gave him a puzzled look, but he saw no reason to explain. "You've got three hours," he said, and turned away abruptly to set to work at lowering the *Sea Hawk*'s small dinghy.

She gasped. "Three hours! But that's outrageous. I—" The rest of her protest was lost in the rattle of the dinghy's chains. He was aware of her, gray eyes flashing, nostrils flaring as she fumed silently beside him until the rattling stopped. She began again, "If we had made an earlier start—"

"We didn't." The dinghy launched, Jack dangled the rope ladder over the side, and turned to face her. "The climb up to the crater's rim shouldn't take you more than forty-five minutes, and it'll be quicker coming down. That gives you a good hour and a half to look around the summit, and make sketches of the Faces of Futapu or whatever it is you plan to do up there, and still be back on the beach in three hours."

She obviously wasn't used to being dictated to. She glared at him, her chest rising and falling with indignation, her grip on the strap of her knapsack tightening until her knuckles showed white. If she'd had his neck in her hands, he'd be dead. "And if I'm not?"

Jack gave her his meanest smile. "Then I'll assume someone's made you his dinner, and the *Sea Hawk* sails." He let the smile fade. "Understood?"

Her lips pressed together into a thin, hard line. "Quite."

~~Chapter Five

To INDIA'S RELIEF, it was Patu and not that vile Australian who rowed her over to the stretch of gleaming white coral sand that formed the bay's shoreline.

"There's a path by that stream," Patu said, helping her out onto the beach. "It'll take you around the side of the mountain and up to the top."

India let her head fall back, her gaze lifting above the beach's fringing palm trees to the darkly jagged peak towering overhead. She'd read about this path, which was said to have been made by the natives of the island. The cannibal natives. As far as they were concerned, Mount Futapu was a kind of god. In times past, they had been known to throw living sacrifices into the volcano's crater.

From the deck of the *Sea Hawk*, the island had looked wild and beautiful, like something from a dream. Now, as she stared up at its steep cliffs of naked rock and gorges choked with impenetrable jungle, it seemed to have acquired a darker, faintly menacing aspect. It was all this talk about cannibals, she decided. It had made her fanciful, something she heartily despised and was not normally inclined to be.

"You will be back in three hours, won't you, miss?" said Patu.

India touched one hand to the watch she wore pinned to her bodice, and smiled. "I shall be ever vigilant of the time." Her boots sinking in the loose sand, she turned to go, then paused to look back and ask, "Would he really leave?"

"I suspect he would, miss."

India nodded. "I thought so."

She found the path easily enough. At first the climb was gentle, an idyllic stroll through groves of coconut palms with high feathery tops that murmured softly with the breeze. Brilliantly hued butterflies danced and played about her while, overhead, a vivid blue and yellow parrot peered down at her with arched head and open beak, his scolding cry echoing exotically through the jungle. India looked up at him, and laughed.

Farther inland, the track steepened, the palms giving way to moss-covered giant trees hung with pendant ropes of lianas and a tangle of unknown vines and creepers. The distant boom of the surf was still audible, but lessened here, even her footfalls seeming hushed. India lengthened her stride, oblivious to the whine of mosquitoes and the steamy heat that was gradually becoming more oppressive as she moved away from the shore. This was what she loved, this heady, heart-pumping sense of adventure, the excitement of experiencing the unfamiliar and the unexpected. At a turn in the path she came across a half-hidden, breathtakingly beautiful white orchid and longed to sketch it, but the weight of the watch pinned to her breast filled her with an uncomfortable awareness of the passage of time, and she kept walking.

Something like halfway up the slope, she stopped beside a rocky stream to rest and make some quick notes in her book. Before she left, she reached down cupped hands to bathe her face and found the water surprisingly warm, hot even. Continuing on her way, she wasn't surprised when, a few minutes farther up the trail, she came upon a bubbling hot springs, and as she neared the summit, she found another spring, the water in the small pond beside it percolating as if at a low boil. The unmistakable odor of cooking meat impregnated the warm, moist air. India stopped short, her gaze riveted on the flat stones lining the water's edge where, half obscured by the steam that floated in drifting wisps over the churning surface, someone had placed what she realized must be some kind of flesh, wrapped in leaves.

Cannibals. The word leapt immediately into her head, bringing with it a stomach-wrenching, blood-chilling, finger-tingling wave of primitive terror that swept through her body and left her winded and trembling.

"Don't be ridiculous," she told herself out loud. One hand pressed to her heaving chest, she deliberately straightened her spine. A visitor to the South Seas was in far more danger of being gored by a wild pig than of being eaten by cannibals, and she certainly wouldn't allow the presence of a few pigs to dissuade her from her inspection of the Faces of Futapu. In fact, it was probably nothing more than a side of pork steaming by the hot springs right now. She remembered with another sick twist of her stomach that a cooked human being was cavalierly referred to in this area as "long pork," but she thrust that thought from her mind. She was not some fainthearted miss, forever shrieking and going into hysterics. She was India McKnight, travel writer, and it was just this sort of experience that added spice—another unfortunate word, given its associations with cooking—to her writing.

She glanced about the clearing, but it appeared peaceful and deserted, and she told herself cannibals normally roasted their victims, anyway. Reassured by this thought, India adjusted the straps of her knapsack and canteen, straightened her pith helmet, and continued on her way.

"It's the *Barracuda*, all right," said Jack, lowering his spyglass. "Of all the bloody luck."

Patu leaned his elbows on the rail, his gaze on the brilliant white sails in the distance, and shrugged. "They should be long gone by the time we leave here."

"They should be." Jack raised the glass again. "Although if I didn't know better, I'd say they were headed right this way."

"That corvette, she's too big to fit through the passage."

"Mmhhmm." Jack watched the British ship plunge through the swells, and knew a deep, disturbing sense of uneasiness. "But her jolly boat isn't."

Patu's eyebrows drew together in a quick, worried frown. "Why would the *Barracuda* want to come here?"

"I don't know." Jack swung around to stare up at the steep, jungle-clad slopes of Mount Futapu, and swore under his breath. If it weren't for that bloody writer, he would weigh anchor right now and sail away, just to be safe. But however much of a pain in the ass India McKnight might be, Jack wasn't the kind of man to abandon a woman on a cannibal-infested island.

Swearing again, he raised the glass to his eye and watched the sails of the *Barracuda* grow larger, and larger, and larger.

There was no doubt about it, India decided, her heart soaring with excitement: the so-called Faces of Futapu were an entirely natural rock formation, not the work of long-vanished Polynesian stonecutters at all.

She worked her way around the massive twin pillars of stone, analyzing them from every angle and carefully studying their surfaces for signs that shapes naturally occurring in the rocks might have been exploited and exaggerated by human tools. But she could find nothing. Nothing at all. From the distance, these folded, upthrust remnants of some ancient eruption did look uncannily like two human heads, the faces long and narrow, the noses and eyes stylized and yet remarkably evocative. But the effect was entirely coincidental, like the face of the man in the moon. From certain angles, in fact, the resemblance disappeared entirely.

Buzzing with elation, India pulled out her notebook and found a flat rock on which to sit while she began making a series of quick, rough sketches. Thanks to Mr. Ryder, she would need to wait until later to make a more complete, careful rendering from her notes.

For perhaps the hundredth time, India lifted the watch on her chest and studied it carefully. She still had two hours, but India McKnight was not one to run unnecessary risks by cutting things close. She had every intention of leaving for the beach with plenty of time to spare.

The wind gusted up, bringing her the fresh, briny scent of the sea and the distant sound of the surf. Raising one hand to shade her eyes from the glare of the sun, India glanced down at the bay far below, and was surprised to see a ship riding at anchor just off the entrance to the passage through the reef. The sight gave her pause for a moment, but by squinting, she was able to make out the white ensign of the Royal Navy fluttering reassuringly from the ship's mast.

She watched, surprised, as the ship's crew went about the business of lowering the jolly boat. Then she went back to her sketching.

~~Chapter Six

ALEX PRESTON STOOD on the *Barracuda*'s deck and stared at the steaming, green-black mass of mountains rising above the palm-fringed shores of Takaku. The savage beauty of the island attracted and yet repelled him, like the seductive, dangerous call of some mythical temptress of old. He ached with a desire to both know it and tame it, as if by subduing its wild bestiality he could somehow conquer all the primitive, frightening urgings within himself.

"I'd like to be a member of the boarding party, sir," he said as Captain Granger prepared to join the armed seamen in the jolly boat.

Simon Granger glanced up from buckling on his sword, the fierce tropical sunlight falling full on a face that was still surprisingly young for a ship's captain. He was probably no more than thirty, Alex thought, just eight years older than Alex himself. But Granger's clearthinking leadership in those long, tortured weeks following the sinking of the *Lady Juliana* had not only made him a hero, it had also been very good for his career. Looking at him now, Alex felt a vague stirring that was part envy, part determination. It would be very good for Alex's career if the *Barracuda* were to succeed in nabbing Jack Ryder—particularly if Alex himself could have a hand in the man's capture. It would justify his being here now as first lieutenant, and quiet those who said he was too young, too inexperienced for such a posting. Those who kept whispering about his family's connections. They didn't understand, those people who whispered, the weight of such advancements, and the expectations that came with them.

"Very well, Mr. Preston," said the captain. "If Ryder's not on the *Sea Hawk*, you may remain on board the yacht with a small contingent while the rest of us go ashore."

Alex swallowed a surge of disappointment. "I'd like to go ashore myself, sir."

"Why?" The captain's eyes narrowed, as if he could somehow peer into the tortured recesses of Alex's soul. "To see the island? Or for the righteous satisfaction of being there when we capture Ryder? No, don't answer that," Granger added, throwing up one hand when Alex opened his mouth to do just that. "Tell me this instead: Have you never done anything wrong, Mr. Preston?"

Alex hesitated. "Nothing of great magnitude, no, sir."

"No? Then you've been fortunate." The captain turned

toward the ship's ladder. "Come along, Mr. Prescott. Let's hope that life continues to be so kind to you."

Jack paused with one booted, canvas-covered leg thrown over the *Sea Hawk*'s rail, a machete strapped to his side, and watched the British corvette in the open water on the far side of the reef launch its jolly boat with a rattle and a splash. "Bloody hell. I can't believe this. What the blazes are they doing here?"

Oars in hand, Patu looked up glumly from the dinghy. "I did try to warn you. You said you weren't worried."

Jack scrambled down the rope ladder and dropped the last few feet into the yacht's small boat. "If I didn't know better, I'd swear Simon and that bloody Scotswoman set this whole thing up as a trap."

"Huh," Patu grunted, pulling hard on the oars. "I thought you said you and Granger were old friends."

"What does that have to do with it?"

"Because if it'd been me, I wouldn't have expected a woman like Miss McKnight to interest you."

"What the hell are you talking about? That woman doesn't interest me. I did this for the money, remember?" Frowning, Jack stared up the steaming summit of Mount Futapu. The way he figured it, he was looking at a two-to three-day overland trek—he refused to think of it as a *flight*—to the French port of La Rochelle on the northern end of the island. It would be up to Patu to deal with the British boarding party and see that Miss McKnight made it back to Neu Brenen. Damn the woman with her bloody theories of Polynesian migration and that infectious, beguilingly attractive glimmer of excitement in her eyes.

"And if Captain Granger figures out where you're going and has the *Barracuda* patrolling off La Rochelle when I come to pick you up?" Patu asked. "What then?"

Only two usable channels cut through Takaku's fringing coral reef: the pass here, at Futapu Bay, and the wider break in the north that led to the harbor of the French trading post of La Rochelle. There was a third passage, a small, tortuous route barely wide enough for an outrigger canoe, that lay on the windward side of the island, but no one in their right mind would think of taking it, especially at this time of year.

"Then I guess I'll just have to hang around La Rochelle until the *Barracuda* goes away."

Patu grunted again, and ran the dinghy into the beach. "That could take a while."

Jack swung out of the boat and splashed ashore. "It's better than the alternative."

"Which is what?"

"Hanging." Gripping the sides of the dinghy, Jack made ready to push it off.

"Is it true," Patu said suddenly, his hands slack on the oars, "what they say about the natives here? That they've taken to eating people again?"

"Not people. Just missionaries." Jack gave the boat a hard shove that sent it shooting away from the beach.

"Don't worry," he called. "No one's going to mistake me for a missionary."

"No." Leaning into his oars, Patu threw a quick glance toward the reef, where the *Barracuda*'s jolly boat was already threading its way through the passage. "But someone might easily take Miss McKnight for one."

Jack stood for a moment, the waves breaking at his feet, his gaze fastened on the approaching jolly boat. A blinding flash of sunlight glinted as if off the lens of a spyglass, and a shout went up to mingle with the roar of the distant surf and the buffeting of the fresh sea breeze.

Jack took off across the beach at a run, dodging through the thinly scattered coconut trees, his boots kicking up sprays of soft sand that fanned out behind him. He followed, for now, the same path India McKnight had taken, for it would lead him around to the other side of the mountain where he would find another trail he knew that would take him north.

As the trees thickened, he slowed to a steady dogtrot, but it still wasn't long before the sweat was sticking his shirt to his back and rolling down his face and into his eyes. Bloody hell, he thought, sucking in air. Too many late nights drinking brandy or kava. There'd been a time, once, when he could run for miles and miles without giving it a thought.

At the junction of the two paths he paused, his head down, his hands braced on his thighs, his eyes closed as he gulped in air. Swiping an arm across his dripping forehead, he opened his eyes and found himself staring at footprints. Not the even, artificially rounded prints he'd seen left by Miss McKnight's sensible lace-up shoes in the muddy stretches of the path from the beach, but big, splayed-toed, natural footprints, the kind left by bare feet. Lots and lots of bare feet. They'd come through here before Miss McKnight, but not long before.

"Bloody hell," Jack whispered, his gaze following the footprints—one set shod, the others not—up the trail that led toward the summit. Straightening, he stood at the juncture of the two paths, torn between the driving urge to keep going north—deep into the safety of the jungle and far, far away from Simon Granger and the jolly boat full of armed British sailors who were doubtless at this very minute swarming over the *Sea Hawk*—and another compulsion, a compulsion that was unwelcome and crazy to the point of being suicidal.

He told himself he could be wrong, that the natives who'd left these footprints might not be cannibals—or even if they were cannibals, they might not be hungry. He told himself Miss India McKnight had known all about the danger of cannibals when she'd made up her stubborn, opinionated mind to come here and study the Faces of Futapu. He told himself she'd be down the mountain soon enough, anyway. Jack knew her type, always double-checking everything and arriving early for any appointment. And if she did run into trouble with the natives, she had the bloody British navy sitting right offshore, to rescue her.

Except, of course, that Simon Granger might not believe Patu. What if the British thought Patu was lying
about the existence of a Scotswoman in a split tartan
skirt and pith helmet? What if the *Barracuda* forced Patu
to up anchor and sail away before the three hours Jack
had given her were up?

What would happen to Miss India Bloody McKnight
then?

For a dangerously long moment, Jack stood at the
crossroads, wavering, turning first one way, then the
other. He even took three decisive steps on the trail north,
away from Simon Granger and India McKnight and the
men who'd left those ominously numerous footprints.
Then, swearing, he swung around to start the steady
climb up to the smoking summit of Mount Futapu.

Her sketches of the so-called Faces of Futapu complete, India glanced at her watch and decided she still
had enough time left for a closer inspection of the rim of
the volcano.

Futapu's crater was a good three-quarters of a mile
wide and about half as deep, a poisoned-looking area of
bare stained rock and gray ash half obscured by hiss-
ing steam. Venturing as close as she dared, India stared
down into a fiery cauldron of red and orange molten
rock, and knew a moment of humbling awe. Here were
the very bowels of the earth, she thought, laid bare to the
eyes of man. As she watched, a fountain of orange lava
shot out of one of the crater's holes with an explosion

that was like the firing of a cannon. Flaring and spitting, the fiery eruption climbed higher and higher, then suddenly plopped back to earth, blackened and spent.

It was then that India noticed what looked like a stone platform, some three or four hundred feet away, near the gurgling, glowing hole. She couldn't be certain from this distance—if only she weren't cursed with this blasted eyesight!—but it looked very much as if the platform might not be entirely natural. Her curiosity piqued, she glanced at her watch, and pursed her lips in indecision. By rights, she should be getting ready to head back toward the beach. If she went to investigate the platform, she'd be cutting things tighter than she'd like. But she had been planning to leave sooner than she really needed to, and it wasn't *that* far to the platform. If it took her longer to reach it than she expected, she'd simply turn around and go back.

Thus reassured, India set off along the rim of the volcano, her attention divided between minding her steps in the treacherous landscape and keeping an eye on the passage of time as recorded by her watch's slowly moving hands.

She wasn't there.

Standing in the shadow of the Faces of Futapu, Jack turned in a slow circle, his gaze spanning the windblown expanse of pink- and white-stained rocks and vivid blue sky and tangled green jungle set against an endless sea. Not a scrap of tartan in sight. Where the hell was she?

The natives' footprints had veered off the trail at a point near the hot springs, but Jack hadn't been reassured. He hadn't liked the smell of whatever it was someone had left steaming on the rocks. Even as he searched the surrounding brush for signs of the pesky Scotswoman, he was also keeping a lookout for telltale flashes of dark bare skin. The idea of ending up in a cooking pot really didn't appeal to him.

The ground fell away here in a bare precipice toward the bay below, so that he also had to be careful to keep out of sight of any sharp-eyed mariners who might happen to be looking up—the idea of swinging from the end of a British yardarm not appealing to him any more than a native stew pot. Flattening himself on his stomach, Jack crept closer to the cliff's edge and saw that the jolly boat had left a couple of sailors and an officer aboard the *Sea Hawk* and was now headed toward the beach. A familiar figure stood tall and stiff in the boat's prow, sunlight glinting on the barrels of the well-oiled rifles that bristled among the men behind him.

So Simon had come himself. Jack had known he would.

They'd been as close as brothers once, Jack and this man who had been sent to see him brought back and hanged. When they'd first met as young midshipmen assigned to a quick-tempered, cantankerous old captain named Horatio Gladstone, they'd despised each other, for their backgrounds, temperaments, and attitudes couldn't have been more different. As the younger son of an old and proud Hampshire family, Simon had grown up in a world of neatly hedged, misty green fields, where tenant farmers pulled their forelocks and everyone who was anyone went to Eton, or Harrow, or Winchester. But Jack was a product of the Australian outback, his childhood memories of wide-open spaces and cattle musters and Aboriginal corroborees. His family might have been successful, but they were also boisterous and relaxed and peculiarly proud, in their own way, of the transported London pickpocket and Irish whore from whom they were descended. The antipathy between the two midshipmen had been instantaneous and intense, but it hadn't stopped them from eventually forming a bond they'd once sworn would last forever.

As if sensing Jack's eyes upon him, Simon looked up, his gaze raking the craggy heights. Jack ducked his head and pulled back, intensely aware, suddenly, of the heat of the tropical sun on his shoulders and the hard, insistent pumping of his own heart. If he hurried, he'd have just enough time to make it back down to the path heading north without meeting Simon and his boys coming up from the beach. Oh, they might try to follow him, but Jack had spent years in the jungles of the South Pacific, while Simon was, and always would be, a navy man.

A sea tern circled lazily overhead, drawing Jack's attention to the far rim of the volcano, where a woman in a tartan skirt stood, sketchbook in hand, her attention fastened on something he couldn't see. What the hell was she doing over there? he wondered, momentarily diverted. She should by rights be headed back down by now.

One hand on his machete to keep it from knocking noisily against a stone, Jack scooted away from the cliff's edge and straightened carefully. He had every intention of going off and leaving Miss India McKnight to the heroics of Simon and his boys in blue, when something else caught his attention, something he realized was a man's naked black buttocks, liberally smeared with mud and moving stealthily in her direction.

~~Chapter Seven

BAD EYESIGHT WAS a severe handicap to a travel writer, particularly to one without the fortitude to venture too close to a volcano's edge. Or rather, the foolhardiness; India told herself it would definitely be foolhardy to risk sliding to such a terrifyingly hideous end.

Standing well back from the steaming rim, she balanced the edge of her notebook against her midriff and squinted at the rock ledge that jutted out precariously over the bubbling, rumbling inferno. It must be from this very rock, she thought with a thrill of illicit excitement, that the natives used to hurl sacrifices to the fiery god below. Was the ledge a natural formation, or not? Impossible to tell from here, yet impossible to get any closer to make certain. She thought wistfully of Jack Ryder's spyglass, and decided in future to add one to the collection of necessities she carried in her knapsack.

Ever mindful of the oppressive, ticktocking passage of time, India set to work capturing the image before her in quick, bold pencil strokes. One more minute. All she needed was one more minute—

"What the bloody hell are you doing up there?"

The harsh, colonially accented voice, so unexpected and so near, broke her concentration. With a startled gasp, she swung about so quickly her boots slid on the scattering of small stones at her feet and she had to throw out her arms in a panicked and rather undignified maneuver to preserve her balance. Her fingers tightened on the edge of her notebook just in time to keep it from flying into the glowing red oblivion below. Her gaze fell on Jack Ryder, clothed, for once, in the attire considered suitable for his culture. True, his shirt hung unbuttoned halfway down his dark chest, and the sleeves had been rolled up to reveal tanned, muscular forearms. But he was wearing rugged canvas trousers and—wonder of all wonders—boots. She watched him climbing purposefully toward her up the blighted crest of bare rock that rimmed the volcano's edge, and a surge of indignation swelled within her. "Of all the inconsiderate, unthinking—"

"Shut up and get down here, fast, or I swear to God, lady, I'll let them eat you."

"Them?" she repeated in a squeaky voice that was not at all like her, for what she saw in his face took her breath away.

"So far, I've seen three natives, all watching you." He paused just below her, one hand on the machete at his side, his sweat-streaked features lifting into an odd, chilling smile. "And you can bet your bustle there's more."

All her senses brought to instant, quivering attention, India stood perfectly still, only her eyeballs moving as her gaze searched the edges of the dark tangle of rain forest surrounding the open summit.

"No, don't look. Just get down here, now."

Hastily stowing the notebook in her knapsack, India plunged down the rocky slope, sliding the last few feet to his side. As she reached him, his hand closed over her upper arm, his fingers digging in hard. "We're going to walk fast, but not too fast," he said in a low, calm voice. "We don't want them to think we're scared."

Scared? She was so scared, her fingers were tingling, but she forced herself to walk beside him with calm dignity. "The death grip on my arm is unnecessary," she said after a moment when he continued to hold on to her as they crossed the bare stretch of poisoned rocks that yawned between them and the path back down to the beach. "I understand the gravity of the situation. If you had explained yourself more clearly at the outset, then I—"

"Save your breath. We might need to run."

India saved her breath. Her long legs in their split skirt easily matched his man's stride, but the pace he set was brutal.

Leaving the sun-blasted bare rock face of the summit behind, they plunged again into the dark thickness of the rain forest, the tall, creeper-hung mass of beeches and laurels and pandanus instantly cutting off sight of the shimmering sea and the cooling trade winds that blew across it. Here all was shadow and steamy, smothering heat and the heavy smell of damp, fecund earth. Plunging down the steep, rocky hillside, they passed the bubbling thermal pond with its faintly lingering odor of cooked meat, and then the first hot springs India had seen. And still the primeval forest yawned around them, seemingly empty and silent except for the furtive rustling of small unseen creatures, and the loudly screeched complaint of a vivid-hued parrot.

"Are they following us?" she finally asked, when she could bear the suspense no longer.

The man beside her didn't slacken his pace, although he did throw her an amused look. "Shall we linger for a while and see what happens?"

She lapsed into silence again. The path here ran through an area of rocky outcroppings beside sheer, unexpected drop-offs, and she was finding it difficult at such a pace to keep her footing on the steep, muddy path. Once, her foot slid in an unexpected patch of muck and shot off into space, and she found she was grateful for the tight grip he'd continued to hold on her arm, even though he almost dislocated her shoulder pulling her back up beside him onto the trail.

She grabbed a handful of the loose cotton shirt at his chest and held on to it as she swayed slightly, her breath coming in ragged gasps. He gripped her other shoulder to steady her, his straight dark brows drawing together as he studied her. "You doing all right?"

She nodded, determined. "Yes. Thank you. I simply needed a moment to catch my breath. I—"

The crack of a rifle shot echoed through the jungle. Bark flew from a tree just feet from India's face, and she let out a startled yelp.

"Bloody hell," swore Jack Ryder, and yanked her down behind the nearest boulder.

India pressed her back against the moss-covered rock. Her heart was pounding so hard, it hurt. "Those aren't cannibals," she said in a strangled whisper. "Who—"

"Hold your fire, you fool," shouted a crisp, vaguely familiar English voice from below, a voice India had last heard on the docks of Rabaul Harbor. "You could have hit Miss McKnight."

"Good heavens," said India. "It's Captain Granger."

She was aware of the man beside her stiffening, his head whipping around to pin her with a deadly blue stare. "Friend of yours?" he asked in an unpleasant drawl.

India shook her head, confused and more afraid, suddenly, than she had been up there at the summit, surrounded by cannibals.

Jack Ryder's hands descended on her shoulders, jerking her forward so that she fell into him, one hand splayed against an intimidatingly hard chest, her head forced back at an awkward angle as she stared up at him. She knew a fission of fear that took what was left of her breath and left her shaky and cold. "You bloody well set me up, didn't you?" he said, his words low and even, his lips curling back from his teeth in a fierce smile. "You bloody bitch."

India's mouth went dry. She'd thought him easygoing and lazy, an annoying but essentially harmless degenerate. Now she stared into eyes that were glittering and dangerous, and knew how wrong she'd been. She shook her head. "I don't know what you're talking about."

"You might as well give it up, Jack," called the English voice from below. "I've six armed seamen with me. You so much as stick your head around that boulder, and you'll lose it. This is checkmate, Jack."

He seized her wrist, spinning her around in an elbow-wrenching maneuver she didn't even comprehend until she felt her back slam against his chest and heard the bare blade of his machete whip through the air to come to rest a whisper below her chin. "You got me into this," Jack Ryder hissed in her ear, his hard arm crushing her breasts as he pinned her back against him in a deadly parody of a lover's embrace. "You can bloody well get me out of it."

"But I didn't—"

He swung his head away to shout to the men below. "You're forgetting something, aren't you? I have Miss McKnight."

There was a pause, filled with the furtive hush of the jungle around them. Granger said, "You're bluffing. You wouldn't hurt her. I know you, Jack."

"You *knew* me." He waited, as if giving time for his

words to sink in. Then he said, "I'm standing up now, Simon, and I'm bringing Miss McKnight with me, which means that anyone trying to take off my head is liable to take hers, too. And did I mention she has a machete dangerously close to her throat?"

India tried to hang back, but his grip on her tightened brutally, drawing her up with him, the sharp edge of the machete close enough that she could feel the cold bite of it against her skin. She let out a little whimper of protest, which was all she could manage. Her fear was like a suffocating weight, stealing her breath, squeezing her chest.

She could see them now on the narrow trail just below, Captain Granger, his hand clenched in furious impotence around the pommel of the sword at his side, and six seamen, their rifles pointed unwaveringly at India and the man who held her. For one unbearable moment, Ryder and the captain simply stared at each other, and it seemed to India that the very air between the two men vibrated with the violent intensity of their emotions. She was aware of the rise and fall of Ryder's hard chest against her back, the warmth of his breath against her neck, the power of the dark, muscular arm that pressed against her breasts and held her pinned back against him.

"Tell your men to lower their rifles. *Now,*" Ryder added sharply when the seamen continued to hold their guns at the ready.

Granger turned his head, the muscles in his lean cheek bunching tight. "At ease, men."

Six muzzles lowered, and India remembered to breathe.

The two men's gazes met again, and clashed.

"Now tell them to lay down their guns."

The tall blond captain's hard stare never wavered. "Do it," he said out the corner of his mouth.

"Nice and easy," added Ryder, his hand shifting on the handle of the machete at India's throat. "I'm a very nervous man. Somebody startles me, and Miss McKnight here might end up with a nasty gash in her neck."

It was said for effect, of course; the fiend who held her was neither nervous nor easily startled, and India knew it. In another situation, she might even have admired his calm coolness. But she also had no doubts about his ruthlessness. He wouldn't hesitate to spill her blood if he thought he needed to. The seamen carefully laid down their guns, and she let out a soft, relieved sigh.

"Now step back. You, too, Simon. That's right, gentlemen, keep moving. There, that'll do." His voice had changed, taking on a vaguely rollicking tone that puzzled her until he said, "Now, gentlemen, you're going to take off your clothes."

The fair-haired captain was so startled, he jerked, while behind him, the seamen murmured and exchanged wary looks.

"That's right," said Ryder. "Don't everyone rush to strip off all at the same time. We're going to do it one by one. Starting with you, Simon."

The tall Englishman gave a curt, mirthless laugh, and

crossed his arms at his chest in a blatantly defiant pose. "Over my dead body."

"A laudable attitude, I'm sure. But you're forgetting Miss McKnight's throat." The man behind her shifted and India felt the blade bite, a gasp escaping her lips before she could press them tightly together. "What would the Admiralty have to say about that, hmmm?"

Granger's teeth clenched. "You bastard."

"Just start with your sword, Simon. Easy," Ryder added warningly as the captain moved with seething resentment to comply. "Now throw it over that cliff."

For a moment, Granger hesitated, then sent the sword sailing out into space. India could hear it clanging and bouncing on the rocks below.

"Now your jacket."

It wasn't until the captain was unbuttoning his shirt with quick, jerky movements that India thought to squeeze her eyes shut out of consideration for the unfortunate man's modesty. But even though it was self-imposed, she found the isolating darkness oddly terrifying. In the end, she reluctantly opened her eyes again, but she kept her head tilted back, her gaze fixed on the thick green canopy overhead.

"Now you," Ryder said, nodding to one of the seamen after the captain's smallclothes had joined the rest of his possessions in a heap at the base of the cliff. "That's right. You. Start with your boots."

India kept her gaze resolutely fastened on the tropical

tangle of leafy branches overhead, but Ryder's low-voiced, explicit instructions and the subtle sounds of clothing being removed in response kept her painfully aware of what was happening.

He took them, one by one, through the same slow striptease. At first India thought he did it to humiliate them. But then she heard him say, his voice deadly cold and even, "Move one step closer to that rifle, sailor, and we'll all have a chance to see what color a Scotswoman's blood is." And she realized that this was the only way he could hope to keep control of the situation, that in the confusion of seven men moving about undressing it would have been all too easy for one of them to make a lunge for the rifles that still lay on the jungle floor.

The strain of keeping her head tipped back was starting to give India a cramp in her neck, but she refused to look down. She would not look. . . .

"You there," Ryder said, when the last of Her Majesty's men had stripped to the buff.

A high-pitched voice squeaked, "Me?"

"That's right, you. I want you to pick up each of those rifles, one at a time, and toss them over the cliff. "Look lively now."

There was a pause, then the sounds of shifting underbrush and a muffled "Ouch!" that told her the man in question must be moving, barefoot, to comply.

"And remember," said Ryder, "try anything, and Miss McKnight here will pay for it."

In spite of her best intentions, India's gaze wavered.

She had one swift, shocking impression of a group of red-faced, white-bodied men standing rigidly erect, elbows bent, hands folded over their crotches, and another man, fair-haired and rib-thin, his body hunched over, one hand still protectively cupping his privates as he bent to retrieve a rifle. Then her gaze snapped back to the jungle canopy overhead.

"I think that will be all, gentlemen," said the hatefully laconic voice behind her when the last of the rifles had clattered down the cliff face and an expectant hush fell over the jungle.

India felt her body tense up, tighter and tighter, in anticipation of what would happen next. She'd been wondering for the last ten minutes what she would do if he ordered her, too, to strip. She'd finally decided he could slit her throat with his machete if he wanted; she wasn't removing so much as a handkerchief.

"You may leave now," she heard him say. "One at a time. Just turn around and walk back down the trail single file. No, not you," he added softly in her ear, his voice deepening with amusement and his hold on her tightening when India would have moved away from him.

She was no longer bothering to keep her gaze carefully trained on the tangle of vivid green vegetation overhead. Suddenly, the men's nakedness was of far less importance than what was about to happen to her. She could see them scurrying away, one after the other down the trail, their unshod feet slipping in the muck, their bare bodies glowing a discordant bluish white in the jungle gloom. Only Simon Granger stood his ground, his hands no longer shielding his groin but clenched instead into two fists at his sides. "And Miss McKnight?" he said, his head held high, his voice strained but crisp.

Jack Ryder's reply was slow and taunting and laced with a smile. "She's coming with me."

~~Chapter Eight

INDIA LET OUT a gasp that brought the strained sinews of her neck into uncomfortable proximity to the machete's sharp edge. She went instantly, quiveringly silent.

Captain Granger said, "You can't be serious."

Jack Ryder let out a low, mean laugh. "When she's the only thing standing between me and a hangman's noose? Of course I'm serious."

"You want a hostage?" The Englishman spread his arms wide in a gesture of surrender. "Take me. But let the woman go, Jack."

The despicable fiend holding her laughed again in what struck India as an unnecessarily hearty—and heartless—manner. "Nice of you to offer, Simon. But you're not exactly dressed for a jungle trek."

A muscle bunched along the Englishman's clenched jawline. "I never thought I'd see you hiding behind a woman."

"Yeah?" The rollicking tone vanished, leaving in its

place a cold, lethal timbre that sent a chill through India's veins. "Well, there was a time I thought I'd never see you *killing* women, which just goes to show how wrong one man can be about another."

"I was only following orders, and you know it."

A dangerously volatile hum of anger coursed through the man behind her. India knew a stab of raging panic, then felt him relax, his voice sounding unutterably sad and weary as he said, "Just get out of here, Simon."

For a long, silent moment, the two men stared at each other. Simon Granger said, "I won't quit. You know that, Jack."

"I know it."

The Englishman turned to leave, and it was only by sheer force of will that India managed to hold herself still, her jaws clenched together to keep from crying out, *No! Don't leave me here with him!* She watched in sick, stomach-wrenching despair as Simon Granger maneuvered his way with rigid care down the slippery, narrow trail, his tall, naked white body flickering ghostlike through moss-covered tree trunks and vivid green creepers. Then an outcropping of rough volcanic boulders hid him from her sight, and she was alone in the jungle with a mad, machete-wielding Australian renegade and an unknown number of watching cannibals.

Jack kept his grip on Miss McKnight's wrist, the weight of his arm across her rib cage holding her back pressed tightly to his chest, his machete at her neck. He waited until Simon had disappeared from sight and the only sounds to be heard were faint jungle whisperings and the labored breathing of the woman he held in his arms, her full breasts rising and falling with each intake of air. Then he let her go and stepped back warily.

He wasn't sure what he expected her to do. Faint maybe, or fall into hysterics, or maybe even try to make a frightened run for it. He should have known better.

She stood rigidly erect, her back still to him, one hand rubbing the wrist he'd held so tightly, the other hand coming up to touch fingertips to her neck. When she finally turned, it was to show him a pale but composed face. "So, Mr. Ryder," she said in that tart, Sunday-school teacher voice of hers. "What do we do now, given that a return to the *Sea Hawk* is obviously no longer an option?"

Jack let out a soft laugh and drove his machete back into its scabbard. What now, indeed? When Simon and his bluejackets had appeared below them on the trail, Jack's only thought had been to get himself out of a tight situation alive and with as much of a chance of getting away as he could manage. It was only now, as he stared at the pith-helmeted woman who stood before him, her shoulders determinedly straight, her fine gray eyes flashing scorn and contempt, that the magnitude of what he'd let himself in for burst upon him.

For the next two days, he was going to be tramping through a cannibal-infested jungle in the company of the most aggravating, sharp-tongued Amazon he had ever had the misfortune to encounter. And as if that weren't bad enough, he'd be willing to bet his machete that as soon as Simon and his men scrambled into new clothes and rearmed, they were going to be hot on Jack's trail. Simon would have been after him in any case, but it didn't help that to his already long list of crimes, Jack had just added the offense of kidnapping a popular lady travel writer.

"What we do now," said Jack, taking her by the elbow and propelling her with gentle insistence down the path, "is move. Very quickly."

She removed her elbow from his grasp, but kept walking. "And precisely what is our destination?"

"La Rochelle."

"*La Rochelle?*" She stopped abruptly and swung to face him. "But . . . that will take *days*."

"Two, by my reckoning. If we move it."

"*Two?*" She drew back her shoulders and crossed her arms beneath her impressive breasts in the manner of a Valkyrie preparing to do battle. All she needed was a sword and a skull cup flowing with mead, Jack thought, and the image would have been complete. "I'm not going."

Jack eyed the statuesque, strong-jawed woman before him. A smaller, weaker female he might have bullied, but this one was almost as tall as he was—besides which, he didn't think anyone had ever successfully bullied Miss India McKnight in her life. He tried a different tack. "You want me to leave you here, do you? Alone?"

"I am not afraid of being alone."

"You're forgetting about the cannibals."

Her lip curled in scorn. He'd known men who could do that, but never a woman. "Do you really think me such a fool as to fall for that tale twice?"

"Tale? You think it's a tale? And who do you think left that footprint?" He jabbed a pointed finger toward a muddy patch on the trail, where the imprint made by a bare human foot showed clearly.

"Obviously, one of those poor unfortunate men you forced to disrobe."

"Their feet were bare going *down* the hill, not up it."

She gazed at him with cool disbelief. "You realized you might need a hostage, and—"

"A hostage?" Jack leaned into her. "Bloody hell. If I hadn't been so bloody worried about you getting yourself eaten, I wouldn't need a hostage now."

He swung away from her, his head falling back, his gaze taking in a whirl of vibrant, tangled greenery before he spun back suddenly to pin her with a hard, suspicious stare. "Exactly what do you think I'm planning to do to you, anyway? Drag you off into the jungle and rape you?"

He watched a flush of maidenly modesty color her cheeks, her breath hitching in an unmistakable betrayal of fear.

"Jesus. You do." He set his jaw, one pointed finger coming up to waggle beneath her thin nose. "Well, let me tell you something, lady. I'm not that hard up. This is the bloody South Pacific, remember? These islands are full of naked, willing women. A man doesn't need to resort to kidnap and rape to get a little around here." He paused, his gaze sweeping over her to linger just a shade longer than he meant it to on her full, heaving breasts. "And even if I did, I wouldn't pick some frigid, supercilious, bloody-minded Englishwoman!"

She stared at him, her color becomingly high, her breath coming hard and fast through parted lips. But all she said was "I am Scottish, not English."

A breeze blew up suddenly, rustling the leafy canopy overhead with a movement that must have brought down a coconut somewhere nearby, for the crash of it echoed and reechoed through the jungle. Jack threw a quick glance up at the patch of sky just visible through the overarching mass of branches. From the sounds of things, there was a squall blowing in. Smothering a crude oath, he drew his machete from its scabbard and straightened his arm until the point rested against India McKnight's breast, just above her heart. "Look, Miss McKnight, I don't give a rat's ass if you're English, Scottish, or Transylvanian. Just move."

She went a shade paler, but she didn't move. "You're bluffing. If you kill me, you won't have a hostage, so what would be the point?"

"You willing to bet your life on that?"

They stared at each other. The wind died, and in the sudden stillness the steamy heat seemed more oppressive than ever. He watched a bead of sweat form on her forehead and roll down her temple. Just when he thought she was going to call his bluff, after all, she blinked and looked away.

"Very well, Mr. Ryder. You may put away your machete." Turning on her heel, she stalked off down the path ahead of him, her shoulders pulled repressively back, her pith-helmeted head held high. "But when they hang you, I intend to be there."

Jack swiped one forearm across his hot, sweaty face, and followed her. "They need to catch me first."

He'd expected her to dawdle along, deliberately trying to delay him, but she kept pace with him easily, her long legs matching his stride for stride. Watching her, Jack came to the conclusion she was one of those women with a naturally long, mannish gait. He suspected she was constitutionally incapable of walking slowly, no matter how much she might have wanted to. The thought brought an odd smile to his face, a smile that faded to leave a lingering, unexpected ache that was both wistful and sad.

At first, she stomped along in an angry, detached silence, no doubt indulging herself with satisfying images of his lifeless body twisting at the end of a hangman's rope. But it wasn't long before her interest in her surroundings reasserted itself, and several times he had to prod her on when she would have stopped to investigate a peculiar form of mushroom growing on a moldering log, or to watch a red parakeet flitting through the branches of a giant breadfruit tree. He supposed it was inevitable that she would, eventually, turn her overly well-developed sense of curiosity to him.

"Why are you wanted by the British navy?" she asked as they pushed through a stand of enormous old native pines mixed with native oaks and laurels and tree ferns.

He glanced back at her in surprise. "Didn't you even bother to find out, before you agreed to help Simon capture me?"

There was a long, uncomfortable pause. Then she said, "I was having difficulty finding someone willing to take me to Takaku, and Captain Granger suggested you. I didn't know what he intended."

He didn't want to believe her, but studying her half-averted profile, Jack thought she was probably telling the truth. She was too determinedly straight-laced and bloody-minded to ever lie convincingly. He wondered idly if he would have drawn his machete on her and taken her hostage if he hadn't thought, in that first rush of blind fury, that she'd deliberately set him up. He was still pondering the question when she said, "Were you actually an officer in the British navy?"

The way she said it, one would think it the most unimaginable thing in the world. He grunted. "Once."

"Did you jump ship?"

"Not exactly."

"So what happened?"

"My ship sank."

She turned her head to look at him. "Was it your fault?"

"The Admiralty thinks so."

She kept her gaze leveled on his face. "Was it?"

He gave a low, harsh laugh. "In a sense, yes."

"In what sense wasn't it?"

It was a perceptive question, but not one he intended to answer. A silence dragged out between them and lasted so long that Jack decided she'd forgotten the subject. She hadn't. All of a sudden, she said, "He told me he was once your friend."

"Simon? He was."

"It was a vile thing, what you did, forcing him and his men to walk back to their ship in such a state."

"Natives spend their entire lives running around the jungle bare-assed. Why not Simon and his bluejackets?"

"Because they're white men."

"What's the matter? Never seen a naked white man before?"

"Of course I have."

Jack laughed. "I guess you saw me, all right."

"I wasn't referring to you."

He turned to stare at her, and was surprised to discover a faint hint of color staining her cheeks. If he hadn't known better, he'd have said Miss Indomitable McKnight was blushing. "My dear Miss McKnight, you are full of surprises. Where?"

Her gaze met his, then veered away. "I don't see how that is any of your business."

"How old was he? Two?"

Instead of answering him, she continued to stare off

into the jungle until her toe caught on a root and she tripped.

"It helps if you watch where you're going," he said pleasantly, but she simply threw him a withering glance, and kept walking.

India had formulated and discarded four different plans for her escape before she finally settled on the only course of action that promised any reasonable chance of success.

They had long since veered away from the trail she had originally followed and onto a narrower path that snaked its way toward what she supposed must be the northern end of the island. At first, the path ran along the steep side of the volcano's slope, then plunged down into a jungle-filled glen that separated Mount Futapu from the craggy heights of the next, even higher volcanic peak. With every step she took, India was painfully conscious of the growing distance that separated her from the *Barracuda* and the safety it had come to represent. But if she were to have any chance of escaping this vile, machete-wielding madman, she would need to pick her moment very, very carefully.

Her chance came at the base of the glen, where they ran across a small stream, gurgling clear and sweet between moss-covered, fern-draped banks. Jack Ryder knelt on a flat stone to cup his hands in the burn and splash water on his face, his worn cotton shirt pulling taut against the muscles of his chest as he shut his eyes and let the water run in glistening rivulets down his tanned cheeks and corded throat. But India hung back, her voice tight with an embarrassment that was only half feigned as she said, "I need a few moments to myself behind those rocks there."

He glanced up at her, his dark brows drawing together as he regarded her thoughtfully. "You wouldn't be so stupid as to try to run off, now would you?"

She let out a short, mirthless laugh. "How far would I be likely to get?"

"Before who caught you? Me, or the cannibals?"

Not even bothering to dignify that remark with a reply, India moved toward the pile of massive, moss-covered basalt boulders that effectively hid the trail that led back to the bay from his sight.

"I don't care which rock you choose," he called after her, "as long as I can still see the top of your pith helmet when you squat."

"You, sir, are disgusting."

"No. Just very untrusting."

Ducking quickly behind the rocks, India cast a frantic glance around for some sort of prop, and found it in the form of a stout length of bamboo. Driving it deep into the soft, spongy earth, she began, very carefully, to remove her pith helmet.

"Don't take too long, you hear?" Jack Ryder called.

"I . . . I fear I am rather unwell," she replied shakily. "Do have patience, Mr. Ryder."

She heard him mutter something in response, but she didn't think he really expected her to run away from him. He wasn't even looking toward the rocks when she slipped away, leaving her pith helmet swaying gently in the afternoon breeze.

~~Chapter Nine

THE WAY INDIA figured it, she had at best five minutes before he discovered she was gone.

Every nerve in her body was screaming for her to run, but she forced herself to concentrate on moving as quietly as she could until she had put some distance between them. The dank, steaming jungle closed around her, dark and dense, swallowing sound and light. She threw one quick, apprehensive glance over her shoulder, and broke into a run.

On and on she ran, her knapsack banging awkwardly against her hip, her feet sliding on the muddy path, her world a blur of varying hues of vivid green that swirled in a hooting, rustling rush around her. She had always considered herself a strong, fit woman, but as the path angled sharply upward, weaving between tropical beeches and mountain pandanus and swaying vines, her breath began to come in ragged, agonized gasps. And still she pressed on, her lungs bursting, her face hot with sweat, loose strands of hair slipping from her prim chignon to plaster against her wet neck.

She had no illusions about her ability to outrun him. Her skirt might be split, but it still didn't give her the freedom of movement a man would enjoy. And after what she had seen both yesterday and this morning, she had no doubts about the condition of this particular man's powerful, leanly muscled body. If he came after her, he would catch up with her eventually.

But she didn't think he would come after her. She'd already served her purpose. He'd used her to escape Simon Granger and his men, and while her presence might be a handy bargaining chip in a similar situation, she didn't think Jack Ryder would risk taking the time to turn around and come after her. Oh, he might flail about, swearing, for a few minutes, looking for her. She smiled quietly to herself, delighting in the thought of his impotent fury when he realized that she'd tricked him. But she was confident that he would waste little time before pushing on toward La Rochelle.

India's toe caught on a root and she stumbled, pulling herself up short. Her heart was pounding so hard, her entire body was shaking and she was starting to feel light-headed. With a groan, she leaned her back against the trunk of an aito tree that grew beside the path, the muscles in her legs quivering, her eyes squeezing shut as she drew great, exotically scented gulps of steamy jungle air into her aching lungs. Just half a minute, she told herself. She would rest here for half a minute, and then she would press on.

Perhaps it was the sudden stillness of the primeval forest around her that warned her, or perhaps it was the unexpected and entirely instinctive shiver of fear that licked up her spine. India felt her breath back up in her throat, choking her. Slowly, and quiveringly afraid of what she would see, India opened her eyes.

The breath she'd been holding expelled itself from her mouth in a queer rushing sound of terror as she stared with wide-eyed, paralyzing horror at the dark-skinned, naked men who stood in a tight half circle not five feet from her.

Jack squinted up at the thick canopy of entwined leaves and branches overhead. The rain had held off so far, but he could smell it coming, and feel it, too, hanging over the island like an oppressive hush.

"Bloody hell, woman," he shouted. "How much more time do you need?"

The gentle murmur of the stream beside him filled the answering silence. He stood abruptly, an awful suspicion forming as he stared at the rounded, unmoving crest of that bloody pith helmet. "Miss McKnight? You'd better say something quick, because if you don't, I'm coming around to the other side of those rocks."

Even as he said it, he knew there would be no answer. He was alone in the glen, and if he hadn't been sitting there lost in dark, useless thoughts of the past, he'd have realized it sooner.

Swearing softly to himself, Jack sprinted around the side of the pile of silent boulders. The pith helmet was there, carefully propped up so that it just showed above the rocks. But Miss India McKnight was gone.

"Sonofab—" He swung around in a circle, his gaze sweeping the dense stand of mara and hutu trees thickly undergrown with ferns and orchids and native jasmine. There was only one way she could have gone: back up the path, toward the bay and the *Barracuda*.

For one, ugly moment, Jack hesitated, his gaze narrowing as he stared at the steep trail that led back the way they had come. She might be all right, he told himself. She might even meet Simon and his boys coming up from the bay. But as hard as he wanted to believe it, Jack knew she didn't have a chance. He hadn't seen the natives who had been shadowing them for the last hour or more, but he'd known they were there, watching.

He told himself that she wasn't his responsibility. She was the one who had insisted on coming to this bloody island. He'd warned her about the cannibals, hadn't he? And yet there was no denying, either, that she wouldn't be in this situation now if he hadn't stopped her from leaving with Simon when she'd had the chance.

With one last, despairing glance toward the north, Jack loosed the machete at his side and set off at a slow trot back toward Mount Futapu.

* * *

Alex stood in the open doorway of the captain's quarters and watched as Simon Granger quickly thrust first one foot, then the other into his spare pair of boots. "Let me come ashore with you this time."

The captain's fair head fell back as he looked up and grinned. "I think I should have let you come with us last time. Being forced to strip bare-assed naked in the middle of a cannibal-infested jungle is quite an experience."

Alex felt himself go red in vicarious humiliation. "It was a shocking thing the man did. Disgraceful."

"And very clever."

Puzzled, Alex gave the captain a long, steady look. "One might almost think you admire him."

A strange, not altogether pleasant smile curled the other man's lips. "Oh, I have always admired Jack Ryder's cleverness." The smile faded. "But don't make the mistake of thinking I have any intention of letting him get away from us."

Alex nodded, although he wasn't entirely convinced. "One shudders to think of the shocking indignities to which that poor woman will be subjected in the meantime."

"Miss McKnight? Jack won't rape her, if that's what you mean."

It was exactly what he meant, of course, but Alex knew a moment's discomfort at the other man's plain speaking. He cleared his throat. "You can't be certain of that."

The captain stretched lazily to his feet. "You forget, I know Jack Ryder."

Alex cleared his throat again, his hands clasped tight behind his back. "You haven't said if I may join the landing party, sir."

A strange light gleamed in the other man's eyes. "By all means, come with us, Mr. Preston. I think you need it."

They tied her hands and feet together and hung her, pig-fashion, from a pole slung between the shoulders of two of the men. *Long pig,* she thought with a bubble of what must be hysterical laughter. But the laughter never erupted because she had her teeth clenched firmly together. She had to, to keep from screaming.

She hadn't fought them. It would have been useless, in any case, and would simply have earned her a whack on the head from a war club, which might have killed her, or at least rendered her insensible. And India had no desire to be insensible. She was going to need all of her wits if she was to have any chance of getting herself out of this alive.

It was an uncomfortable way to travel through the jungle, hanging from a pole, her hands and feet quickly going numb, each step taken by her captives setting her to swaying back and forth in a hideous evocation of a rocking baby's cradle. They left the main path almost immediately, striking out along a trail so obscured by tall cane grass and pendant ropes of lianas that no one but a native could ever find it. And with each step they took, India knew, her chances of rescue grew fainter and fainter. Bent as they were on their pursuit of Jack Ryder— and thinking her with him—Simon Granger and his men would rush right past this hidden trail. And as for Jack Ryder himself, well, any man who would threaten to sail off and abandon a woman on a cannibal-infested island was not likely to play the part of a rescuing hero.

The realization that he had been telling her the truth about the cannibals did nothing to improve India's disposition toward him. He had known there were cannibals out there in the jungle, watching them, and still he had deliberately, wantonly exposed her to this danger by kidnapping her and forcing her to embark on some wild overland journey to the north. If there were any justice in this world, it would be Jack Ryder, not her, who would end his days in a cooking pot.

But there was no justice in this world, and India knew it.

The intensely green, swaying branches overhead blurred, and she blinked furiously. She would not cry. She would not scream, and she would not cry.

She became aware, slowly, of the scent of smoke overlaying the other jungle smells, and knew they must be nearing the native village. She heard women's voices, and a child's shrill laughter, and the banked terror within her flared up hot and bright and so all-consuming that the blood roared in her head and her stomach clenched so violently she almost vomited.

She could see it now, a small village of no more than a

dozen huts made of thickly woven palm leaves lashed to pole frames and elevated some five feet off the jungle floor. Everywhere was a stinking litter of fish bones and putrid breadfruit and blackened banana peels, the women and children of the village wading unconcernedly through the muddy filth as they came to crowd around her. Her world filled with the reek of hot sweaty bodies and wild wooly hair and black, flat-nosed faces, eyes wide and excited, open mouths jabbering all at once. A grubby hand closed over the watch pinned to her bodice and tore it away. Fingers poked her hips, her midriff, as if assessing how much meat she had to offer.

"Don't touch me," she said in a tight, carefully controlled voice, except of course that no one here understood English, and she frantically searched her memory for an appropriate line in Pidgin, the lingua franca of the South Seas. One of the men, an unusually tall and skinny man with the ashen white skin of an albino and hair dyed a frizzy ginger color, pinched her breast hard enough to make her eyes water. "*Yu gettim bek,*" she shouted in his face. He laughed, showing her a mouth full of rotten teeth stained red from betel-chewing. But he didn't pinch her again.

She remembered reading, once, about a German botanist trekking through the jungles of the Solomons who had come across two women staked out up to their necks in a stream. Every bone in their arms and legs had been broken, but they had still been alive, for it was said that exposing an animal to the action of running water before killing it made the flesh more tender for eating. She wondered with a rising spike of horror if these people meant to do that to her, but then the men carrying the ends of her pole dumped her ungently into the muck beneath a pawpaw tree. Her back hit the ground hard enough to knock the breath out of her. She was still gasping for air when they jerked her into a sitting position and yanked her numb hands over her head again to lash them high up to the tree's trunk.

She sat there, panting, her arms over her head, her hair hanging in her face in tangled, sweat-soaked strands, and stared at the men, women, and children who meant to eat her.

They were a small, short-legged, heavily jowled people, their faces savagely decorated with tattoos on their foreheads and bones through their noses and ceremonial scars on their cheeks. The bare-breasted women wore tattered grass skirts, but the men were nearly as naked as the children, their only covering a penis purse made of grass and held in place with a length of twisted vine. Nambas, they were called. *Namba* meant number, and there was a time India had found that funny.

She didn't find it funny anymore.

She swallowed hard, her throat so dry it hurt, but she had no intention of asking this ring of curious, hungry-looking man-eaters for water. Gradually, they began to drift away in groups of twos and threes, their interest in her waning as she simply sat and stared back at them. A couple of little boys amused themselves for a time by picking up pebbles and tossing them at her, laughing when she twisted this way and that in an effort to avoid the sharp sting of the rocks. But they soon tired of the game and went away, too. After that, no one paid her any more attention than they might have given to a tethered goat, or a cow.

Beneath her terror began to build, slowly, a deep and powerful rage. She was a human being, not a walking piece of meat, ready for the slaughter. She had tried, always, in her travels and in her writings to respect the various traditions and customs of the different societies she encountered, but she found it impossible to dredge up anything except revulsion for these people, who lived in filth and ate their own unwanted babies, and disposed of the aged or sickening members of their families by stoning them to death. They seemed devoid of so much that she had always thought typified her species, and it was profoundly disturbing to realize that the Eden-like beauty of these islands could have produced something so dark and terrible. Or was this, she thought with a strange, hollow weight of inner despair, the natural state of man?

Surreptitiously, she began to move her hands, testing the bindings on her wrists. They seemed tight and unbreakable, but she kept moving her hands anyway, trying to loosen them. She had no real hope of being able to escape these cannibals in the daylight, but perhaps tonight, when everyone was asleep . . .

Always assuming, of course, that they didn't have her for dinner.

A fly buzzed with annoying persistence around her sweaty face, attracted by the blood trickling from a cut on her forehead where one of the boys' stones had hit. India shook her head, trying to chase it away, then stilled when she realized she was being watched by one of the women seated nearby weaving a mat from palm leaves. Like all the older women in the camp, this one's body was terribly bent from years of carrying loads of yams and other labors, for it was obvious that here, as in most Melanesian societies, it was the women who did all the work, while the men stood around with their killing clubs and watched for enemies. Women didn't count for much in Melanesia, their worth being reckoned at slightly less than that of a full-grown pig. After all, pigs had more meat on them.

At the thought, India felt a fresh tide of panic swell within her, but she resolutely pushed it down and concentrated, instead, on slowly moving her hands as soon as the bent old woman looked away again. She would not think about what they were going to do to her. She could not think about—

A blast from a conch shell cut through the murmuring voices and desultory activity in the village. India froze, while all around her, hands weaving palm mats stilled, heads lifted, squabbling children broke apart and stared at the entrance to the village clearing.

A man strode from out of the jungle gloom, a tall,

dark-haired, sun-bronzed white man carrying a half-grown, squealing, thrashing pig slung across his shoulders the way a shepherd might carry a tired lamb. *"Me kum buyim dim-dim meri,"* he said, lowering the pig before the tall albino with the ginger hair who stood in the center of the village, flanked by some half a dozen cannibals, their war clubs held at the ready.

India blinked away a film of sweat mingling with sudden, startled tears. *Dim-dim* was what the Melanesians called a white, while a *meri* was a woman. And she realized, with a swift, joyous surge of incredulity and exultation, that Jack Ryder had come to rescue her, after all. He was proposing to buy her. For a pig.

～～Chapter Ten

I N THE NEXT instant, that brief wild flare of joy disappeared beneath a surge of renewed horror and despair so overwhelming, it took India's breath.

They're going to kill him, she thought with a sickening twist of her stomach. He might have come—unexpectedly, unbelievably—to rescue her, but these savages had no reason to bargain with him. They would simply kill him, and then they would eat him, too. The man had to be mad, India decided, watching him stand there, his hands resting lightly, almost casually on his hips. Only a madman would stroll into a camp full of cannibals and expect to achieve anything other than his own death.

She sat tensed, waiting for the thrust of a spear, the dull thud of a falling war club to end his life. Instead, the albino prodded the bawling pig at his feet with one bare big toe and said something India didn't understand, but which Jack Ryder answered with a flood of Pidgin. The albino shook his head and held up two fingers. And India began to realize with a resurgent spark of hope that the men were wrangling over her price.

The problem, evidently, was the size of the pig. It wasn't big enough. India's own command of Pidgin was limited, but there was no misunderstanding the derisive way the albino sneered down at the poor, bawling animal at his feet, then held up his hands some six inches apart. The men in a half circle around him laughed, their hideously carved war clubs jiggling menacingly up and down.

Jack Ryder shook his head and said something India couldn't catch, something about copra, and the *Sea Hawk*. The albino jabbered quickly in response. Reaching into the bag he wore slung across one shoulder, he pulled out a round, flat object that he thrust in Jack Ryder's face. It was a curious bag the albino wore, made of some pale leather, and the longer India stared at it, the more convinced she became that it was made of human skin. A white man's skin.

The Australian blinked at the ship's biscuit held just inches from his nose. "*Orait,*" he said. All right.

All right? India's hopes soared so high she was practically wriggling in the mud, tethered only by the plaited vines tying her to the tree. Did that mean they'd come to an agreement? Had he actually, somehow, managed to save her?

Abruptly, the albino withdrew the biscuit and tucked it away in that revolting bag. Turning, he called to a nearby woman, who scuttled forward, back bent nearly double, to take possession of the pig. The half circle of men drifted away, swinging their war clubs in idle boredom, while the women of the village turned their attention back to their work.

From the time Jack Ryder had first sauntered into the clearing, he had looked at her only once—a quick, assessing glance thrown her way before he'd tossed that poor pig at the albino's feet. Now he swung toward her, and what India saw in his face was enough to make her wish for one, craven instant that he hadn't rescued her.

He stopped in front of her, his arms crossed at his chest, his gaze traveling over her, from her loose, tangled hair to her ripped bodice to her crumpled, mud-streaked tartan skirt. His eyes were cold and hard, but it was the wry smile of amusement twisting his lips that dried up every word of profuse gratitude that had been trembling on the tip of her tongue.

"Don't say it," she snapped, her neck arching back awkwardly as she stared up at him.

"Say what?" Easing his machete from its sheath, he hunkered down beside her to slice neatly through the twisted vines binding her ankles. "That you must be six kinds of an idiot, to go running off by yourself into a jungle full of cannibals?" He cut the cords holding her arms suspended high over her head. "Or that it would have served you right if I'd let them eat you?"

Whatever retort she might have made was lost in the agony of the sensation of the circulation flowing back into her cramped arms and numbed hands. She bit her lip to keep from crying out.

An ungentle hand closed around her upper arm, hauled her to her feet. "Can you walk?"

The muscles in her legs were cramped, her feet tingling painfully, and the long hours of unspeakable terror had left her feeling weak and shaky, but she tightened her jaw and nodded resolutely. "I can run if I must."

"That's good, because thanks to your little adventure, we're probably going to have to." He eased the machete back into its sheath, then tightened his hold on her arm, jerking her toward him so that she half fell against him, her free hand splaying against the solid muscles of his chest. She stared into narrowed, dangerous blue eyes, and knew a stab of renewed fear. "But understand this," he said, his lips drawing back into a nasty smile as he enunciated each word with awful clarity, "You run away from me again, and you're on your own." He threw a telling glance over one shoulder, to where some of the natives had begun to gather together again and were now staring at India with an expression on their dark, sullen faces she didn't like. "They can baste you in butter or sacrifice you to the gods of Mount Futapu if they want, and I won't lift a finger to stop it. Is that clear?"

India met his icy stare without flinching. "Quite clear."

"Good." He thrust a satchel at her, and she realized with a sense of shock and profound gratitude that it was her own knapsack. She had dropped it back on the trail, when the cannibals had seized her, but until this moment she'd scarcely given it a thought.

"My notebook," she said, her still-numb fingers clumsy as she tried to open the satchel's flap. Most of the material she'd gathered for her book so far was safely back in Neu Brenenberg with her trunk, but she'd been writing and sketching in this particular notebook for over a week now, and the thought of how close she'd come to losing it made her sick. "Is it—"

"It's there." He thrust her forward with an ungentle push. "Jesus Christ. You can do an inventory later. Let's get out of here before your friends change their minds and decide to have us both for supper."

"Why didn't they eat you?"

It was a puzzle that had been bothering India ever since they'd left that squalid village with its sullen man-eaters and darkly huddled huts and smoking cookfires. Now that her legs had finally stopped shaking, and the constriction of terror squeezing her throat had begun to ease, she asked the question out loud.

Up ahead, Jack Ryder paused, his machete held high, a small quirk of amusement lifting his lips when he glanced back at her. "What do you mean?"

The obvious amusement in his face irked her to no end. She'd found a straight pin at the bottom of her knapsack and used it to repair the damage to her blouse. She'd washed her face, and made an attempt at putting up her hair again, but she was uncomfortably aware that she still looked more like a waterfront doxy who'd just lost a catfight than the coolly efficient travel writer who'd set sail from Neu Brenenberg that morning.

"The cannibals," she said severely. "One look at me, and all they could think about was dinner. Yet they never laid a hand on you."

He brought his machete down in a practiced swipe at the thick stand of fern that all but obscured the narrow track they'd been following. "I do business with them."

"You *what*?"

"The women harvest copra from fallen coconuts and haul it down to the bay. I buy it from them."

India stared at the broad back of the man ahead of her, the muscles beneath his sweat-stained shirt bunching and flexing with each swing of his machete. He did business with cannibals. Traded with them. Regularly. "What do you pay them with?"

He shrugged. "Different things. You cost me an extra crate of ships' biscuits."

They were revolting things, ships' biscuits, a kind of hardtack—inevitably infested with weevils—that was traditionally fed to sailors on a long voyage. A sudden and unaccountable wave of indignation swept through her. "You bought me for a crate of ships' biscuits?"

"Mmm. And a pig. Don't forget the pig."

India thought about that bawling, terrified pig that would be eaten in her stead, and she wondered if she would ever be able to bring herself to touch meat again. "I'll never forget that poor pig."

He had a crooked way of smiling that brought an unexpected dimple to one tanned, lean cheek. "Made you feel a certain kinship with the edible beasts of the world, did it?"

"Yes, it did."

A silence fell between them, filled only with the swish of Jack Ryder's machete and the hot steamy drip around them. The track they followed had at first dipped downward, but it seemed to India that they'd been climbing sharply now for half an hour or more, the thick stands of fern and creeper-choked ironwood, sandlewood, and pine allowing only occasional distant glimpses of a sunsparkled, cobalt blue sea. And she realized, suddenly, that this was not, as she'd first supposed, the same track down which she'd been carried by the cannibals.

"Shouldn't we have made it back to the main trail by now?"

"We're not going that way."

"We're not?"

He took another swipe with his machete, and grunted. "Too risky. In the time I spent tracking down you and your friends and finding that damned pig, Simon and his boys could have easily made it back to their ship and reoutfitted. You might be anxious to run into them again, but I'm not."

"So we're striking out *overland*?"

He swung his machete with a hefty *whack*, and grunted. "There's a trail here. It should intersect with the main track just before the river."

India tipped back her head and stared up at a jungle canopy so thick that only a faint suggestion of daylight filtered through to bathe the air around them in an eerie greenish glow. "There used to be a trail," she said, unable to resist the urge to goad him. "I think either it has petered out or you've lost it."

He replied with a muttered oath and a savage swing of his machete that told her he'd been thinking the same thing. "Hell, if it hadn't been for that stupid stunt of yours, I'd be halfway to La Rochelle by now."

She stopped short. "If it weren't for me?"

"That's right." He turned to face her. He was drenched with sweat, his shirt open halfway down the front to show a bronzed chest that lifted with each breath. Swinging a machete was hard work. "If you hadn't got yourself nabbed by cannibals—"

Jerking her gaze away from that exposed, aggressively masculine chest, India stabbed the air in front of his nose with one pointed finger. "If you hadn't forced me to go with you, none of this would have happened."

"Bloody hell!" He swatted her accusing finger away as if it were an annoying gnat. "If it hadn't been for me, those cannibals would have grabbed you off the summit of Mount Futapu."

"Right." She rocked back on her heels, her hands on her hips. "So they grabbed me at the base of Mount Futapu instead!"

He leaned into her, his strong jaw clenched tight enough that she could see the muscles throbbing along the line of his lean cheeks. "If you'd just stayed with me instead of running off at the first chance you got, you'd have been fine."

"And that's supposed to make what happened to me all my own fault, is it?"

"A share of it. You know, you might try being just a tad grateful for what I did. You haven't even bloody said thank you."

India let out a low, derisive laugh. "Indeed, Mr. Ryder? Would you have me believe your rescue was motivated by chivalrous impulses?"

"What the hell else do you think *motivated* me?"

"Pure self-interest, of course."

He flung back his head. "Self-interest?"

"That's right. You believed possession of a hostage would facilitate your escape, and so you were—"

"*Facilitate* my escape?" Swearing foully, he swung away to take a series of vicious swipes with his machete at the tangled undergrowth before spinning back around to face her again. "Jesus, woman. Do you always talk like that?"

"Like what?"

"Like you're delivering a bloody lecture to the local scientific society or something."

India held herself quite still. "You shock me, Mr. Ryder. Do you mean to imply that you have actually *attended* such lectures? Judging by your language, I had assumed your exposure to conversation must be limited to barrooms and seamen's quarters."

For a long, charged moment, he stared at her, his chest heaving, his nostrils flaring with each indrawn breath, a faint, unexpected stain of color appearing to ride high on his cheekbones. "Sonofabitch," he said suddenly, and turned uphill again, his machete chopping savagely at every creeper in their path.

She followed him, the silence between them heavy, the steamy jungle hushed and oppressive around them. After a moment, he said, not slackening his pace, "You know what's wrong with you, don't you?"

"No," said India, pushing determinedly after him. "But I've no doubt you have every intention of telling me."

"It's the same thing that's wrong with every spinster I've ever met. It makes you all sour and cranky, and—"

"I am not sour and cranky—"

"—frustrated."

India stopped short. "And precisely what is that meant to imply?"

"You know what I'm saying." He didn't miss a beat with his machete.

Muttering softly to herself, India pushed after him up the steep, overgrown mountainside, swatting angrily at every stray branch and hanging liana in her way. So he thought she was sexually frustrated, did he? He thought all she needed was to allow her body to be frequently used to sate some man's revolting lust, and she would turn into the kind of gentle, docile imbecile men seemed to prefer? "Indeed, Mr. Ryder?" She glared at that broad, hateful back ahead of her. "Judging from the evidence

I've seen, you could hardly be said to be suffering from any such *frustration*, yet you are still as cranky and sour as they come."

"Judging from what evidence?"

"Your numerous half-native offspring!" she snapped before she could stop herself.

She expected him to laugh at her, maybe even make fun of her for her shock. Instead, he went very still, his arm arrested in midswing. Then he let the machete fall in a smooth, carefully controlled arc, and his voice, when it came, was cold and hard and more precisely modulated than she had ever heard it. "I have but one half-native offspring, Miss McKnight, and as I haven't seen her myself for almost ten years, I wonder how you came to be aware of her existence."

India knew a swift stab of some emotion she could not name. There was no doubt in her mind that he spoke the truth, which meant that neither the bare-bottomed baby she'd seen on his veranda nor the boy, Patu, who had helped sail them here, were his. And she knew, too, that while she had struck out at him blindly in furious and embarrassed self-defense, she had hit a nerve far more painful and raw than she had ever intended.

The silence between them returned, and this time, neither one broke it.

It was some three-quarters of an hour later, when they were working their way down a high, windswept slope sparsely covered with gorse and tree ferns and tall stands of kunai grass, that Jack Ryder's hand suddenly closed around India's arm to pull her back behind the wide buttressing roots of a big lone mountain pandanus.

"Sonofabitch," he swore softly beneath his breath, his gaze fixed on some point far to their right.

"What is it?" she whispered, her heart beginning to beat in quick, painful lurches as she squinted hopelessly into the distance.

He shifted, his gaze flicking over her in a quick, assessing glance. "Can't you see?"

"No, of course I can't see," she said impatiently. "What is it?"

He leaned forward until his lips were only inches from her ear. "Cannibals."

"Oh my God." She couldn't go through that again, she thought in quiet despair. She simply couldn't. "I thought you said you and the cannibals were business partners. That they wouldn't attack you. That as long as I was with you, I'd be safe."

Unbelievably, the edges of his mouth quirked up in amusement. "They're not exactly predictable, cannibals." The smile faded as he gazed into the distance again. "Try to keep as low as you can, but hurry. With any luck, they won't see us until we're near enough to the gorge to make a run for it."

She'd heard it for a while now, the growing roar of a mountain torrent, somewhere up ahead. She turned to fix him with a steady, suspicious stare. "Gorge? There's a gorge?"

"Wairopa Gorge." He propelled her on with a gentle but insistent pressure in the small of her back.

India didn't know much Pidgin, but she knew enough to make her stomach twist with an old, shameful fear. "Why is it called Wairopa Gorge?"

"Because a Scandinavian expedition that came through here some years back erected a bridge of fencing wire and braided vines over it."

"Fencing wire and—" Her voice broke, so that she had to swallow hard before she could continue. "How many years ago?"

"I don't know. Four. Maybe five."

"Five years?" She stumbled over a half-buried stone and would have pitched head forward down the slope if he hadn't still been holding her arm. "You want me to use a wire and vine bridge that's five years old? How deep is the gorge?"

"Six hundred feet. Maybe a little more."

She could see it now, a great, nearly vertical chasm of moss-covered black rock that split the mountain in two. "Oh my God," she whispered, her voice lost in the violent booming rush of the river far, far below.

"Don't tell me," said the hateful man beside her, his smile broadening as he studied her face. "Miss Indomitable McKnight is afraid of swinging bridges."

"I can't cross that thing," she said, her voice tight, her gaze fixed on the bridge of knotted vines and rusting wire and primitive, hand-hewn planks that dangled over an ominously thundering void. "I can't." Her step faltered, her head shaking slowly back and forth.

He threw a quick glance over his shoulder, his mouth tightening into a hard grin. "It's either the bridge, or the cannibals. Take your choice."

She was close enough now to see the zigzag of slippery, nearly vertical moss-covered stone steps that snaked down the side of the cliff, toward the raging river far below. Cut directly into the rock face, they were primitive and dangerous and yet, somehow, still preferable to the creaking, rotting bridge that swung sickeningly with every buffet of the wind. "There are steps," she said, just as a shout went up from behind them, followed by another.

"Shit. They've seen us." Jack Ryder's hand closed hard on her arm, jerking her forward. "We don't have time for the bloody steps. *Run. Now.*"

~~Chapter Eleven

JACK TOOK THE bridge at a rush, hoping to get India McKnight across it before she lost her nerve—or caught sight of who was really behind them. But they'd only made it something like three feet out onto the bridge's slippery, swaying planks before she balked, her hands closing convulsively over the vine-wrapped sides of the bridge, her face going pale and slightly greenish.

"*Don't look down!*" he shouted when she let out a low moan, her eyes widening as she stared at the tumbling, rocky torrent of frothing white water far below. "And don't look back, either," he added when she twisted her head to glance at the exposed, windswept rocks of the mountain behind them. "Just give me your hand and we'll get over it together. *Now*, damn it," he added, his voice sharpening as first one man, then another appeared up the main trail from Futapu Bay. "*They're coming.*"

He expected to have to pry one of her hands loose from the bridge, but she reached out to him, her gaze lifting to meet his. Her eyes were dilated wide with fear, her breath coming in jerky gasps. He took her hand in a fierce grip, and urged her forward. "Easy now," he murmured, as if coaxing a nervous horse. "Just hold my hand and put one foot in front of the other."

With each step, the wires jerked in all directions, so that it was like trying to walk on the thrashing tail of a giant crocodile, but she didn't scream. She was not the kind of woman who would ever scream, he thought with an unexpected and unwanted surge of admiration as he watched the way her square jaw tightened with determination, her thin nostrils flaring with each intake of breath. She was one hell of a woman. Aggravating and cranky and opinionated as all get-out, but with enough guts to put ten men to shame.

They were still a couple of yards from the end of the bridge when Simon's voice reached them, barely audible above the roar of the river far below. *"Hold your fire, men! He has Miss McKnight with him."*

"What?" she said, her face going slack as she started to twist around.

Tightening his hold on her hand, Jack jerked her onto solid ground with a force that sent her flying past him, so that she lost her footing and went down on her hands and knees in the trail. Yanking his machete free, he was about to bring the blade down on one of the main bridge supports when she scrambled to her feet and threw herself against him.

"You told me it was *cannibals*!" She hit him hard enough that he staggered, his breath coming out in a startled *oomph*. "You filthy, lying *beast*."

Wrapping his left arm around her waist, Jack swung India McKnight behind him and raised the machete again, just as Simon ran out onto the swaying, moss-covered planks of the wire bridge. His momentum propelled him almost a third of the way across before he stopped short, his gaze riveted on Jack's upraised machete. Then his eyes shifted to meet Jack's and the two men stared at each other, chests heaving with labored breathing, faces drawn and hard. Beside him, India McKnight went suddenly, breathlessly still.

"What's stopping you?" called Simon, a muscle jumping along his tight jaw. "You killed the better part of an entire ship's company. Why balk at one old friend?"

Jack's fist tightened around the machete. The bridge was old and rotten. One blow would be enough to send the rusted fencing wire and ancient planks and the man on them hurtling down into oblivion. For one haunting moment, Jack was vividly aware of the woman behind him, her breath coming hard and fast, and the bluejackets bunched up behind another officer, a slim, dark-haired young man of perhaps twenty or twenty-two who hesitated, wide-eyed and apprehensive, on the far side of the bridge. Then, suddenly, all the leaves in the forest

behind them began to rustle, the bridge swaying ominously back and forth as the squall finally blew in.

Dark and gray, the clouds moved rapidly to obliterate
the blue sky and vivid golden sunlight. "Sonofabitch,"
Jack growled, and shoved to his feet. The machete still in
his fist, he grabbed India McKnight's hand again and
yanked her with him in a scrabbling rush.

"After him, men," shouted Simon. "Quickly. But hold
your fire!"

Jack expected her to try to hang back, or break free
of his hold. She did neither. Hand in hand, they fled
down the main trail and into a dark gloom of thick,
moss-covered trunks and looming vines and great arching ferns as the rain forest closed in around them once
more. Overhead, they heard the excited flutter of hundreds of birds as the creatures of the jungle rushed for
cover. Then the sky opened up, and it poured.

The heat of the day vanished. The rain teemed down,
soaking them instantly. An endless curtain of giant drops
pelted through the overhead canopy of native oaks and
beech, drummed on the giant leaves of the spreading
understory, filled the air with the smell of wet vegetation
and dark earth. Even with the rain, the going was easier
now that they'd struck the main trail again. But with
every step, Jack was aware of Simon's men, pounding behind them.

"Why don't you just give up?" India McKnight shouted,
the rain coursing down her wet face, her voice a breath-

less rasp as she slipped and slid behind him in the muck. "You'll never get away."

Jack gritted his teeth and plowed on, his boots slapping through the puddles, the rain running in his eyes as he tipped back his head to search the rocky, vine-covered hillside on their right. "If I can just find— Ah," he shouted in triumph as a black void opened up beside them. Tightening his hold on India's hand, he pulled her off the path through a tangle of wet creeping fig and into a dank, dark world of sweating stone and cool stale air that closed in around them like a tomb.

Her steps slowed as she looked around in wide-eyed wonder. "What is this place?"

"It's an old lava tube."

"It's a burial chamber," she said, her voice hushing with excited awe as the fading light from the receding entrance revealed a scattering of skulls and long bones, ribs and disjointed vertebrae, some gleaming white, others turned green with mold and age. Then the tunnel widened out into a chamber whose very walls seemed to be composed of nothing but row after row of gape-eyed, grinning skulls, hundreds of them, looming, towering, peering. She stopped cold. "But this is fascinating."

"Not *now*, for Christ's sake," he swore, sheathing his machete. With one swipe of his arm, he sent the nearest wall of skulls shivering and clattering and banging to the stone floor of the cave behind them in an avalanche of chattering jawbones and cascading craniums.

"What are you *doing*?" she cried, her voice rising in horrified indignation. He jerked her forward, but she twisted around, trying to peer behind them. "This is a gravesite you're desecrating. How would you like it if these were the bones of your ancestors?"

Jack let loose an inundation of green leg and arm bones that rattled and rolled away into the darkness. "Hell, I'd set every one of them to dancing on a gibbet if I thought it would save me right now."

His hand tightening around hers, he dragged her on. The last faint glow of light from the entrance was almost gone, and as the tunnel narrowed and twisted to the left, he whacked his forehead on a low protrusion of stone and said, "Shit."

"Huh. Serves you right," she whispered in that censorious, Sunday-school teacher voice of hers. "And exactly how do you propose to see where we're going now?"

They could hear a renewed rattle and crash of bones followed by the painful thud of soft warm bodies hitting stone as Simon's men, swearing and shouting, stumbled into the bouncing, sliding phalanx of dead man-eaters.

"I don't need to." Beneath his feet, the solid stone floor of the cave changed, suddenly, to soft sand. Dropping to his knees, Jack groped blindly along the dripping rock face on his left with the splayed fingers of his free hand. Already he could feel the moisture seeping into the sand beneath him, wetting his pants legs. "Now, where the hell— Ah." His hand slid over the smooth wet stone to shoot into a yawning void, and he let out a satisfied exhalation of breath. Yanking on India McKnight's hand, he pulled her down beside him. "Lie down."

She half fell against him, her hand gripping his shoulder, her head coming up as she stared at him, a vague shadow, peering at a shadow. "I beg your pardon?"

"Now, damn it!" Bearing her down into the soft, wet sand, he pinned her woman's body beneath his.

She squirmed furiously against him. "What are you doing?"

"Shhh," he hissed, and clamped his hand over her mouth. "Just keep your head down, and watch your elbows."

She murmured something indecipherable against his hand, her palms flattening against his chest as she tried to push him away from her. But already he was moving, only just managing to duck his head as he rolled with her beneath the curtain of rock that separated the lava tube from the cave that lay beyond it. He heard her elbow whack painfully against the stone, then they were through.

He landed on top of her, his arms braced wide on each side of her shoulders to take some of his weight as he kept his hand pressed firmly over her mouth. Their faces were inches apart, so close that he could feel the flutter of a stray lock of her hair against his cheek when he breathed out. He lowered his head until his mouth was about where he assumed her ear must be, although he couldn't be certain, for the dim gray glow of the lava tube had been replaced by an impenetrable blackness that seemed to press in on them, thick and damp. "Don't make a sound," he whispered.

It was so quiet he could hear the steady *drip, drip, drip* of water as the rain from the storm outside trickled its way into the cave and ran in growing streams down the wall to pool beneath them. He could hear the strained rasp of her breathing, feel the rapid beating of her heart. Painfully conscious of his own heart pounding in his chest, he listened to the scrabbling of boots and jingling of scabbards as Simon and his men rushed past, kicking up sand that sprayed through the low opening in the cave wall to scatter over Jack's bare forearm in a fine, damp layer. The woman beneath him had gone utterly, completely still.

"It's no use," he heard Simon say, his voice echoing queerly from the adjoining chamber. "We need light. Brooks, O'Neal—go back to the entrance and fashion us some torches."

"It's raining, sir."

"I know it's raining, damn it. Just do it."

"We could easily have passed up several side passages already," said another voice, a young, educated voice that Jack didn't recognize.

There was a pause. Then Simon said, "You're right. We'll go back to the last bone chamber and await the torches there."

The voices and tramp of feet receded into the distance. Jack let his hand slip from India McKnight's mouth.

He heard her take a deep breath, and hold it a moment before releasing it. "I am lying in what appears to be a rapidly growing pool of water," she said in a tight, strained voice. "Do you intend to move anytime soon?"

Something about the way she said it made him suddenly, intensely aware of the soft warmth of her breasts, pressed against his chest, and the intimate way her legs had tangled with his. He stood abruptly, his hand clasping hers so that he drew her up with him. "If we don't move soon, we're going to drown."

"Drown?" She surprised him with a short, dry huff of laughter. "Of course."

Jack peered into the darkness, trying to see the woman beside him. She was wet and cold; she'd been shot at, and captured by cannibals, and chased by Her Britannic Majesty's navy over a thundering gorge and through a cave full of the moldy skeletons of generations of man-eaters. Most women—most *people*—would be fainting with fear, or sobbing hopelessly with reaction. But India McKnight could still laugh at the absurd thought of now drowning.

Reaching out blindly, he found her arm, then slid his fingers down her sleeve until his hand captured hers again. "Let's get out of here," he said gruffly.

"*Is* there a way out of here?"

Jack took a step forward, whacked his knee, and grunted. "Just hold my hand. And keep your voice down."

"You do realize, of course, that you've only bought yourself a few more minutes," she whispered, her hand obediently gripping his as he began to inch his way forward. "As soon they bring up torches, they'll see that opening, and our tracks in the sand, and know where we've gone."

"Uh-uh," said Jack, water gurgling around his boots as he carefully felt his way forward. "All they'll see is a pool." It had always surprised him, how rapidly the pool in this cave could fill when it rained. Another half minute, and they wouldn't have been able to make it through that passage without swimming.

He took another step, and a strange, eerie music moaned through the cavern, rising and falling, echoing and re-echoing.

"What's that?" she whispered, her hand tightening around his.

"They call this place the Cave of Songs. When the water is deep enough, the waves strike the walls of the cavern and make music."

He became aware, slowly, of a faint, barely perceptible lightening in the darkness, and a breath of fresh air that touched his cheek and fluttered the surface of the pool behind them to unleash a new crescendo of uncanny, ghostly notes.

"How did you know about this cave?"

He shrugged. "I hid here once, for a time."

He could feel her staring at him. "When you were on the run from the British navy?"

"Yes."

He expected her to pursue that, but she didn't. "Where will we come out?"

"On the other side of the mountain."

"And the lava tube?"

Jack laughed softly. "This mountain is honeycombed with lava tubes, all intertwined. Simon and his men could spend the rest of the week stumbling around in them. And they all lead back toward the gorge."

From the mouth of the Cave of Songs they could look out over the entire north end of the island stretching far below them, a mist-swirled land of steep, rain forest–filled ravines widening out into verdant valleys and thickly matted swamps. Far to the northeast lay the tiny French trading hamlet of La Rochelle, its golden beaches and emerald lagoon sheltered by the nearly unbroken, half-submerged reef against which the trade winds drove the surf in a never-ending crash of spray and fury.

Standing beneath the sheltering overhang of the cliff face, Jack squinted up at the sky. The rain had stopped, but the world still rang with the splash and drip of running water. It looked as if it had rained for a hundred years, he thought, rather than a mere thirty or forty minutes. The path snaking its way down through the soggy, dripping tangle of green was a quagmire of mud and slippery rocks, and the air still held a definite chill. Then the sun broke through the parting clouds, and the dark wet rocks around them began to steam.

Swearing softly beneath his breath, Jack kicked off his boots and socks, unbuttoned his wet shirt, and pulled it off. He had his trousers half undone when India McKnight said, *"What are you doing?"*

His thumbs hooked in his waistband, Jack looked up to find her watching him with wide, scandalized eyes. "What the hell do you think I'm doing? I'm taking off my bloody clothes. They're soaked."

She'd been bedraggled enough when he'd rescued her from the cannibals, with her blouse torn and her pith helmet gone and her hair coming down in stringy, sweat-dampened hanks. Now, drenched by the rain and smeared with wet sand from the cave, she had the rakish air of a shipwreck victim. Or maybe a guttersnipe. But she hadn't lost one iota of her starch. "And so you just strip them off? In public?"

He laughed out loud. "This isn't exactly Piccadilly Square." He pushed his trousers and smallclothes down over his hips. "There's a reason the natives on these islands run around bare-assed, you know. A wet man with clothes on is a hell of a lot wetter than a wet man with no clothes on, and a hell of a lot more likely to get sick." Hopping around on first one foot, then the other, he finally managed to peel the wet material off his legs.

When he straightened, it was to find her staring resolutely off over the dripping, vivid green leaves of the banyan tree below them. The color was high in her cheeks, her chest lifting with her labored breathing, her wet blouse clinging to her in a way that he couldn't help but notice. And he knew it again, that swift, unexpected, and totally unwanted surge of sexual awareness. She was not at all the type of woman who interested him. She was prudish and bossy and determinedly, aggressively virginal. But there could be no denying the effect she had on him, however impossible it was to understand. Dropping his arms so that his bunched wet trousers strategically covered the growing evidence of his wayward thoughts, Jack gave her a crooked, provocative grin. "If you had any sense, you'd strip off, too. Spread out on the rocks, that outfit of yours'll dry in no time. But you're looking at a long, cold night if you insist on keeping your clothes on."

She wrapped her arms around her chest, as if she was afraid he might try to take her clothes away by force. Or maybe she was just cold. "Some of us are made of sterner stuff than others."

"So that's what it is, is it? *Sterner stuff?*" With a sodden plop, he spread his trousers out on a nearby rock to dry. "And here I thought you were just being stubborn and stupid."

She swung to face him, her eyes narrowed, her magnificent breasts rising and falling with each agitated intake of air. "Stupid? Is that what you call decency? Prudence?"

Deliberately, Jack turned his back on her. "Prudence. Now, that's an interesting choice of words. What the hell do you think? That I'd be so overcome by lust at the sight of your naked body that I wouldn't be able to stop myself from ravishing you? Believe me, after twelve years of living in these islands, the sight of a naked woman doesn't even turn my head anymore. Besides—" He hung up his shirt in the golden rays of the setting sun, where the breeze would catch it. "You're not my type. I like women who like the way a man's body looks—the way it feels. Women who actually enjoy what happens when a man and a woman's bodies come together. Women who don't just lie back and think of England, and wait for it all to be over."

"What makes you think you know what type of woman I am?"

He threw a quick glance at her over his shoulder, and huffed a laugh. "Hell, just look at you, swathed in a bloody tartan skirt in the middle of a tropical jungle, with your collar buttoned up so high around your neck it's a wonder you don't choke."

"I'll have you know that my Expedition Outfit is imminently practical."

"Practical?" Bending over, he picked up a dry branch that had fallen beneath the overhang of the cliff, and looked around for more. "It's a wonder you don't have a heat stroke. There's only one reason a woman would wear a getup like that, and that's as a signal to men. It's like wearing a sign tattooed across your forehead that says, *Warning. Frigid virgin. Do not touch.*"

"Huh." She swept up a branch to add to the pile he'd been accumulating on the flat shelf of rock at the cave's entrance. "Just goes to show how much you know."

Forgetting he had a growing reason to keep his back to her, Jack straightened slowly, his gaze narrowing as he took in her heightened color. "Ho. What are you trying to tell me? That you're not a virgin?"

"That is none of your business," she said, and tossed him what he realized only in the last instant was a waterproof tin of safety matches.

He was so surprised he just managed to catch them out of the air. "Where the hell did these come from?"

She shook her hair out of her face in an unexpectedly feminine gesture, and gave him a slow smile. "I keep them in my knapsack. I'm *practical*, remember?"

It was the first time Jack had seen her smile like that, and the effect it had on him was both unwelcome and potentially embarrassing, given his current state of undress. Swearing silently to himself, he crouched down beside the pile of firewood, one knee strategically raised to hide his crotch, and wondered how long it would be before he could comfortably put his bloody trousers back on.

It took a while, but he eventually managed to coax a sluggish flame from the damp wood.

"You're not worried someone might see the smoke?" she asked, coming to stand on the far side of the fire, her arms still wrapped around her chest.

Jack looked up, and shook his head. "If I know Simon, he'll have his men combing those lava tubes till dawn."

"And the cannibals?"

He added another branch to the growing flames. "I trade with all the mountain tribes, and the natives on the northern end of the island have been Christianized. Which means they now symbolically eat the son of God, rather than each other."

A shiver wracked her tall frame, and she stretched her hands out to the blaze. She'd made an attempt at fixing her hair and brushing the worst of the mud and sand from her clothes, but she was still soaked to the skin. In the faint light of the fading day, her hands looked almost blue. Jack sat back on his heels, his gaze on the curve of her cheek, where a smudge of dirt stretched from her ear to the angle of her strong, square jaw.

"Why did you do it?" he asked suddenly.

"Do what?"

"Run with me. You know as well as I do that if you'd hung back, I'd have had to let you go."

She kept her attention fixed on the dancing flames, her voice crisp and matter-of-fact. "Without me beside you, Captain Granger's men would have shot you."

"And you'd have cared?"

Slowly, she raised her gaze to meet his. "You saved my life. Twice. And even if one of those episodes was entirely your fault, it still seemed a shabby way to repay you, by letting you be killed. Even if you did deserve it," she added.

He laughed. Then the laughter died on his lips as he stared at her reflectively for a moment or two, thinking oddly and with no apparent connection that he hadn't noticed what a wide, full mouth she had, and that maybe he hadn't been wrong after all when he'd decided, after reading that book of hers last year, that he'd like this woman if he were ever to meet her.

≈≈Chapter Twelve

INDIA WAS COLD. She was cold and she was wet and she was so hungry, her stomach kept growling.

Sitting as close to the flames as she could without actually catching on fire, she slipped her notebook from her knapsack and subjected it to careful scrutiny. The edges of the pages were a bit wavy, but the waterproofed canvas had kept out the worst of the wet. She propped the book open beside her, the pages turned toward the fire.

"I guess if we run out of wood, we can always use that," said Jack Ryder.

India looked up. He sat cross-legged near the entrance to the cave, his back propped against a rock as he worked at doing something with a long stick. Much to her relief, he'd finally put his trousers back on, but he was still bare-chested, the fire and the setting sun combining to drench his smooth, tanned flesh in a deep golden light.

"Huh," she said, because she knew him well enough by now to realize that he was only trying to get a rise out of her. "Why not burn your clothes instead? You never seem to wear them, anyway." She thought about poor Captain Granger and his men, forced to strip and walk back to their ship in the nude, and then the cannibals with their mud-smeared black buttocks and pandanus penis purses. Her day had been bizarrely filled with naked male bodies. And it occurred to her, as she watched the muscles in Jack Ryder's upper arms and chest flex and bunch with each pass of his knife over the tip of the stick he was working on, that his male body was by far the most attractive she'd seen.

It was a thought that brought with it a strange inner clenching that stole her breath and lingered like a slow heat, low in her belly. Aghast, she comforted herself with the thought that such a primitive, physical reaction was to be expected, considering the savage environment in which they were stranded. She told herself her unwanted, scandalous interest in this man's hard, bronzed body was a natural result of her having seen—literally—so much of him in the last thirty-six hours. But as she watched his eyes narrow in amusement, watched a dimple appear, fleetingly, in one lean, tanned cheek, she knew she was only lying to herself.

"If you had any sense, you wouldn't still be wearing yours," he said, and so wayward were her thoughts that it took her a moment to remember they were talking about clothes.

She glanced away, more embarrassed by her own thoughts than by his words. "I will survive, Mr. Ryder."

"Oh, you'll survive, all right. But you might pick up a nasty fungus. They're bloody hard to get rid of in the tropics."

India knew a hollow sense of dread. They could be unpleasant things, tropical fungi.

"There was a missionary's wife over on Tanna who got a fungus on her foot," he was saying. "Ate up half her leg before—"

"I don't need to hear this, Mr. Ryder."

"Actually, I think you do."

India kept her gaze fixed on the darkening lowlands stretching away from the base of the mountains, to the north. A moment ago, the world had been awash in golden light. Now the sun was only a faint memory on the far horizon as the distant sea turned into a surging swath of pink-tinged silver, broken here and there by the dark ragged outline of faraway islands. In the trees below, a native nightingale began to sing, while all around them, a myriad of night-blooming flowers filled the air with an exotic medley of sweet scents. India sat very still, awed to silence by the beauty of the moment.

Jack Ryder broke it. "How do you expect to be able to write anything meaningful about the South Seas when you've never felt a tropical breeze on anything more than the bare skin of your face?"

"I have a very good imagination," she answered tartly, glancing back to where he still sat, doing whatever he was doing to that stick.

"Huh. You can imagine what you've never known, can you?"

"I have been cold before."

He let out a short laugh. "It's not cold. You're only cold now because you won't take off your wet clothes." He ran his hand up the stick to test the point. "I'll bet you didn't even take off your clothes the time you did it."

There was no mistaking which *it* he was referring to. She should have told him she had no intention of discussing anything so personal, and that if he were a gentleman, he never would have made such a remark. Instead she demanded, "How do you know it was only one time?"

He looked up then, the firelight gleaming in his dark eyes. "Well, you obviously didn't enjoy yourself. And if you didn't enjoy it, then why would you do it again?"

India stared at him, uncharacteristically bereft of speech.

"Well?" he said, going back to work on his stick. "Did you?"

"Did I what?"

"Did you take off all your clothes?"

"Of course not."

"Why not?"

"I'm not having this conversation," India said, pointedly turning her back on him to stare off over the darkened treetops. The moon was full tonight, the sky so full of stars that the heavens glowed.

"I don't believe you even did it," said the hateful, irrepressible man behind her. "I mean, why would you?"

"Presumably for the same reason anyone does," she answered tartly, before she could stop herself.

"In my experience, people do it for one of two reasons: either out of a sense of duty, or because they succumb to passion. But since you've never been married—" He paused. "You haven't been married, have you?"

"Of course not."

"I thought not. So, since you obviously didn't do it out of duty, one would think you must have succumbed to passion. But people who succumb to passion usually take off all their clothes—unless they're so excited they're in too big of a rush, of course. But since you weren't excited, and you say you didn't take off your clothes, I'm wondering why you—"

"I was curious," she said, twisting around to face him again. "Is that so difficult to understand?"

"Curious?"

"Yes, curious. Having made up my mind never to marry, I decided I wanted to see what *it* was like—so I'd know what I was missing. I decided I wouldn't be missing anything."

He stared at her for a moment, then let out a short bark of laughter. "Only you would approach something as sensually sublime as lovemaking as if it were a scientific experiment."

Sensually sublime. It wasn't an expression she would have expected him to use. But surprise didn't account for the strange, not unpleasant flow of liquidlike warmth his words sent coursing through her. "It wasn't a scientific experiment. It was . . ." India paused, chagrined. It might not have been scientific, but it had definitely been an experiment, of sorts.

"So, how was it?" he asked.

"I beg your pardon?"

He looked up, a slow smile curving his lips. He was really quite devastatingly attractive, in a rakish, dangerous way. "What was the result of the experiment?" he asked.

She kept her voice crisp, analytical. Detached. Everything she wasn't at the moment. "I found the entire episode unutterably boring." And embarrassing, she thought, although she didn't say that. "Frankly, I fail to understand either the attraction or all the hoopla surrounding what is basically a rather unpleasant and messy activity."

He reached to put away his knife, which she realized he wore sheathed in his boot. "So because you made the mistake of selecting a man who was a bad lover, you gave up on the whole thing, did you?" He stood, reaching his naked, well-muscled arms over his head in a lazy stretch that was both entirely natural and intensely, breathtakingly sensual. "Don't you think that was a bit hasty? Scientifically speaking, of course."

India stared up at him, her eyes narrowing against the smoke. "And what makes you so sure he was a bad lover?"

"You just said so."

"I didn't."

"Yes you did. If he hadn't been a bad lover, you wouldn't have found the whole experience *unutterably boring*. You just didn't know he was a bad lover because you had nothing to compare him to." In one fluid motion, he bent to catch up the stick he'd been sharpening and straightened to give her a slow smile. "Now, let's go catch some dinner, shall we?"

"I don't think we should stop yet, sir," said Alex, gritting his teeth to keep them from chattering.

Captain Granger turned, the makeshift torch in his hand sputtering and flaring to send ghoulish patterns of light and shadow over the gray rock face behind him. "The men are still wet from the rain, Mr. Preston, and it's damned cold in these caves. An officer must always remember to take into consideration the needs of his men."

Alex felt a flash of heat at the rebuke, yet couldn't stop himself from saying, "Ryder must be here somewhere."

"Then we'll find him in the morning, won't we?" The captain swung toward the cave's distant entrance. "Come, Mr. Preston. Your enthusiasm and determination are commendable, but one should never forget the importance of wisdom."

It was a direct order, however lightly he'd phrased it. Alex had no choice but to obey.

They camped for the night at the entrance to the lava tube. As soon as the fires were lit, most of the men stripped off completely, propping up their clothes on sticks to dry. Even Captain Granger undressed down to his small-clothes. But Alex removed only his jacket, although the rain had seeped through to the shirt beneath and his wet trousers chafed him painfully with each unwary movement. Just because one was in a jungle, he reasoned, and wet, was no excuse for indulging in conduct more befitting a savage than an Englishman.

But he'd been foolish to question the captain's decision to call off the search for the night, Alex realized, as he watched the tired, hungry men tear with gusto into the baked red mountain plantains and native oranges the captain had directed them to gather. With more seamen from the ship, they'd be able to search the warren of caves far more thoroughly, come morning. And in the meantime, Ryder wasn't going anywhere.

But when he ventured to say as much to Captain Granger, the other man only shook his head. "I don't intend to waste any more time searching these caves."

"But sir!"

Simon Granger glanced up from tending the leaf-wrapped breadfruit he was baking in the coals of the fire. "Jack Ryder knew what he was doing when he ducked into that lava cave. Unless I miss my guess, he'll be halfway down the other side of this mountain before the sun's been up an hour."

"So you think we should continue to work our way around to the northern end of the island?"

Captain Granger busied himself with his breadfruit.

"Tell me something, Mr. Preston: Where do you think he's going?"

"I don't think he has any real objective, sir. I suppose he hopes simply to hide out in the jungle until we give up and go away."

"Never make the mistake of underestimating your opponent, Mr. Preston," said the captain, raking the steaming package from the coals. "Believe me, Jack Ryder knows exactly where he's going."

Alex eyed the other man in disbelief. "And where's that, sir?"

"La Rochelle."

"La Rochelle?"

The captain unwrapped the steaming fruit with studied care. "As I understand it, the previous French commissioner was a good friend of Jack's—and no friend of the British," he added.

"But he's not there anymore?"

"No. No, he's not." Simon Granger handed Alex an unappetizing-looking lump of mush heaped on a broad leaf. "Here. Try this."

Alex wrinkled up his nose, and felt his stomach heave in warning. "I'd rather not."

"Try it," the captain repeated, more sternly.

Alex's gaze faltered beneath the other man's steady stare. "Yes, sir." His insides skittering in anticipation, Alex took a tentative nibble and realized, for the first time, why they called this unattractive lump breadfruit. "It's not bad," he said around another mouthful, as he suddenly remembered just how hungry he was. "Rather like toast." He took another bite. "Oddly crossed with new potatoes."

"Don't sound so surprised."

Alex looked up to find the other man smiling faintly. "Where did you learn to fix this?"

For one, brief moment, a sad, faraway light shone in the other man's eyes, before he hid it with a careful lowering of his lids. "Jack Ryder taught me."

The sharpened stick was a spear, India came to realize. Ryder used it to skewer a species of plump native fish as they came up to feed in a nearby moonlit mountain pool overhung with soft ferns and trailing vines of white flowering native jasmine and sweet laurel.

To her relief, he kept his trousers on, simply rolling them up to the knee before wading out bare-chested to a flat-topped rock, where he stood motionless yet utterly relaxed, eyes alert, spear poised high in a natural huntsman's posture that India, watching him, decided must be as old as time.

With a quiet ripple and a flick of its tail, a silver fish broke the surface. The muscles and sinews of the man's bare, sun-bronzed back flexed and lengthened. The crude spear shot through the air in a swift, clean strike. And India McKnight, watching fascinated and oddly humbled from the mossy bank, felt something quicken within her, a primitive and unwanted admiration of male beauty and grace and some other quality she could not quite identify but that had something to do with a strong, skilled male's ability to protect and provide nourishment for a female. Once, she would have scoffed at the idea that she might find such a characteristic even faintly attractive. But the allure was there, powerful and subconscious and no less real for being innate.

"Where did you learn to do that?" she asked when he came to hunker down in the shallows and clean his catch.

"On Rakaia," he said, his attention all for his task. "It's an island near Tahiti."

"Is that where you lived with the cannibals?"

He looked up, the mingling moonlight and star shine limning the sharp bones of his face as he stared at her through dark, narrowed eyes. "Who told you I lived with cannibals?"

"Captain Granger." She held herself quite still, caught off guard by the intensity of his reaction. "He said you lived with cannibals for two years."

Jack Ryder went back to cleaning his fish. "The people of Rakaia haven't been cannibals for half a century or more."

"But they were, once?"

He rolled one shoulder in a dismissive shrug, but she could feel the tension in him, the simmering anger, even if she couldn't explain it. "All the natives of the South Pacific were cannibals once, Melanesians and Polynesians alike, from Rabaul to the Sandwich Islands."

"Did you ever wonder why?"

He straightened, his lips quirking upward in a smile. "Maybe they got tired of pork," he said, then laughed when India couldn't quite keep herself from shuddering in response.

She was glad to get back to the fire, and stood holding her hands out to the flames while he set the fish to roast on a spit propped between rocks. The short walk down to the pool and back had been unexpectedly difficult, for the split petticoats India wore beneath her tartan skirt were soaked through and the wet cotton had chafed the tender flesh of her inner thighs with every step. Even her corset was wet, its baleen ribs rubbing her torso painfully raw. She was sore and cold and very, very tired of being wet, and if it hadn't been for the presence of Jack Ryder, she would gladly have stripped off blouse, skirt—everything, so overwhelming was the urge to release her body from the wet, clinging embrace of wool and cotton and whalebone.

"What exactly are you wearing under that outfit of yours, anyway?" he asked, glancing up at her.

India stiffened. "I beg your pardon?"

"You hobbled up here from the pond like an old bow-legged stockman just off a four-week muster. All those wet female *accruements* of yours are starting to get a mite uncomfortable, are they?"

"My 'female accruements' are none of your business, sir." She meant to say it loftily. Instead it came out sounding petty and more than a bit childish.

He gave her that nasty grin of his. "Uh-uh. Anything that slows us down is my business."

India felt her heart give one, unsteady lurch. "Which means?"

He was smiling still, but his eyes were narrow and hard with a look she was learning all too well. "Which means you can put that damned wool skirt and your blouse back on if you insist. But you either take off those wet petticoats and all that other nonsense now and let them dry overnight, or you take them off in the morning and simply leave them behind. The choice is yours."

≈≈Chapter Thirteen

INDIA OPENED HER mouth to say, *And if I don't?* Then she read the determination in his eyes, and swallowed instead.

"That's right," he said, as if he knew the train of her thoughts exactly. "If you don't take them off, I'll take them off for you."

He stood slowly, the firelight gleaming over his bare, well-muscled chest. She was suddenly aware of the breathless stillness of the moment, broken only by the crackle of the dancing flames and the *creak-creak* of some exotic creature lost in the vastness of the surrounding rain forest. The velvety darkness of the tropical night seemed to press in on them, making her excruciatingly conscious of their isolation and his power and her own vulnerability. And the thought of facing him, of facing the night to come, without the rigid, protective confines of her corset and all those layers of petticoats awakened once more that strange, unfamiliar coil of tension, low in her belly.

"Well?" he asked softly. "Which is it to be?"

She eyed him consideringly. "You're not that much taller than I."

"Nope. But I'm bigger. And I don't fight by the Marquess of Queensbury Rules."

The implications of his words seemed to hover in the moonlit night between them, along with the image they provoked, of him wrestling with her, his big, half-naked body rising over her, pinning her down, his lean, sure hands seeking out buttons and ties. And India felt it again, a strange inner heat that rippled not unpleasantly downward to meet and be passed by a surge of panic that spiraled contradictorily upward.

"Turn around," she said, coming to an instant decision.

He eyed her with unconcealed suspicion. "Why? So you can skewer me with my spear? Or just run off into the night?"

"Exactly how far do you think I could run in these wet clothes?"

He grunted noncommittally. "And the spear?"

She raised her chin so that she could look down her nose at him in a haughty gesture of disdain. "You have my word as a gentlewoman that I will accompany you safely to La Rochelle."

"Your word as a gentlewoman," he repeated.

"That's right."

He hesitated a moment, then swung around to stare off at the distant shimmer of moonlit sea, his arms folded across his chest. She studied the broad expanse of his bare shoulders, aware for the first time of just how much he was trusting her by turning his back on her like this.

Then he said, "Remember: I have very quick reflexes, and my sense of hearing was honed by some two years of living with ex-cannibals."

"You should write a book about your experiences, Mr. Ryder," she said, unbuckling the wide belt she wore at her waist, and quickly going to work on the row of buttons down the front of her blouse.

"A book?"

"Yes." She hesitated a moment, then peeled her blouse down over her shoulders, sighing softly with relief as the stiff, wet material came away from her arms. The night air felt warm and sweet and vaguely sinful against her bare flesh, so that her voice quavered slightly when she said, "There have been numerous accounts written by missionaries who worked among the various peoples of the South Pacific, but your experience of actually living with the natives as a renegade must be unique."

"I wasn't a renegade at the time."

"You weren't?" She twisted around to find him staring out over the dark valley, his hands resting lightly on his lean hips, his powerful body held almost painfully still.

He shook his head. "A seaman by the name of Toby

Jenkins and I were washed overboard in a storm. It took the British navy the better part of two years to figure out we were still alive, and track us down."

She wanted to ask him more, but something about the taut line of his back and the harsh, flat tone of his voice discouraged her. With one more quick, apprehensive glance at his motionless back, India took off her camisole and set to work loosening the hooks of her corset. This was easily accomplished, for she was far too practical a woman to ever indulge in that ridiculous affectation known as *tight lacing*. She wore her corset not to exaggerate the female curves of her body, but to present a rigidly proper silhouette to the world. It was like a shield, her corset, and as she stripped away the wet, heavily ribbed material, she felt exposed, vulnerable—oddly naked, despite the presence of the thin chemise she still wore.

"Why don't you put on my shirt?"

India froze, the corset clutched to her chemise-covered breasts, her gaze lifting once again to the man who still stood staring off into space, his back to her. "I beg your pardon?"

"My shirt. Why don't you put it on until yours dries?"

"I couldn't do that."

"Would you rather I did it for you?"

She snatched up his shirt from where it lay draped over the top of a nearby boulder. "That will not be necessary." Turning her back on him, she yanked the hem of her damp chemise from beneath the waistband of her skirt and quickly stripped it off, as well.

A warm breeze kicked up, caressing her naked breasts with an erotic, compelling touch. Shocked at the new and unfamiliar sensations the experience awakened within her, India thrust her arms into the sleeves of his shirt and hugged it close against the dangerous seductions of the night.

The shirt was warm and dry and smelled not unpleasantly of him. She buttoned it swiftly, then loosened the waistband of her split skirt. The heavy tartan smelled pungently of wet wool, but she was determined to put it back on once she rid herself of the petticoats, no matter what Jack Ryder threatened to do to her. Casting a quick glance at him over her shoulder, she wriggled the wet cloth down over her hips, quickly followed by her three petticoats. Then, after only a brief hesitation, she also rid herself of the damply clinging cloth of her drawers.

The exotically scented breeze stirred the thick canopy of the surrounding primeval forest, whispered softly over the bare flesh of her thighs to seek out the intimate, secret places of her woman's body. She was peculiarly, unexpectedly aware of the dark presence of the man who stood behind her, of all the breathless, forbidden possibilities of this moment. Then a laconic male voice said, "If you don't hurry up, the fish is going to burn."

India thrust her legs back into her tartan skirt, dragged

the wet, scratchy wool up over her bare flanks, and hastily cinched her belt around the voluminous fabric of his shirt. "I've finished," she said, busying herself with the task of spreading her clothes out to dry. She could not look at him. He might have kept his back turned throughout the entire procedure, yet nothing could mitigate the fact that she'd just stripped essentially naked while this man stood scant feet from her. It was a dangerous thing, she decided, this relaxation of the normal standards of decent, proper behavior, this overly familiar knowledge of each other's bodies brought about by the forced intimacy of their sojourn alone together in the jungle.

"Jesus," he said with a soft whistle. "You were wearing all of that?"

"I'll thank you not to ogle my undergarments, Mr. Ryder."

He huffed a soft laugh and went to hunker down beside the fire. "You planning to fuss with those things all night, or are you going to come sit down and eat?"

"I do not *fuss*." She came to sit opposite him, the wet wool of her tartan scratching her bare legs unmercifully with every step.

"You fuss." He handed her a chunk of neatly filleted fish on a bamboo-leaf plate. "All old maids fuss."

"I have always despised that expression," she said loftily. "*Old maid*. It makes any woman who never marries sound like some pitiful, passed-over creature, her life lived solely in desperate expectation of a moment that never arrives."

He looked up from filleting the second fish, his eyes gleaming softly in the light cast by the glowing embers of the fire. "I remember now, you—how did you put it?—made up your mind never to marry. Now, why was that, I wonder?"

"Do you indeed, Mr. Ryder? When a man and a woman marry, they are legally considered to have become one person, and the husband is that person. Is it any wonder that I should be reluctant to cease to exist as an individual? That I should object to my personal property immediately becoming some man's, to do with as he pleases? That I should not wish to give some man the power to direct the course of my life, to *beat* me if he should so choose?"

"When you put it that way, no, I suppose it isn't such a wonder." He handed her another hunk of fish. "How'd your family feel about your decision?"

"According to the Reverend Hamish McKnight, a woman owes her husband the same obedience and submission due her Lord, and the idea of any female existing outside the control of some male is more than an aberration, it's an abomination."

"I take it the reverend isn't too favorable."

"Wasn't. My father is dead now."

"I'm sorry."

"Don't be. We were never close."

She'd meant it to come out sounding casual, even flippant. But she knew when she looked up to find Jack

Ryder staring at her, his eyes narrowing as he studied her face, that she hadn't succeeded.

"And your mother?" he asked quietly. "Did she agree with the reverend?"

India felt the hard line of her lips relax into a smile, and shook her head. "My mother is the one who named me India."

"Ah."

"She always dreamed of traveling the world," India said, a deep ache in her heart. "I think it was one of the reasons why she married my father. He talked of devoting his life to missionary work in Africa or the Pacific."

"But he never did?"

"No. My mother never traveled any farther than London."

"She's dead, as well?"

India nodded. "She died when I was fifteen."

"I was thirteen when my mother died." It was simply said, but the pain was still there, in the tightness of his voice, in the way his chest lifted.

A silence settled between them, a silence filled with the gentle crackle and pop of the fire, and a companionable recognition of shared pain and life-shattering loss. With an unsteady hand, India set aside her makeshift bamboo plate. She had not thought of this man in this way, as someone who had once known a mother's love, someone who still mourned that mother's passing, even after so many years. It made him seem both more vulnerable and more human, and she wasn't sure she wanted that. It

would have been much easier—and more comfortable—
to continue thinking of him as a renegade, a man without
any past that didn't involve nefarious deeds and dark
secrets.

"And your father?" she asked after a moment. "Is he
dead, as well?"

"Nah. He says he plans to live to be a hundred, and
he's just ornery enough to do it." He smiled when he said
it, his voice rough with an affection he wasn't quite able
to hide. And India thought, What would it be like, to
have that kind of bond with your father? To know the
closeness that smile hinted at, rather than grow up hurt
ing and angry and alone.

Aloud, she said, "He's still in Australia?"

"He has a station, in Queensland."

India stared at the man who sat across from her, firelight gleaming a hellish red over his naked shoulders.
"You grew up on a sheep station?"

He grunted. "That surprises you, does it?"

"It's an unusual background, surely, for a naval
officer?"

He shrugged, and reached for one of the oranges
they'd collected on their walk back up from the pond. "I
have four older brothers. And I always liked the sea."

"I never had any brothers or sisters," she said, before
she could stop herself.

He threw her an orange. "I figured as much."

India caught the orange, its sweet, tangy scent filling

the air as she set to work boring its thick peel. "How could you possibly know?"

"It shows."

India resisted the urge to press him for more of an explanation. The combination of food and fire and dry clothes had warmed her, and she realized that he'd been right, that despite the elevation the night was still comfortably balmy. Quietly sucking on the orange, she stretched her bare toes out to the fire, finding it both decadent and oddly pleasant to be sitting here in the open night air, sensuously aware of the naked flesh of her thighs and hips, covered only by the thin folds of her tartan. With every breath, her bare breasts brushed the rough cloth of the man's shirt she wore. Never before had she been so conscious of her own body. It was as if, along with her corset, petticoats, and drawers, she had divested herself of some of the restraints of the civilization of which they were a part. It was a thought that both frightened her and excited her.

She stole a glance at the dark man who sat, silent now, on the far side of the fire. He had one hand dangling idly from a bent knee, his head half turned away from her as he stared out over the distant moonlit seas, so that all she saw was his profile, nose straight and long, chin strong, cheekbones flaring wide and high. It was a striking face, made even more striking by the unusual, unexpected jolt of those vivid blue eyes. She wondered suddenly how old he was, and decided he probably wasn't much above thirty, if that. He was such a mystery to her, his life an intriguing whisper of terrible crimes and dark secrets. She knew a swift, unwelcome yearning to understand those secrets, to know the reason for the anger and pain she sometimes glimpsed lurking behind the lazy, habitual smile in those blue, blue eyes.

He turned his head then, and caught her watching him. The fire crackled and flared between them. The warm wind sighed. "I haven't thanked you," he said suddenly.

She shook her head, not understanding. "For what?"

"For staying with me, back there at the gorge. For saving my life. Thank you."

She felt a strange smile tug at her lips. "So now we're even."

An answering gleam lit his eyes. "Are we?"

"I think so." She held her hands out to the fire, although she was no longer cold. "Tell me about your ship," she said, her gaze carefully fixed on her spread hands. "When it went down and you were blamed. How did it happen?"

Whatever comfortable camaraderie had developed between them was gone in an instant, leaving a chill so palpable that she shivered, feeling suddenly intrusive and insensitive. He stood abruptly, the dancing flames throwing dark shadows across the hard features of his face. "You'd better get some sleep."

She stayed where she was, her head falling back as she looked up at him, her heart surprisingly heavy with regret. "And you?"

"Don't worry about me," he said, and walked off into the night, leaving her alone with the fire and her thoughts, and a strange, inner yearning that she came to realize was something she'd always sworn she never suffered from.

Loneliness.

~~Chapter Fourteen

FROM WHERE JACK sat, the distant sea was an undulating, moon-shivered expanse of midnight blue that seemed to stretch out, empty, forever. But he knew it was an illusion. There were thousands of landmasses out there, including one small jewel of an island named Rakaia, its volcanic slopes and fertile valleys cloaked in luxuriant tangles of green, its reef-sheltered lagoon teeming with a life-giving abundance. If he closed his eyes, he could see it, see its palm trees dancing in a warm wind, see Titana's beautiful, beloved face, so pale and deadly still.

Usually, Jack was careful not to close his eyes.

It was at night when the memories came crowding in on him, bittersweet memories of peace and love and laughter, and a soul-deep grief that haunted him still. When they grew unbearable, he drowned those memories with alcohol, or numbed himself with kava. But sometimes, as now, he forced himself to look back, to remember. And the cost was, inevitably, this blinding, wracking pain that distorted his vision and pounded through his head like a self-imposed penance, a kind of mental flagellation that left him weakened but cleansed.

He tipped back his head, his eyes open wide as he stared up at the star-filled darkness. Ten years. Ten years was a long time to run, to hide from the past. He found himself wondering, idly, about India McKnight, about what her reaction would have been if he had answered her, if he had told her the truth about what he had done. And then he wondered at himself, for he was not usually given to thoughts of that kind.

The pain in his head was growing worse, making sleep impossible. He sucked in a deep breath of warm, tropically scented air, then let it out slowly in a sigh. It was going to be a long night.

After Jack Ryder left her, alone beside the fire, India decided to haul out her pencil and set to work jotting down notes in her clothbound book until he returned. But she'd written no more than half a page when her head began to feel heavy, and the words on the paper blurred. Her pencil slipped from oddly nerveless fingers. She thought about retrieving it. Instead, she laid her head down on her open book, and slept.

She awoke to a chorus of exotic birdsong and the steamy golden heat of the rising sun. Sudden memory of where she was, and why, jerked her up into a sitting position. She threw a quick glance around, and found that she was still alone.

A hideous, heart-stopping, breath-stealing fear bloomed within her, the fear that Jack Ryder had abandoned her here in the middle of this sodden, dripping rain forest, within uncomfortable proximity to any number of cannibals, practicing and Christianized.

She rose shakily to her feet, her back pressed against the smooth stone wall of the mountain behind her, one splayed hand against her heaving chest as she stared out over the twittering, swaying, intimidating mass of jungle green that separated her from the tiny French outpost on the lagoon-sheltered coast far, far below. "Oh my God," she whispered.

A cheery whistle warbled vaguely to the tune of "I'll Take You Home Again, Kathleen," split the exotically scented air, then ended abruptly as Jack Ryder materialized out of the dark green gloom. "I thought you might like some breakfast," he said, swinging a stalk of bananas down from his shoulder. "They're a bit green, but the rats get them when they're completely ripe." Knife in hand, he hunkered down on the far side of the dead fire, then paused to slant a lazy grin up at her when she stayed where she was, frozen by an odd combination of relief and indignation. "What's the matter, then? Did you think I'd run off and left you to fend for yourself?"

She pushed away from the rock face and tried to act nonchalant, which wasn't easy when her hands were still shaking. She shoved them behind her back. "Why didn't you?"

He settled on his heels, his eyes narrowing as he stared up at her. "You're still wearing my shirt, remember?"

She'd forgotten that. Running her hands self-consciously up the sleeves of the man's shirt that covered her arms, she turned to the tumble of surrounding boulders where she'd laid out her clothes to dry last night. Her boots and stockings were still there, and her blouse, and her chemise and drawers. But her camisole, corset, and every single one of her petticoats were gone.

She spun to face him. "What have you done with my clothes?"

He sat at his ease with one hip propped on the edge of a rocky ledge, a half-eaten banana in his hand. "Reduced their weight."

A wave of impotent fury threatened to swamp her. "You had no right."

He took another bite of his banana, and let out a sound that was halfway between a grunt and a low laugh. "You'll still be wearing twice as much as you ought to be."

"As much as I ought? I'll have you know that when I fell into an animal pit in East Africa, I would have been killed if the thick, multiple layers of my clothing hadn't kept me from being impaled by the sharpened stakes at the base of the trap."

"Yeah? Well, the islanders here don't dig animal traps, so you shouldn't have anything to worry about. It's a wonder you don't have a heatstroke, tramping through the jungles of the world wearing what must be a goodly percentage of one day's productive capacity of Britain's mills on your back all at the same time like that."

"Don't be ridiculous." India snatched up what was left of her clothing, and retired behind the nearest large boulder to put them on with quick, angry jerks. It said something about the effects of her forced intimacy with this man over the past twenty-four hours that she did so without a second thought.

His voice reached her from the far side of the rocks. "Believe me, when we get down into the lowlands, you're going to thank me."

India yanked her chemise on over her head. "I doubt it."

"Well, let's put it this way: you would if you were honest."

"If you knew me better, Mr. Ryder, you would realize that I am always scrupulously honest. And that I never accept heat or discomfort as an excuse for abandoning the trappings of civilized deportment and behavior."

"Jesus. You remind me of someone I used to know."

"Who's that?" India asked, wriggling her split tartan skirt up over her drawers. "Your mother?"

"No." He paused. "Simon Granger."

In the act of buckling her belt, India looked up, then cinched it tight. "I am ready," she said, and stepped from behind the rock.

He straightened slowly. He didn't say anything, but a

strange smile played around the edges of his lips, deepening the dimple in his cheek and bringing a soft light to his eyes.

"What is it?" she demanded, resisting the urge to cross her arms over her full, corsetless breasts.

"Nothing. Here." He held out a banana, his smile broadening to show his teeth. "You'd better have something to eat."

They followed an old, overgrown fey trail that wound along the crests of ridges of gray granite darkened by lichens and only haphazardly shaded by carabeen trees and pines undergrown with mountain palms and native rhododendrons and dracophyllums, all twisted and stunted by the endless force of the trade winds. The air here was clean and clear, the view out over the sun-warmed massed green of the lowland rain forest and the sparkling, purple-blue tropical seas beyond so impossibly gorgeous that it took India's breath.

"Need to rest?" Jack Ryder asked, glancing back at her as her steps faltered.

"No," India said with a smile, and brought up one hand to catch back the hair blowing loose around her face. "It's just . . . beautiful."

"Yes, it is," he said softly. Something in his voice made her glance over at him, but by then he'd already turned his back to her, and they pushed on.

As they dropped down into the foothills, the undergrowth of palms and ferns gradually became more lush, the smooth-barked, buttressed trunks of the satinash and carabeens and cedars stretching high overhead to form an increasingly thick canopy of intertwining green. For a time, the trail they followed ran beside a mountain stream that sometimes whispered softly over smooth jumbled stones, sometimes tumbled away into short thundering waterfalls that filled the air with a sweet, cooling mist.

It was beside one of these waterfalls that they paused to eat, the clear, calm pool at its base shaded by filmy ferns and orchids and deep green mosses that almost hid the remnants of an ancient stone house platform built at the top of the stream bank. The bamboo-and-grass hut it had once supported had long since vanished back into the tropical growth of wait-a-whiles and pepper vines and creeping figs that rampaged over it.

India had noticed several such platforms as they worked their way down from the highlands. Now, nibbling absently at a papaya plucked from a nearby tree, she drew out her notebook and began making a quick sketch of the abandoned ruin.

"Where did they go, do you think?" she asked, her attention all for her sketch. "The people who built these stone foundations, and the fey trail we've been following?"

"I think we met a lot of them in that cave."

She glanced up to find him leaning against a boulder, his head tipping back as he drank deeply from their canteen. "They were the victims of warfare, you think?"

He lowered the tin container, and shrugged. "Some, maybe. But disease is more likely. They say there were no mosquitoes in these islands before the white man brought them. No elephantiasis. No malaria. No venereal disease or influenza."

"A Garden of Eden," India said softly. "Where people ate each other."

He let out his breath in a huff of what might have been laughter. "You just can't seem to get past that, can you?"

India's pencil slashed across the page in broad, agitated strokes. "I have always sought to understand and sympathize with the various cultures I encounter on my travels. But I draw the line at people who want to eat me."

"Maybe. But think about this," he said. "Those natives who captured you, they might have been planning to eat you, but it would never occur to them to let anyone in their tribe go hungry. All their food—everything—is shared equally. Yet when I was in London, I used to see rich, fat men in silk waistcoats and gold watch chains walk right past ragged women and children who were starving in the streets. Starving to death. In the midst of so much wealth and plenty." He pushed away from the rock. "And we call these people savages."

India sat silent, her notebook forgotten in her hands, and watched him stoop beside the pool to refill the canteen. And it occurred to her, suddenly, that she had seriously underestimated this man when she'd dismissed him as a careless, heedless renegade.

Replacing the canteen's stopper, he rose to his feet. "Are you about finished there? I would like to reach La Rochelle sometime before the monsoons hit."

She smiled softly, for the monsoon season was still a month or more away. "What makes you think you'll be safe in La Rochelle, anyway?" she asked, tucking her notebook back into her knapsack as they started downhill again.

He shrugged. "This is a French island. Which means that unless the *Barracuda* is willing to provoke an international incident, their ability to act here is limited. And international incidents aren't good for a navy man's career."

"They do marvelous things for the sale of travel books, though."

He glanced back at her and grinned. "What made you decide to choose this way of life, anyway? I mean, traveling around the world by yourself, writing travelogues."

"When I was a little girl, I wanted to grow up to be Marco Polo."

He laughed softly. "Now, that's a rare ambition. How did you manage to come so close to achieving it?"

India stepped carefully over a fallen log. "My aunt was married to a man in the British foreign service. After my mother died, I went to Egypt, to live with them." Her father had *sent* her to live with them—sent her away from him, away from her home, away from everything and everyone she'd ever loved, but she wasn't going to tell Jack Ryder that. "I seized every available opportunity to explore the country, and I wrote about my experiences in a book I called *Up the Nile to the Valley of the Kings*. It was successful enough to enable me to finance an expedition to Russia."

"*In the Land of the Tsars.*"

She was so surprised, she drew up short. "How did you know?"

"I read it," he said, not pausing. "You were young, to be traveling by yourself."

"I was eighteen." She moved to catch up with him. "My aunt and uncle were childless, and they'd never been particularly happy about having me come to live with them. I think they were relieved when I wanted to go off by myself." While her father . . . her father hadn't even responded to her letter telling him she was going.

"It seems an unsettled, lonely way of life," he said, his attention all for the vines in their path.

She looked at him in surprise, for it was not at all the sort of thing she'd have expected a man like him to say. "You're alone. And relatively unsettled."

He let out a sharp laugh. "I'm a wanted man. Besides . . ." He paused to dash his shirtsleeve across his forehead. "I have Patu."

"Why is he with you, if he's not your son?"

He gave a careless shrug that struck India, watching him, as entirely too calculated to be casual. "I woke up one morning after drinking kava, and found him piloting my yacht for me. He said I needed someone to look after me, and I couldn't seem to convince him that I didn't."

The airy way in which it was said didn't fool India. The man could easily have rid himself of the half-European, half-Polynesian boy if he'd really wanted to. The fact that he hadn't said something about the kind of person he was, something that made her look at him in a way she didn't want.

India watched the man ahead of her, watched the way the iridescent green light filtering down through the leafy canopy above danced over his broad, strong shoulders, watched the way his head fell back, his tanned cheek dimpling into a fleeting smile as he studied the vivid green and yellow parrot flitting through the branches of the giant satinash overhead. And she found herself wondering at what point in the past twenty-four hours she'd gone from fantasizing about seeing this man hang to hoping he somehow managed to get away.

She said, "Even if you escape the *Barracuda* this time, they're not going to give up trying to capture you. You know that, don't you?"

He glanced back at her, his smile broadening into a devil-damn-the-world grin. "I know it."

"It doesn't worry you?" It would terrorize her, the knowledge that someone was after her, waiting for her, watching for her to make one unwary step.

He shrugged. "What's the point in worrying about it?"

"You could do something about it."

He gave a low, harsh laugh. "Like what? Try to prove my innocence?"

"Could you?" she asked on an unexpectedly emotional exhalation of breath.

For one, tense instant, he paused in the path ahead of her, his back held rigid, his fist tightening around the handle of his upraised machete. Then he let the machete fall, his shoulders rolling into that careless shrug that was so un-British, and so much a part of who this man was. She expected him to say it would be too much trouble, or maybe that it was useless to try to change the opinion of those in power. Instead, he said, "I'm not innocent."

It was only then that India realized the full truth, that not only did she want this man to escape, she wanted him to be innocent of the terrible thing of which he'd been accused. Somewhere between that tension-filled moment on the edge of Wairopa Gorge, when she'd watched him sacrifice his own chance to get away rather than destroy the bridge and kill the man on it, and now, she'd somehow convinced herself that he hadn't done it, that he wasn't responsible for the sinking of that ship and the death of all those men.

And as she followed Jack Ryder down into the dripping, sultry, insect-buzzed heat of the lowland rain forest, she realized also that a part of her didn't believe what he'd just told her. A man who would risk his own life to save a woman he barely knew and didn't even like was not the kind of man who would deliberately, knowingly send a shipload of his comrades to their deaths.

Something had happened all those years ago, something dark and secret and shameful. But she couldn't believe that this man had committed what amounted to mass murder.

She refused to believe it.

By early afternoon, India had to admit—at least to herself—that she found the absence of all those layers of petticoats and the close confines of her corset a relief.

As they descended from the relative coolness of the trade-wind-bathed highlands to the jungle-choked valleys of the interior, the heat became oppressive, the very air a sultry, suffocating blanket that soon had her bathed in a sticky film of perspiration. Her hair stuck to her face, and her remaining clothes hung like a sweat-dampened, uncomfortable shroud that made every step a labor. Once, she made the mistake of resting her hand against the trunk of a nearby pandanus tree, only to let out a yelp as dozens of giant, biting ants leapt upon her. But the worst part, by far, was the mosquitoes. They whined about her in an angry, annoying cloud that would provoke a saint to madness. And India was no saint.

"I think I've figured out why the inhabitants of all these islands are cannibals," she said, batting uselessly at that endless, whining, bloodsucking assault. "They've been driven insane by the mosquitoes."

Ahead of her, Jack Ryder swung his machete at a curtain fig that had virtually obscured the path ahead, and laughed. "If they like you that much, you'd better hope we reach the coast before dusk."

India studied the man ahead of her through narrowed, hostile eyes. His half-open shirt and rolled-up sleeves exposed vast swathes of naked, succulent flesh, yet the mosquitoes seemed to have no interest in him at all. "When do you think we'll reach La Rochelle?" she asked, trying hard not to sound too anxious.

"Sometime tomorrow morning, I hope."

Catching the tip of her boot on the root of a vine that snaked across the path, India pitched forward, just managing to catch herself with her outflung hands before she landed flat on her face. "And precisely what do you plan to do if the *Barracuda* prevents Patu from being there to meet you?" she asked, gritting her teeth to hold back the most unladylike curse that threatened to erupt as she picked herself up from the thick leaf mold and brushed off a rat-sized hairy brown spider she found crawling up her tartan.

"I can wait." He glanced back at her. "You all right there?"

"Quite fine, thank you. Does it occur to you, I wonder, that you might not be welcome in La Rochelle? I've heard unflattering things about the French commissioner on this island."

"Georges Lefevre? He's not so bad."

Something in his voice made her look at him with interest. "Is he a friend of yours?"

"We fought a duel once."

"A duel?"

"I made a derogatory remark about Brie, and he challenged me to a duel. To defend the honor of French cheese."

He wasn't making this up. She stared at him. "You fought a duel over *cheese*? Who won?"

He laughed. "Georges is at least sixty now, and he weighs a good twenty stone and is blind in one eye. But he's a hell of a swordsman. It was only sheer luck that we both passed out before any blood was spilt."

"You were drunk?"

"Of course we were drunk. Do you think we'd have been fighting about cheese if we hadn't been?"

"I think you delight in behaving abominably," she said, knowing she should be shocked and censorious, and trying to sound it, although she couldn't quite keep the amusement out of her voice.

"Why do you do that?" he asked suddenly.

"Do what?"

"Try so hard to sound like a sour old maid. You're what? Twenty-four? Twenty-five?"

"I am six-and-twenty," she said, all sense of amusement vanishing in a blaze of anger and some other emotion she didn't want to understand, didn't want to feel. "And I have already given you my opinion of that expression."

"Then why deliberately make yourself into something you don't want to be? You harp on about *propriety* and *decency* as if they were the gods to which you've sacrificed your existence, when the truth is, your own life has been pretty damned irregular."

She stopped short. "There has been nothing *irregular* about my life—"

"Oh, yeah?"

"—and it is not only *old maids* who are concerned with such guiding principles as propriety and morality and decency."

He swung around to give her a slow, lopsided grin that brought the roguish crease to his cheek and a beguiling light to his impossibly blue eyes. "Old maids and missionaries."

India stared at him, and felt her heart begin to pound slowly, painfully within her. He was too near, and she was too undeniably aware of the muscled power of those bare, masculine forearms visible beneath his rolled-up sleeves, and of the way his half-opened shirt revealed the bronze, sweat-slicked expanse of his chest. She sucked in a deep breath of air, and her senses filled with the earthy intoxication of the virgin forest around them, the darkly filtered green light and heavy, exotic scent and steamy, primeval heat. She was suddenly, deeply afraid, of herself, and of the dangerous drift of her feelings for this man, and of where the increasingly easy camaraderie of their conversations might lead her heart, if she didn't do something about it.

"Obviously," she said, making her voice as prim and repressive as she could, "one can't expect a man like you to be overly familiar with the opinions and habits of respectable women."

"Ho. A man like me?" He put his hands on his lean hips and rocked back on his heels in a rollicking stance that seemed to accentuate everything about him that was so quintessentially, aggressively male. "What's that supposed to mean?"

"You know full well what I mean." She swept one hand through the air before him in a gesture that was meant to take in every reprehensible thing about him. "From what I can see, your life is dedicated to nothing more productive than drinking and gambling and consorting with native women."

He was still smiling, but in a cold, dangerous way that sent a warning tingle down India's spine. "That really scares you, does it? The thought of a white man and a dusky-skinned woman together?"

"I don't think *fright* is the word I would use to describe my reaction."

She swept past him, meaning to continue down the path, and felt his hand close around her arm, hauling her about to face him again. "What word would you use, then? Mmm? *Disgust?*" She tried to yank away from him, but he held on to her, his fingers tightening around the muscles of her upper arm. "Tell me, exactly what is so bloody disturbing about the thought of a white man lying with a native woman?"

She stared up into his hard face, and felt her breath leave her chest in a whoosh. "It's . . . it's just not proper."

"Why not?"

"What do you mean, why not?"

"I don't think it's a particularly obtuse question." He leaned into her, so close she found herself mesmerized by the movement of his lips as he said, "What's so damned improper about it?"

"The commingling of the races!" she exclaimed desperately.

"Yes, that's what happens when white men lie with dark women. But you still haven't explained what's so shocking about it."

She stared at him, her lips parted, her breath coming hard and fast, and found herself unable to utter a word.

"It's because you have some lofty, arrogant notion that the white race is superior, don't you? You think it's wrong for a man to pollute his fine, Anglo-Saxon blood with that of a second-rate people."

"What I think is wrong," she said, enunciating her words carefully, although her voice was shaking, her entire body trembling with fury and fear and this powerful, unwanted attraction, "is for a man to use some simple, primitive creature as an object upon which to slake his lust."

His teeth flashed white in his tanned face as he gave a harsh laugh. "I don't suppose it ever occurred to you that it's often the other way around? White men being used by dark-skinned women to slake their own lust?"

"Don't be ridiculous."

"I'm not." He studied her through narrowed, intense eyes. "That's what really scares you, isn't it? The terrifying idea that *primitive*, dark-skinned women are somehow more sensual, more *sexual* than white women. You just can't stand the thought that a white man might actually prefer a dusky, responsive woman to some rarified white *lady* who just lays there like a dead fish and waits for it to be over."

He let her go so suddenly she stumbled back, her hand coming up unconsciously to touch her arm, where he had held her. "I did not lay there like a dead fish!" she shouted after him as he swung away from her and continued on down the path.

"Didn't you?" he said, without looking back at her. "Hell, you were so unexcited and uninvolved, you didn't even take off your clothes."

She stomped after him. "Exactly what is it you men expect a woman to get excited about, anyway? What is so *sensual* about being crushed and salivated over and pawed at? Maybe your *dusky women* are just better actresses than you give them credit for being."

His head tipped back, the softly filtered jungle light dappling warm and golden over his arched, tanned throat as he laughed out loud. "Oh, no," he said, smiling still as he glanced back at her. "That's a white woman's trick. If an island woman doesn't like your performance, she'll tell you."

"Indeed? And have any of your island women ever

told you that your *performance* wasn't quite up to her expectations?"

His smile widened. "Nope."

India felt a rush of impotent fury, mingling, disastrously, with the insistent promptings of a growing curiosity. "You really think you're good, don't you?"

"I know I am."

She stopped in the middle of the overgrown trail, her hands on her hips as she watched him saunter ahead of her. "All right. Prove it."

⌒⌒Chapter Fifteen

THAT STOPPED HIM.

He swung about, no longer smiling. "What did you say?"

"You heard me." Her heart was pounding so hard and fast she was shaking, but she had no intention of backing down. "Show me how good you are." She lifted her chin tauntingly. "Kiss me."

Sheathing his machete, he brought up both hands, palms forward, as if warding her off—or surrendering. "Oh, no." His head swiveled slowly back and forth. "You're not going to make me part of one of your bloody experiments."

She gave him the tightest, most supercilious smile she could summon up. "Now who's afraid?"

His eyes narrowing down into dangerous slits, he walked right up to her, until his thighs pressed hard against her tartan skirt and his bare, sweat-slicked chest was so close it seemed to fill her vision. Somehow, she managed to hold her ground, but she felt her smile slip as, hot and unexpectedly predatory and fiercely blue, his gaze captured hers, and held it. She watched his thin nostrils flare when he breathed, watched his lean, tanned cheek crease with a crooked smile that stirred a strange, hungry yearning deep within her.

"All right," he said, one hand closing behind her head to draw her toward him. She felt her breasts flatten full and aching against his solid, nearly naked chest, felt the hard proof of his arousal—shocking, thrilling, frightening—as he settled her into the cradle of his spread thighs. "Just remember you asked for it." She knew one piercing moment of raging, blood-thundering panic. Then he dipped his head, and kissed her.

His lips were hard and yet soft, so soft, and took hers in a magical caress of heat and tenderness and raw, savage wanting. Stunned, she opened her mouth in a helpless whimper, and he filled her, with his tongue and his fire and the intoxicating, tangy taste of him. She was drowning in his kiss, drowning in him, in the smell of him and the feel of him and the piercing, erotic intimacy of that kiss.

Her hands clenched, once, at her sides, then came up to touch his chest, his shoulders, hesitantly at first, then tightening, her fingers digging into the hard flesh beneath the rough, damp cotton of his shirt. She felt his fist tighten in the hair at the nape of her neck, pulling her head back as he deepened the kiss, his mouth slanting roughly over hers, devouring her, stealing her breath and her sense and her consciousness of anything but the exquisite mating of his mouth with hers.

She felt his hands come up to cradle her face, holding her as if she were something precious as he kissed her eyelids, her nose, her cheeks. "Jesus," he whispered into her open, trembling mouth. He brushed her swollen, aching lips with his once, twice more, then let her go and took a step back.

His eyes were dark and a little desperate, the color high on the sharp, flaring bones of his cheeks, the pulse beating hard and fast in his neck.

She knew she should feel chagrined, that he had proven her more wrong than she could ever have imagined she might be. Yet she saw no sense of triumph on his face, only a stunned wariness that mirrored her own.

"I'm sorry," she said, her voice sounding rusty, as if she hadn't spoken for decades. "I shouldn't have provoked you into doing that."

He sucked in a hitching breath that jerked his chest oddly, as if he were having a hard time getting enough air. "I don't think either of us expected this."

She shook her head. She was suddenly, exquisitely embarrassed, and feeling awkward around him in a way she never had before. "We should keep moving," she said, "if we're to reach the coast before nightfall."

"Yes. Yes, of course."

They turned by mutual consent. It had been only a kiss, she reminded herself. Only a kiss. And yet it had changed everything, and they both knew it.

*   *   *

The sun was hanging low in a clear tropical blue sky when they came to a freshwater lake that separated them from a band of palms and pandanus and parau trees, beyond which they could hear the gentle swish of the lagoon and, beyond that, the thundering of the surf against the offshore barrier reef.

Hunkering down near the shore, India bent to scoop up handfuls of cool water and splash her face. The lake was a crystalline blue, its banks fringed with white lilies and yellow hibiscus that nodded gently in the evening breeze. Yellow and green noisy pitas and small brown swallows called sweetly from the branches of overhanging paperbarks draped with vivid green mosses and tree ferns, and India settled back on her heels, overcome by the calm, pristine beauty of the moment.

"Well, shit," said the man behind her.

For the first time since that disastrous episode on the trail, India looked directly at him. He had his hands on his hips, his head tilted back as he squinted into the dazzling golden light of the westering sun. His dark, shaggy hair was tangled and worn far too long, the hard line of cheek and jaw shadowed by two days' growth of beard, his bare, tawny torso sweat-slicked and streaked with dirt. And still she felt it, that tightening in her chest, that clenching, inner heat that caught her breath and made her want to do all sorts of wayward, forbidden things.

Jerking her gaze away from him, India rose quickly to her feet. "We're almost there. What could be wrong?"

He swung his arm in a sweep that took in the sun-spangled water and gently drooping lilies and hibiscus, and the thick growth of trees beyond. "In case you hadn't noticed, there's a lake in front of us."

India laughed. The lake might be wide, but they should have enough time to skirt its shores before night was upon them. "So we go around it. What's the problem in that?"

His strong, warm hands fell on her shoulders, twisting her around toward the south. "See those Alexandra palms and paperbark trees there, growing over those sedges and fan palms?" He pivoted her around to face the northern end of the lake. "See them there? Hear the ten billion frogs that live there croaking so happily? That's palm swamp. You try to go through that and you're liable to be sucked clear through to South America. It's going to take us a good two hours to work our way around this." He nodded toward the glowing west, his hands slipping from her shoulders so slowly that the movement was almost a caress. "And we don't have two hours."

A mosquito whined in India's ear and she swatted at it with a tired, shaky hand. "I don't think I want to spend the night in a swamp."

He gave her a smile that crinkled the skin at the edges of his deep blue eyes. "Can you swim?"

India turned to stare out over the sparkling clean water. She thought of what it would be like, to strip off her hot, sweat-soaked clothes and slip her tired naked body beneath those cool, gentle waves. A near-desperate yearning rose up within her, a yearning she ruthlessly squashed. "When I was trekking cross-country in Malay, we came to a very large lake in the foothills. It was essentially impossible to go around it, due to the verticality of the slopes rising up on the other side, so my guide built a kind of a raft out of banana stems."

He fixed her with a hard, steady stare. "Banana stems."

"Yes. Trussed together with vines. I sat on top while my guide swam and pushed the vessel from behind." She paused as a thought occurred to her. "You can swim, can't you?"

"Yes."

"Well then, I think it should be fairly easily accomplished. I did get wet in the crossing, but when we reached the other side, my guide lit a fire by rubbing one end of a stick with great rapidity into a hole made in a flat piece of driftwood. As soon as the sawdust began to smoke, he added dried leaves, then swung the wood around his head until it burst into flame."

"I think I'll stick to matches," he said dryly, and slipped his machete from its sheath.

While Ryder cut down the banana stalks, India gathered vines that she stripped of leaves for the lashings. She was helping him tie the last stalk in place when something made her look up to find him watching her with an odd, intense expression sharpening his features.

"What?" she asked, a shy smile trembling on her lips. "What is it?"

He shook his head, and grinned. "I think we're ready." Stretching to his feet, he hauled off his shirt.

"What are you doing?" she asked, her voice ending in a squeak.

Spreading the shirt out on the grass, he pulled off first one boot, then the other. "Ever try to swim in clothes?"

"No. Why? Is it difficult?"

Dumping the boots in the middle of his shirt, he pulled off his socks, and glanced up at her. "Did this Malay guide of yours keep his clothes on?"

India swallowed. "He was wearing a loincloth."

"Yeah?" Ryder's hands dropped to his belt buckle. "Well, I don't have a loincloth."

India swung around to stare off over the lake, its brilliant blue surface ruffled now by an evening breeze. "Why does everyone keep taking off their clothes?"

He laughed, a rich, throaty sound that seemed to vibrate in her blood. "This is the South Pacific. If you had any sense, you'd take yours off, too. You're going to get wet."

Without looking at him, India bent to strip off her own boots and stockings, then swooped up the bundle he had made of his clothes. "I shall endeavor to keep your things out of the water."

"You *endeavor* to do that." She heard him splash into the water, the makeshift raft floating at his side. "Are you coming?"

She tried, she really tried not to look directly at him. But he was there, big and bronzed and naked, the hard thighs of his spread legs far too near when she waded into the water, her tartan skirt already heavy and dripping as she scrambled onto the lashed stems. The makeshift raft tipped violently back and forth, then settled into a gentle rocking. India grabbed the lashings with one hand, and used the other to balance his clothes, her boots, and her knapsack on top of her head, like a Senegalese vendeuse on her way to market.

"If this thing falls apart—" he began.

"It won't fall apart."

"Yeah. Well, if it does"—he pushed the raft ahead of him and waded deeper, the sun-spangled water rippling out around his lean hips—"just relax and let me get you to shore."

"I am capable of executing a crude dog paddle."

His only response was a noncommittal grunt. The water was lapping against his chest now. He struck out into an easy sidestroke, half pushing, half pulling the lashed banana stalks beside him. A good inch or two of water washed over the green ribbed surface, but it stayed afloat. "If you ask me," he said, "the weight of that damned wool skirt of yours is liable to sink us before we're halfway across the lake. You should have taken it off."

"The lake in the mountains of Malay was much wider than this one, and we crossed without incident."

"Yeah?" He ducked down to skim along just below the surface, then rose, shaking his dark head, fine droplets flying out to sparkle in the sun. "Well, maybe Malay banana stems are more substantial than Takaku banana stems."

Beneath her, the banana stalks groaned and shifted ominously. India cleared her throat and threw a quick glance around. "There aren't crocodiles in these waters, are there?"

He laughed. "Now you decide to start worrying about crocodiles, do you? When you think you might go swimming? What about me?"

India tightened her hold on the lashings and felt them loosen beneath her grip. "Mr. Ryder," she said, trying to keep her voice calm, "are there or are there not crocodiles in these waters?"

He gave her a wide, nasty smile. "Not to my knowledge."

India squinted toward the slowly approaching shore, trying to gauge the distance. The water flowing over the top of the raft grew deeper. "And how extensive is your knowledge, precisely?"

"I think you're about to find out," he said, just as the lashings gave way and the separating rows of banana stalks rolled slowly from beneath her.

~~Chapter Sixteen

RATHER THAN PLUNGING dramatically beneath the waves, India simply subsided inexorably into them. When the water reached her breasts, she kicked out with both feet, one hand flailing in an awkward attempt to keep herself afloat. She let go of her boots, his bundle, everything except the knapsack, which she held desperately aloft, her arm thrust straight from the water like the mast of a doomed ship.

"Bloody hell, woman," she heard him yelp beside her. "My clothes."

"*Damn* your clothes," she said with a gasp, then choked when she swallowed a backwash of lake water. "My notebook."

"Give me that." He yanked the knapsack from her grasp, and she let out a faint mew of protest, fearing he meant to toss it away. Instead, he held it easily above the surface of the lake, his legs and one arm moving effortlessly through the water as she thrashed and splashed beside him. "Can you make it to shore by yourself?"

She nodded, afraid to open her mouth lest she swallow more water.

He took her at her word and struck out toward the bank, only occasionally glancing back to where she flailed along in his wake. Her wool skirt was unbelievably heavy, dragging her down, making each kick, every movement a weighted chore. A wave slapped her in the face and she faltered, her head sinking, briefly, beneath the surface. She sputtered up, blind now to the blue sky and the tree-fringed shore, to anything except water. Water splashed in her eyes, washed into her mouth, stretched out endlessly before her.

"If you put down your feet," said a low, amused voice beside her, "I think you'll find you can touch."

She reached down with one foot, tentatively, doubtfully, and found solid ground beneath her. "Oh, God," she said with a heartfelt gasp, and felt Ryder's arm come around her waist. "Oh, thank God."

For one weak, shameful moment, she allowed herself to collapse against him as he hauled her coughing and gasping into the shallows. She hunched over, hands on her shaking knees as she sucked great droughts of clean, fresh air deep into her lungs. At first, she was only dimly conscious of the man who stood behind her, his strong arm holding her braced against him, one hand keeping the loose tangle of her hair back from her face as she retched and choked.

But as her breathing slowed and her fear subsided, she found her attention captured, inexplicably, beguilingly, by the bare male foot that nestled casually beside hers. She straightened slowly, her hands closing around the muscled forearm that rode low on her waist, every fiber of her being aware of the power of the hard, naked thighs pressing so intimately against her flanks. It was as if time ground down and slowed to a heart-pounding tempo played by the whisper of the wind through the sun-kissed palms and the exotic pulse of the nearby surf. Then he said, "I think you need to improve your dog paddle," and the moment was broken.

She pushed away from him, her wet skirt hanging heavy about her legs, tripping her as she slogged up onto the grassy bank toward where he had thrown her knapsack.

"Either that," he added, splashing behind her, "or learn to take off that damned tartan before you go swimming."

"I hadn't intended to go swimming, remember?" She fell to her knees beside the knapsack, water streaming from her hair, running down her arms, dripping off her nose as she wrenched open the flap and peered desperately inside.

"You're going to get it wet."

He was right, of course. She sat back on her heels, her upper body twisting around as she stared back at the sun-dazzled surface of the lake. She had suddenly remembered what else she'd been holding. "I've lost my boots."

"Your boots?" His low, throaty laugh drew her attention to where he stood at the water's edge, his hands on his hips, his legs planted wide. For one stolen moment, she let her gaze rove freely, almost hungrily over the lean, naked length of him, over his strong, muscled back and narrow waist, the enticing curve of his buttocks, the long, powerful line of thigh and calf. He was as sun-bronzed as a native, his skin tight and smooth and golden, and the beauty of him, the raw sensual power of him, stole her breath all over again. "You lost my bloody clothes."

"Huh. That will teach you to strip them off at every opportunity that is offered. Some of us have more sense."

"*More sense?*" He swung around, and she quickly lifted her gaze to the feathery tops of the palms waving against the deep blue sky. "That damned wet tartan of yours is what sank the raft."

India straightened slowly, her split skirt and shirt hanging limp and dripping about her. "You could dive for them, couldn't you? I remember when I was in Bangkok, I watched the children there diving for coins tossed into the harbor. And the water in Bangkok's harbor is considerably murkier than that of this lake."

He was silent for so long that her gaze drifted downward for one, unguarded moment before resolutely snapping back to the treetops. "Well? Couldn't you?"

"I tell you what," he said, his voice taking on that rollicking, teasing edge she was coming to know so well. "I'll make a deal with you."

"What kind of a deal?" India asked warily.

"I'll dive for your boots, if you agree that when we get down to the beach, you'll take off that damned wet skirt and blouse."

"*What?*"

"You heard me."

She was no longer making even a pretense of not looking at him. Slack-jawed and wide-eyed, she stared at him, at the long, lean, gloriously naked length of him, and felt her heart begin to beat so hard and fast she was practically shaking.

"You can leave on your underthings, if you insist," he was saying. "They'll dry soon enough. But everything else has to go."

"But . . . why?" Her voice ended in a pleading wail.

"Because," he said, walking up to her, "that damned skirt will never dry otherwise. Because it's more dangerous than you seem to realize, wearing wet clothes in this climate." He was so close to her now that his hard, naked thighs were pressed against hers and his warm breath caressed her cheek as he leaned into her. "And because you can't write anything meaningful about the South Pacific when you've never known the warm touch of a tropical breeze against your bare skin."

She shook her head slowly from side to side. Every nerve in her body was quiveringly, achingly aware of his nearness, of the heat of his naked body and the dangerous, unwanted, inexplicable power of the undeniable attraction between them. "No."

Dark, wicked amusement sparkled in the depths of his impossibly blue eyes. "It's a risky thing, you know, walking along the beach without shoes. A coral cut can take years to heal. And if you step on a stone fish . . ." He shrugged.

India swallowed, hard. "This is blackmail. Extortion."

A nasty smile curled his lips. "Yes."

She watched the water drip from his dark, wet hair to trickle down the golden flesh of his cheeks and throat. She felt his bare chest lift against hers as he drew in a deep breath of air, felt her senses reel as she, in turn, breathed in the hot, heady scent of him. She saw his eyes narrow, his lips soften. And in that moment, she would have done almost anything, said anything to break the unbearable tension of the moment and put some distance between them.

Besides, she needed those boots.

"All right," she said, her hands coming up to flatten against his bare chest, her head nodding once in curt agreement as she pushed him away from her. "It's a deal."

It was a good thing it wasn't far to the beach, Jack decided as he watched India McKnight limp down the path ahead of him, her boots making light squishing sounds, the wet, heavy wool of her split skirt rubbing audibly with every step she took.

She had insisted on walking ahead of him as soon as she found out he had no intention of struggling back into his own soaked shirt and trousers. But then, a man would have to be a fool to subject his body to the kind of discomfort she was undergoing. He supposed her maidenly modesty recoiled at the thought of walking behind a naked man and being forced to stare without respite at his bare ass. But he wondered if she might not have found it the lesser of two evils if she'd realized the explicitly carnal nature of the thoughts running through his head as he watched her.

She might not be naked, but without the rigid shield of whalebone once provided by her corset, her wet blouse and chemise clung to her in a way that revealed every natural swell and hollow. And the natural curves of Miss India McKnight's body were mighty fine indeed, her breasts full and rounded and firm, her stomach flat, her legs strong from years spent trekking through the jungles and deserts of the world.

She was not at all the type of woman he normally found himself attracted to. He kept telling himself that. Oh, she was strong and gutsy, with a quick mind and a wry, dry sense of humor that he couldn't help but like and admire. But she was too out of touch with the woman she was born to be, too tied up in all sorts of knots by her attempts to conform to the image she'd created for herself of a proper but determinedly single Scotswoman, upright and asexual and unassailable.

And yet . . . There was the interesting matter of that *scientific experiment* she'd once conducted to discern for herself exactly what she was missing by eschewing the marital act. Then there was that kiss.

Every time he thought about that kiss, he felt his blood surge, his chest lift on a ragged breath. It had been wine and honey, that kiss, sweet and hot and so damned over-whelmingly erotic that it haunted his every step. He watched her pause ahead of him, her head turning, a quiet smile lifting the edges of her lips as she watched the sun sparkle golden and brilliant on the outstretched wings of a white-breasted sea eagle, and he wanted . . .

He wanted to lay her down on the soft sand of a se-cluded beach, with the whisper of the surf beside them and the wind warm and gentle in the palm trees above. He wanted to strip away what was left of her confining, oh-so-proper European clothes and let the sun dance golden and free over all the secret, hidden places of her body. The smooth flesh of her beautiful breasts would be white, almost translucent, he thought, her thighs long and lean and strong. He wanted to touch her, to taste her there, and there . . . everywhere. And the image of it, the savage heat of that wanting was so intense, so powerful, that he shuddered with it.

"Thank God," he heard her say, and he realized sud-denly that the path beneath their feet had turned to sand. Looking up, he saw the limpid turquoise of the lagoon, visible through the screen of ferns and broad-leafed shrubs that grew thick beneath the overarching palms.

Cool and sweet, the sea breeze wafted over them. She paused at the edge of the rain forest, her head falling back as she drew the fresh, salt-tinged air deep into her lungs. She had her eyes closed, her neck arching invitingly. And it occurred to him, as he watched her lips part, her breasts lift with her breathing, that maybe it had been a mistake to make her agree to take off her clothes.

∼∼Chapter Seventeen

JACK SPREAD HIS clothes to dry on the bleached white branches of an old driftwood log half buried in the sand. The sun was a giant orange ball hovering just above the misty line where water met sky, and he moved quickly to gather dried coconut fronds and pieces of driftwood, and build up a fire before the rapid descent of darkness.

Kneeling in the sand with India McKnight's waterproof match tin in his hands, he glanced up to find her staring out over the gold-washed, gently lapping waters of the lagoon, to where the surf beat in thundering, white-spray savagery against the offshore reef. She might have her back to him, but the taut line of her shoulders and spine told him that she was as aware as he of all the subtle nuances of the night to come.

That kiss had changed everything between them. Oh, the attraction had been there before, there was no denying that, for all they'd both worked so hard to suppress it, to disallow its very existence. But the raw, naked power of that one moment had stripped away all the pretenses, all the unconscious subterfuges thrown up by their instinctive rivalry and petty bickering. Now sexual awareness crackled in the very air between them, underlay every movement, every word.

"We had a deal, remember?" he said softly, and smiled when she spun to face him, her eyes widening with what looked very much like panic. He'd seen her deal with hungry cannibals and rotting bridges and sinking banana-stem rafts, but the thought of being reduced to nothing more than her chemise and pantalets had her in a gut-terror.

She hugged her arms across her chest and gave a little shiver, as if she were cold, when he knew damned well she wasn't. "I'm waiting until you get the fire going."

He grunted, his attention all seemingly for the task of coaxing his small flame to flare up hot and bright and spitting. "The sun might be setting, but it's still hot. You're just stalling. Besides . . ." He sat back on his heels and reached to tuck the matches into her knapsack. "The fire's going."

She swallowed hard, the muscles in her slim white throat bunching and flexing. She waved one hand through the air in a vague, conjuring gesture. "Shouldn't you go . . . catch some fish, or something?"

"After you get out of those wet clothes." Jack stood up, his hands dangling loosely beside his naked thighs. Her gaze snapped away to some indefinable point over his left shoulder, but not before he knew what she'd been looking at. He had to try really, really hard not to smile. "Need some help?"

Her gaze wavered back to meet his, her breath coming short and fast, her lips parting in that way that made him think of what it would be like to touch her mouth, gently, with his fingertips. What that mouth would feel like, hot, wet, on him. And then he wondered what she must have seen in his face, because she said, "Turn around."

"What?"

"You heard me. Turn around."

"If you think I'm going to keep my back to you all night—"

"Obviously not. But I can't undress with you watching me like this. Turn around."

He turned around. The setting sun drenched the sand with a rich golden light that picked out the vivid yellow flowers of the red beech and the golden orchids that grew in breathtaking masses at the edge of the rain forest. He felt the evening breeze skim across his bare skin, heard the rustle of the gently swaying fronds of the palms. Someplace in the distance, a curlew cried, its call low and haunting.

"If you don't hurry, you're going to be gathering coconuts by moonlight," he said.

Her only answer was a swish of sand. Then she said, "There," and he swung slowly around.

The lagoon had turned into a rose-tinged sheet of undulating silver reflecting a pink-washed sky against which the black silhouettes of the palms shifted back and forth in a slow, seductive dance. She stood with her head held high, a defiant challenge in her eyes. Her long, chestnut-shot dark hair was loose and half-dry, and billowed enticingly about her shoulders. But the fine cloth of her chemise and pantalets still clung, damp and revealing, to every swell, every curve of the body beneath.

It seemed impossible, looking at her, to remember the woman he'd first met, the prim, frigid Scottish travel writer with her voluminous tartan and stiff, whalebone-reinforced silhouette. The India McKnight who stood before him now was a wholly natural and unconsciously seductive woman with full, high breasts and swelling hips and the kind of slim, long legs that were made to wrap around a man's waist and hug him tight. Jack looked at her, and he wanted her so badly in that moment, he ached.

"I think I'll go—" His chest felt tight, as if he'd run out of air. "—catch some fish, or something."

He caught a big fat sea trout that he roasted on a spit over the fire and served up on banana-leaf plates, with roasted breadfruit and water scooped from a nearby stream with coconut-shell cups.

She was unusually quiet while they ate, lost, he supposed, in her own thoughts. He didn't realize her thoughts were of him until she said, suddenly, "Where is she now?"

Jack looked up, a tender bit of trout suspended halfway to his mouth. "Who?"

"You said you had a daughter. Is she with her mother?"

Swallowing slowly, he stared out at the black line of silver-crested breakers that threw themselves with an incessant boom and crash against the distant, offshore reef. Somehow, he managed to hold himself deceptively still. Only he couldn't seem to control the painful beating of his heart. "Her mother is dead."

"Oh." Beside them, the fire crackled and spit, flaring up in a quick flash of golden red light that danced over the delicate European features of her face. "I'm sorry."

"Are you?"

"Yes."

"Why should you be?" His voice came out harsher than he'd meant it to. Harsh and hurting. "Why should you care just because one beautiful, vibrantly alive young Polynesian girl is dead?"

"Because it's obvious that you care," she said, her gaze steady and solemn on his face. He thought she'd drop the subject then. She didn't. "So where is she now? Your daughter, I mean."

"On Rakaia." A few days' sail to the west of Tahiti, Rakaia was a small island of clear turquoise lagoons and sparkling white sand and palm trees that waved gently against a clear tropical sky. An island of laughter and love, and sudden, violent death that came in a hail of bullets unleashed by a curt, English command.

"You left her there?" The shock in her voice surprised him.

"Ulani was a baby, and I was a wanted man, on the

run. I left her with my wife's family." Those who were still alive. "It's where she belonged."

She stared at him, her eyes huge in an oddly pale face. He thought perhaps she was appalled to hear that he had taken a native woman to wife. But what she said was, "You could have gone back for her."

He shoved what was left of his meal aside. "I'm still on the run, in case you hadn't noticed."

"But to abandon her—"

"I didn't *abandon* her." He stood abruptly and went to wash his hands in the moonlit, slowly surging surf of the lagoon. "Ulani is far happier growing up on Rakaia than she would ever be someplace like London or Sydney, where little girls are expected to wear corsets, and breathe air fouled with coal smoke, and spend their days sewing seams and learning catechisms."

"How do you know?" She waded into the sea beside him, the lace-trimmed hem of her pantalets floating on the surface of the water as she bent to wash her own hands. "Did you ask her?"

He straightened slowly. "What are you saying? That while no one would have questioned my leaving a baby daughter with her mother's family in someplace like London, it was wrong to leave her on a South Pacific island? That I've somehow failed her, by letting my daughter grow up in a *primitive* society?"

"No. That's not what I'm saying at all. I just think it must be hard for a child, growing up knowing she has a father out there, somewhere, and thinking that he doesn't love her enough—" He heard her voice crack with emotion, although he couldn't begin to understand why. "—that he doesn't *care* enough about her to want to be with her."

He stared at her, at the way the mingling moon- and star-shine played over the fine features of her face, the flaring cheekbones and wide mouth and the strong, square chin. Her hair was dry now, blowing free and beautiful around her bare shoulders, curling seductively against the swell of her full breasts, so obvious beneath the thin linen of her chemise. He felt the anger drain out of him, knew the renewed surge of throbbing desire. And he realized, suddenly, that the anger had been just a defense, a shield, against the desire.

"I care," he said. "It's because I care that I have stayed away from her." Turning, he waded farther out into the lagoon, the water rippling cool and soothing over his hot skin.

"What are you doing?" she called.

"Going for a swim." He dove beneath the lagoon in a shallow arc that brought him back up to the surface. Shaking his head, he opened his eyes and looked back at where she still stood, bathed in the misty glow of moonlight. "Join me," he said, before he could stop himself.

She shook her head, although he noticed she waded a bit farther out into the lagoon, her fingertips trailing over the surface of the dark, star-spangled water. "If I didn't know better, Mr. Ryder, I'd suspect you of trying to seduce me."

He laughed, because of course it was exactly what he was trying to do, and they both knew it. Raw sexual awareness hung in the air, throbbed with the surge of the surf and the brutal crash of breakers against the off-shore reef. "I'm just trying to seduce you into enjoying yourself."

"I've swallowed enough water for one day, thank you."

"It's not deep." He let his feet touch bottom, and raised his arms wide. "See?"

She took another step toward him, the fine linen of her pantalets billowing out around her hips as the water rose higher.

"You must like the water," he said. "Where did you learn to dog paddle?"

"I employed the services of a bathing machine at Brighton."

"I think you'll find swimming in this lagoon a lot more pleasant than hanging off the end of a bathing machine in the English Channel."

"I'm not so sure." She took another step toward him. "Brighton was . . . bracing."

"And what is this?"

She stood before him, the water lapping at her breasts, her eyes huge and dark in a pale, moonlit face. "Sensual."

"You say that as if it were a bad thing."

"It can be."

"Only if you think it is."

She didn't say anything, but it was obvious from the

angle of her jaw and the stiffness of her shoulders that as far as India McKnight was concerned, sensuality was an enemy to be guarded against at all costs. And he knew then that she would never relax, never enjoy the beauty of the warm water and velvety tropical night air, unless he helped her.

"Turn around," he said.

"What?"

"I want to show you something. Turn around."

She hesitated, then did as he asked, her body tense and wary as he moved up beside her until his lips were scant inches from her ear. "Now lay back and simply let yourself float. Don't worry," he added when she remained rigidly upright. "I'm here to support you if you need it."

She hesitated another moment, then leaned back, her body held stiff and unnaturally tight as his arms came up to cradle her back. "Relax," he said with a soft laugh. "Let yourself enjoy it, India."

He thought, for a moment, that she wouldn't be able to do it. But the moonlight and the gentle caress of the water were working their own magic, and he felt the resistance and need for control drain out of her, until she floated freely beside him. Slowly, he lowered his arms away from her, and took a step back.

"It's beautiful," she said on a soft expulsion of breath, her eyes wide, her lips parting with awe as she stared at the sky above.

Tipping back his head, Jack gazed up at a deep purple-blue night so full of glowing stars that there seemed scarce any space between them. Heavy with all the sweet, spicy scents of the island, the tropical breeze whispered around them. He felt the warm water lap against him, wash away the sweat and dirt and pain of the hot, exhausting day. And heard her whisper, "Thank you."

He lowered his head, his gaze locking with hers as she let her feet sink slowly toward the bottom. He reached for her, his hands sliding over her wet shoulders, drawing her toward him just as, out of the corner of his eye, he saw a triangular-shaped fin slice through the calm, silver-shimmered water some two hundred feet offshore.

≈≈Chapter Eighteen

JACK LET HIS fingers slip down her arm to close around her hand. "I think we'd better get out," he said, plowing through the water, toward shore.

She hung back. "What's the matter? What are you doing?"

"There aren't any crocodiles on this island," he said, his voice calm as he dragged her behind him. "But every once in a while a shark gets into the lagoon."

"A shark!" She whirled around, her hand clutching his, her long dark hair whipping through the air as she stared out across the moonlit stillness of the water. "Where?"

He shook his head, his eyes narrowing as he scanned the now flat, empty surface. "All I saw was a fin."

"A fin? Oh my God." She broke into a run, stumbling in the shallows as the sand shifted beneath her feet, the gentle waves sloshing around her as she fell to her hands and knees at the edge of the surf. Reaching down, Jack grasped her hand to help her up, then paused as a sleek, rounded body broke the surface of the lagoon. For one, miraculous moment, the porpoise soared through the air, moonlight glimmering on its dark, wet hide as it arced gracefully back into the water with a gentle splash.

"Oh, Jesus," Jack said, laughing. "It's a bloody porpoise."

"You—you *fiend*." She tightened her grip on his hand and pulled, and it was so unexpected, he lost his balance and crashed, still laughing, into the surf beside her. Low and husky, her laughter joined with his, so that the sound of their laughter floated together out over the warm, moonlit lagoon. And then they weren't laughing anymore. She was staring at his mouth, her expression still and intense.

He brought up one hand to spear his spread fingers through the heavy fall of her hair, drawing it back, his grip tightening as he cupped her head in his palm. In the glow of moonlight, he saw her eyes dilate until they looked black, saw her slim white throat work as she swallowed. The sea sighed around them, warm and soft. And still he waited, giving her time to pull away from him, to end the moment, if that was what she wanted.

She didn't pull away.

He leaned forward, his gaze locked with hers. He heard her make a breathy, wanting sound, deep in her throat, felt her hand slide up his bare, wet chest to wrap around his neck and draw him to her. Then he tipped his head, and kissed her.

Her lips were sweet and welcoming, and opened beneath his. His hand spasmed in her hair, once, then swept down her back to draw her body up against his. She was warm and pliant and soft, so soft against the hard length of him, only the wet clinging linen of her chemise and drawers coming between his nakedness and hers.

Groaning, he deepened the kiss, his tongue mating with hers as she rolled onto her back, drawing him with her. He covered her, felt her thighs part beneath him as he settled his weight over her, and the kiss turned into something hot and hungry. The surf crashed against the distant reef with a wild, thundering roar, and the warm sea spilled around them.

He tore his mouth from hers, her head tipping back, her neck arching as he kissed her throat, his lips brushing against her thrumming pulse point before traveling lower, to the tender flesh that showed above the delicate lace edging her chemise. She tasted of the sea and the warm night air, and of herself, and the need in him, the need to have her, to surround himself with her moist heat, to join her body with his, was so powerful, so damned near overwhelming that he shuddered.

He lifted his head and stared up at her. Her lips were parted, her face pale and beautiful in the moonlight. "Make love to me," he said softly.

She bracketed his face with her hands, cradling him as if he were something precious and dear. "I can't."

He swallowed, hard. His skin felt so hot and tight, it hurt, but somehow, from somewhere, he managed to dredge up a crooked smile. "I notice you didn't say you don't want to."

Her eyes were wide and solemn, her breath soughing as hard and heavy as his own. "We both know that would be a lie."

He dipped his head, his lips brushing hers in a soft, tender kiss. "Make love to me, India," he whispered, kissing her trembling eyelids, the curve of her cheek, the tender flesh at the base of her ear. "Here, tonight, with the moonlight soft on your face, and a tropical breeze warm against your bare skin."

He felt her shudder beneath him, her hands desperate and seeking as she ran them over his shoulders, down his back, then up again to touch his face. And he knew, even before she said it, what her answer would be.

"No."

He kissed her once more. Then he pushed himself up and rolled away from her. While he still could.

"You're thinking of what I told you," she said. "About that man I was with, before."

He swung his head to look at her over his shoulder. She sat at the surf's edge, her arms wrapped around her bent knees to hug them close to her chest. "No." He shook his head, once, from side to side. "That was an experiment. But this . . . *this* would be for pleasure, and you're only allowed to break the rules if you don't enjoy it." He paused. "Isn't that right?"

She lifted her chin in that way she had, that way that

used to annoy him and now only made him want to kiss her again. "I don't break society's rules."

He laughed, and stood up. "Don't you? In a society that expects a woman to devote herself exclusively to making a home and caring for a family, you travel the world by yourself—a single woman, with no escort, no companion. You say you have no intention of ever marrying because, with the law the way it is, you'd be giving up not just your independence, but all control of your life, and you refuse to do that." He felt the surf curl around his ankles, the receding wave sucking at him, beckoning him. "And then you say you don't break society's rules."

She stared up at him, her nostrils flaring wide as she drew in a deep, shuddering breath. "Don't you see? That's precisely why I must maintain a reputation for strict moral rectitude, why people must see me as an essentially sexless being, a travel writer. Not some amoral female who wanders the world, scorning her proper place in society and taking a lover in every port."

He felt a sad, wry smile twist his lips. "And do you care so much about what other people think? I wouldn't have expected it of you."

She held herself very still. "You're only saying that because you want me to make love to you."

"I want you. But that's not why I said it."

He turned, conscious of her watching him as he waded out into deeper water. Then he dove beneath the surface of the lagoon and let the gentle waves wash over him, warm and soothing.

He didn't sleep.

India thought, at first, that he had gone to stand there, on the rocky spit of sand jutting out into the lagoon, because of what had happened between them at the water's edge. For the longest time, he watched the sea, and she watched him, a dark solitary figure silhouetted against the silver path spilled across the water by the westering moon. She supposed he thought that if he stayed away, she might somehow manage to fall asleep. Only, how could she sleep, knowing he was out there, wakeful, alone? How could she sleep when his kiss, his touch, the very scent of him had awakened within her such heat, such aching desires as she had never dreamt could exist?

It was good, she decided, that tomorrow would mark the end of their journey together. She would never see him again. In time, she told herself, she would forget this tight, painful need that burned within her, forget the magic of his touch and the intoxicating vortex of his kiss. Forget the way he could warm her heart with just a smile. She told herself these things, to reassure herself. She was unprepared for the yawning, bitter sadness, the desperate yearning that rose up within her, sweet and hurting.

She tossed from one side to the other, sleep continuing to elude her despite the scented softness of the bed of ferns he had heaped up for her beside the glowing embers of the fire. On this balmy night, with the tropical breeze a warm caress that brushed sinfully across the bare flesh of her arms and legs, the fire was for comfort more than anything else, a defense against the savage darkness of the rain forest and the yawning emptiness of the sea.

The thought drew her attention, inevitably, back to the man who still stood looking out across the wide Pacific. Her gaze roved over him, over the lean, taut line of his back, the dark angle of his profile as he stared at the blackness of infinity. And she knew then that while he had left her alone so that she might sleep, it was also true that wakefulness was his constant companion. He rarely slept.

She sat up, her arms wrapping around her bent knees, her thoughts on the things he had told her, about the girl child he had abandoned on that faraway, mysterious island, about the beautiful woman he had loved, and who had died.

His wife.

It was not shock India had felt when he told her of the island girl he had taken to wife. Not shock, but an emotion more intimate, more powerful. And India realized now, as she listened to the gentle slosh of the ocean beside her, that what she had felt was something she didn't often experience, something she was ashamed, even now, to own. Because what she had felt was envy. Envy for this man, who had once loved so deeply, so vibrantly. And envy for the woman he had loved with such a powerful passion that he had flouted every expectation, every rule of his society and service, to make her his own.

India had never considered herself an impulsive person. But she could not have said what it was that caused her to stand and walk toward him. It was not a conscious decision. It was a need. A need to understand this man, whose life had become so unexpectedly, so fundamentally entwined with her own.

∼∼Chapter Nineteen

SHE COULD SEE him standing at the water's edge, his body taut as he watched her walk out to him. The air was soft and warm and sweetly scented with brine, the sea a dark, star-glittered presence that stretched beyond tomorrow.

"Why don't you ever sleep?" India asked, pausing only a short distance from him.

A flicker of a smile lightened his eyes. "I do sometimes."

"It's because of what happened on Rakaia. Isn't it?"

He didn't answer her, but she knew from the tightening of his jaw, the cording of the muscles in his throat as he swallowed, that it was true.

"Tell me," she said. "Tell me how your wife died."

He turned, his gaze sweeping the distant line of breaker-shattering reefs. "You don't want to hear it."

"Tell me."

He swung his head to look at her over his shoulder, his gaze narrow and piercing. "You want to hear? You want to hear how three sailors from the *Lady Juliana* raped an island woman so viciously that she died?"

India felt a sick, hollow dread settle heavily within her. "Not . . . not your wife?"

"No. Another village girl. But the Rakaians handled the situation badly. They thought the island was theirs, you see. They thought they had the right to exact their own justice on these visitors who had broken the island's laws."

"They killed them?"

"Yes."

It would have been the penalty for such a crime in England, of course. But the captain of the *Lady Juliana* wouldn't have seen it that way, India knew. He'd have seen three British sailors murdered by hostile natives. "The captain . . ." Her voice was a scratchy, broken whisper. She thought, too late, that he'd been right: she didn't want to hear this. "What did the captain do?"

Something flared in Jack's eyes, something that blazed up, deadly, then grew cold and hard. "He lined up thirty of his men and ordered them to open fire on the village. Men. Women. Children. It didn't matter. Those who could ran for the edge of the forest. Only, Titana couldn't run very fast. She was a month away from delivering our second child." He drew in a long, ragged breath, then let it out in a rush. "She was eight months heavy with child, and they shot her down like a rabid dog. Like she was nothing. Because to them, she was nothing."

"I don't believe it," India said, although even as the

words left her lips, she knew what he'd told her was true. She simply didn't want to believe it.

He shifted to face her, his hard gaze locking with hers. "Why can't you believe it, India? For the same reason you can't believe that thirty years ago in the Subcontinent, a British squadron strapped the Sepoy rebels they'd captured to the mouths of cannons and literally blew them to hell? For the same reason you can't believe the good, God-fearing Puritan colonists of New England had a nasty habit of surrounding native villages and burning their inhabitants alive?" He took a step toward her, his eyes blazing. "What do you believe? That the world is divided—simplistically, dangerously—into good and evil? That the white men represent the force of civilization and good, which means the darker races of this world must be barbaric and evil?"

She stood her ground, although her heart was beating so hard and fast, her chest ached. "You are wrong about me. I have seen the ruins of the once-great cities of Central and South America that were laid waste by the brutality of conquerors *from Europe.* I have walked the mosaic floors of Arab homes that were old when Englishmen still wore uncured animal skins and roasted people in primitive trials by ordeal." She brought her hands up together, as if in prayer. "Don't you see? One of the reasons I am driven to write is because I want to try to dispel all the comfortable delusions people like to live with, to challenge their preconceptions and prejudices, to help those who are unable to travel understand the other peoples with whom we share this world. You can accuse me of many things, but don't you dare accuse me of cultural elitism."

The air seemed to echo with the thrum of her emotion, mingling with the distant crash of the breakers and the slosh of the surf at their feet. She watched as a strange, unexpected smile curled the edges of his lips. "Except, of course, when it comes to cannibals."

She was surprised into a shaky laugh. "Yes. Although perhaps by the time I sit down to write this book, I will have come to a more philosophical, less personal perspective of anthropophagy."

He reached for her, his hands closing over both of hers to draw her closer. At some time, he had put his trousers and shirt back on, although he wore the shirt unbuttoned and loose, so that it flapped in the warm breeze. She was intensely aware of a haunted, almost desperate glow in his eyes, and the way the moonlight glazed the dark sinews of his throat, his collarbone rising and falling with each breath. "I think it would have been better," he said, his voice a husky whisper, "if I had continued to think of you as an arrogant, self-righteous Scotswoman, convinced of the superiority of her race and scornful of any unfamiliar culture."

"Better why?" she asked, her hands trembling within his, although she made no attempt to remove them. "So that you could continue to keep me at a distance?"

He gathered her hair in his hands and lifted it from her neck before letting it fall down her back again in a soft, sensuous tumble. A dimple slashed one lean cheek. "And here I thought I was trying to seduce you."

"That's just biology." She touched his beard-roughened cheek, gently, with her fingertips. It was something she'd been wanting to do for what seemed like forever, although she'd resisted the impulse. Now it seemed the most natural thing in the world. "You blame yourself, don't you?" she said quietly. "You blame yourself for your wife's death. Hers, and all those who died with her."

His hands stilled in her hair, his eyes narrowing, his nostrils flaring as he drew in a quick breath. "Wouldn't you?"

It would have been easy to say, *No, of course not,* to tell him that the blame was not his, that responsibility for that dark day lay with the captain of the *Lady Juliana* and the men who had followed his order. But India knew something of what it was like to bear a burden of guilt, and so she said, instead, "I don't know."

"I think you do." A ghost of a smile softened the fierceness of his features. "I might blame myself for Titana's death, but you blame yourself for your mother's life." He shifted his hands to her shoulders, holding her close when she would have stepped back in surprise. "You think that if she hadn't had you, your mother would have left your father. That without you tying her to that cold, narrow house in Edinburgh, she could have had the life of adventuring she'd always dreamt of."

"How?" India whispered hoarsely, her gaze wide and

frightened as she searched his face. "How could you know?"

"Because we're alike, you and I," he said softly, his hands moving over her shoulders in a gentle, caring caress. "We've simply found different ways of punishing ourselves."

She watched, breathless, as the warm tropical breeze ruffled the dark hair at his forehead. She watched his head dip, his features taut with a hunger she understood. His eyes looked as black and wild as the sea, and for one, dangerous moment, she almost fell into them. Then he brushed her parted lips with the pad of his thumb, and said, "You need to go back now. Before biology gets the better of us both."

She could have stayed. A part of her wanted to stay, to taste again the wickedness of his kiss, to know the magic of his hands and the secrets that his body could show hers. But everything she'd told him before was still true, and so were the other things, the things she hadn't told him and that he hadn't guessed. And so she turned and walked away, and left him there, with the wind, and the sea, and his past.

The passage through the barrier reef off La Rochelle was wide and easy, the lagoon opening out into an arcing, white-sand-rimmed bay that formed a natural harbor. The air blew off the sea cool and salty-sweet, the high feathery fronds of the palms overhead shifting lazily with the trades. Backed as it was by a thickly overgrown series of low foothills that rose lush and green above the clear, vivid turquoise waters of the bay, the village could have been beautiful.

It wasn't.

Pausing upwind of the settlement, Jack let his gaze drift over the rotting lumber hovels roofed with rusting sheets of imported iron that straggled away from the beach. Lacking both the shabby elegance of an English colony and the neat prosperity that characterized the German settlements in the Pacific, the French trading post of La Rochelle was simply squalid and sad, and half-obscured by indiscriminate piles of rotting garbage that included what looked like the bloated corpse of a man, floating facedown just offshore.

Jack saw India's eyes widen as she stared at the corpse gently rising and falling with the placid surf, but she didn't mention it. All she said was, "Patu isn't here."

Jack squinted out over the sun-sparkled harbor. A battered old sloop rode at anchor on the far side of the bay, and some half a dozen native outrigger canoes lay propped up on forked branches stuck in the white coral sand. But other than that, the bay was deserted. "He will be," Jack said.

It was close to midday by now, and blazingly hot. Anyone with any sense had long ago disappeared into the lavender-colored shadows of the mangoes or one of the ugly plank buildings strung out along the bush track that passed for the settlement's main street. He knew that. And yet . . .

"What is it?" she asked, her brows drawing together as she studied his face. "You think something's wrong, don't you?"

He shook his head, his gaze lifting to the walled French compound that had been sited, with deliberate intimidation, at the top of a low rise. "I'm not sure. It just seems . . . different."

"Why? Weren't there dead men floating in the bay the last time you were here?"

He glanced over at her, and smiled. "You're going to put that in your book, aren't you?"

"Of course," she said, her sensible boots kicking up loose sand as she set off down the beach again. Her voice drifted back to him. "Right after the part about the cannibals."

His smile fading slowly, Jack watched her walk away from him, her back straight and tall, her head held high, her knapsack with its precious notebook gripped securely to her side. He watched the sun warm the curve of her face, glint in the chestnut highlights of her hair, and he knew a surge of regret, an unexpected and baffling desire to reach out and hold this moment before it could slip away. Hold her in his life.

It was a strange, useless thought. He was a renegade, a hunted fugitive doomed to a short, violent life spent alone and on the run. While she . . . she roamed the world freely, deliberately. And while Jack yearned, secretly, desperately, for a home and a family, he knew that

India was determined never to tie herself down to any place, anyone . . . any man.

The call of a seabird drew his attention, briefly, to the sun-dazzled bay, where a tern sailed low and graceful on an updraft. Jack watched it come in, its wings spread wide as it glided to water level. Then he started down the beach, toward the acacia-shaded path that led to the French compound.

～～Chapter Twenty

BUILT CRUDELY OF saplings bound together with vines, the gates to the French commissioner's compound hung open and untended in the thick, sun-baked air. Once, the high, spiked walls had provided a refuge for European traders and missionaries in times of unrest. Now the gates were used mainly at night, their purpose less to protect the lives of the compound's inhabitants than to guard their property. The island's Melanesian peoples, who judged a man's worth not by the number of possessions he accumulated but by the generosity with which he gave his bounty away, had never quite been able to bend their minds around to understanding the white men's possessive attitude toward things.

With India at his side, Jack paused in the compound's open, muddy courtyard, his gaze flicking from the tangled, rioting ruin of Georges Lefevre's once well-tended garden, to the empty, fly-buzzed blue shadows of the main bungalow's bougainvillea-draped veranda. For a moment, he turned, his eyes narrowing as he stared, again, at the nearly deserted lagoon below the settlement, where a scrawny native dog could be seen foraging for scraps on the refuse-strewn beach.

"What is it?" India asked, touching his arm.

He shook his head. "I don't know." Crossing the court and the untidy, overgrown garden beyond it, he climbed the wooden steps to the bungalow's veranda two at a time. "Georges?" he called. In the hot, heavy silence, his footsteps echoed hollowly. "Georges? *Ou est tu?*"

A whisper of white muslin lightened the dark, open doorway before him as an unexpected but wholly familiar scent came to him, the scent of lilies of the valley and talcum powder; a European woman's fragrance, mingling oddly with the tropical scents of frangipani and gardenia, honeysuckle and stephanotis wafting up from the rioting garden below.

"Hello, Françine." Jack paused at the edge of the veranda, one hand still resting on the weathered wood of the rail. He was intensely conscious of the presence of India in the garden below, her gaze riveted on the petite, exquisitely fair Frenchwoman who came to trail one hand down Jack's arm in a familiar, almost intimate caress.

"Jacques," said Françine Poirot. "You look as if you've spent the last month in the jungles." Her small, turned-up nose crinkled. "And you smell like it, as well, *mon ami.*"

Jack caught her hand in his, then let it go. "What are you doing here, Françine?"

"You did not know?" She pursed her full lips into a pouty moue that had once heated Jack's blood, but now made him feel only wary and uncomfortable. "Pierre is Takaku's new commissioner."

Jack let his gaze drift, again, around the compound that was not, he now realized, as deserted as he had thought. Two gendarmes had appeared near the gates; another waited, silent and hard-jawed, at the end of the veranda.

"I suppose I should congratulate Pierre, but commiserate with you. Pepeete might be a backwater, but it's better than this." In the courtyard below, India McKnight had not moved, but he knew from her tense, still posture that she was as aware as he of the gendarmes, and all the implications of their presence.

Françine shook her head, as if overcome by sadness. "You should not have come here, *mon ami.*"

"I could leave," Jack said amicably.

"Actually, I don't think you could."

Another gendarme appeared from around the side of the bungalow, then another. "Five men," said Jack. "Pierre must think I'm dangerous."

"He knows you are."

"I have no quarrel with the French."

"*Non.* But there were some Englishmen here this morning, a Captain Simon Granger and his lieutenant, a fiercely passionate young man who takes himself far too seriously. They say you are a wanted man."

"Wanted by the English. That's nothing new." Jack

brought his gaze back to the Frenchwoman's delicate features. "Since when have the French turned themselves into Her Britannic Majesty's policemen?"

"There's a diplomatic revolution under way in this world," said a heavily accented, masculine voice. "Had you not heard?"

Shifting slowly, Jack met the gaze of the man who had appeared in the bungalow's open doorway. He was a slim, darkly handsome man, Captain Pierre Poirot, with fierce eyes and an aristocratic nose and a perfectly proportioned physique. It wasn't until he limped across the veranda floor to pause behind Françine that it became apparent he stood only a few inches taller than his incredibly dainty wife.

Jack gave Takaku's new commissioner a tight smile. "Cheeky of the Germans, isn't it, to decide at this late date in history to unite, and upset the Franco-Anglican domination of the world?"

A muscle bunched along the other man's clenched jaw. "Where you made your mistake, Monsieur Ryder, was in leaving Neu Brenen. No German gunboat here."

Jack swung to gaze out over the palm-fringed, sun-spangled turquoise waters of the lagoon. "No Royal Navy corvette, either."

"The *Barracuda* will be back." The Frenchman smiled. "After I've arrested you."

Jack raised one eyebrow in mild inquiry. "On what charge?"

"The forced and violent abduction of a British travel writer."

"That's ridiculous," said India in her crisp, Scots-accented voice. "Obviously, there's been some sort of misunderstanding. Do I look as if I have been kidnapped?"

Turning, Jack watched her climb the stairs, her sensible, lace-up boots treading firmly on the plank steps. Her hair might be bound in a simple plait secured at the end by a twisted vine, her Expedition Outfit might be ripped and muddied and reduced in volume and propriety by well-intentioned theft, but it would take more than cannibals and jungles and Aussie renegades, Jack thought with a private smile, to diminish the powerful, no-nonsense presence of Miss India McKnight. She had her head held high, her piercing gaze fixed on the Frenchman. As she reached the veranda, it was Pierre Poirot who swallowed hard, and took a step back.

"As a matter of fact, mademoiselle," said the commissioner, his eyes widening as he assimilated the wonder of that tattered, jungle-stained tartan skirt and belted shirt, "you do."

"Nonsense." She planted herself directly in front of the French commissioner; the top of his head came up just shy of her shoulder. "I did have a spot of trouble with the cannibals on the southern end of the island, but Mr. Ryder acted the part of the rescuer, not the abductor."

Tipping back his head, Pierre Poirot stared up at her, his jaw slack with bemusement. "You are Miss India McKnight?"

She held out her hand. "How do you do?"

After the briefest of hesitations, Captain Poirot took the proffered hand in a limp clasp, quickly released. "And you say this man did not kidnap you?"

"That is what I say, yes."

A light feminine laugh drew everyone's attention, for a moment, to Françine Poirot. "Really, Jacques," she said softly, her head tipping to one side in a practiced artifice that reminded Jack of a small bird contemplating a choice morsel. "I would not have thought her your type. Yet you appear to have seduced her quite effectively."

Pierre Poirot's skin darkened perceptably as a muscle jumped along his suddenly tightened jaw. He did not look at his wife. "Thank you for your information, Mademoiselle McKnight. But Monsieur Ryder is still under arrest."

"This is absurd," said India in her best Sunday-school teacher voice.

A curt jerk of the commissioner's chin brought the gendarmes in a slow advance across the compound. "You can go willingly," he said to Jack, "or you can fight."

"Well," said Jack, glancing from the gendarmes on the veranda to those still in the garden, "since you put it that way . . ." He ducked and stepped back to bring his fist up into the nose of the first gendarme who reached for him. "I guess I'll fight."

There were only five of them, after all, and Jack had grown up with four older brothers who'd taught him all he needed to know about using his fists and his feet. He tripped the second gendarme, then sent the third spinning back into the first as, blood spilling down his face, the bellowing Frenchman came at Jack again in a blind, angry rush.

Wrapping his hands around the rail, Jack vaulted off the veranda to land in a hibiscus- and fern-breaking crouch in the garden below. A roundhouse kick in the stomach sent the fourth gendarme back into the fifth, and bought Jack enough time to deal with one of the men from the veranda who came charging down the stairs with a howl of rage. Jack stopped him with left clip that caught the man under the chin and sent him sailing into a bed of rioting zinnias. Spinning around, Jack knocked down the gendarme who had just managed to come flailing out from beneath the prone body of his comrade.

A sweat-dampened lock of hair fell into Jack's eyes and he shook it back, assessing the distance to the open gates and the welcoming darkness of the jungle beyond. But behind him, Pierre Poirot picked up one of Georges Lefevre's clay flowerpots and dropped it in a shower of dirt and crimson geranium petals and cracking terracotta onto the top of Jack's head.

He saw a flash of brilliant light, felt a stunning wave of pain. Then he saw nothing, and felt nothing.

A cool, wet cloth touched the back of Jack's head.

He became aware, slowly, of the fact that he was lying on his stomach, his nose pressed against what must be a mattress, thin and noisome and thrown directly on a flagged floor. He tried to move, but his muscles were curiously unresponsive and his gut heaved alarmingly, taking away whatever inclination he might have had to move again or even open his eyes.

He contented himself with a soft groan.

"And you call me stubborn and stupid," scolded a familiar, stern voice, the Scots accent unusually thick. "I'd like to know how you'd describe that stunt."

Jack heard a trickle of water, then the cloth touched the back of his head again, stinging like crazy. "Ouch," he said. "That hurts."

"Stop whining. The flesh is broken, and there's dirt in the wound that must be cleaned out. The last thing you can afford at this point in your adventurous and disreputable career is a tropical infection."

Jack opened his eyes. He had a vague, pain-filled vision of India's tight, concerned face leaning over him. Behind her rose nondescript piles of shadowy objects and the contrastingly bright glare from a small, barred window. Then his stomach heaved again and he squeezed his eyes shut against the light. "Where am I?"

"Locked in the storeroom of the local Chinese trader's shop. It seems to be the most secure establishment in the settlement."

"It usually is."

"How's your stomach?"

"Rebelling. Why?"

"I'm afraid you might have a concussion."

By clenching his teeth, Jack was able to summon up

the courage to roll over and open his eyes. A dusty ceiling swam sickeningly overhead, then the world righted itself, and he sighed. "What happened to Georges? Did anyone say?"

India dipped her cloth in the water again, and laid it on his forehead. It felt cool, and so good he changed his mind about telling her to stop fussing over him. "I gather he was recalled to France. Something about a duel."

"And the powers that be decided to replace him with Napoleon Poirot." Jack gave another low laugh. "Now, how's that for irony?"

"I thought the commissioner's name was Pierre."

"It is."

"Huh." She stood abruptly and went to stand by the window. "Madame Poirot tells me her husband limps because you shot him."

He wished she'd come away from that damned window. The light hurt his eyes, and he had to twist around in an awkward angle to see her. "He challenged me to a duel."

She swung to face him, her elbows cradled in her palms, her features in shadow. "Are all French trade commissioners so enamored of the practice of dueling, or only the ones who have the dubious distinction of encountering you?"

Jack sighed. "Georges Lefevre wasn't trying to kill me. Napoleon Poirot was."

"Why? For calling him Napoleon, or for sleeping with his wife?"

Jack slewed around on the torn, filthy mattress to stare at her, but he still couldn't see more than the sun-dazzled outline of her head. "How the hell did you know that? Did she tell you?"

"Do you think she needed to?"

"Obviously not."

"One might have expected even you to have more sense than to seduce the French commissioner's wife."

"He wasn't a commissioner at the time. And you've got it all wrong. She seduced me."

She let out another one of those scornful huffs of hers, like she didn't believe him or something. And it came to him in a kind of wonderment that she was jealous. He might even have smiled about it, if the back of his head hadn't felt as if he'd been scalped. He rolled gingerly onto his side. "Come away from that damned window, would you? The sun hurts my eyes."

"The wages of sin," she said crisply. But she came away from the window.

She was still wearing her Expedition Outfit, although she had washed her face, and wound that glorious fall of thick, chestnut-shot hair back up into its customary neat, controlled chignon. "How long have I been in here?" he asked suddenly.

"Less than an hour. The *Barracuda* is expected after six, when the tides change."

Jack nodded. The tides here in the South Pacific were solar, cresting regularly at midnight and noon. "I'm surprised Napoleon let you in to see me."

"He didn't want to. But I reminded him that you were a British subject, and as the only other British subject currently on the island, I had a responsibility to see to your needs."

"I wouldn't have expected that argument to impress him much."

"It didn't." Her lips curled into that slow, secret smile that he liked, the one that had first told him she wasn't nearly as proper and starchy as she chose to appear. "So I thought it best to let him know about the chapter I was thinking of adding to my book, the one about the shocking corruption and abuse of power prevalent among the French colonies in the South Seas. That convinced him."

Jack laughed softly. "You're a dangerous woman, Miss McKnight."

Her smile faded slowly, leaving an intensely earnest expression in its place. "Does the Admiralty really mean to hang you?"

Jack met her gaze squarely. "They do indeed."

"For causing the sinking of your ship, and the death of all those men?"

"Yes."

"And did you do it?"

He looked away, his chest lifting as he sucked in a deep breath and let it out slowly. "Those men who died . . . they were my shipmates, my friends. And yet . . ." He paused, his jaw hardening. "I was glad to see them die. Yes."

She came to kneel on the hard, dirty floor beside him,

her features pinched with an unexpected sadness. "They had just killed your wife, and your unborn child," she said softly, her hand coming out to touch his shoulder, briefly, before drifting away. "I can understand that you might in your grief have found some grim satisfaction in what happened to them." She paused. "But did you cause it?"

He swung his head sideways to look at her. "And if I said I didn't, would you believe me?"

She didn't even blink. "Yes."

"Not many would."

"Perhaps." She held his gaze steadily. "Did you deliberately sink that ship?"

He swallowed, as if he could somehow swallow the old, old pain that welled up from deep within him. "I was responsible, yes."

Reaching out, she touched her fingertips to his lips. "I didn't ask if you felt responsible. I asked if you deliberately sank that ship."

He could hear, in the distance, the sound of the surf crashing against the offshore reef, and the rustling of the fronds of the wind-ruffled palm trees edging the beach. Even here, in the Chinese trader's locked storeroom, he could smell the familiar, evocative fragrances of the South Pacific, of frangipani and gardenia and orange blossom, and, beneath it all, the briny breath of the sea. A strange, weightless kind of dizziness engulfed him, until along with the thrum of the surf and the whispering of the palms, he thought he heard, for one brief, heart-breaking moment, the sweet lilting of a woman's laughter, lost all too quickly in a roar of guns and the sucking, deadly cold rush of water.

"No," he said at last, his lips moving against her fingers. "No, I didn't."

~~Chapter Twenty-one

THE STORE WAS run by a tall, incredibly-thin Chinese man named Johnny Amok. He had pale, parchmentlike skin and a pair of gold-rimmed glasses he wore perched on the end of his nose, and could have been anywhere between fifty and eighty in age. While a gendarme stood guard, it was Mr. Amok who had wielded the long iron key that admitted India to Jack Ryder's prison, and Mr. Amok who locked the thick door again when she left—all without uttering a word.

"I should like to make a few purchases," India said when the trader would have turned away.

He paused, then nodded silently, leaving her to follow as he shuffled up the muddy, hibiscus- and acacia-shaded path that led to the trading post's crooked veranda.

Inside, the shop itself was every bit as dusty and cluttered as the storeroom that served as Jack Ryder's prison. Looking around, India saw hemp bales and fencing wire, cook pots and tins of canned beef, all jumbled together in what appeared to be an untidy confusion. "First of all," she said, extracting from her pocket the list she had prepared, "I require a dress. No, not that sort," she added briskly when he held up a dark red, voluminous Mother Hubbard. They were ugly, shapeless things, Mother Hubbards, developed by the missionaries to clothe the scandalous nudity previously practiced by island women. India had never considered herself vain, but she had her limits, and she drew the line at wearing a Mother Hubbard. "What else do you have?"

Mr. Amok regarded her unblinkingly for a moment, then turned away. After some minutes spent rummaging through an odd assortment of yellowing, smashed boxes, he held up a fine white linen shirt, meticulously worked with neat stitches and little pleats down the front. It was beautiful—but it had never been intended for a woman.

"That's a man's shirt," India said.

Mr. Amok shrugged, and put it away. Then he turned to look at her expectantly, his hands folded into his long, flowing sleeves.

She stared back at him. "You don't have anything else?"

He shook his head.

India glanced at the next item on her list, *new pantalets,* and sighed. "How much is the shirt?"

She waited, expecting him—finally—to open his mouth and say something, but he didn't. Picking up a pencil, he scratched a figure on a slate lying on the counter, and shoved it toward her.

She'd come to the conclusion the man simply couldn't speak when, twenty minutes later, as he was wrapping her purchases up into a brown paper bundle, he suddenly peered at her over the rims of his glasses and said in perfect, Australian-accented English, "Are you Jack's friend?"

Caught in the process of opening her purse, India jerked in surprise, the movement sending a shower of coins to bounce and ring all over his counter. "Yes," she answered unhesitatingly. "Why?"

He regarded her steadily for a moment, his dark eyes unblinking. Then he answered her question with another question. "How good of a friend?"

Since the trading settlement of La Rochelle lacked anything even remotely resembling a rest house, India had no choice but to accept the commissioner and his wife's reluctantly offered hospitality in the French compound's bungalow.

"I would have lent you one of my own gowns to wear," said Madame Poirot, lingering in the doorway of the small guest room while a young, dark-skinned girl in a loose-flowing gown of brightly patterned cotton hauled in bucket after bucket of lukewarm water to fill the tin hip bath, "but you are so much bigger than I, *n'est pas?*"

"*N'est pas,*" agreed India, unwrapping her brown paper bundle. "Fortunately, Mr. Amok was able to furnish me with a shirt and sundry other necessities."

Françine Poirot crinkled her little nose as India spread her purchases over the white counterpane of the high, turned-post bed. "But it is a man's shirt. And—*alors!* A man's smallclothes."

"I noticed that."

"I suppose you do not mind," she said slowly, as if reaching to try to understand this enormous peculiarity, "since you already wear the trousers."

"It's a split skirt." Turning away, India emptied her knapsack of the few personal items she carried. "Not trousers."

"And do you wear it always, this split skirt?"

"Only when trekking through jungles, or in other rugged terrain."

"You do this often?" The shock in the other woman's voice was profound.

"It's how I make my living. I'm a travel writer."

"It is a strange thing for a woman to do, to willingly travel to such dangerous and unpleasant places."

India looked up. "I enjoy it."

Françine Poirot blinked at her. "You never married?"

"No."

She sighed in sympathy. "*C'est dommage.*" It's a pity.

"Is it?" It struck India as a strange thing for the woman to say, given the obviously unhappy state of her own marriage. But then, for most women, an existence outside of marriage was unthinkable. They identified themselves by the man to whom they were attached, and so did society. "Tell me," India asked, "how do you happen to know Jack Ryder?"

A secret smile played around the other woman's lips. "My father is the commissioner in Tahiti, at Papeete. Jacques spent some months there once."

Taking the pins from her chignon, India let her hair fall about her shoulders, and set to work brushing it. "And did you find him a good lover?" she asked with studied casualness.

The boldness of the question brought a heat of embarrassment to India's cheeks, for she was not at all the sort of woman who normally indulged in discussions of this nature. But it was obvious Françine Poirot found nothing either untoward or awkward in the topic. As India watched, the other woman's lips parted, her half-closed eyes gleaming with the banked fires of a long-ago passion and remembered ecstasy. And India, her brush clutched forgotten in her hand, knew a swift, unexpectedly vicious stab of emotion that left her throat feeling tight and painful.

"*Mon Dieu,*" said Françine on a soft, breathy sigh, her smile turning wistful as she wrapped her arms across her breasts and hugged herself. "I have never known another such as he."

India stared at the other woman, and found herself struggling to suppress all sorts of improper questions that threatened to come tumbling off the tip of her tongue.

What makes a man a good lover, as opposed to a bad one? How was Jack Ryder different from the other men you've known? And, *How many have you known?* Instead she said, only a slight tremble in her voice betraying the extent of her agitation, "Then why didn't you marry him?"

Françine's peal of laughter was instantaneous and unforced. "Marry Jacques? *Mais non.*" Her open hand flashed through the air in a very Gallic gesture of dismissal. "He is an adventurer, a renegade, a penniless fugitive. *Vraimant,* he is dashing and exciting, but one does not marry men such as this." She wrinkled her nose in that way she had that somehow managed to be both attractive and endearing, whereas India knew that if she tried it, she'd only succeed in looking as if she'd smelled something foul. "At the moment, Pierre's position is not so good, but he is his uncle's heir. One day, he will be rich."

Of course, thought India; in a world where a woman is identified by her husband, it made sense that the choice of that husband be guided largely by financial considerations.

"Besides," the Frenchwoman added, a wry smile touching her lips, "Jacques never asked me."

India met her gaze in the mirror. "Then why the duel?"

Françine jerked her shoulder in a dismissive gesture. "Pierre was jealous."

Pierre was obviously still jealous, India thought, but she didn't say it.

Françine tipped her head sideways, her expression growing thoughtful as she studied India. "I would not have thought it, but I see you are a romantic, *n'est pas?* You would marry for love."

"I have no intention of marrying at all," India said, jerking her brush through her hair in long, quick strokes.

"But only because you have not been in love, hmmm?"

India turned away to test the temperature of the water in the tub. "I don't believe in love."

"I think perhaps you do." Françine smiled. "If you did not, you would not have been shocked that I chose Pierre Poirot over Jacques."

India straightened slowly, her gaze caught by the view through the open window, where a slice of palm-fringed turquoise waters was just visible over the top of the palisade. As she watched, the westering sun struck the sails of a British naval corvette, the billowing sheets of white canvas turning to gold. In the corvette's wake came a sleek little schooner-rigged yacht, its masts stark against the tropical blue sky. The *Sea Hawk*.

"It's the *Barracuda*," said Françine, coming to stand beside India.

Her gaze still fixed on the sun-spangled lagoon below, India curled her hands around the rolled metal edge of the tub and gripped it tightly. A moment ago, she had been thinking about how different they were, she and this petite, beautiful, pragmatic Frenchwoman. Now she realized they were not so different, after all. They stood as if one, united by a mutual, unspoken concern for the man who lay on a filthy mattress in Johnny Amok's storeroom.

"Will they take him tonight?" India asked after a moment.

Françine Poirot shook her head. "*Non*. It must all at least be seen to be legal. In the morning, Pierre will hold an official hearing, decide that Jack is an 'undesirable element,' and order him expelled from Takaku—on the *Barracuda*."

"It doesn't sound exactly legal."

Again, that Gallic shrug, although there was no missing now the distress that pinched the woman's pretty face. "It doesn't matter. No one will care as long as the correct forms are observed."

"I care," said India softly.

The other woman turned to regard India though wide, steady eyes.

"What is it?" India prompted when Françine Poirot said nothing.

But she only shook her head, and smiled an odd, sad smile. "I think it is something you must discover for yourself, *n'est pas*?"

Confused, India pressed the other woman for an explanation. But she never did get one.

"It bothers you, doesn't it?" said Alex Preston, glancing sideways at his captain's hard, closed face. "Having the French take Ryder?"

Simon Granger kept his gaze on the back of the unkempt, potbellied gendarme who had been detailed to escort them from the island's French compound to Jack Ryder's makeshift prison. Alex had expected the commissioner himself to accompany them, but the handsome little Frenchman had declined. They had left him sitting alone in the darkened office of his bungalow, his frowning gaze fixed on a pair of dueling pistols that hung like crossed swords on the wall opposite his desk.

"Smacks a bit more of revenge than of justice, don't you think?" Granger said after a moment.

Alex shrugged. He didn't know exactly what had happened between the French commissioner's wife and Jack Ryder, but he'd heard and seen enough to figure most of it out. "Pierre Poirot's revenge, perhaps. But British justice."

"Yes, of course," said the captain, although Alex heard the unmistakable note of doubt still in his voice.

Located strategically between the island's two small churches, one Catholic and the other Protestant, the store run by the local Chinese trader stood at the far end of the row of half-dozen or so ramshackle plank and iron-roofed houses that formed the settlement of La Rochelle. Here and there, in the fork of an orange tree, or nailed to the side of a building, someone with a perverse sense of humor—presumably the departed Georges Lefevre—had stuck up a series of crudely lettered boards that read AVENUE DE TRIOMPHE, or BOULEVARD DE STE. MARIE, although as far as Alex could tell, the muddy, rubbish-strewn bush track they followed was the only street in the place.

Detouring around the pig snorting through a pile of fly-buzzed garbage rotting in the hot sunshine, Alex followed the gendarme to the stout plank door of a stuccoed lean-to jutting out from the back of the store. There they were met by a tall, scholarly-looking Oriental man with a thin, lined face and a queue that hung limply in the moist, hot air.

"*Donnez-moi la clef*," growled the gendarme, his stubble-covered jaw jutting out in an ugly scowl as he took a menacing step toward the Chinese trader. Producing a long iron key from his sleeve, the trader opened the door's rusting old lock with an audible click, but whisked himself sideways when the gendarme made a grab for the key.

"*Donnez-moi la clef*," snapped the gendarme again, but the old man tucked the key once more up his sleeve and silently shook his head, his face set in enigmatic lines.

"Wait out here," Granger told the gendarme in that stern, slightly bored voice that so effectively intimidated every seaman and officer on the *Barracuda*.

Responding instinctively to the tone of command, the gendarme pulled back his shoulders and clicked his heels as he stood aside to let them pass. "*Oui, monsieur.*"

After the glaring brilliance of the tropical light outside, the interior of the storeroom was dark, stifling. Giving his eyes time to adjust, Alex paused just inside the doorway and heard a glib, broadly accented voice say, "Do come in, gentlemen. I hope you won't take offense if I don't get up, but my head hurts like a sonofabitch."

Alex stared with interest at the man who sat on a filthy mattress thrown into one corner of the room, his back braced against the wall, his legs sprawled out in front of him. He was ragged and unshaven, his dark hair too long, and clumped with sweat and blood and dirt. More blood and dirt stained the ripped remnant of the shirt he wore hanging open halfway down his chest. He looked degenerate and disreputable; everything Alex had expected of such a man, and then some.

Simon Granger stopped a few feet shy of the mattress, his face unreadable as he stared down at his former friend. "I heard you'd resisted arrest."

An unexpected smile curled the edges of the Australian's mouth. "Only to be felled by a flowerpot. I must be getting old."

To Alex's surprise, the captain laughed. "What did it do to your head?"

"Miss India McKnight thinks I'm concussed, but I expect I'll live long enough to hang."

Simon Granger's smile faded. "It was wrong, what you did to that woman. Dragging her through a cannibal-infested jungle for the better part of three days."

"I know." The other man's chest jerked with a cynical sound that might have been a laugh, but wasn't. He tipped back his head, his eyes gleaming in the dim light.

"And it wasn't wrong of you to use her as live bait in a trap to catch me?"

"I didn't expect you to hold a machete to her throat."

"You should have."

Simon Granger brought up one hand to rub his forehead in an oddly uncharacteristic gesture. "I understand she's saying you didn't abduct her."

"Have you spoken to her?"

"Not yet. But it doesn't make any difference what she says. You're going to swing, anyway. For what you did to the *Lady Juliana*."

The man on the mattress sat quite still, only his chest rising and falling with the effort of his breathing. But as Alex watched, the man's face seemed to alter, as if pain had somehow stretched the flesh more tautly over the skull, causing the ridges of his cheekbones to stand out sharp, stark against the tanned skin. "I didn't send that ship up onto the reef, Simon."

With a sigh, the captain went to stare out the small, barred window. From where he still stood, Alex could see only a shimmering sliver of the distant sea, almost the same color as the darkening sky.

"I heard you myself," Granger said softly, his hands clasped behind his back, his gaze still fixed on the mist-shrouded horizon. "We all heard you tell Captain Gladstone that the charts were wrong. I know the state you were in that day, Jack. What Gladstone did to that native village was—" He paused, and a shudder passed over his face, an echo of a revulsion so profound, it sent an answering shiver down Alex's spine. "—an abomination. But that doesn't excuse what you did. You sent that ship onto the reef deliberately. Knowingly. You *killed* those men, Jack. You killed them. And now you're going to have to pay for it."

One hand braced against the wall for support, Ryder staggered to his feet, his face paling alarmingly as he stood swaying, his breath coming heavy and ragged. "Damn it, Simon, listen to me. The charts *were* wrong. Don't you understand? The old bastard changed his mind. He ordered the helmsman to keep to the originally plotted course, and *that's* why the ship missed the passage through the reef."

"You dare, sir!" Alex started forward, his clenched fists coming up. "That 'old bastard' you are attempting to slur was my mother's brother."

Granger's splayed hand slammed against Alex's chest, stopping him. "Lose control like that again, Lieutenant, and you'll be waiting outside with the gendarme."

Heat burned Alex's cheeks, but he set his jaw hard, and drew himself up tall. "Yes, sir."

The captain frowned at the pale, ragged man leaning against the wall. "Even if it were true, Jack . . . there's no way you can prove it."

"But I can."

"How?"

"What's left of the *Lady Juliana* is still caught on that reef. All you need to do is compare the ship's position with its charts and log, and you'll see I'm telling the truth. Gladstone followed the charts, not me."

Alex glanced from one man to the other. He was finding it increasingly hard to breathe in the hot, close atmosphere of the storeroom.

The captain's lips thinned into a tight smile. "The *Lady Juliana*'s charts and log are at the bottom of the ocean. Along with whatever's left of her captain."

Ryder leaned his shoulders against the wall behind him, his hands flattened at his sides, his chest lifting with his labored breathing. It occurred to Alex that someone really ought to advise the man to sit down again, but the words stuck in his throat.

"That's just it, they're not," said Ryder. "Toby Jenkins has them."

Granger's brows twitched together. "Toby Jenkins? The seaman who spent those years on the island with you?"

Ryder nodded.

"And where is Jenkins now?"

"He's still there. On Rakaia."

Alex gave a small start of surprise, quickly suppressed. On the way out from Rio, the *Barracuda* had anchored at Rakaia, looking for Jack Ryder. They'd found the island deserted.

"You haven't heard, I take it?" said Granger.

Ryder's eyes narrowed, his body tensing, his voice low and wary. "Heard what?"

"Rakaia was hit by an epidemic. Four, maybe six

months back. It's completely uninhabited now. Anyone who was there is dead, Jack. Jack?"

Granger surged forward, but Alex got there first, catching Ryder beneath the arms just as the man pitched forward in a dead faint.

～～Chapter Twenty-two

CLAD IN AN exquisitely tailored man's white linen shirt and her own tattered but well-brushed tartan split skirt, India sat on a driftwood log that had been thrown up by some past storm into the shade of the line of towering coconut palms fringing the lagoon. From there, she was able to watch Captain Granger when he left the storeroom and took the rutted, refuse-strewn path that led down to the beach. He had another officer with him, a younger man, with light brown hair and a sharp-boned, earnest face. The two men were obviously arguing, the younger officer's hands flashing through the air in short, emotional chops.

They were too far away for her to hear their words, but India knew by the sudden turning of the captain's head and the break in his stride that he had seen her. Pausing at the edge of the beach, he said something to the other man and, after a moment's hesitation, the younger officer continued to the waiting jolly boat drawn up on the golden-white sand, while Captain Granger turned aside, the last rays of the setting sun falling golden and warm on his craggy face as he walked toward her.

"Miss McKnight." He paused some half-dozen feet from her to stand with his hands clasped behind his back and his legs braced wide in the manner of a man who'd spent most of his life on the pitching deck of a ship. "I was hoping to have the opportunity to speak with you."

His discomfiture was obvious, and if she'd been feeling more in charity with the man, India would have said something to put him at ease. Instead, she merely tipped back her head and gave him a steady stare. "Captain Granger."

He cleared his throat awkwardly and fixed his gaze on some point over India's left shoulder. "To beg your pardon after all you have been through seems woefully inadequate, I know, but you must allow me to do so, nonetheless. I can only assure you that I would never have involved you in this affair had I imagined that the consequences to you might be either dangerous or unpleasant."

India studied the man's face, tanned dark and lined by years spent squinting into sun and salt spray. "Do you honestly believe that? Or are you simply hoping that I will believe it?"

A muscle bunched along his tight jaw. Then a wry smile touched his lips and he shook his head. "You're right. I saw a way to get my hands on Jack, and I seized it. And the devil take the consequences."

India kept her gaze on his face. "I don't understand. Why are you so determined to capture him? Why now, after all these years?"

"My orders come from London."

"And do you always go to such lengths to carry out your orders?"

He swung to look directly at her. "I volunteered for this assignment. Did you know?"

India shook her head. "No."

"Most people thought I seemed the obvious choice, given what I'd been through because of Jack. But there were some who weren't so sure. They remembered that Jack and I had once been friends, and they worried I might not pursue him with as much energy as I ought." He nodded toward the jolly boat pulling away from shore, and the young officer who stood stiff and erect at its prow. "Even my first lieutenant suspects me of cherishing dangerously tender feelings toward my quarry."

"And so you're determined to prove them wrong, is that it?"

Simon Granger drew in a sharp, deep breath and let it out in a sigh. "What I'm determined to do is to get my hands on Jack before London decides I'm not trying hard enough, and sends someone else. Someone who might not be as careful as they should be."

India felt a chill touch her heart. "You mean, someone who would just as soon kill Jack Ryder as capture him?"

"What Jack did . . . Well, let's just say there are a lot of people in the Admiralty who would like nothing better than to see him dead. With or without the benefit of a hearing."

"He says he didn't do it."

The Englishman's gaze met hers. "And you believe him?"

"Yes. I do."

"That's because you don't know what happened."

"Then tell me," she challenged him. "Sit down, and tell me what happened. From the very beginning."

"It's a long story."

"Don't you think I deserve to hear it?"

He hesitated, then came to sit beside her on the white, wave-smoothed old log. For a long moment, he simply stared out at the reef, where the surf broke in a savage, noisy barrage of upflung spray and swirling foam. Then he said, his voice hushed, hoarse, "We were two days out of Tahiti when a storm blew up, fast." He paused, and India knew from the faraway look that crept into his eyes that he was hearing, again, the relentless shrieking of the wind, the thundering roar of foam-flecked, storm-blackened waves that could crush even a mighty ship of the line into kindling. "I'd been in the navy since I was thirteen, but I'd never seen anything like that typhoon. For a good thirty-six hours, it was all we could do to keep from disappearing into a cross sea. We had no idea where we were."

Leaning forward, he rested his elbows on his knees, his clasped hands dangling loosely between them. "It was on the morning of the second day when the wind brought down the foremast and swept one of the men overboard, an old seaman by the name of Toby Jenkins. He was still alive, caught up in the rigging we were trailing, but with the seas the way they were, Captain Gladstone decided it was too dangerous to ask the men to try to haul him in."

India felt a wry, sad smile tug at her lips. "So Jack Ryder volunteered to do it."

He nodded, an echo of her own smile lightening his face, only to fade again. "He almost had the man pulled in when the ship swung around in the wind and a wall of water swept over the deck. What was left of the rigging tore free, and took Jack with it." Granger stared out over the distant sea, peaceful now in the rapidly gathering twilight. "We tacked back and forth for hours, trying to find them, but . . ." He shook his head. "It was useless. No one looking at that sea would ever imagine they could have survived."

"So how did they?"

He shrugged. "The rigging would have kept them afloat for a while. But even then, they wouldn't have lasted long. It was just sheer luck that at the time they were lost overboard, the *Lady Juliana* was only a few hundred yards off an island. We simply didn't know it."

"The island was Rakaia?"

Granger nodded. "It wasn't until almost two years

later that we started hearing rumors about a couple of Europeans who'd been lost off their ship in a storm and were living with the natives on one of the islands. Even then, it took another couple of months to find the right island."

India kept her gaze on the *Sea Hawk*, rocking back and forth in the gentle, blue-green waters of the lagoon. A light had appeared on the foredeck, a lantern that shone across the gathering gloom. Patu would come ashore after dark, Amok had told her; India had only to wait here, and he would meet her.

"When the *Lady Juliana* sailed into the lagoon," Granger was saying, "Jack came paddling out to meet us in one of those native outrigger canoes. At first, I didn't even recognize him. He'd always preferred going barefoot to wearing shoes, and he'd just as soon do without a shirt most of the time, as well. But after two years on Rakaia . . . Well, he looked like a Polynesian. A blue-eyed Polynesian with an Aussie accent."

"He told me he had married one of the native women," India said, her tone carefully kept emotionless, impersonal. "Had a child by her."

Simon Granger nodded. "He was glad enough to see us, but he really didn't want to leave. Not permanently. He was talking about getting out of the navy. Coming back to Rakaia to live."

"He loved her," India said softly, a strange pain squeezing her chest. "He loved her, and because he'd come to the island, because he brought the Royal Navy to rescue him, she died."

Simon Granger stared out over the distant sea, blue-black now in the starlit twilight. There was something strangely revealing about the tense, still way he held himself, and suddenly, India knew. "You were one of the thirty men who opened fire on that village," she said. "Weren't you?"

His jaw tightened. "The islanders had killed three British seamen. Captain Gladstone felt they needed to be taught a lesson."

"A lesson? Is that what you call it?"

"That's what the Admiralty called it."

India kept her gaze on the man beside her. "But how could you? How could you do such a thing? Innocent men, women, children . . ."

"It was an order."

"An order to commit a massacre," India said with feeling.

"Yes." His voice was hushed, torn. "Yes, it was." He sat silent for a moment, staring off into the starlit darkness. "You can't imagine what it was like," he said at last. "The sun was just coming up, spilling a golden light across the water when we were rowed ashore and ordered to form a line across the front of the village. I remember watching the morning breeze ruffle the fronds of the palm trees along the sand, and thinking how beautiful, how idyllic and peaceful it all looked. Like paradise." Simon Granger blew out his breath in a long, painful sigh, and dropped his gaze to his clenched hands. "Then the shooting started.

"The native huts, they were never made to stop a bullet. Some of the islanders were killed even before they made it to their doors. But Jack's wife . . . she came out running. I think she must have been trying to make it to the shelter of the trees, but she was heavy with child and she had the little girl in her arms, too." Granger paused, his voice becoming hushed, torn. "She must have been hit four, maybe five times."

"And Jack Ryder?" India asked quietly. "Where was he?"

"Captain Gladstone had sent him ashore with a detail of men, to gather fruit for the ship. He wanted Jack well out of the way before the shooting started, but they hadn't moved that far from the village."

"Did he see it? Did Jack see what happened?"

Granger's chest jerked with a deep, quick breath. "He ran straight into the line of fire. It's a wonder he wasn't killed himself before the seamen realized what was happening and stopped shooting. He probably saved the lives of half the natives by dashing into the village like that. But by the time he got to his wife, she was already dead. The little girl was screaming. When I saw Jack lift her up, covered in blood, I thought she'd been hit, too." The Englishman's face convulsed with a spasm of emotion, quickly suppressed. "But it was the mother's blood."

"I don't know how he bore it," India whispered.

Simon Granger shook his head. "He didn't. He went berserk. He must have wounded half a dozen seamen before they were able to wrestle him down, and even after we had him in irons and were dragging him back on board, he kept thrashing about, swearing he was going to kill Gladstone and every man on the ship."

"He was out of his mind with grief. You can't assume from what he said in such a moment that he then deliberately sank the ship."

"It's not an assumption." In the bleak moonlight, his face looked stark, cold. "We were supposed to set sail that morning, but the seas were running rough, too rough to navigate the passage through the reef by sight, the way we'd done coming in. Gladstone was planning to follow the charts, but Jack, he suddenly stops raving and says the charts are wrong, that if we try to follow them, we'll end up on the reef."

"And the captain believed him?"

"Not at first. But in the end, Jack somehow convinced him. Gladstone ordered the helmsman to steer by Jack's reckoning." He swallowed, the muscles in his throat working painfully. "The *Lady Juliana* ran right up on the reef."

India was silent for a moment. "You said half the ship's company died. Why? Were the seas so rough?"

He shook his head. "The first lifeboat cleared the reef without much trouble. But by the time the second boat was filled, the natives had realized what was happening and launched their war canoes.

"We tried to put back, to come to their aid, but the seas were running against us. All we could do was watch." He swung his head to meet her gaze. "They killed them all, Miss McKnight. The captain, and the rest of the ship's men. The only survivors besides those of us lucky enough to have made it into the first boat were Jack Ryder and Toby Jenkins. The islanders spared them."

India stood abruptly, her tented hands coming up to cover her nose and mouth, her boots sinking into the sand as she took a hasty step away from him. "If you told me Jack Ryder had killed a dozen seamen in a grief-stricken rage, then I might believe you. But to deliberately, diabolically plot to sink a ship? No. That's not Jack."

Simon Granger sighed. "He says Gladstone changed his mind. That the helmsman steered by the charts, and that's why the *Lady Juliana* hit the reef. But there's no way to prove it."

India swung to face him again, her hands falling to her sides. "There must be. Has anyone ever been back to Rakaia?"

He nodded grimly. "The *Barracuda* put in there just a few months ago. What's left of the *Lady Juliana* is still caught on the reef. If we had the ship's log and charts, the question would be answered in an instant. But as it is . . ."

India felt a hollow sense of dread, low in her stomach. "They were lost?"

"Everyone assumed they were. Captain Gladstone had them in the lifeboat that was attacked by the natives. But according to Jack, Toby Jenkins found them, and kept them."

"So where is Toby Jenkins now?"

"He was on Rakaia."

"Was? He's not anymore?"

Simon Granger shook his head. "The island is deserted. Completely deserted."

India stared at him in frustrated, frightened bewilderment. "How can that be?"

"I've seen it happen before. Sometimes it's typhoid, or influenza. But it doesn't need to be that serious. Something as simple as the measles or even a cold can wipe out the entire native population of an island in a matter of weeks."

"But—" India broke off as a new thought struck her, a thought that took her breath and brought a sick wrench of compassion and sorrow to her stomach. "Jack's little girl—the one his wife died trying to protect—he left her with his wife's family. On Rakaia."

"He told me."

The wind kicked up stronger, swelling the waves and setting the dark fronds of the coconut palms to dancing back and forth above them. India came to sink back down on the log, her gaze caught by the squalid outline of Johnny Amok's storeroom, all but lost now in the thick, hot night. She thought about the man who lay there, alone in the darkness, and her heart ached for him. "Does he know?" she asked at last. "Does Jack Ryder know about the epidemic on Rakaia?"

"He does now." The English captain's face was tight, shuttered.

Dear God, thought India. *Dear God.*

Granger glanced toward the beach, where the lazy surf of the lagoon whispered gently in and out over sand bathed in white moonlight. The jolly boat had long since returned for him, its seamen lounging at ease, only the occasional restless clunking of an oar against the boat's wooden sides ringing out in the warm tropical evening. "He asked me to take him there, to Rakaia. Before we sail for London."

India swung to fix a steady stare on the man who sat beside her. "Will you?"

"What would be the point?"

"But if the charts and logs are there—"

Granger shook his head. "If they ever were on that island, they obviously aren't there anymore."

"If? You don't believe him?"

A wry smile tightened the captain's lips. "There are some people in this world who simply don't believe in playing by the rules, and Jack's one of them."

"You think he's trying to trick you?"

"I think Jack would do anything, say anything to keep from hanging—and to get back to that island and see what happened to his little girl."

"Don't you think he should be allowed to find out for certain? Before you carry him off to London?"

"I have my orders, Miss McKnight. And they don't call for using a royal corvette to escort a Colonial renegade halfway across the South Pacific in a quest to discover the whereabouts of his abandoned half-native offspring."

"But the *Lady Juliana*'s charts—"

Simon Granger stood abruptly. "Were lost ten years ago."

"You don't know that," India said, almost pleading with him. "A man's life is at stake."

Granger glanced back at his ship, his voice crisp, hard. "I have my orders."

"Yes, of course," India said. "Your orders."

He left soon after that, standing stiff and upright in the prow of the jolly boat as the seamen from the *Barracuda* leaned into their oars and the dark water curled away from the boat's sides in twin phosphorescent waves that washed out in an ever-widening V across the smooth surface of the lagoon. But India stayed where she was, her head falling back as she stared up at the waving fronds of the coconut palms silhouetted black against the purple, starlit sky. The night was full of the sounds of the sea and the scents of strange flowers and a throbbing, aching kind of sadness that seemed to emanate from the island itself.

After a time, she heard again the splash of oars and looked out over the lagoon to see a small dinghy pulling away from the darkened hull of the *Sea Hawk*. She stood then, and walked down to the beach, her boots sinking into the soft sand until she reached the wave-darkened, hardened verge where the lagoon lapped against the shore and Patu ran his boat up beside her.

~~Chapter Twenty-three

H E HEARD THE whispers first.

Jack was lying on his back, blood trickling down from a cut on his cheek to seep into the mattress below, when he heard a low-voiced murmur. He tensed, wondering how many more nocturnal visits he was going to have to endure. Then he heard India's hushed but unmistakable Scots accent, coming up the path toward the storeroom, and relief mingled with confusion and a surge of powerful, contradictory emotions he didn't want and couldn't even afford to contemplate.

Lifting his head, Jack squinted toward the door. He thought about trying to stand up, because he really didn't want her finding him like this. But it all seemed more trouble than it was worth, and so he simply lay there in the close darkness and listened to Johnny Amok's key grate in the rusty old lock.

The door swung inward, admitting a flood of moonlight that fell on his face. "Oh my goodness," exclaimed

India. She paused for a moment, her statuesque shape silhouetted against the moonlight in a way he would have appreciated if his ribs hadn't been aching like a sonofabitch. Then she came across the dusty flag floor in a rush and fell to her knees beside his filthy mattress, her hands hovering over him, but not quite touching him. "What happened? Who did this?"

He gave her a crooked smile that pulled painfully at his cut lip. "Did what?"

It was Johnny Amok who answered her. "The commissioner paid him a visit. Along with three of his gendarmes." Two to hold Jack up, his arms tied behind his back, and one to hit him. Again. And again.

She twisted around to stare at the trader. "And you let him?" Her voice quavered with a sense of outrage and betrayal, as if Amok could somehow have stopped the French commissioner from beating up one of his prisoners. "You let them do this?"

"It's not as bad as it looks," Jack said, struggling to sit up, although actually, the reverse was true: the damage to his face had been peripheral, almost accidental. With the British navy taking him in the morning, Poirot hadn't wanted to mark Jack up too badly. The French were very good at making a man hurt in ways that wouldn't necessarily show.

She touched her fingertips to his cheek, but jerked her hand back when he winced. "Can you walk?"

Instead of answering, he looked from her to Amok, and back. "What are you doing here? What time is it?"

"Just after midnight."

Through the open door, Jack saw only dark shadows and a distant moonlit sliver of the sea. He was aware, suddenly, of the hush of the settlement around them, a stillness that spoke of closed doors and deep sleep, and he realized he must have passed out after Poirot and his boys had finished with him. "Where's the guard?"

The lenses of Amok's glasses flashed in the night as he went to sit on an upturned barrel near the far wall. "One of the village women is—" He glanced at India, and seemed to reconsider what he'd been about to say. "—entertaining him."

"She'll tell on you."

"No, she won't. I've promised her two new Mother Hubbards, a silk shawl, and a case of corned beef every year, for as long as she keeps her mouth shut."

Jack grunted. "That will cost you plenty."

Amok smiled softly into the night. "I reckon you're good for it, mate."

Jack laughed, then regretted it when a red-hot pain curled around his side to take his breath away.

"Can you walk?" India asked again.

"Walk, yes." By gritting his teeth, Jack managed to struggle to his feet. "But run . . . I don't think so."

India stood beside him. "You only need to make it as far as the lagoon. Patu says there's another passage through the reef, on the northeast end of the island. He's arranged for you to borrow one of the natives' outriggers. The owner is a man named Savo, and he's on the *Sea*

Hawk right now. He'll help Patu navigate through the main channel out of the bay, then paddle himself back to shore when we meet you outside the windward passage on the far side of the island."

Jack stared at her. "The *windward* passage?"

"Yes. Patu says it will be difficult, but he's confident in your ability to navigate it."

Something about the way her gaze skittered away provoked Jack into asking, "What else did Patu say?"

Her brows drew together in a worried frown as she brought her gaze back to his. "He said that given a choice between drowning and hanging, he thought you'd prefer to drown."

"Well, he's right about that."

She touched her hand, gently, to his cheek, and he knew, from the sorrow in her face, what she was going to say before she said it. "Captain Granger told me about . . . about Rakaia. I am so sorry."

Jack looked away from her, out the open door, to the moonwashed sea. "My daughter's not dead." He said it fiercely, firmly, because it must be so. Surely he would have known it if it wasn't so? Surely he would have *felt* it, deep down in the soul of him? For ten long years he had gone through the motions of his life, laughing, drinking, sailing into the sun with a sea breeze fresh in his face. Ten long years of living. Yet always, always, a part of him had belonged to that little blue-eyed, dark-haired girl who was a mingling of him and the woman he had loved and lost.

Sometimes, when the trades were blowing wild and free from out of the east, he would stare off across the ocean and try to imagine what she looked like, what she was doing at that moment. Ulani laughing in the sun. Ulani, her lashes long and dark against her cheeks as she drifted off to sleep. He had to keep reminding himself that as the years passed for him, they were passing for her, too. And so he would be careful to try to picture what she must look like. Ulani at four. Ulani at eight. Ulani, now almost twelve. And it would scare him, and sadden him, to realize that she would soon be a woman grown. All those growing-up years, lived without him.

But always, always, the certainty that she was alive glowed warm and true within him. And so he said it again. "I know she's not dead."

India nodded, although whether in agreement, or simply in sympathy, he couldn't have said. He took an awkward step toward the door, but had to stop and suck in his breath when the movement jarred his sore ribs and set his insides on fire. Her arm came around his waist, catching his weight as he wavered, his vision blurring, the storeroom whirling giddily around him.

"You *are* hurt."

He didn't want to lean on her, but he was afraid that if he didn't, he might topple over backward. "Why are you doing this?" he finally managed to say, his hand gripping her shoulder as he twisted his head to meet her gaze.

She was so tall, her eyes were nearly level with his, which he figured was probably a good thing, seeing as how his weight would have crushed a smaller woman. "Because it's the right thing to do," she said simply, her gaze holding his steadily.

He shook his head. "I can't ask this of you. I can't run away and leave you and Amok to face the British and the French in my place."

"No worries, mate," said Amok, settling more comfortably on his barrel. "I'm the victim here. First I'm assaulted in my bed and threatened with all sorts of bodily mayhem if I don't hand over the storeroom key to your friends, and then what do the ruffians do but lock me in my own storeroom." He shook his head sadly. "It's shocking, the breakdown of law and order in the islands these days."

Jack smiled at his old friend. "Huh. So what's your excuse going to be for not having set up a shout once these 'ruffians' had gone?"

His glasses winking in the moonlight, Amok extracted a small porcelain bottle from his sleeve, and held it up. "Given a choice between getting a bloody bump on the head and surrendering to the sweetly scented dreams of opium, what alternative did I have?" Unstopping the bottle, he tilted back his head to down the contents, then looked at them and grinned. "Don't forget to lock the door on your way out."

Jack shifted his gaze to the tall, determined woman beside him. "He might get away with it, but you won't. They'll know you helped me."

Urging him none too gently out the door, she turned

the key behind them, then swung to fix him with a steady stare. "Why is it that you credit me with absolutely no intelligence, simply because I'm a woman?"

Jack felt the earth shifting dangerously beneath his feet, and it had nothing to do with his concussed head or cracked ribs. "What the hell kind of question is that?"

"Shhh," she hissed, her arm tightening around his waist as she steered their steps down the shadowy path to the lagoon. "Keep your voice down. We've planted evidence to suggest that you took to the jungles again, and the men Captain Granger has watching the *Sea Hawk* will be able to report that Patu and I sailed alone. No one will suspect me."

"Simon Granger is letting the *Sea Hawk* go?"

"The navy has nothing against Patu. He told Captain Granger the *Sea Hawk* is partially his."

The path they followed ran through the line of pandanus and coconut palms that edged the lagoon, heading out toward the northeastern end of the village. Away down the beach, he could see the shadowy silhouette of an outrigger canoe, drawn up on the sand just beyond the water's reach. Jack frowned into the moonlit darkness. "Then who the hell is supposed to have helped me escape?"

"Your business partners," she said, her head half turned away from him, her eyes narrowing as she squinted at the long stretch of white sand bathed in moonlight and washed by the gentle swish of the dark, foam-flecked surf.

"My business partners?" They left the shadowy shelter of the trees, and Jack stumbled in the soft sand and would have fallen if her arm hadn't still been around his waist. The resulting jerk seared his insides with white hot pain and took his breath, so that he was still gasping when he said, "What business partners?"

She swung her head to meet his gaze. The moonlight fell full on her face, illuminating the smooth planes of her cheeks and showing him her smile. The smile he liked. The one that caught at his gut and squeezed his heart and threatened to steal his soul.

"Why, the cannibals, of course," she said, the smile widening into something at once naughty and delicious. "Who else?"

As they neared the canoe, a shadow separated from the dark line of the outrigger and stepped forward.

"Holy moly," said Patu, the whites of his eyes shining wide in the moonlight as he stared at Jack. "What did they do to you?"

"I'm fine," said Jack.

Detaching himself from India's side, he went to brace his arms against the outrigger and, leaning over, proceeded to be violently, noisily sick. "Oh, Jesus," he groaned, hanging on tight to the poles, his forehead pressed against the smooth wood. It felt as if he'd vomited up his ribs, and that they'd torn apart his insides on the way. For one hideous moment, his sight dimmed, and all he could hear was the sucking, hollow rhythm of the sea. Then, from an unfathomable distance, came the sound of India's voice.

"This afternoon, I thought he had a concussion," she was saying, her Scot's accent curt and crisp with censor, as if his broken head was all his own bloody fault or something. "Now I think he's added a couple of cracked ribs."

There was a long pause, then he heard Patu expel his breath in one of his hard, worried sighs. "That windward passage," he said, "it makes the channel through the reef at Futapu Bay look like nothing. The cross tides are deadly. If he gets sick or passes out at the wrong moment . . ."

Patu's voice trailed off, but his words seemed to hang in the air, the implications of what hadn't been said weighing down on them. "Then I'll have to go with him," India said calmly.

Swallowing the rebellious heavings of his stomach, Jack roared, *"Are you out of your bloody mind?"* and swung around so fast the stars and the moonlit swells of the sea and the shadowy waving fronds of the line of palm trees blurred into one spinning mass that spiraled down to a pinprick of light, and went out.

When he finally came to, he and Patu both argued with her. But in the end they had to acknowledge that India was right.

He would make it no other way.

~~Chapter Twenty-four

THEY MADE GOOD time at first, running up the shallow, reef-sheltered lagoon on the port tack. The outrigger had no jib sail, only a sprit main, so that while India knelt awkwardly at the front of the narrow dugout, her hands clutching the thong-laced, hand-hewn planks that had been used to build up the gunwales, Ryder perched like a native with only his left knee in the canoe itself, his bare right foot stuck out to grip the left rail while he trailed the paddle behind to starboard as a kind of primitive rudder.

But then, long before dawn, the light wind died, leaving the night calm and turning the lagoon into a shimmering black mirror that reflected the stars overhead in a myriad of jewellike flashes. Only the ceaseless crash of the surf against the offshore barrier reef broke the silence, and, nearer, the splash of Jack Ryder's paddle joined with the soft ripple of twin waves curling away from the outrigger's prow as it cut through the water.

Turning her head, India watched the shore slide slowly past, white sand gleaming in the moonlight, the feathery, exotic silhouettes of coconut palms and pandanus trees rising dark and still behind. And she thought, How strange it all is, and how beautiful, and she was seized with a profound awareness of how ominously fateful this night had become.

There could be no going back from this moment. She'd known that when she'd made the decision to accompany Jack on his desperate bid for freedom. The seamen Simon Granger had left aboard the *Sea Hawk* would know Patu had sailed without her, which meant that when Jack Ryder was found missing in the morning, they would know she'd been responsible for his escape.

"Regrets?"

India shifted her gaze to where Jack now knelt, the paddle in his hands flashing back and forth with all the skill and thoughtless ease of a native islander. "No."

"You haven't seen the passage yet."

She shook her head. "I'm not afraid to die."

A strange smile curved the ends of his lips and brought a hint of a dimple to one cheek. "Why not?"

"We all die."

"Some sooner than others."

She nodded toward the glorious firmament overhead. "And how much difference do you think thirty or even fifty years make, when measured against eternity?"

"It makes a difference to you."

"I'll be dead."

The dimple deepened, then disappeared. "Would no one mourn your death?"

"I suppose my publisher might regret the demise of my books."

He gave a short laugh, and for one telling instant, the smooth, flawless rhythm of his paddling broke. It resumed almost immediately, but not before she'd seen the way he clenched his jaw, his breath hitching as if in pain.

"Your ribs are hurting you," she said, reaching for the paddle. "I wish you would let me do that. It's why I'm here."

Her hand closed over one of his where it gripped the smooth wood, and he stopped paddling, the outrigger canoe gliding lazily through the calm, dark water. His gaze met hers, and something arced between them, something that made her exquisitely aware of the male power of the hand beneath hers, and the gentle kiss of the moonlight, and the stillness of the warm tropical night around them.

"I'm fine," he said, his voice husky. "You're only here in case I pass out, remember?"

"Precisely. And don't you think I should learn how to do this before I'm faced with the prospect of having to maneuver through the passage with you out cold?"

His eyes held hers a moment longer, then he eased his hand from beneath hers. "All right. But you're going to need to turn around—preferably without capsizing us," he added when the canoe rocked dangerously as she moved to position herself about a foot in front of him, her back to his chest.

"You need to get closer than that," he said.

She scooted backward, and heard the amusement in his voice when he said, "Closer."

She threw him a glance over her shoulder. "If I move any closer, I'll be almost on top of you."

She saw his teeth flash in the moonlight. "Don't worry. I know from experience that it's not a good idea to make love to a woman in an outrigger canoe."

She inched backward until she felt the warm, hard length of his thighs bracketing hers. "And I'm supposed to be reassured by that statement, am I?"

He gave a soft laugh. "Just take the paddle. No, not like that," he said, when she whacked him in the elbow. "Here. Like this."

She felt his arms come around hers, his cheek pressing against her hair as his hands closed over hers, guiding them into position on the smooth shaft of wood. She felt the calloused strength of his hands covering hers, and the hardness of his chest pressed against her back, and knew the power of a response within her that was no less compelling for being animalistic and primitive and unwanted.

"Loosen up," he said as she continued to move the paddle from one side of the canoe to the other in awkward, labored jerks. "Just let your body move with mine."

She tried. She really tried to imitate the graceful shifts of his body, but it didn't work.

"You're fighting it," he said, "making it harder than it should be. Let your body find its natural rhythm. Feel it.

Then surrender to it." He breathed, and his warm breath tickled a stray curl that lay against her cheek. "That's it," he coaxed as her body began to glide sinuously with his. "Feel the rhythm. Feel it."

Once she let herself go, India discovered it was all too easy to do, to relax against him, to let his body guide hers into a primitive cadence of thrust and pull, thrust and pull, that seemed to call to the building need within her. For one moment out of time, she lost herself in the magical glow of the moon and the whisper of the waves and the intoxicating sweetness of being cradled in the arms of this man, with the tropical night warm around them.

Then he said, "If we come through this alive . . ."

India let her head fall back to touch his shoulder, her eyes squeezing shut against an unexpected upsurge of emotion. "No." She shook her head. "Don't say it."

It was all still there—the pearling of the waves, and the sweet spicy scent drifting from the palm-fringed shore of the rugged island gliding past beside them. But the moment was no longer one out of time. She was suddenly, gut-wrenchingly aware that this man—this man whose kisses set her on fire, whose body moved now in such intimate, perfect rhythm with hers—was a hunted fugitive, and that they might both die tonight, trying to fight their way through the treacherous windward passage ahead of them.

"All right," he said. "I won't say it." She turned her head against his shoulder to meet his gaze. In the silvery light of the moon, her eyes found his, and she saw there the need, and the want. "But that doesn't mean you're not going to have to decide what your answer will be, when the time comes."

The sun rose as quickly as it had set, splashing the world with a fiery, richly saturated red glow that gave way all too soon to a clear, brilliant light.

Squinting against the glare off the glasslike lagoon, Jack Ryder stared up at the limp sail, and swore. "At this rate, the tide will have turned before we get there."

India studied his tightly set face. She had insisted, at one point, on paddling by herself for a while, but they made so little headway that he'd soon taken over from her again. Now the rising sun showed her all too clearly the twin grooves dug between his brows by pain, and the unhealthy pale tinge that had crept into his face. She wanted to tell him that he needed to rest, that he'd been badly hurt. But his life depended upon their reaching the northeast passage in good time, and so, to a certain extent, did hers.

"How bad will that be?" she asked. "If the tide has turned?"

"With the incoming tide meeting the strong current pouring out through that narrow channel?" A cold smile curled his lips. "Bad."

India shifted her gaze to the line of breakers thundering against the string of low islets and half-submerged coral shelves that formed the surf-battered barrier some quarter of a mile or so offshore. "Does he know about the northeast passage through the reef? Simon Granger, I mean."

Jack grunted. "No one in their right mind would try to make it through that passage at this time of year. Besides, even without steam up, the *Barracuda* is a hell of a lot faster than the *Sea Hawk*. He'll think all he needs to do is sail straight for Rakaia, and wait for me there."

It was a possibility that had been secretly troubling India all night, but she was surprised to hear him give voice to it with such careless unconcern. "Then we can't go there," she said, leaning forward earnestly.

"We're not. We're going to Waigeu."

They swung around a wide rocky headland, and a faint whisper of a breeze ruffled across the still, shallow waters of the lagoon. India looked up, the sail stirring as the first breath of the trade winds touched the limp canvas. "Waigeu?"

Suddenly, the wind snatched at the sail, and Jack moved quickly to shift his weight to the port rail. "It's an island between Rakaia and Tahiti. There's a priest there, a Father Paul." He wrapped his free hand around the pole. "Or at least I hope he's still there. He counts something like a dozen islands and atolls as part of his parish. Rakaia is one of them."

"I don't understand."

He glanced down at her, the sun gleaming on his sweat-sheened, sun-bronzed skin, the wind catching at his ragged, open shirt and billowing it out behind him. "According to Simon Granger, Rakaia is deserted. Which means that either the entire population was wiped out in the epidemic, or else those who survived have fled elsewhere."

"You think this Father Paul will know if Toby Jenkins is still alive, and where he might have gone?"

"Toby, and Ulani."

"Ulani is your daughter?"

She saw the answer in his face, and the naked pain it revealed was so profound that she had to turn her gaze away, to the turquoise-tinged water sliding past beneath them. The lagoon was transparent enough that she could see, quite clearly, the white sandy bottom, nearly covered by bulbous sponges and feathery groves of pink and blue and yellow coral. Here and there, bright flashes of color reflected the light, schools of brilliantly green trumpet fish and tiny jewelfish, and one fat white spotted puffer who swam lazily by.

She became aware of a new sound building, mingling with the snap of the small sail and the gentle rippling of water around the outrigger and the crash of the surf against the reef. "What's that noise?" she asked, looking up.

He nodded beyond her, to where a turmoil of dark water snaked its way out to the open sea. "The passage," he said, his voice grim. "What you hear is the tide, rushing in through the channel. It's after six."

"We can't make it through that," India said, her throat tight as she twisted around to stare at the narrow, churning pass through the ominously dark, semisubmerged bulk of the coral reef. "We'll have to wait until the tide shifts again."

His chest lifted with a huff of what might have been laughter as he looked out at the open, purple-blue sea beyond the reef.

"What is it?" she asked, peering desperately into the misty distance. "What do you see?"

"Sails," he said after a moment, a strange curve of amusement pulling at his lips. "Coming around the headland from La Rochelle."

"The *Sea Hawk*?" India asked, although even as she said it, she caught sight of the sleek little yacht already riding at anchor, just outside the passage. "Oh, God," she whispered, her stomach hollowing out with fear. "Tell me it's not the *Barracuda*."

He swung his head to meet her gaze, and gave her such a rakish, devil-damn-the-world smile that her breath caught in her throat, and a painful and totally unwanted realization clutched at her heart, taking her by surprise and bringing a sting of tears to her eyes. "It's the *Barracuda*."

≈≈Chapter Twenty-five

JACK STARED AT the wind-whipped surf breaking hard against the coral rocks on either side of the dark, roiling waters of the passage, and swore softly beneath his breath.

Patu had been right: given a choice between a relatively quick, watery death, here, with the tropical sun warm and golden above him, versus the kind of ugly, humiliating end the Admiralty had planned for him, Jack had nothing to lose. But he wasn't about to risk India's life by trying to make it through that channel against the tide.

He shifted his weight to bring the canoe's prow about, and heard her cry out. "What are you doing?"

"Heading toward the beach."

"Don't." The outrigger rocked as she leaned forward to close her strong hand over his, stopping him. "I'm here to help you escape, not to be responsible for your recapture."

He met her gaze squarely. "I could lose myself in the jungle. Wait until—"

"No." She shook her head, her hand tightening around his. "You're hurt. How far do you think you'd get?"

Not far, Jack knew. The pain in his head seemed to reverberate through his body, tightening into a dizzy whiteness punctuated by bolts of red fire that speared his chest every time he breathed. And the problem was, this time it wouldn't only be Simon and his boys on Jack's trail. With Poirot's consent, the men from the *Barracuda* would be able to hire natives to track Jack. And if they caught Jack, they would also catch India. By helping him escape, she had put herself on the wrong side of the law, and they both knew it.

He hesitated. "Do you see those boilers?"

Her calm, determined gaze never wavered from his face. "Can we make it?"

Jack pursed his lips, his breath coming in a long, painfully drawn-out sigh as he stared at the churning passage, the wind-whipped waves leaping and crossing each other in an angry, racing swirl. "Maybe."

"Then I say we try."

He brought his gaze back to hers. Her eyes were deep and still in a pale, beautiful face, her dark, chestnut-shot hair blowing wild and free about her. Reaching out, he cupped the back of her head with his palm and drew her to him, his mouth taking hers in a hard, crushing kiss that was savage and life-affirming and over all too quickly.

"Hold on," he said as he let her go, and sent the outrigger racing toward the dark, torturous waters of the channel.

Lashed along by a strong beam wind, they flew across the water, Jack crouching forward so that he could use the paddle like a pry to throw the bow to one side or the other as dark, menacing heads of coral rushed at them.

It was a race against time—against the *Barracuda*, crowding all sail as she swung around the headland, against the growing strength of the tide, and against the sickening spiral of dizziness and pain that threatened to pull him down into unconsciousness. The sea was a thunderous roar, the high, wind-driven rollers breaking against the surrounding reefs in an endless cannonade that filled the air with spray and the pungent scent of brine. It seemed to Jack that the world had narrowed down until it consisted of nothing but a vivid, crazily tilting blue sky, and water: wind-flung spray, and boiling white foam, and swelling waves that set the canoe to pitching so heavily, the outrigger flew dripping through the air. Water washed over the hand-hewn gunwales, sloshed about their feet. India found a coconut shell in the bottom of the canoe and used it to bail frantically while Jack struggled to keep the wind and the treacherous waves from flinging them against the jagged coral rocks rising beside them.

"Where's the *Barracuda*?" he shouted, not daring to look up.

India's voice reached him over the roar of the waves and the flapping of the sail. "Coming fast."

The canoe crested a wave, then dipped down again with a jarring crash that stole Jack's breath in a flaming agony. Clenching his teeth against the pain, he shot a quick glance toward the open sea, and saw the corvette bearing down on them, her prow lifting high and proud as she cut through the rolling swells. "Shit," he whispered.

Patu had already raised anchor and was setting sail. As Jack watched, the neat little yacht's main sail billowed out white and full as the trades hit it, and the *Sea Hawk* swung away.

"He's *leaving*," India said in an anguished whisper. "Patu is leaving."

"No." Gasping for breath that seemed to keep eluding him, Jack leaned into the paddle and threw the canoe to starboard, then back to port as the channel snaked dangerously first one direction, then the other. "He'll veer around in an arc and come back to pick us up with his sails already set. It's the only chance we have of outrunning the *Barracuda*."

"And how much chance is that?"

Jack started to laugh, then swore instead. "*Bloody hell.*" White and sun-bleached, a clump of coral reared up from the boiling water, straight ahead. He threw all his weight into the paddle, but the churning tides seemed to hold the canoe fast in their grip, spinning it relentlessly toward the jagged, looming mass. Pain stole what was left of his breath, and his sight dimmed.

For one, frozen moment, the canoe surged ahead, caught fast by the current, out of control. Jack leaned into the paddle with what was left of his strength, and it still wasn't enough. He heard the roaring crash of the waves, felt the wild spray wet on his face. Every muscle in his body strained, screaming, desperate. Then, with an odd popping sound, the carved prow swung away. The trades eddied, gusted up again, catching the small sprit main and sending the canoe skimming out across the swelling, suddenly open water.

Jack looked back, saw the breaker-shattering reef behind them, saw the fringed palms of the distant beach rising up feathery and green against a tropical blue sky.

Then the island and the sky and the surf disappeared, and he sank into unconsciousness.

"Jack, *please*. Please wake up."

Jack heard India's tight, desperate voice, felt her fingers dig into his shoulder as she shook him, hard. He groaned, and tried to turn away.

"Jack." The hand left his shoulder, and he sighed. "*Wake up.*"

Wet and cold, water splashed into his face, dripped down onto the bare flesh of his chest. "Bloody hell," he roared, and sat up, shaking his head, droplets spraying everywhere. The blue horizon tilted crazily, then righted itself as his bleary gaze focused first on an unfamiliar Melanesian who crouched, silent and watchful, on the outrigger, then shifted to where India knelt at Jack's feet, a wet coconut shell clenched in her hands.

"Thank God," she said in a harsh whisper. Tossing the shell aside, she gripped his shoulders with urgent fingers. "The ladder. Hurry."

Jack glanced beyond her, to where the *Barracuda* bore down upon them, the wind catching the spray from the water curling away from her bow as she crested the waves. "Bloody hell," he said again, and scrambled for the rope ladder dangling from the *Sea Hawk*'s rail.

He'd made it about three-quarters of the way up the ladder when the world went into a spin and his stomach heaved. He stopped, the rope fibers digging into his clutching hands, his sweat-bathed body swaying in the wind as he hung, suspended, over the surging waves.

"It's about time." Patu's hand closed around Jack's upper arm and hauled him over the rail. "I was startin' to think Her Britannic Majesty's representatives were going to get here before you did."

Jack leaned back against the gunwale, his breath coming hard and fast as he fought down another wave of nausea.

India came up the ladder in a rush. "I thought you said Granger would head straight for Rakaia?"

"I was wrong." Swallowing hard, Jack pushed away from the rail and moved quickly to release the helm from Patu's lashing.

Patu worked at hauling in the ladder, his frowning gaze fixed on the crowding sails of the approaching ship.

"The *Sea Hawk* might be a fast little lady, but she's not going to outrun a royal corvette."

"No. But we can go places they can't."

India knew a niggling tremor of disquiet. "What places?"

"Run up the fisherman staysail," Jack told Patu as the *Sea Hawk*, answering to the helm, swung sharply to port. "It might boost our speed by a knot or so."

"What places?" India repeated.

Jack threw a quick glance back at the *Barracuda*. "The Gods' Pathway."

In the act of running up the staysail, Patu froze. "I think that flowerpot musta hit you harder than we figured."

India glanced at the boy, then brought her gaze back to Jack's face. "What is the Gods' Pathway?"

"That," said Patu, the canvas unfurling as he swiveled to point at the wave-lashed line of green and gold rushing toward them.

Stumbling with the pitch and fall of the deck, India went to wrap her hands around the rail and squint into the distance. "It's a reef. You're sailing right into a reef."

Jack kept a steadying hand on the helm. "It's a belt of reefs. Some with atolls, some just shelves of coral lying below the surface. It stretches for a good twenty-five miles or more. We lose ourselves in that, and the *Barracuda* will never be able to follow us."

"Huh," said Patu. "We slice our hull open on one of those submerged reefs, and the *Barracuda* won't need to catch us. We'll be shark food."

Jack realized India was no longer looking at the ominous outline of the Gods' Pathway. She was staring at a trio of sleek, triangular-shaped fins slicing with menacing silence through the waves off the starboard bow. "Those are porpoises, aren't they?" she said in a tight, controlled voice. "Please tell me those are porpoises."

Jack flashed her a wide smile, and swung the wheel sharply to port in a deft maneuver that sent the *Sea Hawk* slicing through a narrow passage and into the channel of turquoise water running between the line of reefs. "Those are sharks."

~~Chapter Twenty-six

FROM HIS POSITION at the prow of the HMS *Barracuda*, Alex Preston watched the trades catch the *Sea Hawk*'s sails and send the schooner-rigged yacht skimming across the waves. He had seen, through his glass, Ryder's skill as he maneuvered the native outrigger canoe through the treacherous southeast passage. Seen, too, the way Miss India McKnight had taken control of the primitive vessel after Ryder's collapse and brought them safely to rendezvous with that treacherous, lying little Polynesian, Patu.

"Why?" Alex asked, when Simon Granger came to stand at his side, the captain's attention, like Alex's, lifting to the string of palm- and shrub-covered atolls spreading out in a line, directly in their path. "Why would a gentlewoman such as India McKnight help a scoundrel like Ryder?"

The captain swung his head, his eyes crinkling with

quiet amusement as he threw Alex a quick, enigmatic glance. "One presumes she believes in his innocence."

"But how can she?"

Simon Granger raised the spyglass to his eye. "Did you see her? On the beach at La Rochelle?"

"Yes," said Alex slowly, not understanding where the captain was going.

"She didn't strike you as looking . . . different from the woman we first met at Rabaul?"

Alex let out a sharp laugh. "She'd just spent the better part of three days being dragged through the jungles of Takaku as a hostage. Of course she looked different."

"That's not what I—" Granger broke off, then swore long and crudely under his breath. "The sonofabitch. He's not bluffing. He's going to try to lose us in the Gods' Pathway."

Alex lurched forward to grab the rail. "But . . . he can't mean to sail into that! It's a ships' graveyard."

A peculiar smile tightened the ends of the captain's mouth. "No? Just watch him."

Side by side, the *Barracuda*'s first lieutenant and his captain stood at the prow and watched as the little yacht swung sharply between a palm-studded, sandy atoll and a long, surf-frothed reef. Alex kept waiting for Granger to give the order to break off the chase. Frigate birds wheeled overhead, calling, their great wings outstretched against the vivid blue of the sky; the trades blew warm and strong, kicking up little whitecaps on the swells and flapping the sails overhead. The atoll-studded reefs loomed before them, mysterious and beautiful and deadly.

The order to veer never came.

Finally, when he could control himself no longer, Alex said, "You can't mean to follow him in there, sir."

Granger kept the spyglass to his eye, his attention all for the *Sea Hawk*. "Why can't I?"

"Because this . . . this is a corvette!"

"I know that, Mr. Preston."

"But . . ." Alex's hands tightened around the rail before them until his knuckles turned white. "We could sail directly to Rakaia and await him there. We have no need to follow him through those reefs."

Simon Granger lowered the glass slowly, although he kept his gaze on the yacht ahead. "And if Ryder doesn't go to Rakaia?"

Alex felt a sick clenching, deep in his gut, because he knew what the Admiralty—and his own family—would say if the *Barracuda* broke off pursuit now, only to wait, futilely, ridiculously, off the sandy shores of Rakaia for a fugitive who never appeared. They would say that Granger had deliberately let his quarry get away. That the captain of the *Barracuda* had allowed his past friendship with Jack Ryder to interfere with the performance of his duty. And that Alex Preston had done nothing to stop him.

Swallowing heavily, Alex watched the surf curl and break over mile after mile of hidden reef. "And if we tear the bottom out of the ship? What will the Admiralty say then, sir?"

To Alex's shock, the captain laughed. "If we drown, we won't need to worry about the Admiralty, now will we? And if we're only damaged ... Well, then we'll patch her up well enough to limp back to La Rochelle for repairs. And then we'll go to Rakaia."

The *Sea Hawk* sailed up the narrows on a close haul. To windward lay a chain of sandy islets strewn across the turquoise sea like a line of giant rosary beads, while the submerged, milky-jade shadow of a reef lurked quiet and deadly off their starboard side.

"Holy moly," shouted Patu, his eyes widening as he turned from trimming the main. "They're coming in here after us."

"What the hell—" One hand tight on the wheel, Jack slewed around to see the *Barracuda* doubling one of the chain's small islands, her prow sending out a broad, foam-flecked wake as she cut through the waves. Her sails were reduced, but she was still flying more canvas than was prudent with so little sea room. "Sonofabitch."

She was a square-rigged, three-masted warship, the *Barracuda*. With her flush deck and single tier of guns, she was smaller than a frigate, but larger than a brig. She'd been outfitted with engines, but she didn't look to have any steam up. Coal was expensive and hard to get in the South Pacific; a captain could go months at a time without it—even a captain ordered by the Admiralty to apprehend a man held responsible for the death of the Prime Minister's cousin.

India came to stand at Jack's side, her dark hair flying about her head, her cheeks touched with a rosy glow by the salty morning breeze. He watched her eyes narrow in thought, her lips parting as she sucked in a quick, deep breath. "Simon Granger must want you very badly."

"His career depends on it."

She brought her gaze to his face, her features pinching with sudden concern. "You look terrible."

Jack huffed a low laugh, then regretted it when a fiery hot coil of pain whipped around his chest. At least his head was clear. For the moment.

"How long will it take them to come up with us?" she asked.

"If Simon has the balls to keep flying that kind of sail, not long." Jack glanced up at the telltales fluttering from the shrouds. "Ever done much sailing?"

"Some. Why?"

"Because the only way we're going to lose that corvette is by dodging in between these islands and reefs. And that's going to take more than just Patu handling the sheets."

Her gaze traveled over the rigging. "I believe I can do it," she said in that calm, no-nonsense way she had, and Jack felt a wry smile twist his lips.

The wind had blown a heavy lock of hair across her eyes, and he watched her bring up one hand to catch it. She tried to rake her hair back from her face, but it was in a hopeless tangle. Her finely tucked man's shirt was smudged with dirt and seawater, her split tartan skirt ripped, and stained with his own blood. She looked bedraggled and hard-used and, in that moment, utterly sexless. And yet he felt a swelling of emotion that left him feeling winded and awed.

He'd been aware, for some time, of the disconcerting drift in the nature of his feelings for this woman, as admiration and raw desire had begun to mingle, unexpectedly, disastrously, with his earlier exasperation and vexation. He'd known it, and yet he hadn't been prepared for *this*, this sudden, gut-clenching, heart-stopping realization that what had happened to him went beyond lust, beyond desire, beyond even liking, far beyond, into that mysterious, unfathomable realm of the eternal and the sublime.

He couldn't have said why this revelation had come upon him at this moment. He only knew that it filled him with a fierce determination to be done with this endless round of running and hiding, and a profound regret that he hadn't faced up to the charges against him long, long ago.

"They're gaining on us," said Patu, chewing the inside of his cheek.

"Ready to fall off?" Jack said, his gaze narrowing as he caught sight of a break in the long, foam-flecked reef.

India nodded.

He spun the wheel, and the *Sea Hawk* fell off hard to starboard, Patu and India scrambling to trim the sails to a close reach as the hull heeled to leeward. The little yacht leapt forward, her sails spilling the breeze astern.

They cut through a passage in the reef with such clear, crystal blue water that Jack could see his boat's shadow pass over the sand some five fathoms or more below. The air filled with the sounds of the ocean, the gurgling *swoosh* of the bow slicing through the waves, the tapping of the halyards against the masts. Then they were clear of the coral, an atoll rearing up ahead of them, its sun-soaked, sandy shores licked by a lazy surf, a scattering of coco palms waving in the freshening breeze. Jack swung the *Sea Hawk* back to port until they were on a close haul again, running up the lee side of the reef.

Only, by now the wind had shifted, swinging around so that it was coming almost straight out of the east and putting them closer to windward than he would have liked.

"If you're not careful," shouted Patu, "we're gonna be pinching."

Jack's head fell back, his eyes squinting against the sun as he watched the jib for the first signs of a luff. It wasn't going to be easy, short tacking in this narrow stretch of water to windward against a foul tide. And he was starting to get dizzy again, his hair damp with a strange cold sweat. If he weren't gripping the wheel so tightly, he thought he'd probably fall over.

"How well do you know this section of islands and reefs?" India asked, her breath coming hard and fast.

Jack flashed her a quick grin. "What makes you think

I know it?" He threw a glance over his shoulder and saw the *Barracuda*, her crew still scrambling to trim her sails as she swung around into the smooth, bubbled water of the *Sea Hawk*'s wake. "Aw, hell."

The corvette was close enough now that he could see the man who stood at the prow, a speaking trumpet in hand, his voice drifting across the wind-ruffled, vivid blue water. "Ahoy, *Sea Hawk*. Lower your sails and bring to instantly, or by God, I'll sink you."

Jack glanced at India, and it was as if the wind had died, and the earth stilled. "It's your call."

She brought her solemn gaze to his face. "Why mine?"

"Because you have no reason to risk dying."

Her eyes were wide. She was still breathing hard, but a quiet came over her, and she smiled. "Yes I do."

Reaching out, he took her face between his palms, his gaze caught fast with hers as he dipped his head and brushed her lips with a kiss. Then he swung back to the helm.

"Heading up!" he shouted, and veered hard to port.

They pivoted into the eye of the wind, their sails fluttering, the *Sea Hawk* briefly losing momentum as her bow swung through. Then her sails billowed out, and they began to pull away from the wind on a starboard tack through a break in the reef.

This passage through the reef was narrower, shallower. Through the gloriously clear waters Jack could see jagged heads of coral, every color from amethyst to cadmium yellow. Then the colors dimmed and began to blur together, and he had to grit his teeth against a dark wave of dizziness. He was beginning to realize this wasn't one of his ordinary headaches, that India was right, he *was* concussed.

He took in a deep breath that made his cracked ribs ache like the bejesus. Then they were through the passage, and bearing down fast on the long, gently curving string of sandy atolls. "Heading up," he shouted again, and the *Sea Hawk* swung sharply to starboard, heeling low as Jack fought to bring the prow around for a run along the inside of the channel.

But the wind was capricious, the scattering of islets redirecting the breeze so that it eddied and shifted. Suddenly, the freshening wind swung about again until it was coming out of the southeast, and Patu was jumping to let out sail as the wind came over their beam.

Too late, Jack saw the dark head of coral rearing up off their port bow. He spun the wheel, but the *Sea Hawk* was lurching out of control, her hull scraping briefly against the jagged rock with a jolting grind before swinging away into clear water.

Behind them, the *Barracuda* wasn't so lucky. Plowing through the break in the reef, she was caught by the veering wind, her sails filling to send her surging straight across the narrows, toward a coconut-studded strip of sun-sparkled sand. She tried to claw off, to turn to windward, but her bow was only beginning to respond sluggishly to her helm and she went end on for shore.

The corvette gave a violent lurch, her sails shuddering against the blue sky as a grinding screech rent the morning air. She came to an abrupt halt, spars shivering as she heeled sharply offward. They could see the men on her decks jumping to douse the sails and rush to the pumps.

Fighting now for breath, Jack eased the *Sea Hawk* to larboard, curving her around the island to head out into open waters. His eyes burned and his bones felt all loose and disjointed, so that it was only by a sheer, jaw-clenching act of determination that he kept himself standing at the wheel, his hands gripping the spokes tight. He told himself that if he could just make it clear of the Gods' Pathway before he passed out, India and Patu would be all right.

"Shouldn't we go back and help?" India said, her gaze caught fast by the stricken ship, her voice echoing strangely, as if it were floating to him from a long ways off.

Jack grunted. "They're grounded at low tide on a beautiful, sunny day a few hours' sail from Takaku. Even an incompetent idiot could get his men to safety in these seas. And Simon is no idiot."

He could see the open sea now, stretching out purple and wide before the yacht's prow. He let the breath ease out of him, felt the darkness stealing over him, taking him. "Can you handle the wheel?" he said.

India swung her head to look at him over her shoulder. "Can I *what*?"

"Can you take the wheel," Jack said. And then he

stumbled, the mastheads whirling against the blue sky, the deck rushing oddly up to meet him as the darkness slid over him.

This time, it would be days before he awoke.

He dreamt of craggy island peaks wrapped in misty moonlight, of feathery cocos silhouetted against a soft night sky, of snow-white shores and pale green waters filled with rainbow-hued coral and bright small fishes that glowed from within. The trades were warm against the sun-soaked naked flesh of his body, the air sweet with the scent of gardenia and orange blossom and sandalwood. He heard the crash of the breakers against the offshore reef, and the endless rustling of palm fronds mingling with the hiss of the tide washing in and out over the beach.

She was so tiny, the length of his arm only. She had her mother's heavy fall of midnight dark hair and sweetly curving lips, but her eyes were a startling northern blue, her soft, baby-scented skin a pale sun-kissed gold. He saw her, laughing as she clambered into her mother's lap. Saw her long, dusky lashes flutter, then close as she sighed into sleep. Saw Titana brush the hair from the child's forehead, and smile.

Titana. He sucked in a deep breath, and felt a rush of pain, hot, scalding. Moaning, he tried to turn, but his body was oddly unresponsive, the wall beside him hard and unyielding. A cool cloth touched his forehead and a woman murmured something soothing. But the crash of the breakers had turned into the roar of guns, and Titana was running, her eyes wild with terror, her thin arms clutching the squirming child close against her bulging belly. He saw her falter. He thought at first she stumbled, but then he saw her jerk, and jerk again as another bullet, then another slammed into her warm, life-giving body.

He was running. Always, in these dreams, he was running, screaming out an agony that produced no sound. He ran, but his arms and legs were heavy, his movements oddly slowed in time, while her body jerked again, then fell. Ulani screamed, struggling as her mother curled her dying body around the child in a last, desperate attempt to save her. He was shouting. *No. Don't shoot. You bastards, you bastards.* His frantic hands gripped the child. She was covered in blood, but the blood was her mother's, her cries of terror, not pain. He cradled the child and her mother in his arms, but Titana was already gone, her eyes staring and vacant, the child within her never to be born.

The rage that filled him was a black-red, violent thing, a tide of dark passion that flooded his being and subsumed his soul and left no room for mourning. That would come, but only later, when he could bear it, because he could not bear it, not now. And so he let the rage take him, let it pump through him, shuddering him, swirling him away on a surging lust to destroy, to kill, to create a semblance of justice in this world without justice, without reason, without God.

He threw back his head, his agony welling up hot and despairing in his throat. But when he drew breath to scream, all he knew was more pain, and then a deeper, smothering darkness.

~~Chapter Twenty-seven

O N THE EVENING of the third day, the fever broke, and his breathing subsided into the slow cadences of a deep but natural sleep.

Her hands cupping her elbows by her sides, India pressed her back against the steep wooden brace of the companionway, her gaze on his face, quiet now in a dreamless, restful slumber. In the past three days, she had come to understand well the haunted shadows she had previously only glimpsed behind his easygoing smile, the quick laughter and teasing banter. And she understood, too, why he avoided sleep when he could, for his dreams had filled these last days and nights. She had listened to his torn, anxious whispers, watched his features contort in an agony of grief and despair, and she had wondered at the resilience of this man who had suffered so much, and yet still retained the ability to know laughter and joy, to find beauty in the quiet splendor of a tropical sunrise, to touch a woman with tender want.

His face was quiet now in sleep, and she let her gaze rove his features, the straight dark brows, the flaring cheekbones and strong chin. It seemed strange to her that a face that had been unknown to her just a week before should now be so familiar, and so dear. She watched him sleep, and it seemed to India that her heart swelled painfully within her until she could feel each heavy beat shuddering her body, filling her with a pounding knowledge that took her breath and left her both wondrous and terrified.

How had she come to this? she wondered. How could what had begun as simple physical fascination and a primitive hunger have slipped, unawares, into this soul-deep, life-wrenching need? She had traveled the world, proud of her independence, relying only on herself, needing only herself. Never had she considered herself lonely, or felt her existence lacking in any way. She'd had some vague notion that if she should ever grow too old and infirm to travel, she would retire to a place near the sea, a simple cottage filled with mementos of her past travels, and her books, and perhaps a half-dozen or so stray cats. Odd that it had never occurred to her before, when she thought of her aged self, sipping tea beside a warm winter's fire, that she might look back on her solitary life and regret the decisions she had made.

From overhead came a now familiar rattling as Patu took down the foresail, flattened the main, and backed the jib for another night of heave-to. In a moment, his legs, then the rest of his small, lithe body appeared on the steps of the companionway as he peered anxiously into the lamplit gloom of the yacht's small cabin, which served as living and sleeping quarters for them all. "How is he?"

"Better, I think."

Patu shifted his gaze to her face. What he saw there seemed to worry him, for he pursed his lips in concern, and said, "Why don't you get some fresh air while I start supper?"

She nodded, her tired body clumsy as she climbed to the open deck. The sun was just setting, washing the sea with a dark pink. She could see the low shapes of distant islands, invisible with the haze of day but showing clearly now in that magical moment before darkness. She watched a frigate bird glide in to water level, felt the swells roll gently beneath the boat. She breathed in deep, smelled the tang of the sea heavy on the fresh, bracing air. Then the sky turned to silver, and the islands vanished.

Two days later, India was on deck, writing in her notebook, when some indefinable stirring of her senses made her look up to find Jack standing at the top of the companionway. He'd pulled on a pair of trousers, but his feet and chest were bare, the bruises on his ribs a yellowish purple splashed against the sun-browned smoothness of his skin. "You shouldn't be out of bed yet," she said.

"I thought the sun and fresh air might do me some good." A slow smile curled the edges of his lips. "Besides, I was starting to go stir-crazy down there."

He lurched slightly, and she went to slip her arm around his waist and help him sit. He propped his shoulders against the gunwale, his eyes closing as he turned his face to the sun with a sigh. He did look better, she decided, watching the breeze lift the tousled dark hair from his forehead. A faint flush left by the fever still rode high on his cheekbones, but the bruises on his face were fading faster than those on his body.

"How long will it take them to follow us, do you think?" she asked, for the question had been worrying her, all these days.

He opened his eyes, his neck arching as he stared up at the flapping main. They were running with the wind, the air full of the sound of snapping canvas and the whipping of the halliards and the steady rush through the rigging. In the last twenty-four hours they'd covered over 170 miles. But there had been days, just out of the Gods' Pathway, when the wind had all but died and they'd struggled to cover even a quarter of that. He shrugged. "Depends on how badly the *Barracuda* was damaged. A ship like that is designed for speed. Once they get under sail again, they'll be covering twice our distance in half the time."

"Then they could be waiting for us at Rakaia."

"Except that I'm not going to Rakaia. Remember?"

India stared out over the intensely blue, sun-sparkled waves. She wanted to ask him what he would do if Father Paul could tell him nothing of the people of Rakaia, but she couldn't bring herself to form the words, couldn't suggest to this man that both his daughter and the old sailor who held the key to his future might be dead. Instead, she said, "Who was it accused you of sinking the *Lady Juliana*? Was it Granger?"

Ryder shook his head. "When the ship hit the reef, Gladstone himself had me put in irons. He said he'd see me hang."

"But he knew the truth! He knew he'd followed the charts."

A hard smile tightened his lips. "You don't think he'd take the blame for it, do you?"

India opened her mouth to say something, then thought better of it and swallowed instead.

His smile widened into one of genuine amusement. "It's a good thing you don't play poker."

That startled her into a soft laugh. "Why?"

"Because everything you think shows on your face."

She lifted her chin, accepting the challenge. "All right, what am I thinking?"

"You're thinking that with the *Lady Juliana*'s charts and log, I could have proven my innocence anytime these past ten years, and you're wondering how to ask why I didn't, without making it sound as if you don't believe a word I've told you."

India stared at him.

Reaching out, he took her hand in his, and held it. "Not long after the massacre, a sloop carrying some rich Frenchman's son on a tour of the South Seas put in to Rakaia. They offered to take me with them, and I went. I figured the people of Rakaia didn't need any more trouble with the British because of me."

"Toby Jenkins didn't go with you?"

Jack shook his head. "He said Rakaia was as close to Paradise as he was ever likely to come, and he intended to enjoy it for as long as he could."

Beside them, a flying fish leapt from the blue waves, the sun flashing on its wet gray skin before it disappeared again beneath the water. Jack watched it for a moment, then said, "It wasn't until a few years ago that I heard from a couple of sandalwood traders that Toby had been trying to get a message through to me, that he'd found the *Lady Juliana*'s logbook and charts washed up on shore something like six months after I'd left."

They would have been put in a half cask to keep them safe from the water, India knew. She remembered reading once about how the logbook and charts of a West Indiaman, the *Felicity*, had been found almost a year after the doomed ship had gone down. "So why didn't you go back then?" she asked quietly.

He kept his gaze on the sea, although the flying fish was now long gone, leaving only the swelling of the deep blue waves and the sparkle of the sun and, in the distance, a haze of heat where water met sky. For a moment, she didn't think he was going to answer her. Then he said, his voice tight, flat, "A man gets used to running. Sometimes, it takes more courage to revisit the past than to just keep running."

It might have been part of the reason, but India knew

it was still only a part. He stared off across the trackless ocean, far to the east, beyond the sunrise. And India, watching him, found herself wondering if they would be going to look for Toby Jenkins now if the old sailor had still been on Rakaia.

But no sooner had this occurred to her than she knew the answer. Jack Ryder would never willingly return to Rakaia. Because Jack wasn't only running from the British navy; he was also running from that dark, beautiful island and all that had happened there so many years ago. He was running from himself.

With each passing day, Jack grew stronger and his body healed.

Yet there was a coiled tenseness about him, a restless wariness that had replaced the easygoing, ready humor of the man India had first come to know. He ate little and slept even less. Sometimes, in the long dark hours before dawn, she would awake to the creak of timbers and the soft murmurs of the sea, and glance over to find his bunk empty.

Once, late at night, after a heavy squall that had lasted for most of the afternoon and set the small yacht to pitching heavily in a high sea, India awoke to find the *Sea Hawk* riding serenely on a gentle swell. Patu's easy breathing whispered softly from out of the darkness, but she knew even without looking that Jack wasn't there.

Leaving her berth, she slipped into her clothes and moved quietly to climb the steep companionway to the deck above. The night was clear and still, the sky a velvety blue-black scattered with an unfathomable eternity of stars. It was a moment before she saw him, a still shadow standing with one hand resting thoughtfully on the helm.

"What's wrong?" she asked, for there was something about his posture that told her it was concern for the safety of the *Sea Hawk* that had driven him, this time, from his berth.

He shook his head, his fingers running over the smooth polished surface of the wood. "I'm not sure. There's just . . . something different about the way she's been handling lately. I felt it especially today, when the sea was running so heavy."

After they'd lured the *Barracuda* to grief in the Gods' Pathway at the cost of scraping their own side, Patu had put into a quiet cove and spent the better part of the afternoon diving beneath the gentle waves to inspect the *Sea Hawk*'s hull. "But Patu said she was all right. That she hadn't sustained any significant damage."

Jack shrugged. "Nothing he could see."

India stared out into the surrounding darkness. The universe always seemed so much more real at night, she thought. It was easy to forget during the day, when one looked out at swelling blue waves and scattered islets of waving palm trees, easy to forget the existence of everything that was hidden by golden sunlight and distance and the comforting blue arc of the sky. But at night . . . at night, the sun-sparkled waves and peaceful little islands all disappeared, and the surrounding sea turned into a swelling blackness that reflected only the heavens above and made her feel humble and insignificant. And she thought, if the *Sea Hawk* were simply to disappear beneath the waves, here, hundreds of miles from any known landfall, no one would ever know what had happened to it. No one would ever know what had happened to the three of them.

The thought made her shiver. "I'll be glad when we reach Waigeu," she said, and felt the comforting strength of his arm come around her.

"So will I," he said, amusement lightening his voice as he drew her closer to him. She felt the warmth of his breath against her cheek, the brush of his lips against her hair, and knew he was no longer referring to his concerns for the yacht.

It had been a magical time, these last weeks; a South Seas idyll of brilliant blue skies and endless dancing waves and sun-dazzled white sails snapping in the warm breeze. Of days spent running with the trades, and balmy, sweet-scented evenings when the three of them would gather around a flickering lantern to swap stories and play cards and laugh easily with the growing camaraderie of friends. But always—always, in this small boat, there had been the three of them. Never had she and Jack really been alone. Until now.

Raising one hand, she touched his beard-roughened cheek. Her breathing had quickened, growing shallow and ragged. She rubbed her thumb across his mouth, felt his lips so soft and warm. Felt his hand clench, once, in her hair.

Patu's voice, husky with sleep, drifted up from below. "Everything all right up there?"

"Everything's fine," called Jack, his chest jerking with silent laughter as he drew her close enough to plant a quick kiss on her nose. Then let her go.

~~Chapter Twenty-eight

TWO DAYS LATER, they were within several hours' sailing of Waigeu when the afternoon grew increasingly overcast, the sky lowering until it seemed to press down upon them, heavy and airless.

"Shit," said Jack in an undervoice when a huge flash of red lightning crackled across the ugly gray clouds.

India came to stand beside him, her gaze, like his, on the approaching squall. "You think the *Sea Hawk* can't take another bad storm, don't you?"

"I think the impact with that reef strained her timbers." He paused. "I'm not looking forward to finding out how bad."

Almost any other woman—or man—would have fallen apart at the thought of sailing into a storm aboard an unseaworthy boat. But not India. She simply nodded once, accepting the danger. Only the quick flaring of her nostrils as she took a steadying breath betrayed whatever inner trepidation she might be experiencing.

"How bad is the channel into Waigeu's lagoon?" she asked, squinting into the smudgy distance, as if she could will the land to appear before them.

He shook his head. "Waigeu doesn't have a barrier reef. It'll be an easy run into the bay . . . once we get there."

She brought her gaze to his. He saw the flare of interest in her clear gray eyes, saw her hesitate, then succumb to the promptings of her insatiable curiosity. "Are you familiar with Waigeu?"

The *Sea Hawk* lunged through a wave high enough to send spray flying over the deck. "Familiar enough. Why?"

Her cheeks glistened with a faint wet sheen as her lips parted with excitement. "Do you know if there are any maraes or stone carvings on the island?"

He laughed softly. "I was wondering how long it would take before you got around to asking that."

The *Sea Hawk* lurched and pitched heavily with the growing swells, so that she had to make a quick grab for the mast beside them. "Well? Are there?"

"I remember seeing a large marae on the coast near the northern village. But I don't remember whether or not there are carvings associated with it. Patu would know."

The wind was high enough now that it was screeching through the rigging, and Patu was moving quickly to trim the boat down to rail breeze. "Hey! Patu!" Jack called. "Are there any rock carvings on Waigeu?"

The boy turned to look at them, his eyes wide, his answer lost in the flapping of the canvas and the crash of the waves.

"Why would Patu know?" India asked as another flash of lightning lit up the rolling black waves.

"Because he's from Waigeu," Jack said. Then the squall hit, bringing with it a world of rain that poured down in a sudden, roaring torrent.

The squall was fierce but blessedly brief. By the time they reached the open, unsheltered bay of Waigeu, the sea had calmed to gentle swells and the sky cleared to a brilliant turquoise, paling now with the approach of evening.

"We made it," said India, her smile slipping slightly when the *Sea Hawk* gave a peculiar, inexplicable lurch that had her grabbing at the rail.

The island rising out of the sea before them was high and rugged and beautiful. Mist shrouded the towering volcanic peaks of the interior, but the sun shone hot and fierce on the steep, lower slopes and shadowy ravines covered in a lush, dark green tangle of trees and vines and ferns. It wasn't until they drew closer to shore that India realized several of the broad valleys running down to the bay had been stripped of their natural vegetation. The black earth lay open and exposed, like great, ugly slashes only partially covered by pale, oddly tidy rows of green.

"Vanilla plantations," Jack said, coming to stand beside her at the rail.

India glanced at Patu, his face still and closed as he, too, stared at the island before them. "It didn't used to look like this," he said in a tight, broken voice. Then his gaze shifted to the dozen or more small dugouts skimming across the bay toward them, and his expression cleared as the men in the canoes began to shout, laughing and gesturing when they caught sight of him. "Look! There's my uncle," he cried, kicking off his shoes. "And my cousin Timi."

They were a Polynesian people, the Waigeuns, closely related by language and bloodline to the inhabitants of Tahiti, to the east. Golden-skinned, with dark hair and strikingly molded features, the men looked tall and broad-shouldered and hale. And it seemed to India, watching, that she and Jack had become spectators to a scene as old as time: the welcoming home of a wandering, prodigal son.

One of the islanders, a middle-aged man in a scarlet and sapphire pareu, stood up to wave at Patu and shout, *"Mea maitai outou?"* Are you well?

"Ia ora na oe i te atua," Patu called back. Whipping off his shirt, he climbed the *Sea Hawk*'s rail to dive in a graceful, long arc that sent him plunging deep into the purple-blue waters of his home.

The beach rimming the open bay of Waigeu was formed of black volcanic sand lined with coconut palms and puroo, a kind of cross between a mulberry and a fig tree, with giant yellow poppylike blooms touched in the center with maroon.

By the time the *Sea Hawk*'s dingy scraped up onto the beach, Patu was already there, dripping wet and smiling and surrounded by a deep circle of chattering women and laughing men and small, flower-decked children who darted excitely between legs and chased after a barking, half-grown, golden-haired dog that raced across the sparkling black sand toward the bamboo and pandanus huts just visible through a thin screen of palm trees.

"Has it changed so much?" India asked, her fingertips resting easily on Jack's shoulders as he swung her up and over the side of the dingy.

"Well, that wasn't here before," he said, one hand lingering at her waist as he nodded toward a large, white-plank structure with a green painted door and a neatly lettered sign that read DIVINE WORD MISSION.

They called it a himine house, a hymn house. And like the tidy bungalow of milled lumber that stood beside it, its roof of corrugated iron gleaming bright and hot in the tropical sun, it was as alien to this place as the fair-haired woman with corset-stiffened waist and thick layers of dark, voluminous skirts who appeared on the veranda, a hand coming up to shade her eyes.

One of the children, a bright-eyed boy of about ten, with a skinny bare chest and a tiari blossom tucked behind his left ear, noticed the direction of their gaze and paused in his game of chase-the-dog long enough to say proudly, "We're all Methodists now. Even the Cath'lics."

"What happened to Father Paul?" Jack asked, his brows drawing together as he stared beyond the new mission, to a small knoll where what was left of pale pink stucco walls was rapidly disappearing beneath an overgrown tangle of jungle vines.

"Father Paul?" In the act of darting off again, the boy paused to glance back over his shoulder and say something India didn't quite catch, something that sounded like "*pohe.*"

"What does it mean?" India asked, a sense of unease blooming suddenly within her as she lifted her gaze to Jack's hard, shuttered face. "What did he say?"

"He said Father Paul is dead."

"He died four—no, five months ago," said the Reverend William Watson, lowering his slim, small-boned frame into a wooden armchair. He was an earnest-looking man of about thirty, with a high forehead and thin face, and a splendid mustache flowing into a long, light-brown beard. "There was an epidemic of some sort on an island he considered part of his parish. He went to try to help, and took sick himself."

India glanced at Jack, who stood gazing out one of the Watsons' green-painted frame windows overlooking the bay. "That wouldn't have been Rakaia, would it?" he said, his voice smooth and flat and carefully stripped of all emotion.

"Yes. That was it. Rakaia." The reverend rested his elbows on the chair's frame and brought up one hand to stroke his beard. "Sometimes I wonder if there will be any Polynesians left by the end of the century. The population of Waigeu is less than twenty percent what it was in Captain Cook's time. Imagine that! Twenty percent."

Jack kept his gaze leveled on the scene outside the window, where the sun sparkled on the palm-fringed bay, and high white clouds moved serenely with the trade winds. It was India who asked, her throat raw and tight, "Did no one on Rakaia survive?"

The reverend's nostrils flared wide as he drew himself up in his chair, his entire being exuding a peculiar, almost throbbing fury that was part righteous indignation, part personal affront. "A few, but not many. A rascally knave who claims he was once an English sailor brought some of them away in an old jolly boat." Watson let out a harsh laugh and shook his head. "Sailor. Huh. Pirate is more likely."

Jack swung about, his body held so still, India could have sworn he wasn't even breathing. "Was one of them a girl? A blue-eyed girl of about eleven?"

The reverend shook his head. "I wouldn't know. He's not a godly man, that sailor. When I went to try to minister to them, he chased me off with a shotgun. Imagine that! A shotgun."

A step on the veranda heralded the return of Cynthia Watson, the reverend's wife. She came bustling in the open front door, a tray laden with a steaming teapot and a plate of tinned biscuits and a stack of rose-patterned china cups and saucers clutched against her ample bosom. "Here we are," she said, the tray rattling as she set it on the lace-covered table that occupied much of the center of the room. "The tea is fresh from China." She held up a white pitcher. "And the milk is fresh, too. It's from our goat!"

She laughed when she said it, for her demeanor was considerably more merry and open than her husband's. They probably made a good pair, India thought as she went to help the other woman pour tea; while the reverend preached fire and brimstone from his pulpit, his good-natured, round-faced wife would teach the islanders their gospel and help them sew clothes. For those embarked on a missionary life, covering the natives' nakedness was almost as important as converting them.

"Are you saying the survivors from Rakaia settled here?" Jack said, reaching automatically to take the cup India handed him. "On Waigeu?"

The reverend nodded. "The southern part of the island, where no one lived anymore."

Her own teacup in hand, India let her gaze wander around the cozy little parlor, with its white gauze curtains and lovingly polished harmonium and old wooden mantel clock that sat on a shelf and filled the air with an inescapable, ticktocking awareness of the passage of time. They might have been in England, she thought, rather than on this tropical island of bamboo huts and warm trade winds, where time had once been marked by nothing more than the tides, and the coming and going of the hurricane season.

"I met your father once," the Reverend Watson was saying to India. "In Edinburgh a couple of years ago. I always admired his writings, particularly those espousing the importance of missionary work among the darker races. I was sorry to hear of his death."

"Thank you," said India, painfully aware of Jack's hard gaze upon her.

China clinked as Cynthia Watson collected the tea things. "You never considered missionary work yourself?" she asked.

India shook her head. "I prefer travel writing."

The reverend's mustache swished back and forth as he pushed his lips out in a tight frown. "I read your book on East Africa."

"Did you?" India said, both surprised and gratified.

"Yes," said the reverend's wife, hefting her tea tray. "He rather enjoyed the first part. But after he read what you had to say about the missionaries you met in Nairobi, he ordered me to burn it."

"What did you say about the missionaries in Nairobi?" Jack asked, a smile crinkling the skin at the edges of his eyes as they made their way back down to the beach.

India laughed softly. "I believe I said something to the effect that while missionary work might be well-meaning, it doesn't alter the fact that obliterating an ancient culture and substituting for it an alien way of life is essentially arrogant and destructive."

"No wonder William Watson burned your book." His smile faded slowly. "What did the Reverend McKnight have to say about it?"

India stared out over the dark, violet blue of the sea. The air was sweet with the scent of brine and all the rich, earthy fragrances of the rain forest rising up steep and dense beyond the beach. "I never heard. He died a few weeks after it was published."

"I'd had the impression your father died right after your mother."

India paused, the soft black sand shifting beneath her feet as she turned to face him. "My father was a strong believer in that old dictate 'spare the rod and spoil the child.' When I was a little girl, I was terrified of him. But I always believed he loved me, the same way I believed God Our Father loves His children here on earth. Then my mother died, and my father just . . . sent me away. I'd write to him, but he would never answer." Her throat swelled, her eyes stinging with the threat of tears she refused to let fall. "My aunt used to make excuses for him. Tell me how busy he was with his lectures, his writings. But it wasn't true. The truth was, he'd always been disappointed in me. Disappointed in me for not being a son. For not believing everything he told me I must believe. For not being a credit to *him*."

Jack's hand cradled the back of her head, drawing her forward until her cheek pressed against the warm softness of his shirt and she could feel the rumble of his chest when he spoke. "You were a credit to him," he said softly. "He was just too blind and opinionated to see it."

India shook her head, her hands clutching fistfuls of his shirt as she held on to him, held on to him tight. "I don't care anymore. I quit caring a long time ago."

It wasn't until Jack brushed his fingertips across the curve of her cheek that she realized there were tears there. "Then why are you crying?"

~~Chapter Twenty-nine

THEY FOUND PATU on the beach, near the water's edge. Instead of his usual canvas trousers, shirt, and shoes, he wore a bright red pareu tied about his waist, his bare feet dangling over the foaming surf as it rushed in to swirl about the whitened base of the old driftwood log on which he sat.

"You heard about the people from Rakaia?" he asked, when Jack and India walked up to him. "On the southern end of the island?"

"The Watsons told us," India said, when Jack only stared out over the sea, turning silver now with the coming of the night.

Patu's hands curled into fists that pressed, hard, against the smooth wood of the log. "I asked, but no one seems to know exactly how many survivors there are, or anything about them. The people here say no one has sailed down to the southern end of the island for years." He let out a low, harsh laugh, and shook his head. "Very few of the men even go out with their nets anymore. They live surrounded by all this—" He drew an arm through the air in a wide sweep, taking in the shining sea and the rain-forest-clad mountains rising up steep and dark behind them. "All this, and they work in some Englishman's vanilla fields, and eat tinned fish and corned beef."

A sad silence fell, filled with the swish of the surf and the haunting cry of a seabird. "How's your mother?" Jack asked softly.

Patu's face grew tight, strained. "She cried."

Jack blew out a long breath, his eyes narrowing as he continued to stare off across the darkening waves. "The last time I went back to Queensland, to visit my family . . . everything there was different from the way I remembered it. And I guess I was different, too. That's the problem with going off and leaving the place where you were raised. It's never easy, coming home again. The fit is all wrong. You realize you don't belong there anymore. But you don't really belong anyplace else, either."

Patu nodded, a muscle along his jaw throbbing noticeably as he jerked his chin toward the yacht riding at anchor in the bay. "How long you reckon it'll take us to get the *Hawk* seaworthy again?"

Jack shrugged. "I guess we'll know that in the morning, when we get a good look at her."

"I'm not staying here," Patu said suddenly, as if someone had suggested it. "I can't stay here."

Jack kept his gaze on the sleek, bobbing hull of the yacht. "And your mother?"

Patu blinked. "She'll have my brothers and sisters."

A lilting note, at once mournful and yet oddly joyous, filled the briny evening air. India turned toward the sound, and felt the gentle tropical breeze lift the loose hair from her forehead. "What's that?"

"They're having a luau," Patu said. "To celebrate my homecoming." He pressed his lips together, as if trying to keep back an angry outburst. Then he said, "A couple of the villagers didn't want my family to hold it. They said the Reverend Watson wouldn't like it."

India looked around in surprise. "But why not?"

"You haven't seen one yet," said Jack, amusement lightening his voice. "The music is positively heathen, and the traditional dancing . . . shocking. Shocking and shameful."

"Oh, good." India checked quickly to make certain her notebook was in her knapsack. "I do so love witnessing shamefully shocking displays of heathen culture." Her smile slipped a bit. "As long as no one expects me to eat roast pork."

For the first time since they'd met him on the beach, the frown etching lines across Patu's forehead cleared, and he laughed.

It was the sounds she would remember the most, India decided; the erotic, pulsing beat of the drum, and the hushed whisper of the warm wind sighing through the feathery tops of the palms, and the crackling fires, all played out against the endless boom and swish of the silver-crested surf breaking against that strange black beach.

They feasted on prawns and crabs, and raw fish dipped in coconut milk; on taro, and pumpkin greens, and chicken wrapped in the leaves of the purau tree and baked beneath red-hot shingles and sand. Torches of dried palm fronds, wrapped together into bundles some six feet long and as big around as a man, flamed and snapped and hissed, their golden light flickering over laughing faces and bare brown arms and legs, and banana mats piled high with mangoes and bananas and oranges, guavas and baked fei and pineapples. The air was sweet with the briny tang of the sea mingling with the smell of roasted foods and the heady scent of tiare and gardenia blooming in exuberant splendor from the dark edges of the rain forest, or woven with ferns and hibiscus into wreaths.

India was scribbling furtive notes in her book when Jack's hand closed over hers, stopping her. "Write about it later," he said, the firelight dancing warm and golden over the angles of his face as he leaned into her. "But for now, just enjoy it."

She glanced beyond him, to where two lines of female impersonators bedecked in white tiare blossoms and wearing grass skirts over their pareus were going through a bizarre parody of a French gavotte, taught to them by some long-ago, well-intentioned, but ultimately unsuccessful missionary bent on replacing the lusty native dances with something considered to be more sedate and proper. "I can record what I'm seeing and still enjoy it," she said, as the young men, their faces earnest and serious, the fringed pandanus around their ankles and wrists flaring, executed flawless pirouettes.

"But you can't write and dance at the same time." He drew her up with him, her notebook sliding off her lap into the sand.

"I'm the wrong sex," she said with a laugh.

"No, you're not." He nodded beyond her, to where a circle of giggling men and women was forming. The serious young men executed their last pirouette, bowed to each other, then broke away laughing. Hands began to beat the hard-packed sand, pounding out an ancient, primitive rhythm joined by the tap of drumsticks of braided husk fiber against blocks carved from coconut trunks.

"I can't do this," India said, her stomach fluttering with panic as he drew her into the circle.

He slipped a wreath of tiare and sweet ferns over her head, and brushed her lips with a quick kiss. "Yes you can."

Hands undulating like the waves of a tropical sea, feet shuffling sideways, the laughing circle of men and women shifted to the right, slowly at first, then faster as the beat picked up, became louder, more insistent. *Thrum, thrum* went the drums as India circled forward, then back again, Jack at her side, guiding her with a gentle touch, encouraging her with a smile. She felt her body search for the rhythm, find it. She stopped watching her feet. Her hair slipped from its neat chignon to fall in wind-tossed curls about her face, but she didn't care.

Turning her head, she watched the man beside her. She watched the way the trades ruffled the worn cloth of his shirt, the way his neck arched when he threw back his head and laughed. The torches cast enticing, mysterious patterns of golden light and dark shadow across the strong bones of his face, and it was as if something shifted within her, and broke free.

The sand whispered warm and soft beneath her moving feet. The breeze felt gentle and fragrant against her cheek, the air sweet with the scents of sea and rain forest. She drew in a deep breath, drew it all in, until it flowed into her and she reached out to it, became a part of it—a part of the darkly undulating sea and the palm trees waving gently against the star-spangled tropical sky. She was a part of this place, and it was a part of her. She heard the beat of the drums, felt Jack catch her shoulders, swinging her to face him. Their gazes caught, and held.

Slowly, their gazes still locked, they moved as one, hands clutching hands, hips undulating erotically, suggestively together. The features of his face were sharp, stark, the glow in his eyes fierce, almost predatory. She heard the drums pound louder, faster, their beat primeval, insistent, with a savage sexuality that entered her blood, pulsed through her, through them both. His hands tightened around hers, swinging her halfway about to pull her sharply back against him, her spine pressing against the hard length of him, his arms folded across her breasts, holding her close. Over her shoulder, her gaze met his again. She saw the flash of his smile in the flaring of the torchlight, felt the warmth of his breath against her cheek. The beat of the drums mingled with the crash of the surf and the haunting, unearthly wail of the conch shell. And she thought, This is life. This is life as in the past I might have recorded it, written about it. But I never lived it. Not until now.

"I want you," he whispered, his lips just inches from hers.

"Yes," she said simply.

Gently, his hands cradled her cheeks, urging her around until she faced him. She thought he might kiss her. Instead he said, "There's something I want you to see," and his lips twitched up into a lopsided smile that creased his cheek and stole her heart all over again.

∽∽Chapter Thirty

THEY CLIMBED THE hillside above the village, following a hibiscus- and fern-shadowed path worn smooth by countless centuries of bare feet.

India kept teasing him, trying to worm out of him what it was he was taking her to see, but he only ducked his head in that Aussie way he had of smiling up at her with his eyes, and saying nothing.

The path led to a low, moon-bathed headland that curved out into the darkness of the ocean and protected the bay below from the worst of the surf that crashed itself into a white froth on the rocks of the windward cliffs. On its gentler, leeward side, the promontory was mostly of grass, with only scattered tamanos, and here and there, the vermilion blossoms of the delicate, fernlike poinciana trees, just coming into flower.

"It's beautiful," she said, going to stand on the far side, where the land fell away in a dizzying precipice to the sea-bashed rocks below, and the trades blew wild and free, and she could see nothing but the black undulations of the sea and a universe of brilliant stars that seemed to stretch on forever.

"Yes, it is." He came up behind her, his hands warm on her shoulders as he urged her around to face the end of the cape. "But that's not what I brought you to see."

She saw it now. Bold and proud and unabashedly masculine, it jutted up from the very tip of the cape. As she drew closer, she could see that it had been carved—deliberately, skillfully carved—from a hard red granite, its head swollen and round and cloven like a devil's hoof, its shaft long and straight, thrusting some eight to ten feet up into the air.

"Good heavens," said India, pausing at its base. "It's a giant phallus."

She walked all around it, careful not to get too close to the cliff's edge, then twisted to look back at him. "However did you find this?"

He came to stand beside her, his head tipping back as he stared up at the statue's huge, red head. "Patu told me about it this afternoon. He figures the Reverend Watson must not know about it, or he'd have had the islanders toss it into the sea by now."

India sighed, her head, like his, tipping back as she stared up at the monstrous erection. "It's one of the things making my investigation into the origins of the Polynesians so difficult. Most of the ancient stone statues have been smashed, or at least thrown down. And it's even worse on those islands where the carving tradition was in wood. There, they simply burned everything."

She wanted to reach out and touch the stone, but found she couldn't quite bring herself to do it. Instead she said, "Does Patu know what it was used for?"

Jack shook his head. "No. Navigation, maybe?"

India nodded. "The ancient Greeks had signposts they called Hermac, after the god of travelers. At first, actual statues of the god were used, but eventually they were simply stylized into straight pillars." A naughty smile curved her lips. "Only the peculiarly male portion of the god's anatomy continued to be rendered realistically."

"Don't tell me," said Jack, his gaze no longer on the statue, but on her. "It pointed the way?"

India laughed. "Yes, it did. Unfortunately, the early Christians went around and defaced every Hermes they could find."

"I think the word you want is *castrated*."

India looked at him. He stood with his back to the wind, so that it molded the worn cloth of his shirt about the hard, strong length of his torso and fluttered the ends of his dark hair against the tanned skin of his throat. He was smiling at her, the kind of smile that barely curved his lips, but warmed his eyes with an inner glow that spoke of a man's admiration, and a man's desire.

Feeling suddenly shy and a little anxious, she glanced again at the huge red phallus. "It's very big," she said, her throat so tight, the words quivered slightly on their way out.

"Does it scare you?"

She met his gaze. She heard the surf break against the rocks far below, an endless crash and boom that mingled with the primeval beat of the drums drifting up from the luau on the beach. The wind gusted around them, its caress a warm, sweet whisper of all things wild and exotic and unknown. And still their gazes held, and it came to her that never had she felt closer to anyone than she did to this man, in this moment; that no one had ever known her—really known her—the way he knew her, the way he had always known her.

Reaching out, she took his hand, and put it on her breast. Her gaze never left his. "I'm not afraid," she said, and smiled.

He undressed her slowly, standing there at the cape's end, where land met sea and sky in a tumult of crashing breakers and gusting wind. He unbuttoned the tucked front of her man's shirt, his fingers trembling slightly when he eased the fine linen from her shoulders and arms.

"You're shaking," she said.

He laughed, his breath warm against her ear as he reached for the waistband of her split skirt. "I'm trembling with impatience. What I'd like to do—" He shoved the tartan down over her hips. "—is tear every last stitch right off you."

"You can't." She kicked away her boots and stockings. "I don't have any other clothes. If I lose these, I'll be reduced to wearing one of the islander's grass skirts."

His lips curved into that rascal's smile she loved, the one that lit up his face and made her feel all warm and tingly and naughty inside. "Don't tempt me."

Wearing only her chemise and drawers, India took a step back. She was trembling now, as well, every fiber of her being aware of his hard, hot gaze upon her as she tugged open the ties at the front of her chemise and pulled it over her head. The warm trade winds gusted around her, caressed the bare, moonlit flesh of her arms and breasts. She hesitated only a moment, then loosed the waistband of her drawers and let them fall in a soft white flutter to her feet.

"You're beautiful," he whispered, his chest lifting as he sucked in a deep, half-hitching breath. And in that moment, she did feel beautiful. Beautiful and desirable and very much a woman. His woman.

"Now it's your turn," she said, her voice husky, hushed.

He went to work on the buttons of his shirt, his cheek creasing with a crooked smile as he glanced up at her. "You've seen me before."

"I know. But in the past, I always tried not to look."

"Huh." He stripped off his shirt, the muscles of his arms and chest bunching beguilingly as he went to work on his trousers. "That's not the way I remember it."

She laughed, because while it was true that she had

tried not to look, it was also true that she hadn't succeeded as well as she ought. She watched him shove his trousers down over his lean, naked hips, watched the muscles in his bare brown back flex as he straightened again, and the laughter died on her parted lips.

He reached for her, his palm cupping the base of her head to draw her into him. She went to him, her naked body pressing close up against his, her face buried into the curve of his neck as he hugged her close and held her for a moment. Just held her.

He smelled of the night, and the sea, and himself. Her hands gripped his shoulders, then opened, her splayed fingers and palms gliding over smooth, tanned skin, hard muscle. She touched him with reverence, awe even. She was greedy for the feel of him, wondrous with the delight of touching, and being touched.

For as she touched him, he touched her. He touched her everywhere, with his hands, and his lips. And then, laying her down on the pile of their clothes, he touched her with his tongue, touched her where she'd never even touched herself. He sucked her breasts into his mouth, and smiled up at her with his eyes when she gasped, and gasped again. Then his dark hair slid across her belly, and she lost herself in the magic of his tongue and his lips and the gentle, probing knowledge of his fingers.

When he finally lifted his head and stared up at her, she found the sharp, hungry look of arousal on his face frightening, and yet exciting at the same time. A deep and powerful longing filled her, the need to join her body to his, to join herself to him, to hold him in her arms. To hold him in her life, forever.

She reached for him, drew him up to her, her knees bending and falling apart wide as he covered her with his hard man's body. Much of his weight he took on his forearms, his elbows bracketing the sides of her head as he brushed her hair from her sweat-dampened forehead, and kissed her cheek, and whispered sweet endearments in her ear. *God, I love you. Love you, love you . . .*

He shifted his weight, and she could feel his hardness pressing smooth and hot against her. She saw his jaw tighten, saw his lips curl back from his clenched teeth. Then he pushed himself inside her.

She gasped, then let out a soft whimpering noise when he drew himself partially out and thrust in again, harder, deeper, stretching her, filling her. "Easy, sweetheart," he whispered, his body stilling as he held himself poised above her. He kissed her eyelids, the tip of her nose, her lips. She could feel his rapid heartbeat, thundering in his chest, hear the jagged catch of his rough breathing. "Does it hurt?"

"No," she whispered, although she was, in truth, in a breathless torment. Yet this was not the dry, tearing pain she'd known in the past, but a burning, clenching ache that was more like an unfulfilled need, a wanting that was curling up tighter and tighter, deep within her. She slid her hands around his bare sides, held his body close to hers. "Don't stop. Please . . . Don't stop."

His gaze locked with hers, he began to move, a slow thrust and drag that stole her breath and made her heart swell with a love so tender, it brought tears to her eyes. Then he dipped his head, and his lips took hers in a sweet and gentle kiss that caught fire as the tempo of their bodies increased. Above them, the night sky reeled in a breathless swirl of sparkling stars. She heard the distant, savage beat of the drums, and the violence of the rock-dashed surf, far below.

With a groan, he tore his mouth from hers, his hands twisting in her hair, his thumbs tipping her head back so that he could kiss her neck, and she had to bite her lower lip to keep from screaming with pleasure and need. Somehow, her fingers interlaced with his, her arms stretching high over her head as she reached, reached for something she didn't even understand, something that kept eluding her, enticing her.

Squirming, she wrapped her legs around his waist, drawing him deeper, deeper within her. She felt his breath blowing against the sweat-dampened flesh of her throat in quick, harsh gasps. Felt his hand reach down between them, his palm pressing against her woman's mound, pressing her between the hardness of his hand and the pounding hardness of his man's body. And the pleasure was so exquisite then that she did scream, her hands clutching his sweat-slicked shoulders as he whirled her away to a place where pleasure and pain exploded together in a pounding, pulsing, endless rush of ecstasy.

The morning sunlight, spilling across the ocean from the east, awakened her.

India opened her eyes, a smile touching her lips as she found herself staring at Jack's hard, tanned chest, lifting gently with his slow, even breaths. She lay with her head nestled in the curve of his shoulder, his arm holding her close, her body pressed against the warm length of him. They had fallen asleep here, at the very tip of the cape, with the moonlight soft on their naked bodies and the trade winds warm about them. She knew that he had slept, slept soundly in her arms, because once, during the night, she had come awake and propped herself up on her elbow so that she could look at him.

She had stayed like that for the longest time, letting her gaze rove over the sharp, beautiful bones of his face, the curve of his lips. She had looked at him, and felt a sweet ache swell within her, an ache that was part wanting, and part the sadness that comes when the soul glimpses something it secretly yearns for, yet knows can never be.

She'd been so lost in her own thoughts that it had been a moment before she'd realized that his eyes had opened, and he was looking at her. "What are you doing?" he said, his voice a soft caress.

"Watching you sleep."

He smiled, and reached for her. "I'm not sleeping anymore."

And so she had gone, again, into his arms. And he had shown her that there was still much she had to learn about the joys shared between a man and a woman. She'd learned that she could give pleasure as well as receive it, and what a heartwarming delight that could be. She'd learned that lovemaking can be hot and hungry, as well as sweet and tender. And she'd learned that she could hold this man in her arms for the rest of eternity, and it wouldn't be long enough.

Now, with the sun shining down warm and bright upon them, she twisted around so that she could look over the bulge of his strong arm, toward the bay where the *Sea Hawk* lay at anchor far below.

India straightened her elbow and pushed herself up on her splayed hand, her gaze caught by the way the yacht rode low in the water and listed oddly to one side. "Jack," she said softly. "Jack, wake up."

Something in her voice must have warned him. He sat up suddenly, his eyes narrowing as he twisted around to stare down at the purple-blue waters of the bay below. "What the hell?" he said, pushing to his feet.

India shoved her bare arms into her shirt and reached for her tartan skirt, but Jack had already taken off at a run, his bare feet pounding the hard dirt of the path as he sprinted, naked, down the hill. Far below, as if pushed by an unseen hand, the *Sea Hawk* swung about slowly on its anchor chain, the gentle surf breaking over the unnaturally low deck.

"Oh, shitfire!" Jack screamed. "No." He lifted his arms up, wide, his hands clenching into fists that he let fall, helplessly, to his sides as the *Sea Hawk* gave one last gurgle, and sank beneath the waves.

∼∼Chapter Thirty-one

THEY SAT SIDE by side at the edge of the black sandy beach, their gazes fixed on the empty waters of the bay before them. Even without squinting, India could still make out the shadow that was the *Sea Hawk*, plainly visible through the clear, clean water.

"Is it possible to raise it?" she asked, her arms wrapped around her bent knees.

"Maybe. Patu says the men of the village are willing to help try."

She swung her head to look at him. "How long would that take?"

Jack let out his breath in a long sigh. "I don't know. It's not going to be easy. And God knows what we'll need to get her seaworthy again, even if we can raise her. The monsoon season isn't that far away anymore."

India nodded. The shifting wind brought to them a fine spray that felt cool against her cheeks and smelled sweetly of the open sea. "If I had never come to you, or if I'd listened when you said you couldn't take me to Takaku, none of this would have—"

His fingertips touched her lips, stopping her. "No. Don't say it. Don't even think it. It would have happened. The *Barracuda* came out here under orders to see me brought to justice. The Prime Minister himself is after my blood." His fingers rubbed across her lower lip, then drifted over her cheek and down her neck in a soft caress that was there, then gone. "Ten years is too long to run. I should have faced it all long ago."

She took his hand in hers. It was a big hand, strong and tanned and scarred from his years at sea, his years on the run. "And if the *Lady Juliana*'s charts and log have been lost? If you can't prove your innocence?"

He squinted out over the tropical blue sea. "I don't know. I'm tired of running. Tired of hiding." His hand shifted in hers. "India . . ." He paused. His thumb was making circular patterns on the back of her hand, and he watched it intently, as if it were the most important thing in the world at that moment. Then he lifted his head to look straight at her and said, "Marry me."

India felt herself go so cold and still inside, it seemed for a moment as if her heart had stopped.

I love you, he had whispered to her last night. *Love you, love you.* She'd heard him, but she hadn't really believed him. Somehow, she had convinced herself that the caring was all on her side, that everything was still for him the way it had begun for her—a heat, a wanting. An appetite easily and casually appeased. Nothing more.

"I mean, if I can clear my name," he was saying, his dark eyebrows drawing together as he studied her face. "I wouldn't ask it of you otherwise. I hadn't intended to say anything until I knew what kind of future I had to offer you. But after last night, I thought you ought to know where my heart is."

His words humbled her. She would never have had the courage to say something that had the power to make her that vulnerable. She found her chest ached, and she drew in a deep breath, trying to ease it. When that didn't work, she took another.

Ever since she'd been old enough to consider such things, she'd told herself she would never marry. Not even the dawning awareness of the profound depth of her feelings for Jack had provoked her into changing her mind. Even if she had believed in marriage, she wasn't sure she'd have been able to bring herself to become this man's wife. He was too wild and irreverent, too much a rebel, too . . . dangerous.

The skin beside his eyes crinkled, as if he were thinking about smiling, but couldn't quite manage it. "I don't think I've ever seen you speechless before."

"You know how I feel about marriage," she said finally, grasping wildly for something to say, something that wouldn't require her to be as honest as he was being. "My opinion of what marriage means for a woman."

"Then marry me in an island ceremony. Just you and me, promising our love to each other. No government certification, no one-person-before-the-law-and-the-husband-is-that-person."

"It wouldn't work."

He was no longer smiling, not even with his eyes. "Why not?"

In the blue sky above the bay, a gull soared, riding a warm updraft. India watched the bird wheel, its call so sweet and sad it seemed to tear her heart. "Because . . ." She had to stop and swallow before she could go on. "Because I love to travel, whereas you want nothing more than to settle down and make a home."

"So, we settle down and make a home, and then we travel."

"Settle where?" She let her gaze drift around the bay, struck, as she always was, by the vibrancy of color here. The cobalt blue of the water, the vividness of the sky, the saturated gold of the sunlight pouring down on a tangle of intertwined greens of every imaginable hue splashed with blooms of crimson and cadmium yellow and brilliant, pure white. "In Edinburgh? The sea is gray there. Did you know? The sea, and the sky, and the houses . . . everything is gray."

"I'll go to Scotland, if that's what you want." He paused, then added, his voice tight, "If I can."

India shook her head. She couldn't imagine him in Scotland. He belonged here, in this southern land of waving palm trees and sun-warmed sand, where the trade winds blew wild and free across the ocean, and the sky was so full of stars at night that it made a body feel lonesome and sad, just looking at them. "You might think you could live there, but it would kill you. One day at a time."

"And what do you think it'll do to me, living here without you?"

Her gaze met his, and it came to her that his eyes were the exact shade of blue as a deep, tropical sea, and that she could look at them forever and never get tired of it. She swallowed, trying to answer him, but her throat had become so swollen and tight she couldn't push the words out.

"You're just making excuses," he said suddenly, those vivid blue eyes of his narrowing, darkening. "You know that, don't you?"

She scrambled to her feet, the constriction about her throat instantly gone. *"Excuses!"*

He rose more slowly, his hands settling on his lean hips in that quintessentially masculine stance of his. "That's right."

She brought up one clenched fist and thumped it against her chest for emphasis. "I'm being practical."

"Uh-un." He leaned into her, his nostrils flaring with a quick, angry breath. "The truth is, you're afraid. And you're too bloody dishonest with yourself even to admit it."

She scooped up her knapsack from where she'd left it lying in the sand, and practically shook it under his nose. "I'm not afraid of anything."

He knocked her hand away from his face. "That's bullshit, and you know it. Oh, you might not be afraid of traveling around the world by yourself, or exploring a cave filled with moldy old skeletons. But there's a hell of a lot you *are* afraid of, and I don't mean just reasonable things, like swinging bridges and sharks. You're terrified of being late, or looking foolish, or just simply admitting to anyone, least of all yourself, that you get lonely sometimes. Or that deep, deep down, you really would like to have children, and a man to love you, except that you're too afraid of making a bad choice, the way your mother did."

She let out a bitter, false laugh. "You dare? You dare to lecture me about courage, when you're the one who's been too afraid to go back to Rakaia and face up to what happened there!"

It was a cruel, cutting thing to say, and she would have taken it back instantly if she could, except that it was already too late. A line of dark color appeared to ride high on his sharp cheekbones, and his head snapped back as if she had slapped him.

"At least I know what I'm running from," he said, his voice low and even and carefully, flawlessly modulated. "But you . . . you don't even know you're running."

He turned around then and left her there, at the edge

of that strange black beach, with her knapsack clutched to her chest and a sick weight of despair riding low in her belly. And she realized, as she watched him walk away from her, that never had she felt more afraid, or more alone than she did in that moment.

India hesitated at the base of the bungalow's steps, one hand on the railing, her head turning toward the sound of Cynthia Watson's merry laugh. The woman was standing beside a clothesline strung between two erythrina trees, one of the reverend's wet shirts held, momentarily forgotten, in her hands, her back arching as she looked up at a couple of yellow and green noisy pittas.

Turning, India walked toward her.

India might be critical of many of the results of the missionaries' work, but she still had to admire them. This was no easy life to which the Watsons had dedicated themselves. The islands of the South Pacific were scattered with the graves of missionaries' wives, and their children.

"Miss McKnight," said Cynthia Watson, looking around as India walked up to her. "Good morning! What did you think of last night's luau?"

"It was good material for the book I'm writing," India said warily.

The reverend's wife ducked her head to hide a smile. "William was furious, of course, when he heard they were having it. But I thought you would enjoy it."

"Is there a steamer that comes by here?" India asked, reaching into the basket at her feet and bringing up a wet apron she pegged on the line.

"Going which direction?"

India almost said, *Any direction*. But then she remembered her trunk, sitting in the Limerick in Neu Brenenberg, and said, "West."

"The *Fijian* is due tomorrow or the next day. But it'll probably be the last one until April."

India nodded. They called it the Tunnel, that long, tense period running from December to April, when the rains fell incessantly, and the danger of encountering a fierce storm kept most ships and boats in harbor. It made the isolation faced by those manning these far-flung outposts so severe that white traders and missionaries and their wives had been known to go mad, or simply give up and die, waiting for the Tunnel to end. India had been hoping to make it to Pepeete before the rains came. As it was, she'd be lucky not to be stranded on Neu Brenen.

Mrs. Watson shook out a wet petticoat and hung it on the line. "It's a good thing you weren't still at sea when that boat took it into her head to sink. But William had a look at her this morning, and he says he thinks they should be able to raise her."

"I might not be waiting for that."

Cynthia Watson looked around. "But I thought—" She broke off and bit her lip, then laughed. "Silly me. I don't know where I got the notion you and Mr. Ryder were, well, you know."

India felt her cheeks heat with discomfort. "We only just met. I hired his boat."

"Mr. Watson and I knew each other less than three weeks before we were wed. He was due to set sail for Waigeu when we met, so there was no time for a prolonged courtship."

India stared at the other woman's full-cheeked, merry face. "You weren't afraid?"

"Of coming here? What was there to fear, with God leading our way?"

"I meant, marrying someone you didn't know."

India expected the woman to say she'd had God leading her in that, as well. Instead, a strange, secret smile lit up Cynthia Watson's pale gray eyes, and she said simply, "I knew him."

It was Patu who took India to see the ancient burial complex, the marae, that Jack had told her about.

Built at the edge of the tidal plain below the village, the marae was one of the largest such places she'd ever seen. Thousands upon thousands of dark gray stones had been hauled down from the mountains and piled up to form walls some two hundred feet long and perhaps fifteen feet high. At first, she simply walked around the outside of it, stumbling occasionally over stones half buried in the rioting vegetation of the encroaching jungle, her head falling back as she looked up into the spreading limbs of giant old maape trees thrusting up from inside the enclosure. The whole place looked deserted and forlorn and sad.

"Does no one ever come here?" she asked.

Patu shook his head. "It's taboo." Forbidden.

India glanced over at him. "I thought the islanders were all Christians now."

A smile flashed wide and quick across his face. "So they say. But they still don't come here."

India paused between the two giant slabs of basalt that formed the marae's portal. It was like entering some ancient cathedral, she thought; a cathedral torn open to the sky, a place of peace that seemed, contradictorily, to hum with an energy she found almost frightening.

"You can go inside," Patu said, when she continued to hesitate. "It's all right."

She took a step forward, reluctant to disturb the strange aura of this place, yet oddly drawn by it, as well. Her boots made soft swishing noises in the high grass as she passed through a small antechamber and into the interior courtyard, a vast empty rectangle filled with only maape trees, and a tangle of creeping fig and shrubs, and grasses bending softly in the wind coming off the sea. Here and there, a few fragments of bone showed dull white in the fierce tropical sunlight, splintered shafts of long bones and small, weathered vertebrae and the thin, serrated pieces of a crushed skull. But that was all.

"Where are all the people who were once here?" she asked, her voice echoing oddly in the empty stone chamber.

"Father Paul had the bones gathered up when I was a boy, and given a Christian burial." Patu was prowling about the enclosure, parting bushes and pulling back mats of creepers to study the various tall, upright slabs of stone that had been set about seemingly at random. Suddenly he called out, "Here it is. Come see."

She joined him on the far side of the marae, and found herself staring at an upright stone deeply carved with a relief of a squatting, almost fetuslike creature with enormous round eyes and a wide mouth. His stunted legs were bent beneath him, his hands on his fat belly. He looked both faintly ridiculous and utterly evil. India fumbled in her knapsack for her notebook and pencil. "What god is this?"

Patu shrugged. "I don't know. We used to have many gods. The people thought that a god, if properly worshiped, should serve them and bring luck. If he didn't, then . . . *pffff*." He made an outward sweeping motion with his hands, and grinned. "The god would be abandoned, and a new one chosen."

India laughed softly. "Now, that's a threat calculated to make a god behave." She glanced around the deserted, windswept enclosure, and felt an uncharacteristic shiver dance up her spine. "And the spirits of the people who used to be buried here?" she asked softly. "Where are they?"

Patu's smile faded. "Most have gone to a better place. But not all. Some stay. They call them the tupapau. You see them at night, when the moon is full, in just that moment when it rises above the sea. It's said they sing as sweetly as the wind, their songs ancient tales composed in the old, forgotten languages. But they'll tear open your throat or gouge out your eyes if they see you."

In spite of the hot sun pouring down out of the tropical blue sky, India felt herself shiver. "They're evil, then?"

Patu nodded. "Animal spirits can be friendly, but human ghosts are always evil." He turned, the wind ruffling his long dark hair as he let his gaze travel over the tumbled, moss-grown stones. "Of course, no one believes in the old stories anymore," he said softly.

"Do you?"

He shook his head, his lips pressing together, tight. "They're just legends, myths. And yet . . . they contain some truth within them. Something that shouldn't be lost. Forgotten."

"Jack told me once that you left Waigeu with him because you wanted to learn the ways of your father."

He nodded, his expression growing troubled as he stared down at the image of the ancient, forsaken god at his feet. "And now I want to stay here, to make sure the ways of my mother's people aren't forgotten." He looked at her, his features pinched with indecision and a deep, inner torment. "Do you think that's wrong?"

"No," she said, reaching out to touch his arm. "No, I don't."

*   *   *

After Patu left her, India settled in the shade of a big old papaya tree with her notebook in her lap. She was lost in thought when a sudden, loud braying brought her head up with a start, and she found herself staring at Jack Ryder, seated astride a neat chestnut hack and leading a sulky-looking, dun-colored donkey toward her.

He sat tall and easy in the saddle, his legs long in the stirrups, the reins held lightly in his hands. It occurred to her, looking at him, that he was as at home on a horse as he was on a sailboat. But then, she remembered, he'd grown up on a station in Australia.

"Wherever did you get those?" she asked, deliberately keeping her voice light when he reined in before her. She hadn't seen him since that disastrous conversation on the beach, and she wasn't sure where it had left him. Where it had left them.

There was a tightness about his mouth, a wariness in his eyes that she hadn't seen before. "They're on loan from the vanilla grower."

She glanced up at the peaks rising high and jagged behind the village. Now that they couldn't sail to the south of the island, the only way to get there was by going overland. But he'd only borrowed two mounts.

"Patu's not here anymore," she said, her throat so dry, the words came out raspy, hushed.

"I know. He's going to stay and help with the raising of the *Sea Hawk*."

"Then who's the donkey for?"

He straightened his legs in the stirrups, his weight shifting in the saddle, while India held her breath. "You made something of an outlaw of yourself, by helping me escape from La Rochelle. It occurred to me you might consider you had a vested interest in knowing whether or not I was likely to be able to clear my name."

His words hurt, but she supposed she had them coming. She went up to him, her hands reaching high to close around his, her head falling back as she stared up at him. "Amongst all those reasons I gave down there on the beach for not marrying you . . . I never said I didn't love you."

He met her gaze squarely, his eyes hard and flat, the chestnut moving restlessly beneath him. "No. You never said you did, either."

She looked at him, and felt her love for him swell warm and painful in her breast. She wanted to say, *You were right. I am afraid, so afraid of so many things. I spend my life running from the things I fear, and I have never feared anything or anyone as much as I fear you, and the love you make me feel, and the crazy, impossible things you make me want.* But she could say none of those things. So she slipped the lead from his grasp, and said, "Why do I get the donkey?"

His lips twitched, as if he was thinking about smiling. "The planter says this chestnut, he doesn't like women."

"Huh." India tugged the bad-tempered-looking beast

over to a large stone so she could mount. "Are you sure it isn't just that you don't like donkeys?"

He laughed then, and she knew that things were easier between them.

Easier, but not better.

~~Chapter Thirty-two

THEY FOLLOWED A fey trail up the valley and across the mountain divide. The trail was old, and so overgrown at times that Jack had to get down and hack at the encroaching tangle of creeper fig and wait-a-whiles and rioting, white-flowered native jasmine. But they still made better time mounted than they would have on foot, and it changed what would have been an arduous journey into something that India came to see as almost magical, an enchanted passage through a lush realm of diffused green light, where all sounds were hushed and the sun never shone.

As they rose higher, the dripping ferns and deeply groined trunks of the maape trees gave way to the strange, horizontal paranus and the screw pines, with their cone-shaped baskets of roots and their spiky tufts of leaves lifting up to the sky. And still they climbed, up and up, until they reached the highest ridges, where only the aito, the ironwood tree, grew, scattered among the aeho reeds and thick grasses that matted the steepest inclines. From there, they could look down upon sweeping, dark-green cloaked slopes and wild gorges that plunged to a sea so vivid and blue it made her ache just to look at it.

At the summit, Jack reined in, his hard gaze fixed on the wild southern coast below them. Pausing beside him, India studied his taut, closed face. There was about him an aura of raw tension, of strain that even now, when they were at rest, set his chestnut to sidling uneasily.

She supposed the reason wasn't difficult to understand. After ten years, running can seem almost easy—or at least, easier than the possible alternatives. Such as learning that the evidence a man needs to prove his innocence has been lost. Or discovering that one's only child is dead. It was only now, as she stared down at that distant, surf-beaten shore, that it occurred to India that he must be wondering how Titana's daughter might feel about the father who had deserted her.

"You think she's angry with you, don't you?" India said softly. "Ulani, I mean. Angry with you for going away and leaving her all those years ago, and for staying away ever since."

His head came around, his taut, blue-eyed gaze locking with hers. "Wouldn't you be?"

India stared at him, at the wild, almost desperate shadows that played over his features. "You're a fugitive, Jack. You couldn't possibly have taken care of a baby." Yet even as she said it, India knew the fault in her argument, for until recently, the British government had let their pursuit of him grow cold. And Ulani was no longer a baby.

"Did you ever think," he said, his gaze still on her face, "that your father sent you to your aunt after your mother's death because he was afraid?"

India let out a startled huff of what was meant to be laughter, but came out sounding bitter, and maybe just a bit defensive. "My father? Afraid? Of what?"

He shrugged. "Of doing something wrong. Of not having what it took to be a good parent to a young, motherless girl. Of not being what you needed."

She shook her head. "My father was never afraid of anything. I never knew anyone more certain of himself. Whether he was writing about the White Man's Burden, or the divine origins of the powers exercised by a husband over his wife, Hamish McKnight *knew* he was right."

"A lot of people might think the same thing about you—those who didn't know you too well." He paused. "How well did you know your father?"

"Not well enough," she said, urging the donkey forward. "Not well enough at all."

Even before the row of simple bamboo-and-thatch bungalows edging the beach came into view, Jack could hear women's voices, and the lilting trill of a child's laughter echoing through the shadowy depths of the rain forest. At the sound, he checked involuntarily. Then he became aware of India's gaze on him, and he urged his horse forward.

The gorge they'd followed down the side of the mountain had long since widened out into a lush valley of parau and mango and wild papaya, of vivid red hibiscus, and yellow and white orchids hanging in exquisite, waxlike splendor from the spreading limbs of the giant trees overhead. Now, through the trunks of the palm trees, he could see the vivid blue swath of the sea, its tangy scent carrying lightly on the warm breeze.

The crack of what sounded like a rifle shot reverberated up the valley to send the chestnut into a snorting, head-tossing terror.

"Good heavens!" said India, reining in behind him. "What was that?"

"A coconut." Jack urged his horse forward to where a big coconut, still in its husk, lay in the middle of the trail ahead of them. Tipping back his head, he stared up the long, straight trunk of the nearby palm. A golden-skinned, dark-haired child of ten or twelve stared down at him.

"*Iorana*," said Jack. Hello.

An impish smile curled the child's mouth. "*Bonjour, monsieur.*"

"You speak French."

"*Mais oui.* Don't you?"

"Not very well," Jack admitted. The child laughed, her long dark hair cascading in a wave about her shoulders, and Jack knew a quickening, a wild leap of hope that he quickly suppressed. "I thought only boys climbed after drinking coconuts."

The child clambered halfway down the palm's trunk. "Siti is supposed to be a boy, but he picks oranges like a girl. So why shouldn't I climb palms, if'n I want?"

Jack's heart was pounding so hard he was practically shaking with it, but he still had to smile at the child's faithful reproduction of Toby's crusty Cornish accent. "I'm looking for Toby Jenkins. Can you take me to him?"

The girl came down to earth in a graceful rush, her head tilting as she stared up at him, her blue eyes suddenly serious in her sun-kissed face. "Why you want Mr. Toby?"

Jack sucked in a deep breath. He told himself the blue eyes meant nothing. The child could easily be Toby's. After ten years, the old salt could have produced a good dozen half-native offspring. Or she might be any European adventurer's child, perhaps even the product of one of the casual couplings that had taken place between the women of Rakaia and the *Lady Juliana*'s seamen before the massacre.

"Toby's an old friend of mine," Jack said. He wanted desperately to ask the child her name, but the words stuck in his throat, trapped there by the fear of what her answer might be.

And so it was India who gave voice to the simple question Jack could not bring himself to form. "What's your name?" she asked, nudging the reluctant donkey forward.

The child's head turned, her eyes growing wide as she stared at India's tattered but still splendid Expedition Outfit. And Jack's world stopped turning while he waited for the answer.

Then his daughter said, "I'm Ulani."

By the time they reached the village, they had acquired a laughing, shouting circle of children. The noise brought a man to the doorway of his home, where he paused at the top of the steps, one hand coming up to shade his eyes from the bright tropical sun. He was an older man, close to fifty or maybe even sixty now, although his small, wiry frame was still lean and firm, his skin darkened by the sun to a deep copper color that contrasted strikingly with the white of his hair.

"You took your own sweet time gettin' back here," said Toby Jenkins when Jack reined in at the base of the raised house's ladderlike steps. "You're lucky I didn't up and die on you."

Jack felt a slow smile spread across his face. "Hell, you look better than you did the last time I saw you."

The old man scowled at him, although he couldn't quite hide the pleased twinkle in his eyes. "That may be," he acknowledged. "But you didn't know that afore you see'd me, now did you?"

"I know you're a hard man to kill." Jack swung out of the saddle, and went to help India.

"Good gad." Toby's eyes widened as India slid stiffly from the saddle. "Don't tell me the women in England 'ave taken to wearin' britches!"

"I am Scottish," said India, smoothing her tartan.

Jack ducked his head to hide a smile. "Allow me to introduce Toby Jenkins, formerly of Her Majesty's navy. Toby, this is Miss India McKnight. She's a travel writer."

Toby's bushy white brows twitched together over his bulbous nose. "A what?"

Jack let his gaze drift around the small village. His smile faded. "Is this all that's left?"

"Aye, you're lookin' at 'em. That fever, it did a better job of killin' off the Rakaians than Cap'n Gladstone ever did."

"But why come here? Why leave the island?"

Toby Jenkins tugged at his earlobe. "That was on account of the blackbirders. They musta heard from one of the traders that we was pretty-near wiped out, because I caught the sonsofbitches tryin' to steal three young'uns right off the beach. A couple of me boys and me, we managed to scare 'em off. But I knowed they'd be back. They're like sharks, them blackbirders. They know when you're weak, and that's when they comes at you."

"How many sons do you have?" India asked.

"Five." Toby's chest swelled as he sucked in a deep breath. "And three daughters." The old man's proud gleam suddenly dimmed. "I had four, but I lost one, to the fever. The youngest." He nodded to where Ulani, her interest in the new arrivals long since dissipated, was gathering shells from the line of hard-packed, wet sand left by the receding tide. "I take it you didn't let on to her about who you are?"

Jack shook his head. "I wasn't sure what she'd been told."

"Oh, she knows about you, all right. Titana's sisters and brothers, they used to talk about you to her all the time."

"Used to?" Jack said sharply.

Toby nodded. "They're all dead of the fever. And Ulani's granny, too."

Jack stared out over the surging, purple-blue waters of the Pacific, lit now by the golden light of the fading day. A frigate bird called, wheeling high above the small bay, its call low and plaintive. Jack felt a sigh pull at his chest, a sigh that left behind a heavy ache.

"Ya dinna ask yet about the charts and log."

Jack brought his gaze back to the old man's weathered face. "Do you still have them?"

The old seaman sat down on the top step of his house. He was no longer meeting Jack's eye. "I wasna sure if you'd hear where we'd gone, or if I'd still be kickin' by the time you got around to lookin' us up. But I reckoned you'd have enough sense to figure out where we'd left 'em, if you was ever to go lookin' for 'em."

"You left them?" Jack said, his voice coming harsh out of a suddenly tight throat.

"Aye. On Rakaia."

*   *   *

After that, conversation became impossible, for news of Jack's arrival had spread and his old friends from Rakaia came crowding around. One of Titana's cousins looped a wreath of tiare and hibiscus and sweet ferns around Jack's neck, while a half-grown boy with sun-kissed skin and Toby Jenkin's sharp gray eyes ran a reverent hand along the chestnut's flank and said, "Gore. Is this a 'orse?" Jack was lost in a sea of smiling faces and warm, pressing hands.

Then India touched his arm and leaned in to say softly, "You need to go talk to her. Now."

He looked beyond her, to where Ulani sat on a spit formed by dark rocks that jutted into the bay. She stared out to sea, the breeze blowing her long hair out behind her. The graceful curve of her neck, her regal carriage—everything about her reminded Jack so much of Titana that his chest ached. But there was something indefinable about his daughter that reminded Jack of himself, as well. And it came to him as he looked at her now that it was probably the air of restlessness. And the anger.

Detaching himself gently from his old friends, Jack worked his way out onto the rocks. Gulls wheeled, screeching, overhead, their outstretched wings white against a vivid blue sky. Waves crashed at his feet, the trades flinging the spray cool and damp against his cheeks. He kept his gaze fixed on the girl child perched at the edge of the rocks. She did not turn to look at him, although he knew she was aware of his coming.

It was a scene that had played itself out a thousand

times in his imagination. The temptation to come back had been with him every day these last ten years. There'd been times when he'd wanted to see her, to be with her so badly, he would gladly have died just to touch her cheek, to watch a smile spread across her face, to hold her close and breathe in the sweet scent of her.

And now here he was, and though his throat swelled up with love for her, he was a stranger to her. And all the anger, all the resentment he'd always feared she might feel for him was there to read, in the stiff set of her shoulders, the hard line of her jaw.

She waited until he had almost reached her. Then she said, her gaze still on the distant swell of the sea, "You're him, aren't you?"

He hesitated, wanting to go closer, wanting—*needing*, desperately, to reach out to her, to touch her, yet knowing he must not. "Yes," he said simply.

Her features remained impassive, not even a flutter of an eyelid betraying a suggestion of a reaction. "You came for the charts and log from that wreck, the *Lady Juliana*."

Jack felt a sigh lift his chest. He wanted to be able to say, *I love you. I have always loved you, more even than life itself. When I sailed away and left you all those years ago, it tore a hole in my heart, a gaping wound that never healed and that has always, always ached.*

It was true, all true, and more. Yet he knew how false it would sound, were he to say such things now. So instead he said, "The morning I left Rakaia, you and I walked together down to the beach, just the two of us, hand in hand. The sun was spilling the first rays of light over the sea, and I picked you up and held you while we watched the sunrise. We watched the sea turn from gray to yellow to gold, and then to blue, and I thought about leaving you, about never seeing another sunrise with you, about never being able to hold you like that again. I thought about what it would be like, to never again be able to trace the curve of your cheek, or breathe in the sweet smell of your skin, or hear you laugh, and I almost couldn't do it. I almost couldn't leave."

"But you did," she said, her voice hard.

He nodded, his throat so tight it throbbed. "Your mother's people had already lost . . . so many. I was afraid of what else might happen to them if I stayed, if the British navy came and found me there. I was afraid of what would happen to you. So I walked back up to the village, and I handed you to one of your mother's sisters, and I left."

"My mother's sisters are all dead."

"I know. I'm so sorry."

It was a damned inadequate thing to say, and he wasn't surprised when she continued to stare silently out to sea. After a moment, he went to sit on one of the rocks near her, his gaze, like hers, on the purple-blue swells of the waves rolling inexorably into shore. "I didn't expect to ever see you again. I thought the navy would catch up with me in a couple of months. A year at the most."

The shells she'd been collecting lay in a jumble at their

feet, gleaming leopard and turban shells, and one small but beautifully flawless chambered nautilus. Reaching down, he picked one up, a brilliantly hued abalone shell. "I kept running, moving from one place to the next. Then one day it came to me how many years had passed, and I started thinking maybe I might have a future, after all. I started thinking about coming back for you."

He saw her slender throat work as she swallowed. "But you didn't."

"No." He bounced the shell up and down in his palm for a moment, then closed his fist around it. "You were so little when I left . . . I knew you couldn't possibly remember me. The only family you'd ever known were your mother's people, and Rakaia was your home. I didn't feel I had the right to take you away from everything and everyone you knew and loved."

She turned her head to look directly at him, her eyes wide and dark in a still, pale face. In that moment she looked less like a child and more like a woman, and it came to him that she was almost twelve. At twelve, many of the women in this culture were taking lovers. "You could have come to see me."

"I know." An ache settled heavily on his chest as he thought about all the years of this child's life he had missed, all her growing-up years. "I was afraid."

She shook her head, not understanding him, not believing him. "Of what?"

It was only then, as he stared deep into his daughter's angry eyes, that Jack realized he couldn't explain even to himself exactly what it was he feared, why the mere thought of returning to Rakaia overwhelmed him with such a blinding, head-throbbing terror. And so he said, "I don't know," and although it was the truth, it came out sounding pitiful and inadequate and evasive.

She gave him a long, thoughtful look. "Those things you want, we hid them in a cave on Rakaia. Did you know?"

Jack nodded.

"So you're going to have to go back there now, aren't you?"

The sun was setting, throwing out streaks of glorious color that seemed to set the sky ablaze and turned the sea into a heaving expanse of gold and purple. Somewhere out there was Rakaia. Too far away to see, and impossible to reach, now, without the *Sea Hawk*. "The problem is, I don't have a boat anymore."

Ulani laughed, suddenly very much a child as she slid off the rock and scooped up her shells. "That's not a problem," she said, her long hair flying through the air as she swung around to look back at him. "How do you think we came to be here?"

Chapter Thirty-three

"I FOUND HER washed up on the outer reef, a few years back," Toby said. They were standing at one end of the moon-bathed strand, where what had once been the jolly boat of a frigate called the *Reprise* was drawn far up on the sand, away from the reach of the tides. " 'Course, she were bunged up a bit, but I managed to salvage what I needed to fix her from the *Lady Juliana*."

Jack shifted his gaze to the blue-black, star-sparkled darkness of the sea. "It's a long ways to sail, in an open boat."

Toby pulled at his earlobe. "Aye. It was. But it was either this, or them dinky little outriggers. Or the black-birders." Once, the Rakaians had sailed the South Pacific in great seagoing canoes big enough to transport war parties, or entire families along with their pigs and dogs and whatever else they chose to carry with them when they migrated from island to island. But those days were only distant memories, commemorated in festivals but otherwise as much a part of the past as the windblown, abandoned maraes.

"It took a few trips to haul everyone over here," Toby was saying. "On the last trip, the sea was running a bit rough, and they all started puking like a passel of land-lubbers caught in a typhoon." Toby spat in disgust. "Islanders. Imagine it."

Jack squinted up at the boat's single mast. "Does she still have sails?"

"Aye. Although I can't say they wouldn't rip to shreds in a good gale."

Jack nodded, but India reached out to slip her hand into his and clasp it, fiercely. "You can't mean to go to Rakaia."

Jack searched her eyes, and saw there fear, and something else, something he wanted to think was love, but he couldn't be sure. He wondered if a man could ever be gut-sure of the love of a woman like her. And he knew the terror, and the vulnerability, of loving more than one was loved. Of not being able to live without someone who could get along just fine without him.

With slow deliberation, he lifted one shoulder in a careless shrug. "I don't see as how I have much choice."

Her hand trembled within his. "But the *Barracuda* could easily be there already, waiting for you. You know that."

Jack glanced back at Toby. "How long does it take to make the run to Rakaia?"

Toby screwed up his face with the labor of thought. "If this wind holds? I'd say five hours, maybe less."

"So if we leave early afternoon, we ought to get there around sunset."

"Aye."

In the moonlight, India's face showed pale and tight. "But you could miss the island entirely!"

Jack laughed then, because it felt good to laugh, and if he couldn't laugh, there wasn't much point in living anymore. "If I miss the island, I miss it," he said. "It's missing the passage through the reef that's liable to kill me."

India stood in the purple shadows of a spreading mango tree and watched Jack Ryder's daughter playing in the moonlit surf. A warm wind gusted up, carrying with it the salty breath of the sea and the sound of the child's laughter as she ran from a wave that broke white and foaming against the sand.

One could see the man in the child, India thought, in the high angle of the cheekbones, and the squareness of the jaw. India traced the image of the man she loved in the child he had made with another woman, and she knew the pain of want and longing, and a surge of other emotions that left her confused and shaken.

There had been a feast that night, to celebrate Jack's return to the people amongst whom he had once lived. But the child had held herself apart, always on the edge of the firelight, or absorbed, as now, in some game that seemed to occupy all of her attention. He had borne it well, India thought, laughing with his old friends, remembering past joys, and listening, intent, to their tales of all that had happened since last he'd seen them. But sometimes . . . sometimes she had caught him staring at the child with such naked longing and love in his eyes that it had been painful to see.

He was there now, standing with his back pressed against the trunk of one of the tall coco palms that lined the beach, his gaze fixed on the distant, laughing child. India went to him, her boots making soft shuffling sounds in the loose sand as she walked up to him.

He kept his face turned away from her. He smelled of the sea and the trade winds and the warm, tropically scented night, and she wanted to go to him and slip her arms around his waist and press her cheek against his hard chest. Instead, she wrapped her arms around her own waist, and hugged herself.

"You don't need to go to Rakaia," she said. "You can raise the *Sea Hawk*. Get her seaworthy enough to make it back to Neu Brenen before the monsoons hit."

He swung his head to look at her, his eyes gleaming blue-black in the night. "And then what?"

"Then you stay there, and wait for the *Barracuda* to be called home. This intense interest in you can't last forever."

A cold smile curled his lips. "In other words, I hide."

"It's what you did before."

He turned his gaze, again, to his child. "She thinks

I only came here because of the *Lady Juliana*'s charts and log."

"Then show her that she's wrong. Take her away from here now. Forget about proving your innocence. Just keep yourself safe. For her." *And for me,* she wanted to say. *Please, keep yourself safe, because I don't think I could bear it if something were to happen to you.*

He shook his head. "I won't raise her to think that's the thing to do. To run and hide."

India felt her heart twist with a renewed spasm of panic. "And who do you think is going to take care of her if you're dead? Or rotting in a British prison?"

She saw his nostrils flare on a quick intake of breath. Then his jaw hardened, and he shook his head. "I've spent the last ten years of my life running from what happened." He paused. "Running from myself. I'm not running anymore."

She stared at him. In the silvery glow of the moonlight, the sharp bones of his face looked fiercely drawn, and so dear to her that she felt the sting of tears in her eyes. She let her gaze rove hungrily over him, and the steady crash of the surf against the sand was like the pounding of her heart, dangerous, and wild.

"And if I said I'd come with you?" she somehow managed to whisper, pushing the words out past the fear that was squeezing her throat. "If I said I'd stay on Neu Brenen with you?"

She saw the flare of surprise in his eyes, and the hope that narrowed down into a wariness that was almost like pain. From one of the bungalows down the beach came the sound of a woman's voice, calling Ulani in for the night. His head turned, his chest lifting on a sigh as he watched the child run through the moonlit waves, away from him.

The wind gusted up, rustling the palm fronds overhead and fluttering the ends of his hair where it lay long and dark against his throat. "You'd do that?" he said, his gaze coming back to fix India with a fierce, intense stare. "You'd do that to keep me from going to Rakaia?"

"Yes."

He reached for her, his palm cupping the back of her neck to draw her to him. "Then maybe if I make it back from Rakaia, you'll still stay."

She went to him, her arms sliding around his waist to hold his warm, hard body close to hers. "Jack—"

"No." His mouth took hers in a kiss that was fierce, burning, almost cruel. "No," he whispered again, his lips moving against hers. "Don't try to talk me out of this. Just make love to me, India. Just love me."

The afternoon was hot and overcast, the sky a smudgy gray that hung low and forbidding over choppy seas.

Jack stood at the water's edge, the wind throwing a wild salty spray against his face as he stared into the hazy distance. "We could wait until tomorrow," he said, although he knew that with each passing day, the likelihood increased that he would find the *Barracuda* waiting for him at Rakaia.

Beside him, Toby Jenkins shook his head and spat into the frothing surf. "Ulani tells me she had a look at the sea urchins, and they're still out."

They had an old saying on Rakaia, *The ocean roars and the sea urchins listen.* No Rakaian ever put out to sea without checking first to make sure the echini hadn't crawled into their holes. It was the surest weather forecast Jack had ever known.

He glanced over to where the jolly boat rocked back and forth in the pounding surf, despite the steadying hands of the islanders who had volunteered to sail with them. In the time he'd spent staring out to sea, the boat had acquired two extra passengers. And he understood now why Ulani had been inspecting sea urchins that morning.

He splashed through the fast-running surf to where India and his daughter had taken up positions in the boat's prow.

"We're coming," India said, her gaze locking with his as he walked up to them, "so don't even try to argue with us."

Jack looked from her still, carefully composed face to Ulani's fierce scowl, and back again. "We?"

"That's correct. We arrived at our decisions independently, but we find ourselves in perfect agreement."

He sucked in a deep breath. "Have you taken a good look at that sea?"

"I am untroubled by mal de mer. And I have it on the best of authority that since the echini have not sought refuge in their usual places of concealment, we are unlikely to encounter weather any more severe than this."

"Maybe. But we could very easily encounter a certain royal corvette."

She stared at him with a wide, unblinking gaze. "All the more reason for our presence."

He knew what she was saying, and he didn't like it. "Oh, no. It's not going to happen that way. So you can just get out of the bloody boat right now."

She sucked in a quick, angry breath that flared her nostrils and lifted her breasts in a way that stirred a quick, unbidden memory of the things they had done together last night, with the trade winds warm against their sweat-slicked skin and her breasts soft and heavy in his hands.

"There, you see," she was saying. "It is precisely this sort of autocratic male behavior that has given me a distaste for marriage. I would certainly never presume to order you about in such a dictatorial fashion."

Jack wrapped his hands around the gunwale and leaned into it, his voice pitched deliberately low and even. "India, I'm worried about you. You and Ulani."

Her expression didn't alter. "Thank you for your concern, but if I choose to risk my life, it is my own affair."

His hands clenched the gunwale so tight he wondered it didn't crack. His voice was no longer low and even, but loud and harsh. "And I suppose you're going to try to convince me that my daughter's safety is none of my affair, either?"

It was Ulani who spoke, her gaze lifting beyond Jack, to Toby Jenkins. "You didn't tell him, did you?"

Jack spun around to glare at Toby, who was pulling his earlobe and staring at the wind-whipped sea, and the mist-covered hillside—anything and everything but Jack.

"Tell me what?"

Toby pursed his lips and blew out a long, slow breath. "When we decided to leave Rakaia, I put the *Lady Juliana*'s charts and log back into the old half cask they'd washed ashore in, and asked one of Titana's uncles to hide it in the caves. Ulani here went with him."

"Which cave?"

The old seaman's brine-stiffened whiskers swept back and forth as he worked his mouth. "I don't rightly know for sure. I reckon we could find it, if we looked long enough. But I didn't think you had a mind to linger on the island."

Jack swung back to where his daughter sat, graceful and serene at the prow of the boat, her long dark hair streaming in the wind. He opened his mouth to *order* her to tell him where they'd hidden the cask, but the stubborn tilt of her chin and the flash of anger in her eyes told him he could bluster and yell all he wanted, and she still wouldn't tell him. Not until she was ready.

Then her head turned, her lips parting on a quick intake of breath as she stared out over the heavy sea, and something about the angle of her chin and the curve of her cheek reminded him so much of Titana that his chest ached. "Please," she said, her eyes dark and huge as she looked at him again. "I just want to go back to Rakaia."

He stared at her, at this child he had made, and loved, and forced himself to stay away from for so many years. And it came to him that while a man might think he controls his own life, all he can really do is try to make the right choices. And half the time those are wrong, anyway.

He held her gaze steadily. "You're sure about the echini?"

A slow, triumphant smile curved her lips and lightened her eyes, and she nodded.

Jack slapped the side of the boat and made ready to shove off. "Then I guess we'd better get going."

～～Chapter Thirty-four

ALEX PRESTON STOOD up to his thighs in the gently lapping waters of Rakaia's broad lagoon, his hands braced against his hips as he bent over almost double. When he'd left his shoes and socks on the white sand and rolled up his trousers, he'd only meant to wade out a little ways. He'd felt vaguely foolish, even a bit guilty, doing it, but a quick glance around had reassured him that he was alone. It wouldn't have done for one of the men to catch their first lieutenant in such an undignified posture.

He'd been cautious at first, wading only in the shallows. But the lure of those impossibly clear, magic-filled waters had beckoned him on until a wave sloshed against the rolled-up legs of his trousers, wetting him to his knees. And then he thought, Well, since I'm already wet . . .

Sucking in a deep breath of air that puffed out his cheeks, Alex cinched his lips together tight, thrust his face into the water, and opened his eyes. He saw the spreading jaws of an enormous clam, a hundred years old or more, surrounded by a wonderland of corals in sapphire and yellow, crimson and orange, some high and feathery, others smooth and bulbous. He saw twinkling yellow and green tiddlers, and slow-moving parrot fish, and quick silver flashes of reef trout. Again and again, he plunged his face into the lagoon, raising his head only when he needed to take another breath. He had to step warily, of course, keeping to the narrow patches of clear sand. He longed to strip off his clothes and paddle out farther, to where new wonders beckoned. Instead, he straightened reluctantly, water dripping down his cheeks and off his nose, and headed back to shore.

The pounding of the surf against the island's fringing reef filled the air with an endless boom and crash that mingled with the wheeling calls of the seabirds and the seductive rustling of the coco palms. There was a still, white quality to the cloud-filtered light that told him the sun would be setting soon. Rolling down his wet trousers, he sat on a wave-smoothed rock and thrust his legs out before him to dry.

They had been here for three days now, and still the beauty of this place had the power to take his breath and leave him feeling restless and vaguely sad. The main island was fairly small, a steep-sided mountain cloaked in a velvety green mantle of giant rain-forest trees dripping with orchids and ferns and great pendent ropes of lianas. Along the gleaming white sandy beaches grew the coconut palms, their delicate fronds waving gently in the warm, fragrant breezes, while the narrow valleys abounded with oranges and pineapples, guavas and bananas and mangoes—an endless harvest of sweet fruit, free for the taking.

His trousers were still damp, but he put on his shoes and socks and walked along the sand. In the long, idyll days since the *Barracuda* had dropped anchor in the lagoon behind the island, Alex had avoided this part of the beach. Now he found himself oddly drawn to it. He walked past rows of pandanus-and-bamboo bungalows, standing silent and empty in the gentle evening light. A whisper of sound brought him jerking around, thinking someone was there, but it was only a loose corner of thatch, lifting in the warm breeze.

He walked on. A small chapel built of crudely cut coral blocks stood at the far end of the deserted village, and beyond that, a cemetery filled with row after row of silent mounds of freshly turned earth rapidly disappearing beneath a luxurious growth of running vines and softly waving grasses. Most of the graves were marked with simple wooden crosses. But in the older section of the graveyard, he could see a rough granite slab almost overgrown with creeping fig.

Intrigued, he tore away the vines and found himself staring at a deeply carved inscription. IN LOVING MEMORY OF TITANA AND HER UNBORN CHILD, MURDERED BY THE BRITISH NAVY ON SEPTEMBER 10, 1874. Below that was something else he couldn't quite read. Alex had been making a study of the various Polynesian dialects, and as he traced the crudely incised letters with his finger, it came to him suddenly what it said. *Ari rangi.* Paradise is empty.

Sitting back on his heels, Alex stared at those painstakingly incised words. After so many months at sea, he more than understood the carnal urgings that could drive a man to couple with one of the beautiful, half-naked women with which these islands abounded. But raw sexual hunger didn't explain this, this tortured outpouring of grief and rage and love.

The gusting wind brought him a faint spray from the sea. Lifting his head, he stared off across the pale green waters of the lagoon, to where twin islets of golden sand studded with palms marked the site of the passage through the wave-pounded reef. Yet the position of the islets was deceptive, for instead of lying midway between them, the channel through Rakaia's barrier reef curved unexpectedly close to the western islet. On a calm day, when the lagoon lay smooth and undisturbed, one could clearly see the shelves of coral that rested just below the surface of the water, stretching out far beyond the eastern atoll. But with a storm churning up the sea, those jagged rocks would lurk unseen, a deadly graveyard for the unwary.

There was something about the brooding silence of a shipwreck that caught at a navy man's throat and twisted itself deep down into the guts of him. Alex found he had to force himself to stare at what was left of the *Lady Juliana*, looming up dark and ghostly now in the fading light of the day.

At some time in the past ten years, a storm had ripped the ship in two and carried the prow out to sea, where bits of her perhaps still floated, worn, unidentifiable. Now only the stern remained, the canted lower decks awash with the sea. One more bad storm, Alex thought, and there would be nothing left but that silent, deadly shelf of coral. Nothing to show precisely where the *Lady Juliana* had come to grief. Nothing to prove the guilt or innocence of the man accused of steering her to her death.

Not that Alex believed the man, of course. But Simon Granger must, he realized, or else they wouldn't be here, idling away the days, the *Barracuda* carefully anchored out of sight on the far side of the island, with seamen set to watch the single passage through the reef from sunrise to sunset. Or maybe the captain didn't believe in the existence of those old charts, either. Maybe he was simply counting on a father's love for his daughter to bring Jack Ryder back to this beautiful, deserted island.

Alex thought about those empty bungalows, and the mounds of turned earth. Someone had been left alive, obviously, to bury the dead. But there was no one here now, only a noisy flock of vivid red king parrots, feasting on the fruit of an old walnut tree, and a frigate bird that soared high and lonely above the lagoon turning rose and silver now with the dying of the day.

It was past time to be returning to the ship. Even the men Granger had set to watch the channel would have given up by now. And still Alex lingered, his gaze on the long lines of darkening breakers outside the reef. For a moment, he thought he saw something. The swelling waves of the open sea hid it from his sight, but then it reappeared, not an eddy, or a drifting spar, but a boat. A small, open boat hovering just off the island.

Alex stood very still, his eyes narrowed. At first, he didn't think the boat even had a sail, for there was no telltale flash of white, no billowing canvas to catch the last rays of the setting sun peeking through a break in the cloud cover. He was about to turn away, dismissing the small vessel from his thoughts, when he realized it did have sails. Sails that had been dyed.

It was an old pirate's trick, darkening a vessel's sails, but a trick that every officer in Her Majesty's navy knew, as well. It was said that Nelson himself had once used the tactic, to surprise a French warship on a moonless night.

Alex stood on the beach, the wind flattening his damp trousers against his legs. The glorious palette of gold-streaked vermilion and violet cast across the cloudy sky by the setting sun faded. And still the small boat held off, tacking back and forth just off the entrance to the passage. Alex watched it until he was certain there was no mistaking the vessel's intent. Then he turned away, loose sand flying up to stick to his wet trousers as he hurried along the shoreline to tell Simon Granger that his gamble had paid off.

Jack Ryder had come to them.

The echini had been right. Half an hour out of Waigeu, a brief squall set the jolly boat's short square sail to whipping furiously in the wind and dumped enough rain to soak them all to the skin. But then the storm passed, and though the cloud cover lingered, the sea calmed, and the wind blew light and easy.

By the time the rugged, heavily forested slopes of Rakaia appeared before them, the day had not yet begun to darken toward evening. And so they tacked back and forth off the sandy islets that marked the entrance to the passage through the island's fringing reef, close enough to keep their bearings yet hopefully not so close as to attract the attention of anyone who might be watching for a sleek, schooner-rigged yacht such as the *Sea Hawk*.

But as the sky turned from gray to rose to purple, they had no choice but to draw in closer. There would be no moon that night, and while the darkness would help conceal them from any watching eyes, it would also make it easy to miss the passage entirely and run up onto the reef.

India shifted closer to the prow, her gaze roving over the island before them as the jolly boat came around, the water sucking and splashing against the sides. Even with the sky overcast and the light fading quickly from the day, the island was beautiful, its steep, dark slopes ringed by snowy white coral beaches that glimmered from out of the darkness, and palm trees that bent gracefully in the evening breeze. She could smell the island's sweet spiciness, mingling with the brine of the sea. And she had the most peculiar sensation, as if she were returning to a place she had known before, a place that was somehow more a part of her than what she had left behind.

She glanced at Jack, who sat silent and watchful beside his daughter. It couldn't be easy for him, coming back to this place where so much had happened, and from which he'd stayed away for so long. There was a brittleness about him, a wary tension, as if he were tamping down every emotion, every reaction. Emotions had a way of making a man uncomfortable, making a man feel weak. And so she supposed he had decided not to allow himself to feel anything. She couldn't begin to understand how he could do it, and she thought the costs must be terrible. As they drew closer to the surf-battered reef, even Ulani seemed tense, her eyes wide and still as she stared at the island that had once been her home.

"I don't see no masts," said Toby Jenkins, his eyes narrowing as he peered into the gathering gloom.

Jack shook his head. "If Granger is here, you can be sure he has the *Barracuda* anchored somewhere out of sight."

They were hauling in close to the reef now, and it was so dark India found it impossible to believe that anyone, even a native born and raised on this island, could possibly see the channel. And then, as she watched one of

Titana's cousins lean over the side of the boat, his head tilted to one side, his expression one of fixed concentration, she realized she was right: he couldn't see the channel. But he could hear it; he could hear and identify every eddy and gurgle, every subtle nuance of rushing water and swirling tides, while around them, the air filled with the thundering cannonade of the surf hitting the outer reef.

There was no way of knowing if the *Barracuda* had made it here before them. And so they were careful not to speak, slipping silently past the ghostly hulk of what was left of the *Lady Juliana*, caught forever in her death throes on the edge of the reef. India looked up at the ship's shattered, twisted timbers, and felt her breath back up in her chest.

It was Jack's plan, she had discovered, to be away from Rakaia again before sunrise. But as the jolly boat glided smoothly across the empty lagoon toward the main island's beach and India stared at those dark, wooded slopes, such a scheme struck her as impossible.

"It's too dark," she whispered, leaning in close to Jack. "You'll never find that cave without a moon."

Beside her, Ulani kept her gaze fixed on the high mass of the island, rising up dark and beautiful before them. "I'll find it," she said.

～～Chapter Thirty-five

THEY DREW THE jolly boat up onto the sand beneath the spreading branches of a royal poinciana. The island waited hushed and dark before them, the only sounds the swaying of the fronds of the coconut palms along the beach, and the gentle slosh of the surf in the lagoon, and the melancholy cry of an 'u'upa, far off in the night. They were said to be the shadows of the ghosts that haunt the woods, the 'u'upa, and at the sound Toby Jenkins went utterly still.

"I reckon I'll stay here, with the lads," he said, his gaze sweeping the purple shadows of the acacia and mango trees. "Keep a lookout for trouble."

Jack glanced at Ulani, who stood at the darkened line of sand edging the lagoon, her attention fixed on the row of silent, deserted bungalows that stretched away down the palm-lined beach. "You don't need to come with me," he said softly. "You can just tell me where the cave is."

She turned her head to look at him, her eyes wide and still in the heavy darkness. "I'm not afraid."

"I didn't think you were. But this is why you wanted to come, wasn't it? To be here."

She hesitated, then said, "Uncle Revi told me you used to spend a lot of time up on the point, when you first came to the island. He said you used to sit up there for hours, just watching for a ship."

Jack swung about, his gaze lifting to the rocky bluff that rose high above the village to thrust out like a sheltering arm into the lagoon. In those first weeks after he'd been lost off the *Lady Juliana*, he'd spent every minute he could at the tip of that point, his gaze desperately raking the endless, deep blue waves for a glimpse of white sails billowing with the wind. But then one day Titana had come to him there, and the sense of urgency that had been driving him day and night to try to find some way off the island had melted away in the softly scented heat of her embrace.

Jack felt a shudder pass through him, and he wrenched his mind away from the memory. Too many memories, one leading to the other, until they all ended in that blur of hideously succeeding images that he couldn't revisit. Not here, where it had happened.

He'd been ignoring the pain in his head for a long time now, but it was getting harder and harder to do. He was used to the pain, he could deal with that. The problem was, it was starting to affect his sight. It was as if he were looking through rippling water lit from the side with jagged flashes of shadowed light.

His daughter peered at him strangely, her head tilting as she studied him. He wondered what she could see in his face. "Uncle Revi said you'd know where the cave was."

Jack nodded, his lips pressing together tightly. It was taboo, the cave on the point. He supposed Revi had figured the charts would be safer there because of it. "You stay here. It shouldn't take me long."

He started to turn away, but was stopped by the light touch of a hand on his arm.

"I'm coming with you," India said.

He was having a hard time focusing on her face. "You don't need to do that."

"I think I do."

And so he nodded, because he figured she was probably right.

Toby Jenkins leaned his back against the smooth trunk of a giant coconut palm and tried to get comfortable. From where he sat, the distant breakers smashing against the outer reef were only a vague silver line of curling foam, half lost in the blackness of the night. But he smiled at the familiar sight of it, his eyes half closing as he lifted his face to a gentle night breeze heavy with the scent of the sea and the jasminelike sweetness of the teatea-maowa, its blossoms glowing white and beautiful in the darkness.

They shouldn't have done it, he decided; they shouldn't have left the island. Nothing had been right since then. They'd all been cranky and short-tempered and dismal for months. They all wanted to be home, to be on Rakaia.

It had been Father Paul's idea, their leaving. Toby had been against the scheme right from the start, even when the fever was raging so fierce it seemed there wouldn't be any of them left alive at the end of it. But then the blackbirders had come, and the sight of his own wee lad caught fast in the clutches of some thieving Yankee bastard had rattled Toby more than he could begin to understand.

Yet now, as he stared off across the gently sloshing waters of Rakaia's darkened lagoon, Toby knew it had been a mistake. They never should have let those bloody blackbirders chase them away from here. This was their home. What they should have done was maybe got their hands on some old cannon and mounted it on one of them islets by the passage. Let everyone know they meant business and weren't to be trifled with. He'd put it to the others, he decided, as soon as he got back tomorrow. Put it to them that maybe the time had come to move back here, permanently.

It wouldn't be the same, of course. It would never be like it used to be. Too many were gone, and the islands were all changing, changing fast, in ways he didn't like. Twelve years ago, when Fate had taken a hand in Toby's life and swept him off the *Lady Juliana* and deposited him on this little speck of Paradise, the island had been so isolated that he and Ryder had gone for almost two years without seeing any outsider except for the old French priest. Now Rakaia was on the bloody *map*. The island was too small to ever attract a regular steamer, like Waigeu had, but two or three times a year they had sloops putting into the lagoon, fancy little yachts full of *tourists*, for Christ's sake.

Toby heaved a heartfelt sigh, feeling suddenly old and tired, and maybe a bit hungry, too. Rubbing his eyes against the threat of sleep, he lurched to his feet. The other lads had already nodded off, sprawled in the sand beside the beached boat, while Ulani sat at the water's edge, her arms wrapped about her updrawn knees, her gaze fixed on the darkly surging waters of the lagoon. He thought about going looking for a banana or something, but the unnatural emptiness of the island unnerved him. A vague rustling of the brush farther up the beach had him taking in a quick, startled breath.

They called them the tupapau, and they were the nasty ghosts of those who couldn't rest. Horrible things, they were, with tongues three feet long they used to rip a man's face to shreds. Toby took a step back, wishing he had a couple of bamboo sticks he could rub together and make the tupapau disappear. But then he realized bamboo sticks would be useless, because what he was seeing was not the tupapau, but a line of British bluejackets. The air filled with the metallic, deadly click of a dozen or

more rifles being cocked, and a crisp, authoritarian voice
that said, "Mr. Jenkins, I presume?"

Jack followed a painfully familiar trail that left the
narrow valley floor and climbed steadily, through thick-
ets of tall dripping ferns and dark brakes of giant bamboo canes. Memories kept crowding in on him, images
sometimes sweet, sometimes savage that flicked across
his mind like the flashes of jagged light that zigzagged
across his eyes, nearly blinding him. He kept trying to
push the memories away, but it wasn't working.

At the base of a rocky outcrop he stopped to rest,
his back pressed against the hard stone, his chest lifting
heavily with his breathing. India didn't say anything, just
looked at him in that still, thoughtful way she had. But
when they pushed on, she went ahead of him.

As they neared the top of the ridge, the path grew
steeper, the soft stone crumbling under their feet until
they were grasping at parau branches and the roots of giant ferns to help them scramble up. Through the jagged
flashes of darkness and light distorting his vision, he
could see the spreading limbs of the old screw pine that
grew at the end of the point, its strange tufts lifted up
dark and gaunt to the glowing sky. But it didn't occur to
him that they were losing the protective cloak of darkness until he heard India whisper, "The moon is coming
out."

His head falling back, Jack stared up at a patch of
blue-black sky thickly scattered with stars. The cloud

cover was breaking up, scuttling away on the fast-moving trades. By the time they came out on the steep, windblown bluff, the sky looked as if it had been scoured clean, leaving the edges of the moon as clear and sharp as a razor. "Well, hell."

She went to the edge of the precipice, where the land fell away sharply to the empty lagoon. "There's no one here," she said softly.

Jack went to stand beside her, his gaze on the still, moon-glazed waters below. "No one we can see."

He realized she was no longer looking at the lagoon, but at him. "Your head hurts, doesn't it?"

He turned away from her, to the jumble of volcanic rocks that marked the entrance to a low cave set into the hillside rising above the bluff. He'd brought what was left of India's tin of safety matches with him, and he lit one now, the light flaring up bright and golden to dance over the dark, rough stones that closed in around him. Here and there, propped up in crevices, or set in rows on low ledges like so many precious ornaments, were white skulls that seemed to glow at him from out of the gloom.

He heard India suck in a quick breath behind him. "How old do you think they are?"

"Old. Probably from before Cook's time." Jack lifted the match high, the flickering flame passing over a scattering of loose rocks to gleam dully on a curve of smooth, aged wood. Then the flame burned down to his fingers and he said, "*Shit,*" and let the match fall.

"Here, give me the matches," India said, her voice echoing in the sudden darkness.

He handed her the tin. He heard a scratching hiss, then the small, close space glowed again with light.

Hunkering down on his heels, Jack reached to grasp the old half barrel and felt it collapse in his hands, wood splintering, rusted hoops falling with a clatter against stone. But in that brief instant before the match went out again, he saw it, lying there beneath the shattered staves: a large bundle, wrapped up in an old oilskin tied with braided pandanus.

"Sorry," said India.

Another match flared, chasing away the suffocating blackness. With shaking hands, Jack pushed aside the half-rotten wood and lifted the awkward parcel toward him. His fingers slid over hard edges beneath the worn cloth, his heart pounding with a mingling of relief and a strange, horrified aversion. The images were pressing in on him again, too fast and vivid to push away. He stood abruptly, just as the light went out.

"There's only one match left," India said.

"It doesn't matter. Let's get out of here."

She went ahead of him, ducking her head as she passed through the low opening out into the silvery moonlight. He followed more slowly, the oilskin-wrapped bundle tucked beneath one arm, the other hand outstretched as he felt his way carefully, for he was almost blind now, the jagged flashes of dark and light dancing a furious crescendo of pain across his eyes.

At the entrance to the cave he paused, his outstretched hand flat against the rock face, his chest heaving as he drew the fresh, sea-scented air deep into his lungs and tried to will the memories and the pounding pain they brought to go away.

He wasn't sure what told him something was wrong. He heard the distant thundering boom of the surf hitting the reef, and the sighing of the grass bending in the wind. Slowly, he turned his head to where India stood bathed in the silver-blue light of the night, a gun barrel pressed against her right temple.

"Hello, Jack," said Simon Granger.

∾∾Chapter Thirty-six

ALEX PRESTON STOOD on the moonlit crescent of sand before the dead village. The surf beating against the offshore reef filled the air with a distant thundering roar and the scent of the sea. He kept trying not to stare at the wreck of the *Lady Juliana*, its black hulk grounded in white foam. Then he realized he was looking at it again, and jerked his gaze away to where Jack Ryder's daughter sat on the hard-packed sand at the lagoon's edge.

He found he was glad she was still alive. He couldn't have said why it should have mattered to him, but he thought it had something to do with that painstakingly carved slab of granite behind the deserted chapel. And then he realized the girl was returning his regard with a steady stare of her own.

"You're a British naval officer," she said.

Alex cleared his throat uncomfortably. "Yes."

"My father used to be in the navy." Her English surprised him. He supposed she'd picked it up from that old salt Toby Jenkins. But he thought she must have made a special effort to learn this language of her father. And it struck him suddenly as unutterably tragic, that she should have found her father again now, only to be losing him.

Alex let his head fall back, his gaze raking the bluff above the village. He'd managed to alert the *Barracuda* and make it back here with the captain and a dozen seamen in time to see the old jolly boat putting into shore. Alex had expected Captain Granger to order the men to rush the beach at once, but he hadn't. He'd held them back, watching and listening while Jack Ryder and India McKnight set off through the rain forest. Then he'd ordered Alex to secure the men on the beach while Simon Granger himself followed Ryder, with just two able seamen at his back.

The arrangement made Alex uncomfortable. He couldn't get it out of his head that the captain was allowing his past friendship with Jack Ryder to interfere with the performance of his duties. Alex kept thinking about what would happen to his career if Simon Granger let Jack Ryder slip away from them again. What his family would say if Alex let them down. He felt the weight of their expectations, the urgency of his future, weighing heavily upon him. The captain had specifically ordered Alex to stay here on the beach with the men, and yet . . .

"Nash," said Alex, coming to a painful, heart-thumping decision.

Nash snapped to instant attention. "Yes, sir?"

"Take charge of the men here."

Nash blinked. "Yes, sir."

The path through the rain forest was easy to follow. Alex took it at a dogtrot, not slowing his pace until the trail began to climb steeply, his boots slipping in the damp soil, his hands scrabbling for fistfuls of fern and twisted roots. He kept running over and over in his head what he was going to say to Simon Granger, how he could possibly explain his blatant disregard of a direct order, but he couldn't come up with anything that didn't sound feeble even to his own ears.

At a curve in the trail, Alex hesitated, his breath soughing in and out of his throat, his stomach roiling with a growing awareness of the arrogance of what he was doing and its hideous consequences if he was wrong. Swallowing hard, he stared up at the dark bulk of the point, then back at the distant curve of the bay below. He was within a breath of turning back when an unexplained sound brought his head around, and he saw the outline of a seaman's cap dark against the starlit sky.

"What are you doing here?" Alex demanded, climbing up to where the men, lolling at their ease, suddenly jerked to attention at the sight of him. "Where is Captain Granger?"

"He went on up t' the point, sir," said the younger of the two men, his eyes so wide Alex could see the whites glowing in the dark. "He told us to wait here."

Alex knew an instant of sweet, selfishly-based gratification, followed quickly by a surge of angry indignation. He didn't stop to think about exactly how he intended to keep Simon Granger from helping his old friend. He only knew that the man responsible for that dark, wave-washed wreck beside the passage was not going to leave this island a free man.

Not a second time.

India felt the warm sea breeze flutter a loose lock of hair across her cheek. The gun barrel was cold and hard against her skin, Simon Granger's grip on her upper arm brutal enough that she had to bite her lip to keep from gasping with pain. With pain, and fear, and a deep, abiding sense of foreboding.

"So Toby Jenkins found the ship's log and charts, after all," she heard Granger say. "Who'd have thought it?"

Jack paused in a pool of moonlight just outside the cave's entrance, the oilskin packet gripped in one hand. "Let her go, Simon."

Simon shook his head. "In a moment. As soon as you toss that packet over the cliff."

"No." India bucked against the Englishman's grip, then went utterly still as the rasp of the revolver's hammer being cocked sounded loud beside her ear. She was trembling all over, her voice cracking as she said, "Don't do it, Jack. Don't."

The gun barrel shifted against India's temple, scoring

the skin hard enough that she couldn't quite stop herself from sucking in her breath in a quick hiss. "You know I'm not bluffing, Jack," said Simon. "Throw it. Now."

Jack stood motionless, and it seemed to India as if for one suspended instant the wind ceased sighing through the swaying grass and the surf went silent while the world waited with a breath-held intensity. Then his arm moved, his hand opening to fling the oilskin-wrapped package in an arc that carried it over the edge of the precipice and into oblivion. She heard a succession of soft thuds as it bounced from rock to rock, a clattering of loose sliding stones. Then all was silent again except for the wind and the distant thunder of the surf.

"But why?" said India, her heart aching as if it were being squeezed by a fist. "Why?"

"Why?" Jack stood with his hands hanging empty at his sides. A strange smile curled his lips. "I suppose because Gladstone never did change his orders, did he, Simon?"

The man holding India said nothing, although she felt his chest lift with a sharp intake of breath.

It was Jack who spoke. "I remember how after I warned him the *Lady Juliana* was cutting too close to the eastern isle, Gladstone turned and asked what you thought, if you believed me. And you said no."

"There was no reason to believe you." Granger's fingers were digging into India's arm, the hand holding the pistol to her forehead clenching the handle so tightly it was quivering. "You'd just spent the last hour raging like some kind of a madman, swearing you'd see us all dead."

"But Gladstone did believe me," Jack said softly. "He told you to order the helmsman to cut in close to the western isle. Only, you thought you were right, that I was determined to kill you all. And so you didn't relay the order."

"Gladstone believed you because he didn't know. He didn't know you were planning to come back to this island to live. He didn't know how you felt about the natives we killed, about that girl. He didn't know *you*— what you're capable of. But I knew you, Jack. I knew you."

A quiver of some emotion contorted Jack's face, something India thought might have been an echo of horror, and an old, old guilt. "I won't deny I thought about it. I thought about keeping my mouth shut and letting the *Lady Juliana* rip out her guts on that reef. I thought about it, but in the end I couldn't do it."

"Damn you." A strange, contorted sound slipped from a painful place deep inside Simon Granger's chest. "Damn you all to hell, Jack. How was I to know? How was I to know you'd changed your mind?" The fist pressing the gun to India's temple wavered, as if that awful sound had come from the tearing loose of something inside him, something he'd held in tightly for ten long years.

"So what are you planning to do now, Simon? Kill me?"

Simon's throat bunched as he swallowed hard. "My orders are to take you in to be hanged."

Jack's head lifted, the moonlight limning his cheeks as a ghost of a smile tightened the skin beside his eyes. "And if I tell them what really happened?"

"Tell your tale to the Admiralty, if you wish. No one will believe you."

India pressed her lips together, holding back a useless, angry outburst. Because what he said was true. No one would take the word of a renegade against a British naval captain. A hero. With Gladstone and the helmsman both dead, there was no one left alive to say what had really happened on that awful day ten years ago. No one except Jack, and Simon Granger.

"And Miss McKnight?" Jack's gaze met hers. India stared deep into his dark, intense eyes, and knew what she had to do. "She knows the truth."

The man holding her shrugged, his grip on India's arm slackening. "After what she's done, do you think anyone will believe her? She'll be lucky if she doesn't hang with you."

Bending double at the waist, suddenly, quickly, India jerked her right arm out of Simon Granger's grasp and lunged away from him. The maneuver caught him by surprise. He turned, reaching for her, just as Jack grabbed one of the skulls off a ledge at the cave's entrance and brought it smashing down on the back of Simon's head.

He staggered, his grip on the pistol in his hand tightening as he turned. Jack's foot flashed out. The revolver flew through the air, and the night exploded with noise and fire and the raw smell of sulfur.

~~Chapter Thirty-seven

A DEADLY WHISPER rushed past India's cheek. She heard the clatter of metal striking rock, and the pistol disappeared into the darkness, leaving only drifts of light gray smoke and the smell of burnt gunpowder.

Simon Granger swung to face Jack and caught a boot in the stomach as Jack kicked out a second time. The Englishman went down hard on his back in the rock-strewn grass, the breath leaving his chest in an abrupt *wouff*. For an instant he simply lay there, sucking in air. He was curling up on his elbows when Jack threw himself on him.

Granger's foot came out, catching Jack's fall, his hands grasping folds of Jack's shirt and using Jack's own momentum to send him tumbling in a flip over Simon's head. This time the grunt was from Jack.

Dropping to her hands and knees, India scrambled about in the darkness, her eyes squinting against the night, her hands brushing over rough stones and dried leaves as she searched frantically for the revolver. Then the sound of flesh smacking against stone brought her head up, and she saw that the two men were now grappling with each other on the ground, rolling over and over in the windblown grass, dangerously close to the cliff's edge.

"You sonofabitch," Jack hissed as Granger's big-boned, rangy body pinned him to the ground. "All these years, you let me take the blame for something you did."

"You think you're innocent?" Simon's breath came in a hoarse, wheezing effort, his hands closing around Jack's throat. "You lost sight of where your loyalties belonged, Jack. That's why the *Lady Juliana* ended up on that reef. Because of you."

"No. I tried to save her." Bringing up both hands, he chopped outward at Simon's elbows, breaking Simon's hold and heaving up with a groaning push that flung Simon sideways.

There was a rush of falling stones, bouncing and rattling as the ground gave way beneath the Englishman and he slid backward, his legs and lower torso shooting out into a dark void, his fingers scratching frantically through the grass for a handhold.

"Jesus, Simon." Jack dropped to his stomach at the edge of the precipice, his hand stretched out. "Grab my hand."

Simon's big fingers closed hard around Jack's wrist, his weight dragging Jack forward until Jack's head and shoulders hung over the edge of the bluff.

"Jack!" India screamed, pushing up, running.

"Try to climb back up," Jack said, his other hand wrapping around Simon's, gripping him hard, the toes of his boots digging into the soft earth.

Simon's voice was a tight thread, his feet kicking in space, his fingers showing white where they dug into Jack's wrist. "I can't."

"Yes you can."

"No. I'm going." Something flashed in the Englishman's eyes, something cold and lethal. "I should have died here ten years ago. We both deserved to die . . . along with all those men."

With a welling of terror, India realized that Simon Granger had quit trying to heave himself up. He was using all of his weight, instead, to drag Jack over the edge with him.

Jack's shoulders heaved, his breath coming in rasping gasps as he strained determinedly, uselessly, to pull his old friend to safety. Loose stones rolled, bouncing into the darkness as Jack slid slowly, inexorably out over the edge.

"You stupid bastard," Jack said, his breath wheezing out through gritted teeth. "Don't do this."

Simon's lips peeled away from his teeth in an eerie rictus of a smile. "Come on, Jack. Come die with me."

A curious sound, like a haunted, mewling cry, escaped from India's lips before she could stop it. She thought about throwing herself on Jack's legs, adding her weight to his, but she knew it wouldn't be enough.

She spun about, stumbling over a half-buried stone as she lurched toward the cave's entrance. In the soft moonlight, a row of skulls gleamed white and ethereal. Her hands closed around the first one and she swung about in a running rush to lob it as hard as she could at Simon Granger's upturned face.

She heard the dull thud of its impact, bone striking bone. Heard Simon's startled grunt, then a long, thin scream as he lost his grip on Jack's wrist and tumbled backward into space.

"Oh my God," India whispered, as the ancient skull clattered and bounced down the cliff face.

Scrambling to his feet, Jack caught her in his arms and swung her about to clutch her to him. She grabbed fistfuls of his shirt, holding him close. Their chests shuddered together, their breath coming hard and fast.

"I thought I'd lost you," she said, rubbing her cheek against his, over and over again. "Oh, God. I thought I'd lost you."

An odd, wistful smile lit his eyes. "I thought you didn't want me."

She shook her head, her throat so tight it hurt. "I never said I didn't want you." Tears welled up in her eyes, turning the moon and the distant white-curled surf and the looming mass of the bluff into indistinct blurs of darkness and light. And then she saw a shadow of movement, and knew she was looking at the outline of a man, silhouetted against the starry sky. "Jack," she said, her voice a low warning.

But he was already turning, his body tensing as a young officer with dark hair and a tightly set face held out a pistol gripped shakily in both hands and said, "Don't move."

Alex Preston had never believed in shades of gray. He believed there was right, and then there was wrong, and the line between the two was as clearly drawn and unmistakable as the line between those who were good and those who were evil.

Now he stood on a moon-bathed bluff at the darkened edge of nowhere, and felt as if the earth were shifting beneath his feet, as if the sea-scented wind were ripping him apart, tearing him open and leaving him bleeding.

He gripped his pistol tighter, his jaw clenching as he concentrated all his being on keeping the barrel from wavering.

"I think you must have been there a while," said the man before him, this man Alex had thought a traitor to his own kind. The personification of evil.

Alex swallowed hard, trying to clear his throat of the obstruction that seemed to have lodged there. And still his voice sounded like a hoarse frog's. "Long enough."

Long enough that he had simply watched the two men fight, because he somehow couldn't figure out which one he should be making a move to help. Long enough that his world had come unstrung, cut loose, adrift.

"Simon Granger would never have dreamt of deliberately wrecking that ship," Alex said, because it seemed an important point to make. "But you did. You thought about it. You said so yourself. You said you almost did it."

"Yes." Jack Ryder stood with his back to the black void of space, India McKnight silent and white-faced at his side. Alex was keeping an eye on her, too. The woman was dangerous—not what a woman should be at all. "I thought about it," Ryder said. "But in the end, I didn't do it."

"But you could have. And if you had been deliberately steering that ship onto the reef, then what Simon Granger did would have saved the lives of hundreds of men."

"But he was wrong. He disobeyed a direct order, and those men died."

Alex felt a slow heat crawl up his body. By leaving the beach and following Captain Granger up here, to the bluff, Alex, too, had disobeyed orders. And he had been more wrong in his thinking than he could ever have imagined might be possible. He'd been wrong, and yet, somehow, he'd ended up doing right, which struck him as both ironic and unjust.

And it occurred to him that while it was true that in trying to save the *Lady Juliana* Simon Granger had been doing what he believed was right, that didn't excuse what he'd done afterward. By refusing to own up to his mistake and letting Jack Ryder bear the burden of his guilt for ten long years, Simon Granger had committed a terrible wrong. A wrong that must have eaten away at some place deep and secret inside of him.

It was India McKnight who spoke, her gaze leveled hard and fierce on Alex's face. "What do you intend to do?"

Alex's chest jerked on a quick, desperate breath. "Our orders are to take Jack Ryder back to London."

He tightened his grip on his pistol, hunkering down in preparation for flying skulls and all manner of other unorthodox and uncivilized deportments. Instead, Jack Ryder let out a long, weary sigh, and said, "All right. But I'll go willingly. There's no need for chains."

"*What?*" India McKnight swung to face him, her eyes wide with fear. "You can't. They'll hang you."

Ryder shook his head. "I'm through hiding." Gripping her by the arms, he met her gaze with a fierce intensity that had Alex looking away in some discomfort. "I'm not going to spend the rest of my life watching the horizon. Worrying about what the next tide might be bringing."

"But . . . they won't believe you." Her voice cracked. "You have no proof."

"He has me," said Alex simply.

Jack Ryder's head swung around, his eyes narrowing as Alex met his gaze. "Simon Granger was a popular man. A hero. It'll ruin your career, being known as the officer responsible for dragging his name through the dirt."

Alex eased the hammer back on his pistol and let it fall to his side. There might be shades of gray, he knew. But not here, and not now. "Maybe," he said, his heart heavy in his chest. "But it's the right thing to do."

Dawn spilled a rich orange glow across the sky, bathing the calm waters of the lagoon with color and touching the jagged volcanic peak above with gold. The surf lapped at Jack's feet, a gentle sloshing that was only an echo of the violent cannonade hitting the fringing outer reef. He turned his head, his eyes narrowing against the growing light as he stared at what was left of the *Lady Juliana*.

It was hard now to remember the man he'd been on that day, ten years ago. He could remember the hollow despair of his grief, and the burning depths of his rage, but he couldn't remember the man he had been before his soul had been scoured by that quick succession of linked tragedies. A part of him had died on that reef, he realized, just as a part of Simon Granger had died. It hurt, thinking about Simon, thinking about what the decisions he'd made that day had done to him. Jack kept remembering the way they had been before, and that awful moment on the edge of the bluff when they had both confronted what they had become.

It occurred to him suddenly that he could again see quite clearly, the dark, wave-washed outline of the wreck undistorted by the jagged flashes of light that had almost blinded him last night. At some point his headache had left him, and he hadn't even noticed it. He sucked the fresh sea air deep into his lungs and drew it all in, the boundless horizons and the tangy green scent of the island and the haunting cry of the gull wheeling overhead, its outstretched wings lit by the golden brushstrokes of the rising sun. He felt suddenly, oddly, lighthearted and free. Which was ironic, given that he was about to be taken into custody.

India's hand slipped through the crook of his arm, and he turned to her. Her fine gray eyes were huge, her face held stiff, as if she was trying very hard not to cry. "I'm so afraid, Jack," she said, and because he knew her now, knew her well, he knew how much it cost her to make that admission.

He cradled her face in his palms. "It'll be all right. I'll come back. I promise."

She wrapped her hands around his wrists and gripped him tight. "You can't promise that."

He rubbed his lips against her forehead. "As long as there's life within me, I'll be back. I can promise that."

Tears welled in her eyes. She squeezed them shut and pressed her face to his so that he wouldn't see. "I should be there with you," she said, her voice a torn whisper. She'd said she wanted to come with him, to sail back to England with him. But as the *Barracuda*'s acting captain, Alex Preston had balked at the idea of allowing a woman on board.

Jack brought up one hand to touch her hair. "You need to finish your book."

"I don't care about my bloody book."

He smiled. "Yes you do."

"I could follow you." She glanced over to where Ulani sat on a tumble of rocks near the base of the bluff, her gaze on the *Barracuda*, riding now at anchor just off the beach, her decks alive with seamen preparing to set sail. "We could both follow you."

He shook his head. "It would take weeks. We could pass each other on the way and never even know it." He let his knuckles trail down the long line of her neck. He couldn't seem to stop touching her, her face, her hair. Couldn't seem to stop himself from asking the one question he probably didn't want to hear the answer to. "And when I come back? Then what? Will you marry me?"

She pressed her fingertips to his lips, stopping him. "Don't ask me that. Not now."

"Why? In case you commit yourself to something you afterward regret?"

"Jack—"

She reached out to him, but he was already swinging away, the sand crunching beneath his boots as he crossed the beach to where his daughter sat a distance apart, her head bent over something she cradled in her lap.

He paused awkwardly beside her, his gaze on the top of her bowed head. He could see the part that showed so white against the dark of her hair, and the delicate, vulnerable arch of her neck. He wanted desperately to touch her. Instead, he curled his hands into fists at his sides, and said, "Do you understand what's happening?"

Her head fell back and she looked up at him, the blue eyes that were so much like his own narrowing. "What do you think? That because I'm half Polynesian, and eleven years old, I'm stupid?"

Jack sighed. He seemed to be saying all the wrong things to the women in his life. "You know I have no choice but to go?"

"Yes."

"You know I'll be back, if I can?"

She blinked. "No."

At least she was being honest. He let his gaze drift around the lagoon. In the clear morning light it looked like an emerald, set in ivory. "I suppose I haven't given you much reason to believe me," he said, and the truth of his words was like an ache in his heart. "But I will be back. If they don't hang me."

He brought his gaze to her face, to find her staring at him, her eyes dark and solemn. "You might want to take this," she said, and thrust something out at him.

He stared down at the sandy, damp package in his hands, and such was his state of distraction that it took him a moment to understand what he held.

The *Lady Juliana*'s charts and log.

Palm fronds and low tree branches slapped India in the face, whipped against her legs, but she kept running, her breath soughing in and out as the trail steepened, her hands scrabbling for purchase on twisted roots and rocky outcrops as her boots slid in the thick, rich humus. She was driven, desperate to make it up to the point for one last glimpse of the ship that was carrying Jack away from her.

Up and up she climbed, until the trail emptied out onto the grassy bluff and she felt the gusting force of the trade winds blowing cool and sweet against her sweat-streaked face. Out at sea, the wind kicked little whitecaps off the tops of the waves and filled the sunstruck, billowing sails of the *Barracuda* as the corvette heeled to port. India felt her steps slow, falter. At the tip of the point she stopped, one hand creeping up to hold back her windblown hair.

Her breath was coming hard and fast, her heart pounding fierce enough to shudder her chest. She felt overwhelmed by a sickening succession of unbearable possibilities: that she might never see Jack again, that he might somehow fail in his quest to clear his name and win his freedom. Or that, if free, he would turn away from her, because when he had needed her the most, all her old, suffocating fears had reared their heads and she had been unable to give him the reassurance he had sought.

She gasped, her arms wrapping around her waist, her chest aching as if a great rending tear had cleaved her heart in two and left her shattered and bleeding. And she knew then with sudden, awful clarity that she had made a terrible mistake, that she had allowed her fear of the unknown and the unknowable to stop her from reaching for what she really wanted. Because what she wanted was him, and she thought she had probably known it from that first moment when she had looked up to see him standing at the end of his dock, sun-bronzed and wild and free.

Oh, she had fought it, denied it, tried to escape it. But the reality of it, the inescapable rightness of it had been impressed upon her, over and over again. In these last weeks, they had faced a lifetime of dangers together, had known fear and joy and bitter defeat. She had learned she could trust him with her life, her heart, her soul. Only, she still hadn't learned to trust herself.

Out at sea, the trades were freshening, the corvette now only a flash of white in the distance, soon lost. Yet still India stood at the tip of the bluff, the tropical sun fierce on her bare head, a terrible weight of sadness and regret lying heavy on her heart.

~~Chapter Thirty-eight

He CAME TO her early on a sunny afternoon, when the mango trees were in bloom, and the sea swelled gentle and achingly blue into the distance.

She had sailed over to an island in the Marquesas with Patu and Ulani, to investigate reports of stone statues and record examples of the local folklore. They'd been there almost a week when she discovered the existence of another collection of carvings, high on an open hillside above the deep, violet-blue bay where they had anchored the *Sea Hawk*, rescued from its watery grave and lovingly repaired and refitted by Patu.

She was sketching a giant statue of a turtle, her notebook balanced on one hip, her forehead knotted with the effort of getting the proportions right, when a movement on the hillside below caught her eye. She paused, her head lifting, her pencil stilling. So many times, over these past months, she had caught herself doing this, watching, waiting, hoping. She didn't want to let herself believe it might be him, but her heart was thumping, her breath coming suddenly so hard and fast that she was shaking.

A breeze gusted up, warm and sweet with the scents of the sea and the damp earth and a luxuriant tangle of green growing things. A lock of hair blew into her eyes and she brought up one hand to brush it back, the sun fierce and golden on her upturned face as she squinted into the distance.

It was a man, she saw. A tall man with a long, easy stride and dark hair that fluttered against the collar of the shirt he wore open at the neck. Her notebook slipped from her fingers. For a moment, she didn't think she could move. But then she was running, her hands fisting in her skirt, her knees kicking up high, her legs reaching, reaching.

"Jack," she cried, her heart soaring, bursting with joy and love, so much love. "Jack."

He paused, his head falling back as he looked up at her. Something flashed in his eyes, something bright and hot. He laughed, his arms opening wide to scoop her up as she flung herself at him, his embrace warm and strong, lifting her high, so high her feet left the ground and her momentum spun them both around and around. She braced her arms on his shoulders, her neck arching, her head falling back as her laughter joined his. Then his laugher died, the skin pulling taut across his cheekbones as he let her slide slowly down the length of him. Her feet touched the ground, and she found herself feeling suddenly shy, and more than a little afraid.

She reached up and slid her fingertips across his tightly held mouth. "You came back."

"I said I would." His eyes narrowed, his features tense as he searched her face. He took in a deep breath, his chest lifting as if he was bracing himself, steadying himself for something he didn't want to hear. "Do you still want me?"

She felt her lips tremble into a smile, although her heart was thumping wildly with the terror of what she was about to say, what she was about to do. "I have lived every hour of every day since you've been gone wanting you. I want to wake up in the middle of the night and watch you sleeping next to me. I want to have your babies, and spend the rest of my life laughing and fighting with you, and growing old with you. I want you like I have never wanted anything in my life. But—" Her voice cracked, so that she had to stop and swallow, hard. "But I'm still afraid. So afraid."

And then she felt a curious lightening, deep within her, as if by saying it out loud, she had somehow robbed that fear of its hold on her and made it, oddly, less terrorizing.

His features had softened, relaxed. "People are always afraid, India." He caught her hand in his and brought it to his lips, although his gaze never left hers. "I'm afraid. Afraid of not being the man you think I am, of not being the one man you can love, forever."

He was looking at her with all of his love naked in his

eyes for her to see. She thought she had never known anyone so brave, so comfortable with his feelings for those he loved, so comfortable with himself. It came to her that he was everything she wanted to be, and more. And that forever wouldn't be enough time to get to know him, enough time to spend loving him.

"I love you," she said, trembling with the awful courage of what she was saying. "I love you so much it scares me." She laughed, and he laughed with her, catching her to him, his fingers spearing in her hair to hold her head steady, his eyes growing narrow and intense in that way they did just before he kissed her.

And she knew then that he was right, that fear was a part of life. And she thought that the worst fears were the ones that kept you from doing what you knew was right, or from seizing what you really, truly wanted.

"Marry me," she said suddenly.

He froze, his lips just inches from hers, his eyes flaring wide. "What?"

She laughed, buoyed up by a wave of joy and hope and contentment that seemed to wash over her, warm and good. "I said, marry me. Marry me at a Polynesian luau, or in a colonial courthouse, or on the deck of the next ship that passes by, but just . . . marry me."

Jack took her chin in his hand, his gaze locked with hers. "You don't need to marry me, India, if you're not comfortable with that. I'll understand."

"I know." She wrapped her arms around his neck, holding him close. "This is what I want."

He took her mouth in a kiss that was long and hot and went on forever. Then he lifted his head so he could look at her, and the smile in his eyes warmed her heart and healed her soul, and sent her spirits soaring wild and free.

**Look for these scintillating novels
by Candice Proctor!**

MIDNIGHT
CONFESSIONS

Welcome to the dazzling splendor of
old New Orleans, where the air is fragrant with
mock orange and sweet olive—and danger wafts
on the gentle southern breeze. . . .

Widow Emmanuelle de Beauvais devotes herself to
the sick and injured of a grand city now occupied
by the enemy. Then a night of unspeakable terror
puts Emmanuelle at the center of a murder investigation and under the watchful eye of Yankee
provost marshal Zachary Cooper. Although she
despises the uniform and the war it represents, she
finds the man who wears it impossible to resist.

**Sign up for Pillow Talk,
the romance e-newsletter that gives you the
latest scoop on your favorite authors and books.
Go to www.ballantinebooks.com/PillowTalk.**

Published by Ivy Books.
Available wherever books are sold.

Candice Proctor takes readers to the lush
vistas of Australia in this magnificent tale of
two people who share a love as forbidden
and dangerous as the land that
surrounds them. . . .

WHISPERS OF HEAVEN

After years of schooling in England,
Jesmond Corbett finds little has changed on her
family's estate along the coast of Tasmania.
Betrothed since childhood to a wealthy neighbor,
Jessie comes home determined to conform to the
expectations of her family. But nothing in Jessie's
life has prepared her for the mysterious stranger
who works in the stables, a man with searing eyes
who haunts her dreams and awakens passions
she never knew existed.

Published by Ivy Books.
Available wherever books are sold.

Set in medieval Europe, here is a
superb tale of passion and redemption as one
man's quest for glory becomes an unexpected
crusade to save his soul. . . .

THE LAST KNIGHT
by Candice Proctor

To warn her beloved brother of a political betrayal
that could lead to war, Attica d'Alérion disguises
herself as a young courtier and bravely rides into
the arms of Damion de Jarnac, a rogue and an
ambitious horseman. Working for the aging King
Henry, Damion scouts the hills of Brittany on a
mission to expose the treachery of Philip of
France. There he joins forces with a courageous
lad—who turns out to be the most intriguing
woman he has ever met. But to win the beautiful
Attica's love, Damion must slay the demons of an
unforgivable past.
And to save his doomed country, he must
make a deadly decision that could break
his lady's noble heart. . . .

Published by Ivy Books.
Available wherever books are sold.

Subscribe to the new Pillow Talk e-newsletter—and receive all these fabulous online features directly in your e-mail inbox:

♥ Exclusive essays and other features by major romance writers like Linda Howard, Kristin Hannah, Julie Garwood, and Suzanne Brockmann

♥ Exciting behind-the-scenes news from our romance editors

♥ Special offers, including contests to win signed romance books and other prizes

♥ Author tour information, and monthly announcements about the newest books on sale

♥ A Pillow Talk readers forum, featuring feedback from romance fans...like you!

Two easy ways to subscribe:
Go to **www.ballantinebooks.com/PillowTalk**
or send a blank e-mail to
join-PillowTalk@list.randomhouse.com.

Pillow Talk—
the romance e-newsletter brought to you by
Ballantine Books